PAIN OF BETRAYAL

THE WALLKEEPER TRILOGY BOOK 2

PAIN OF BETRAYAL

CAREN HAHN

Pain of Betrayal by Caren Hahn

Published by Seventy-Second Press

www.carenhahn.com

Hardcover ISBN-13: 978-1-958609-97-2

Paperback ISBN-13: 978-1-958609-98-9

This is a work of fiction. Any references to historical events, real people, or real places are used fictitiously. Names, characters, places, and incidents either are the products of the author's imagination or are used fictitiously.

Cover design by 100covers.

Edited by Rachel Pickett.

Printed in the USA

Dedicated to Carli, whose request for a fairy tale prompted the original idea, and whose enthusiastic critique of my first draft opened my eyes to its potential.

Books by Caren Hahn

*Find Caren's work on
Amazon.com*

ROMANTIC FANTASY:

<u>THE WALLKEEPER TRILOGY</u>

Burden of Power

Pain of Betrayal

Gleam of Crown

<u>THE HATCHED TRILOGY</u>

Hatched: Dragon Farmer

Hatched: Dragon Defender

Hatched: Dragon Speaker

CONTEMPORARY SUSPENSE:

This Side of Dark

What Comes After

<u>THE OWL CREEK SERIES</u>

Smoke over Owl Creek

Hunt at Owl Creek

Visit carenhahn.com to receive a free
copy of *Charmed: Tales from Quarantine
and Other Short Fiction.*

PAIN OF BETRAYAL

THE WALLKEEPER TRILOGY BOOK 2

CAREN HAHN

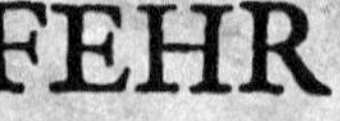

KINGDOM
OF RAHM

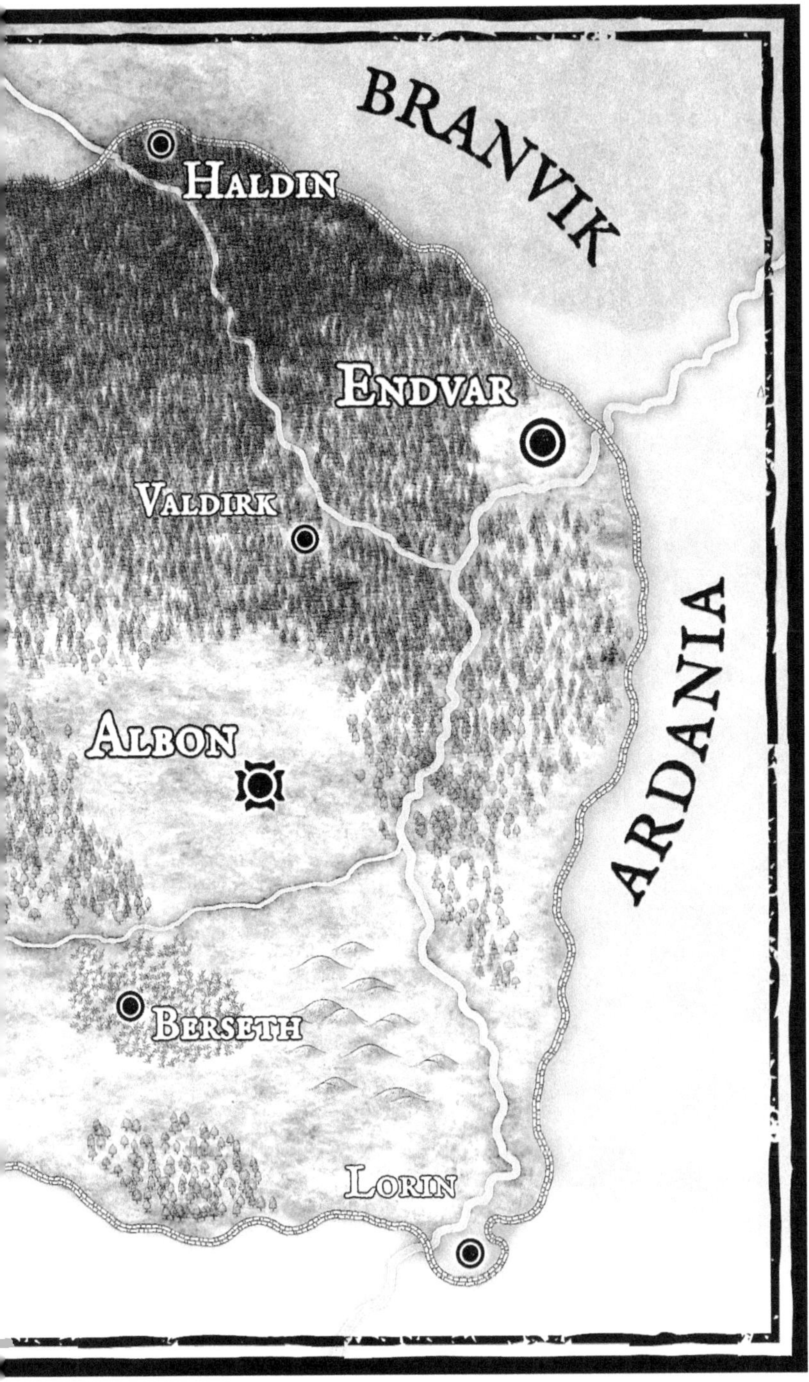

BRANVIK
HALDIN
ENDVAR
VALDIRK
ARDANIA
ALBON
BERSETH
LORIN

ONE

"I can't believe I let you talk me into this," Yulda grumbled. "I was trying to get away from this place!"

Aiya could barely make out the girl's outline in the darkness. With her hood pulled low over her ruined hair and a scarf wrapped around her neck and chin, Yulda's fair skin was well hidden. She was almost indistinguishable from the bulky shape of the woodpile where they crouched, hidden from the open courtyard of Lord Bolen's estate. Once the home of a disagreeable nobleman with criminal connections, it now housed enemy soldiers who had overrun the city of Endvar.

A gentle rain fell around them, and the Ardanians moving in the direction of the grand house hurried to get out of the damp as quickly as possible, their wet boots slapping against stone.

A few of the men were small and dark—Khouri mercenaries—and Aiya tensed when they passed. It was absurd, since their fate would be the same if they were discovered by an Ardanian soldier, but she couldn't help the instinctive response to flee. These were her countrymen, and Yulda said they had been searching for Aiya. Behni knew she was in the city, and he wanted her dead.

"If I had known it would take this long, I would have picked a better position," Yulda muttered, shifting slightly.

"Be still," Aiya whispered, as a gong sounded from deep within the house. "Must you always complain so?"

Yulda sniffed indignantly but fell silent. Over the next few minutes, the traffic in the courtyard slowed, and the night grew still. Another gong sounded, and Aiya idly wondered about the nature of the meeting taking place inside. What secrets might be discussed mere yards away?

But they weren't after secrets, not tonight. When the enemy soldiers sealed Endvar's gates, cutting off help from the nearby garrison, Aiya had been trapped with no hope of escape. Her only companion was Dan, a soldier under Captain Strong who had been charged with taking her to safety. Until they discovered Yulda—Lord Bolen's former scullery maid who had not only been in the tunnels underneath the estate, but had even mapped them out for Rorden. She was their only hope in finding a way out of the city.

A door slammed close by and two shapes suddenly loomed in the darkness before them. Yulda gasped, and Aiya clutched her arm, willing her to be silent. If she didn't move or speak, they shouldn't be noticed here in the shadows.

The voice that spoke was unfamiliar to Aiya, but Yulda stiffened with recognition. "You have not yet been released from your contract. It is dangerous to speak to your men of home when you are needed here."

Another voice responded, and a chill crept up Aiya's neck. She knew that voice. It haunted her memories—memories of fire and death and holding her daughter in her arms as her blood spilled black in the night. Aiya shivered.

"You have your city as we agreed," Behni said in heavily accented Ardanian, his tone full of disdain. "There is nothing further to discuss. It is time for us to look toward home and leave you to clean up your own mess."

"Need I remind you that it was the sloppiness of your men that attracted Strong's attention in the first place? Had you not brought soldiers down upon us, we wouldn't have needed to act before we received confirmation from my master. You will stay and help us hold the city until we receive reinforcements. And you will hope that it will be enough and that he won't hold you personally responsible for nearly unraveling his plans."

Behni spat out a curse in Khouri before returning to Aradanian. "Don't think I will listen to your threats. You who couldn't even manage to take the princess when she practically delivered herself into your hands. Oh yes, I know what happened out there with your bungled ambush. If you want to speak of sloppiness, then I have tales of my own to share with your master. *If* he ever shows his face in this city. I'm beginning to wonder if his secret army exists or if he's as impotent as you are."

The other man stepped forward, and light from a nearby window fell across his profile. Aiya recognized Domar who had infiltrated Lord Bolen's staff as his steward. He looked even paler than usual and moved stiffly as if nursing a wound. "He will come; make no mistake. And when he does, he will reward you if you've served him well. You don't want to risk his wrath."

Behni's posture was aggressive, despite standing more than a full head shorter than Domar. "I am not a fool," he growled. "This is not what we agreed to. I will not wait here until the people of this city grow restless and revolt. My men and I leave in the morning."

He turned and started to walk back toward the door, but the other man's voice stopped him.

"Timar. Rosin," Domar said mildly. "And sweet little Fey."

Behni turned stiffly, his face now illuminated by the lit window. His expression was as hard as steel, but there was a hint of fear in his eyes.

"You may have hidden them from your wife, but my master knows their names. Their ages. And where their mother lives." Domar stepped closer, standing over the Khouri man. "Now, go into that room and explain to your men why they'll be staying in Endvar until our troops come."

Behni knew he was caught. Aiya saw it on his face. He narrowed his eyes and spoke in a harsh whisper that Aiya couldn't hear. But Domar merely smiled a thin, cold smile, and Behni turned on his heel toward the house.

When Domar followed, Aiya let out a sigh of relief.

She realized suddenly that she was still clutching Yulda's arm, and it was trembling.

"Oh, poor thing," she said soothingly, wrapping her arms around the girl and hugging her close. "You're all right; he's gone."

"I shouldn't be here," Yulda shuddered. "I should be far away from here."

"If you want to get away, you must come with us," Aiya said firmly. "When the army gets here, this city will be even more dangerous."

"Army? What army?"

Of course. The men hadn't been speaking Rahmish. Yulda wouldn't have understood a word. "That's what those men were speaking of. There's an army coming."

"When?"

"I don't know. That seems to be a matter of disagreement between the two. But Yulda, if any of us is going to escape, we must do it together."

A movement to the side startled her. Dan crept closer in a crouch, lifting his hood slightly to reveal his face. Aiya was struck by how pleasing his features were without a beard. She smiled a little in greeting, while Yulda sighed in exasperation.

"Did you stop for a drink along the way? What took you so long?"

Dan rolled his eyes at her. "I couldn't find them. Not even a sign that they've been here."

"I told you," Yulda said smugly. "There aren't any soldiers being kept here."

"But I know what I saw," Aiya protested. "They were men of Captain Strong's Wall Guard. Jax was there; I'm sure of it! Perhaps they moved them to another place in the city."

"So, what do we do now?" Yulda asked.

Dan blew into his hands to warm them. "Let's go back to the shop. Tomorrow I'll go out into the city and see if anyone has seen or heard anything useful."

"You'll go out into the city looking like an Ardanian soldier?" Yulda scoffed. "You'll have lots of success, won't you? The people will practically flock to you to tell you all their secrets."

Aiya looked back and forth between the two of them. "None of us can go out and not be noticed. Dan looks too Ardanian without his beard, and I am clearly too foreign. Yulda might be able to manage it if she wore a scarf and hood—"

"—and kept her tongue under control," Dan interjected.

Yulda scowled, and Aiya tried not to smile.

"I'm not sure it matters, though," Aiya continued. She recounted to Dan the conversation she'd heard between Behni and Domar. "If there are more troops coming to the city, this may be our only chance to escape. It would be foolish to delay."

Dan considered this. "If there are more troops coming, this may be our only chance to reclaim the city. Just think of it, Aiya. If we can free Jax and the others, we could mount an assault on one of the gates. We'd just need to seize control long enough for the garrison to enter."

"And somehow get a message to the garrison," Aiya pointed out. "How will we do that without someone on the outside of the city? We still need to find a way out. Besides, those men were not whole enough to mount an assault. Many of them couldn't even stand without help."

Dan tugged his hood forward again, and his face was lost in shadow. Aiya recognized his need for a quiet moment to think.

Yulda did not.

"I'm half soaked in this rain," she complained. "Can we please make a decision and get inside?"

"Just how old are you, child?" Aiya asked her. "Fifteen? Sixteen?"

Yulda's head snapped up. "I'll be eighteen next spring!"

"Ah, a proper woman then. I was married at your age with a child on the way. That is certainly old enough to have learned how to keep unpleasantness to yourself, don't you think?"

Yulda glared in return and fell silent.

"We need you, Yulda," Aiya continued. "You've been in the tunnels. If there is any chance of finding a way out, it will be because of you. But *you* also need *us*. We can help each other, but you have to stop treating us like we're the enemy. Do you think you can try?"

Yulda shot her a hostile glance, but after a moment, she nodded.

Dan shifted, prepared to rise. "All right, Yulda. Let's see if we can get into these tunnels without running into any of your friends."

Two

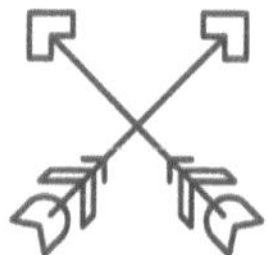

It was early evening when the princess's rescue party rode through the streets of Albon, attracting a following of excited citizens. Just the sort of scene that made Merek squirm. Cheers and applause followed their route, growing louder as the crowd swelled. A few tender-eyed men and women wiped away tears.

Merek kept his eyes firmly fixed ahead of him, gazing above the crowd to avoid making eye contact. But Ria—sitting in front of him on his horse since her injured shoulder prevented her from controlling her own mount—handled it all with customary grace: smiling and nodding with an occasional wave.

When they passed through the gates of Thorodan Hall, the scene changed to one of frantic activity. Servants and soldiers came running from all directions.

Ria turned her head so Merek could catch her voice over the din. "Will you stay long in Albon?"

Merek was momentarily startled by the loveliness of her profile and how her brown hair shone like fire in the golden light of evening. He had buried his feelings deep these past days, so as to not be constantly distracted by her nearness. But there were moments like this when he was caught off guard by the longing that welled up suddenly, and it pained him to have her so near.

"Not long," he answered, keeping his tone even. "I would speak with your father, but then I must return to Endvar."

"I do seem to have a habit of taking you away from your dear city, don't I?" Ria remarked. She was quiet for a moment, and then said, "Please see me before you go. There's a private matter of which I must speak before you leave."

Merek grunted his assent but inwardly wondered if he would even get access to the princess once she was claimed by the king and her attendants.

"Do you see my father?" she asked, looking out over the swarm of people coming to meet them. Merek followed her gaze to the steps of the Hall, but he couldn't make out Sindal's distinctive form or booming voice.

"Maybe word hasn't reached him yet," he said, but he felt a sense of unease. The tall unfinished tower that they'd see on their approach to Albon loomed behind the Hall like an abominable beast crouched to spring.

Merek helped Ria dismount, and her feet had scarcely brushed the pavement when she was whisked away from him by a throng of fretting servants. He watched her go, chiding himself for feeling a sense of loss. He had no right to miss her. His thoughts should be occupied with his duty and nothing more.

Rorden approached, a perplexed expression on his face. "I'm surprised the king isn't here. Do you suppose Captain Drenall's messengers haven't arrived yet? Could we have passed them on the road?"

Merek had no answer for him, but he too was troubled by the king's absence. When the princess's retinue had been ambushed, Captain Drenall had sent messengers both to Endvar and Albon to seek help. Merek considered the reaction of the people as they'd traveled through the city. Their faces were full of concern and relief. So word *had* reached them that the princess was in danger. Where, then, was the king?

"Merek Strong, you dear man!" a woman's voice called out, interrupting his thoughts.

Merek turned to see a plump woman pushing her way through the crowd. It took him a moment to recognize her.

"Lotta!" he said in surprise as she rushed forward and embraced him.

"Thank you for bringing her back to us! I knew you would!" The relief in her voice indicated the opposite, but Merek didn't say so. When she released him, her eyes shone with tears. "I haven't been able to eat or sleep for worrying about my poor girl being hunted in the wild like an animal. My only comfort was knowing that you were looking for her too."

Merek scanned the courtyard over the head of the beaming woman. "Lotta, where is the king?"

Lotta's expression darkened. "No doubt you've seen

the…" She jerked her head to where the tower stood in the distance. "He doesn't leave it these days."

"Not even to see his daughter's safe return?"

Lotta gave a tiny lift of her eyebrows as if to say, *You said it, not me.* "I must hurry to Ria. She needs a woman's care, but I just wanted to give you my thanks. We are all in your debt." She smiled at him, but her smile had lost some of its luster, clouded by the words about the king.

Merek watched her go. "Rorden."

"Yes, sir?"

"Find out if anyone else has seen the king in recent days. Is he ill? Why does he not leave the tower? Learn as much as you can, and quickly."

Two men in the familiar green of the Royal Guard hurried toward him, and Merek recognized two of Drenall's men who had accompanied them on the wall tour.

"Sergeants Nykov, Brandel," Merek greeted.

"Captain Strong! We didn't expect to see you here, not so soon. Do you have news of Captain Drenall?" Brandel asked urgently.

"Drenall is alive. He and his men are being tended by Captain Eldar. It may be some days yet before they arrive. But tell me, Sergeant, why was there no search party sent from Albon? I expected to meet one on the road."

"I can't say, sir," he said, glancing at his companion. His balding head reflected the fading light of the sun.

Nykov looked nervously toward the Hall. "It might be best to speak in private, sir."

Merek nodded, and they stepped to the edge of the

courtyard behind a low building, away from the bustling crowd.

"Have you seen the king since you arrived?" Merek asked bluntly.

Nykov shook his head. "We briefed General Grammel and were told to wait for further instructions."

"But nothing else has happened," Brandel said with frustration. "We were just discussing striking out on our own when you arrived."

"You reported to Grammel instead of the king? Why?"

"We were told the king was indisposed. General Grammel said he would act on his behalf."

"And yet he didn't send out a search party?" Merek was incredulous.

"He urged us to be patient." Brandel's tone was full of disgust. "It's as if we were asking for a great favor, not raising a cry of alarm about the heir to the throne being attacked!"

Merek frowned as he considered these words. Something wasn't right. He turned back to the officers and tried to speak reassuringly. "You've done well. Captain Drenall will be pleased to hear of it when he returns. I'm sure that when the king learns of your role in saving his daughter, he will be very grateful."

Nykov and Brandel exchanged an uncomfortable glance.

"What is it?"

Brandel colored slightly. "Sir, there's talk that the king has gone mad. He won't leave the tower. Meals are brought to him. He sleeps there. No one is allowed to see him. How do we even know he received our message?"

"You say General Grammel is acting on his behalf?"

"General Grammel is one of the few allowed to see the king."

"And this tower? What's its purpose?"

Brandel shrugged. "No one knows. But from the way the servants talk about it, and look over their shoulders, it seems to have taken on a life of it's own. They act as though it's infected his mind."

"Servants can be very superstitious," Merek said drily. "Thank you for your frankness, Sergeant. I would also like to hear more details of the ambush. I couldn't linger to speak with Captain Drenall and didn't want to trouble the princess about it. What can you tell me about those who attacked you?"

The men relaxed a little as they left the uncomfortable territory of their monarch's mental state to relate the tale of the attack. Much of it Merek had surmised from viewing the scene of the ambush, but he pressed them for details anyway. When they had finished, Merek looked around and realized that the activity in the courtyard had quieted. Whatever chaos was going on inside the Hall, there was no sight or sound of it beyond its stately walls. Merek dismissed the sergeants, feeling the weariness of travel descending upon him as surely as the sun descended toward the horizon, casting long shadows across the courtyard.

He started to turn toward the barracks but was stopped by the sight of Rorden trotting toward him.

"Captain Strong, sir," he called. "I've some answers for you."

"Already?"

Rorden grinned. "It's not that hard if you know the right person to ask."

"And by 'person' I assume you mean a young woman?"

"Coincidentally, yes. A chambermaid I've known for some time, though never quite as well as I'd have liked," he mused.

"Careful," Merek warned. "Don't let Biren hear you say that."

"No! Not like that!" Rorden had the decency to look sheepish. "My friend says that very few people are allowed access to the king. He moved into the tower before it was completed, and they've had to work around him while they try to finish it."

"Does she know what its purpose is?"

Rorden shook his head. "Whatever its original purpose, it's now become his living quarters. He has everything to make him comfortable and hasn't left it since."

"Nykov and Brandel say that General Grammel is allowed access. Who else?"

"Old Martin and a few other servants."

"Is Grammel making decisions or acting on his behalf in any way?"

Rorden shook his head. "If he is, he's not public about it. It seems that everything has ground to a halt, with even Galinn being kept at a distance."

"Even the king's steward isn't allowed to see him?"

"Apparently not, which has been a source of great frustration, as you can imagine."

But it wasn't the steward's frustration that concerned Merek. A dreadful thought was growing in Merek's mind, but it was too awful to speak aloud. He'd been at odds with Grammel in recent months, but it was a far cry to go from a minor squabble to accusing him of imprisoning the king to further his own ambitions.

And yet...

"I need to see the king tonight," Merek said, making a decision.

"Yes, sir," Rorden replied, falling into step beside him. "I'll have a bath prepared for you immediately."

"No, there's no time. I'll see him now." Merek turned in the direction of the garden tower.

Rorden paused. "Now, sir? When was the last time you really slept?"

Merek wasn't sure. "Do I look that bad?"

A smile teased Rorden's dimples. "With all due respect, sir, you aren't fit to see the king's footman, let alone the king himself. Let me send word while you clean up."

Merek shook his head. "Prepare the bath. "I'll want it when I get back." Then he broke into a jog, leaving Rorden and his objections behind.

There was only one door at the base of the wide tower, and Merek slowed to a walk as he saw the two guards stationed there. They stood up straighter at his approach and stepped in front of the door.

"No one is allowed to see the king at this time," one said, looking Merek over warily.

"Do you know who I am, soldier?" Merek asked.

The first guard looked uncertain so the second one spoke. "Yes, sir. We mean no disrespect, but the king has requested that no one be allowed to enter after sundown."

This was a matter of some dispute as there were still bright rays of sunlight shining on the upper scaffolding of the unfinished tower. Merek drew himself up to his full height, scowling at the young soldiers.

"I'm Captain Strong, First Captain of the Wall Guard," he growled. "I have a duty to perform as given me by King Sindal himself. I will not wait until morning to see him."

The guards glanced at each other. Finally, the second one moved to open the door. "Please wait here, sir. I'll let him know you wish to see him."

"That won't be necessary," Merek said, moving to the door. The soldier started to put out an arm to stop him, but Merek grabbed his arm and twisted it behind him until the man fell to his knees and grunted with pain. "I don't want to hurt you, soldier," he said calmly. "But I will if you try to stop me. Do you understand?"

The young man nodded, and Merek released him, pushing past him and into the tower. There he paused, feeling as though he had entered a dream world, so familiar and yet so strange it was.

In the center of the large circular room, where the

earth hadn't been disturbed to lay foundation stones, the garden largely remained intact. Trees, tall shrubs, and flowers stood in a rosy haze cast from the filtered sunset coming through slit windows high above. A ceiling overhead hinted at an upper room, and sealed off the plants below from the heavens. Some of the foliage was already wilting without light and water, but much of it looked unchanged. The plants were under siege, and they didn't even know it.

A staircase circled the interior of the wall, built against the stone. Merek climbed until he passed through an opening in the floor above. This room was sparsely furnished, with a pallet bed in one corner, a small wardrobe, and a single bookcase. Two guards sat at a table playing cards before a fireplace cut into the stone while an aging man poured water into a basin. His hands shook, but he managed not to spill a drop.

The soldiers jumped to their feet when they saw Merek.

"You shouldn't be here," Martin said, without turning.

"I've come to see the king." Merek stepped forward into the light cast from two small windows.

Martin turned and his expression changed to one of recognition.

"Ah! It's you, Captain! Did you bring our princess back to us, then? I hope she'll come and see us soon."

Merek was taken aback by the lightness in the man's tone. He spoke as though Ria had been away on holiday. "Where is the king?" he demanded.

Martin smiled brightly. "The king is not available to

visitors. But I will speak to him in the morning, and I'm sure he will see you then."

"I will see him now." Merek strode toward the stairs that led to the next level. The guards rushed to intercept him, barring his way.

"I'm afraid that isn't allowed, young captain," Martin said. "The king has asked not to be disturbed. You will respect his wishes, of course."

Merek whirled on the older man, drawing his sword. The two guards cried out in alarm and stepped forward, weapons in hand.

Merek ignored them, speaking to Martin with deliberate heat. "This is not a social call. I will contest anyone who gets in my way tonight. I just spent five days trying to keep the princess safe from hostile enemies within our borders, and if I find that the king has been harmed in any way, I will consider you party to whatever threat is working against the throne."

"Harmed?" Martin sputtered indignantly. "Why would he be harmed? Your paranoia is as bad as his." But he nodded reluctantly to the soldiers and they moved aside.

Merek took the stairs two at a time with sword in hand until he reached a landing with a large oak door at the top. Heart pounding, he pushed the door open.

This room was nothing like the one below. Large casement windows let in an abundance of light, and the whole room glowed with the last rays of the evening sun. Thick carpets and finely woven rugs covered the stone floor, and elaborate tapestries hung from the walls between the windows. The central piece of furniture was a masterfully carved bed shining with frequent polish and outfitted with rich curtains and linens. A cheerful fire crackled in the hearth.

This was no prison, and the man who stood silhouetted in the furthest window was clearly no prisoner.

Sindal, dressed in fine robes with a golden circlet on his brow, held himself erect and proud.

"My lord," Merek said with relief. He had expected to find the king in distress, not healthy and poised with an irresistible air of authority. Remembering himself, he bowed before the king.

"I should have known you wouldn't give me any peace," Sindal said wearily.

"I mean no disrespect." Merek sheathed his sword, his relief giving way to confusion. "Are you well, sire? Perhaps you didn't hear, but Ria is returned just this evening. Don't you want to see her?"

Sindal regarded him quietly, so changed from the cheerful man who would have once greeted Merek with an exuberant hug. Now he just watched him without speaking.

"Why were you not there, sire?" Merek tried again. "If you're not ill or otherwise impaired, what stopped you from coming to her? If there's one thing I know about you, it's that your daughter means more to you than anything else in the world."

Sindal blinked. "Close the door," he commanded. He stepped away from the window and sat before the fireplace in a cushioned chair. "You may sit if you wish."

Merek obeyed the order to close the door, but didn't join Sindal at the fire. The warmth was welcome after so many days riding in the rain, but Merek despised it. Who was this man who could so casually dismiss Ria's well-being, choosing to sit comfortably at his own fire instead of rushing to her side? How did he dare seek comfort while Ria had been cold, wet, hungry, and afraid?

"I don't know what has wrought this change in you, Sindal," he said. "But Ria needs you. She's been through a trying ordeal, and the only face she cared to see in the crowd was yours. I beg you to go to her."

When Sindal spoke, his voice was laced with suspicion. "Grammel told me you would bring her home safe. I saw it all, from that window. He spoke of conspiracies and hired assassins, and I didn't believe any of it until I saw you ride through the gates with the cheering crowds...just like he said."

The bitterness in his tone made Merek's blood run hot. "I don't know what Grammel could have known of these things. But if you had seen them yourself, Captain Drenall's men would have given you a full report when they arrived."

"Undoubtedly Drenall is party to your treachery as well."

"Treachery? What treachery have I committed? I rescued your daughter from Ardanian ruffians and delivered her safely to your door, and you accuse me of treachery?"

"Bah!" Sindal scoffed. "Ardanians! If you wished your story to be believable, you should have known better than to blame the Ardanians. They're our strongest ally!"

"Do I understand you correctly?" Merek demanded.

"Are you accusing me of planning the attack on the princess?"

"I'm not accusing you of anything," Sindal said, his demeanor suddenly changed. His eyes softened and he shook his head, turning back to gaze at the fire. "If I thought you had orchestrated the attack, I would have had you arrested the moment you entered my city. But Grammel makes a compelling argument, especially since it played out exactly as he predicted. Except for the part where I was supposed to greet you in front of the masses: the emotional father whose grief has turned to gratitude. If what Grammel says is true, I couldn't possibly play into your little drama."

"But to what purpose? What could I possibly have to gain by such a plot?"

The king rubbed his eyes and sighed wearily. "I'm not saying I believe it. I don't know what I believe. But I think it would be best if you left Albon as soon as possible."

"Sindal," Merek said, dropping on one knee before his chair. "What Grammel says is a lie. You know me. I would never do anything to hurt you or your daughter. Talk to Ria. She'll testify that everything I've done was to keep her safe and bring her home to you."

"Perhaps," the king said. He seemed taken aback by Merek's plea, and for a moment there was a trace of familiar warmth in his blue eyes. It passed quickly however, leaving confusion and mistrust in its place. He glanced at the window where the light was fading. "I must ask you to leave now. I need time to think."

Merek hesitated. He needed to tell Sindal about the

plot in Endvar and how the ambush was connected to it, but the king looked so troubled that Merek didn't think he would even listen. And Merek was unnerved by his accusations. He didn't trust himself to keep his tongue if the king dismissed his claims.

Instead he asked, "May I see you in the morning? I have urgent news from Endvar to discuss."

Sindal looked at him sharply, and there was an edge of suspicion to his voice again. "Yes, I expect you do. That should be an interesting tale. Go now. Send Martin up on your way out."

Merek frowned, bewildered by Sindal's changing mood. But he said nothing, only bowed his head respectfully and stood. The sky outside the long windows was now steel blue with twilight, and the only light in the tower was from the fading embers of the fire. They cast Sindal's face into dark shadows, making him seem older than his years. The image haunted Merek, fueling his anger as he left the tower. One thing was certain. He would be having words with General Grammel before he left the city.

THREE

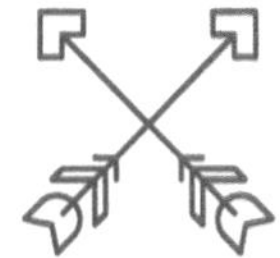

Getting into the tunnels proved to be a lot easier than Aiya had feared. The only inhabitant of Lord Bolen's kitchen was an older woman with a desperate look whose every movement was slow and fearful. When Dan appeared in the doorway and issued a few commands to mimic the Ardanians' broken Rahmish, she took in his appearance and hurried to obey.

"We won't be able to come back this way," Dan whispered as they huddled at the top of the stairs just inside the passageway in the kitchen larder. He closed the door, and darkness descended on them, save for the meager light of the two oil lamps Aiya and Yulda held.

"We are committed," Aiya said reassuringly, but one glance down the long dark nothingness before her made her heart skip a beat.

Stone stairs gave way to a dirt floor as they descended, and the lamplight glistened off rivulets of water running down the walls. Occasionally threadlike roots broke through, reminding Aiya of the weight of a city above them.

Yulda led the way, becoming increasingly confident as time passed. And talkative.

"These lamps are far better than candles, but that's all I dared use so as to not alert Cook. Up here a ways it's going to get a bit wetter. The smell gets worse too. That's when we get to the main part of the tunnels where there are lots of branches off this one. We never got this far with Rorden and the other soldiers."

Dan caught Aiya's eye questioningly as Yulda related an amusing memory from that night. Aiya just shrugged. She couldn't imagine what had brought about the change in the girl, but for all her complaining she clearly had an adventurous spirit. Perhaps Aiya too would have been surly and unpleasant at her age if she'd been trapped as a scullery maid in a gloomy noble house, instead of enjoying the excitement and danger of a thieving ring.

After a time, the floor became thick with mud and the stench of rotting things. *The smell of death*, Hala had described it, and she wasn't wrong. Aiya wished for fresh air to breathe and wondered how far they would have to travel in the dank mud.

Yulda stopped with a gasp. Aiya looked over Yulda's shoulder and saw a dark form on the ground ahead.

Dan stepped around the two women, approaching the bulky shape cautiously. The light from his lamp illuminated the shape of a man. Not just any man. A soldier in the gray and blue uniform of the Wall Guard.

"I recognize him," Dan said grimly. "He's one of Captain Eldar's men."

"That's why you couldn't find them," Aiya realized. "They hid them in the tunnels. But why?"

Dan rolled the dead man over onto his back and examined him. Aiya looked away from the man's face, bloated and ghastly in the flickering light.

"I expect it's an efficient way of keeping prisoners if you don't have enough guards. Throw them in a deep enough hole with no light, food, or water, and they won't be going anywhere."

Aiya shivered at the thought of being trapped here underground in the dark. What they were attempting was going to be challenging enough: navigating an unfamiliar network of tunnels to find an exit that they only hoped existed. But at least they had light.

And Yulda.

Thinking of the girl, Aiya turned and found her cowering against the wall, watching the dead soldier. She looked up and met Aiya's eyes. Aiya waited for an acerbic complaint, but it didn't come.

Instead, the girl swallowed and said, "But how? Why didn't I see them? If they were here all this time, shouldn't..."

"No talking." Dan straightened and glanced over his shoulder at the darkness. "If there are men alive down here, I want to find them."

He didn't need to tell them to be quiet. Aiya had no desire for conversation, and Yulda's chatter had dried up completely. A heavy silence descended over the group, but Aiya sensed an eagerness in Dan. He hoped to find more of his fellow soldiers.

It didn't take long. Around a bend, they came across another corpse. The soldier wore no boots and the flesh on his feet were mottled and swollen in the lamplight. Aiya stepped over them gingerly, refusing to look at his face. She pressed her sleeve to her nose against the smell.

As they passed an opening into another tunnel, Dan stopped, holding up his hand for quiet. A faint snuffling emanated from the dark opening. As Dan moved toward the sound, Yulda grabbed Aiya's arm.

"What if it's them? What if they find us?"

Aiya knew she didn't mean the Rahmish soldiers. She took the lamp from Yulda's trembling fingers before she could spill the precious oil. The sight of death had upset the girl and brought back her fear of being caught by Domar's men.

"I don't think it's them, but stay close to me. You'll be all right."

She hung back a little with Yulda, letting Dan go down the passage until he rounded a corner and was gone from view.

The light from Dan's lamp diminished as he moved further away and then stopped, holding steady. Aiya tried to push away images of nightmarish beasts living in the dark and waiting for fresh prey as she and Yulda crept forward. As they rounded the corner, the murmur of low voices reached their ears.

Here the passageway widened into a small chamber. Rahmish soldiers—nearly two dozen at first glance—

filled the room. Some lay unmoving; others sat huddled together. Many of them shielded their eyes against the light from Dan's lamp, which he'd placed in an open spot of floor. Yulda brushed past Aiya in her haste to snatch it before it was knocked over or swallowed by the mud.

Dan squatted before a group of soldiers, and Aiya recognized Jax. His red hair looked nearly black in the dim light, and his lips were crusted with blood and dried spittle, but his eyes flickered over Aiya in recognition.

Dan murmured a word to Jax, gripping his shoulder before moving to speak to Aiya.

"They need water and food. Especially water." Dan slipped his pack from his shoulder and pulled out a waterskin.

"We don't have enough for all of them," Aiya said with alarm.

"Then we'll get more."

"Where? We don't even know where we are." She tried to snatch the waterskin from him, but he pulled it away.

"These men are dying!" Dan whispered fiercely.

"Yes, but are you saving them from death? Or condemning us to die with them? Think this through, Dan. If all these men need water, how will you choose who to give it to? And how will the others respond?"

"So you would just let them die?"

"No, but we must have a plan so that we don't become trapped here with them."

To her relief, Dan reluctantly returned the waterskin

and closed the pack. "Where's the girl?" he said, looking over Aiya's shoulder.

Yulda had been there a moment before, Aiya was sure of it. But now she was gone, and the other oil lamp with her.

Aiya felt a flare of panic. If Yulda had run off without them, they were doomed. She was the only one who had been in these tunnels before, and their only chance to find an exit.

"I will find her," she said. She handed the lamp to Dan, but he pushed it back at her.

"Take it. You'll need it."

Aiya glanced at the yawning darkness of the passageway through which they'd come. She very much wanted to bring the light, but it seemed cruel to leave these poor men in the dark again. "I won't go far. If I can't find her, I'll return and we can search for her together. Your light will help me find my way back."

Trying not to show the fear she felt, Aiya stepped into the passageway.

The darkness was worse after leaving the light. She waited for her eyes to adjust, but she simply couldn't shake the heavy blindness she felt as the light of the chamber faded behind her. Occasionally she looked back to make sure some of Dan's light was still visible, her beacon to find her way back.

When she reached the tunnel where they had branched off—at least, she *thought* it was the same one —she paused. Dan's light was very dim now, but she could just sense which passage to take. The problem was, she had no idea where to go to find Yulda.

Had the girl fled? Was she exploring? Or was she overwhelmed by the helplessness of the men they'd found? Without knowing her state of mind, it was impossible to guess. And so, counting each squelching footstep in an effort to not get hopelessly lost, Aiya turned and ventured into the darkness.

FOUR

Ria stood at the window, watching the first stars emerge in the western sky. She had never been much of a student of astronomy and couldn't remember the names of the stars or their constellations. But she loved to watch them on a clear night: their varying strengths and brilliance, and the glowing band that stretched across the dark sky as a cold ribbon of light.

"Come away from the window, dear," Lotta said kindly from the doorway. "Your hair will dry faster by the fire."

Of course Ria knew this, but she would let Lotta mother her tonight and relish it. She moved to a backless chair before the hearth, and Biren began combing the tangles from her hair, freshly wet from a long bath.

"Have you seen him?" Ria asked. After fussing over Ria's bath and hovering while the physician examined her shoulder, Lotta had gone to persuade the king to come see his daughter.

"I'm afraid not," Lotta said. "I couldn't even get in through the door. Some nonsense about it being past sundown."

That stung. Why had her father not been the first to welcome her home with open arms? For the first few hours after her arrival, each time the door had opened, she had expected to hear his booming voice. Each time, her disappointment grew.

Lotta sat on a padded stool before her, taking Ria's hands in her own. She spoke with great solemnity which did nothing to ease the gnawing worry in Ria's stomach.

"I didn't want to speak of this until the morning. You need your rest. But I see that you are greatly troubled, and against my better judgment, I'll speak of it now."

Lotta's eyes flickered momentarily to Biren, but Ria shook her head. "Biren may stay. I trust her and her discretion."

Lotta nodded. "Your father," she began uncertainly, "is not well. You spoke to me of the challenges he had before you left. I now believe they may have been more serious than even you knew. In any case, they are very serious now. His nighttime terrors are more violent than before, and the soldiers who guard him are there as much to keep him from harming himself as those who tend him. He doesn't always know what is real and what is false, leading him to behave unpredictably."

The words settled slowly. "Lotta, are you telling me that my father has gone mad?"

Lotta looked pained. "It may not be permanent. The

physician thinks that his current solitude may be healing for him.”

“That’s the purpose of the tower?”

“I don’t know where he got the idea in the first place, but Galinn says he would not be dissuaded. Now that he’s shut himself inside it, by all reports he’s happier, and the damage he can inflict on others is minimized.”

“So everyone is happy to keep him locked up?” Ria felt sick with anguish. “Lock him away so we don’t have to deal with him? Oh, I never should have left!”

“No!” Lotta said, squeezing her hands. “You mustn’t think that. This kingdom needs a leader. You were right to go. It’s good for the people to see you acting in your father’s stead. It’s your rightful place, no matter what Lord Hegrin says.”

Ria looked at her sharply. “What does Lord Hegrin say?”

Lotta grimaced. “My dear, I haven’t been so long from your father’s court that I don’t know the ways of a man like Lord Hegrin. An unprecedented woman heir? The king rumored unwell? It’s the sort of opportunity of which a man like Hegrin dreams. Cast enough uncertainty on your house, and it won’t be too hard to elevate his son as a more worthy heir to the throne, distant relationship notwithstanding.”

Ria stood and moved closer to the fire, her cheeks burning as she remembered dancing with the young Hegrin in Berseth. Had she played into a larger plot by bestowing favor upon him? She glowered at the flames licking the charred wood, her nightclothes giving off a scent of clean linen as they warmed.

In the silence, Lotta offered, "Don't worry too much about Lord Hegrin. It's not he who has the heart of the people. They are eager to accept you if you show that you are ready. Doing this tour was an important step. They will more easily look to you for direction in these uncertain times."

"Uncertain, yes." Ria took a slow breath, speaking her decision aloud. "There may be one thing I can do to help with that. Since the attack, I've been thinking of how tenuous the future of the throne is. Should anything happen to me, there is no clear heir. Now you tell me that my father's reason can't be relied on. But if I were to marry—and soon—and if my father names him a joint heir to the throne, then the line of succession will be secured. In time, we'll produce heirs of our own, and Hegrin and his ambitions will dwindle to dust."

Lotta rested a hand on her shoulder. "We needn't worry about that right now. That's not a decision that needs to be made for some time yet—"

"No," Ria said firmly, shaking off her touch. "I don't need time. I've already made my choice." She smiled, but it felt strained. "I'd hoped to share this news with you in more cheerful circumstances, after speaking with my father. But as he has made that difficult..." She bit off the bitter words she was thinking, nervously tucking her wet hair behind her ear.

Lotta waited expectantly.

"Over the past two months, there is one man for whom my esteem has risen a great deal," Ria said, glancing at her maid with a shy smile. Biren's expression was impassive. "I've decided to marry Captain Strong."

"Oh." Lotta blinked and took a calm breath. "Oh my."

"What is it?" Ria's smile slid away. "I thought you would be pleased."

"Pleased? Yes, well, I didn't expect...He's a commoner. I expected—I think we all expected—someone closer to your own status."

Lotta's veiled displeasure settled sourly in Ria's stomach. She moved away from the fire and sat again before Biren with her wide-toothed comb.

"If he were closer to my own status," Ria said, grunting as Biren worked out the snarls in her wet hair, "he wouldn't possess the qualities I admire. His perspective is unique precisely because his experience is so different from my own. We compliment each other in ways that will be most beneficial. I couldn't ask for a better companion."

"I see," Lotta nodded. "Perhaps you're right. After all, he's no stranger to royal favor. I was half in love with him myself when I was your age. After the people saw you together tonight, they'll be more ready to accept him. Yes, I think they'll learn to love him as you do."

Biren's hands faltered in Ria's hair.

"The people may think what they will, but I cannot lie to you, Lotta. I don't care for him in that way."

The light that had briefly kindled in Lotta's eyes faded. "I don't understand. If you don't love him, why risk the disapproval of the court?"

"Hang the court," Ria said dismissively. "Merek's distinguished career, together with my father's support, will more than compensate for his low birth."

"Perhaps. It will certainly be more complicated than if you had chosen someone from a noble family. And with no affection between you, it will make for a lonely marriage."

"Nonsense," Ria snapped, her irritation rising as Biren tugged at her hair. "Must a woman always be governed by her heart? Why can't you accept that my choice is sound and trust me for it?"

"Forgive me. Of course you know your own mind, but I fear you won't be content to live without love."

"And how well did my father know my mother when they wed? There's no reason I couldn't grow to love Merek as well as any other man...certainly more than a fool like Hegrin."

"Does he agree?"

"We haven't spoken of it," Ria admitted. "I thought it was best to speak to my father first. He may have similar objections, but ultimately, he knows Merek's character better than anyone."

Lotta nodded and patted her hand. "You did right not to speak of it prematurely. But you must remember that Merek Strong hasn't been raised to expect a marriage of the sort you propose. It's likely that he wouldn't find a loveless marriage desirable. Perhaps he even loves another and wouldn't be willing to give her up for the throne. If that's the case, you cannot demand it of him. You must find out what's in his heart and respect him for it."

"Are you suggesting he might refuse me?" Ria hadn't considered this. An image of the beautiful Khouri woman came to mind, and the admiring way Merek had spoken of her. It made Ria feel distinctly uncomfortable, so she pushed the thought away. Even if Lotta was right and his heart belonged to another, she and Merek shared something. A bond. She was sure he felt the same way. It may not be love, but it would be enough.

She would make it be enough.

"I'm merely pointing out that circumstances of birth create different expectations when it comes to marriage. Look at me, for instance. I watched your mother wed your father despite barely knowing him. But she blessed her good fortune—not because he would someday be king, but because of his generous heart and giving nature."

"You always told me theirs was a marriage of great affection," Ria countered.

"Yes, it was, eventually. But your mother knew that she could have had a different fate if your father had been a cruel and selfish man, and she was all the more willing to love him because he was not."

"You see? Why couldn't this be my future?" Ria felt like she was a child again, trying to convince Lotta to let her do her lessons in the garden on a warm summer day.

Lotta paused, waiting until Ria looked her in the eyes. Ria saw such love there that she couldn't help but quiet her tongue.

"My point is simply that when I watched your mother and father together, I knew this could never be for me. A man might offer me the wealth of kingdoms, but I would never marry unless our love was so strong that it made such wealth seem paltry by comparison."

Ria looked down at her hands in her lap. "I never

knew you were such a romantic," she said with a laugh, trying to shake off the unease she felt at Lotta's words.

"Why? Because I married a bald baker?" Lotta's laugh was warm and affectionate, deepening the wrinkles around her eyes. "I count myself blessed each day for my dear Pedr."

"You think Merek may be more like you? Inclined to refuse a princess in favor of a humble commoner?"

"In favor of love, dear, in whatever form he finds it."

"In my experience, love brings nothing but sorrow," Ria said bitterly. "I gave my heart to Artem freely, and it was wounded and scarred in return. The thought of doing that again is terrifying."

"Yes, it is terrifying," Lotta said with a smile. "To love another is the most courageous thing we can ever do. Love brings sorrow and pain and fear, but also the most exquisite joy imaginable. Most who have known love would never settle for some false substitute. You may choose to ignore your heart, but you should be prepared for the possibility that Merek Strong will not."

"Well," Ria said, standing and smoothing her nightclothes. "If that's the case, then I shall just have to be more persuasive than his heart."

Lotta looked at her for a moment, then laughed. "If it's possible, I'm sure you'll find a way. You've grown up so quickly this past year. I'm very proud of you." Lotta put an arm around her waist and squeezed her affectionately. "Now I must pop out for a moment to tell Pedr the good news. I won't be long, but he'll want to know for himself that you are home safe."

As Lotta slipped out the door, Biren turned down

Ria's bed. Slipping between the clean, cool sheets was almost as luxurious as soaking in the hot bath had been. But Ria couldn't fully relax.

"Have I disappointed you very much?" she asked Biren, who was gathering up her dressing gown and slippers.

Biren looked at her in surprise, her light brown eyes rimmed red with weariness. "Not at all, my lady. I think Captain Strong will make a fine king. I had hoped that someday you would marry for love, but I see now it was a naive wish."

"But a kind one," Ria responded with a sad smile. She closed her eyes and tried to shut her mind to Lotta's words about a lonely marriage. She was doing the right thing. Merek would understand her choice, and surely he would welcome the chance to reconcile with her father.

Her father.

An image of the unfinished tower planted over her grandmother's garden rose in her mind, and with it came a strangled feeling of not being able to draw enough air. Lotta had said that Sindal seemed happier in the tower, but how could he be happier away from her? How could he ignore her so completely after what she'd been through?

Solitude was one thing; abandonment was another.

Ria's insides twisted with a mixture of grief and resentment, and despite being exhausted, she couldn't rest. She tried to push thoughts of Merek and Sindal out of her mind, but thoughts of Artem waited to intrude. Thoughts that didn't trouble her in daylight then crept into her mind when she was alone at night with nothing but her doubt and fear for company. *Had* Artem planned the ambush against her? Domar had mentioned that his employer was a prince, but a mercenary like Domar wouldn't be bound to any country. His employer could be anyone. Such a personal betrayal felt too great even for Artem. If it was him, she needed more proof. She couldn't simply accuse him and risk thrusting Rahm into war with Ardania. If only she could speak to her father and seek his counsel.

Which brought her back to where she'd started. With a sigh, Ria rolled over and burrowed deeper into her feather mattress, trying to clear her mind of all thoughts of Artem and Merek and her father. Yet still they clung to her well into the night.

Five

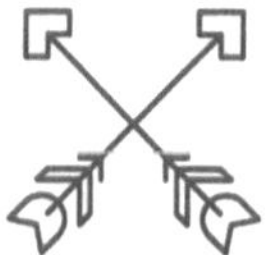

Fifty-seven. Fifty-eight. The darkness pressed in on Aiya. Blood pounded in her ears. She tried to calm her breathing, focusing on counting each step. *Fifty-nine.* Aiya kicked something on the ground, and she jumped back, a small whimper escaping her lips despite her best efforts to hold it in. The blackness was so deep around her that she felt as though she might suffocate from it.

Tentatively, she reached forward with one foot. There was something there, dense but soft. Likely another body. Some poor soul who had tried to find his way out of the maze until he collapsed.

Thinking about the bloated face of the corpse they'd found earlier made the hairs stand up on the back of her neck. If only she could see! Blindly stumbling upon a dead body in the light was ghastly enough. But here in the dark when she could only guess as to what lay before her—

A groan filled the air and something pawed at her ankle.

Aiya shrieked and scrambled backward, tearing away from the creature. She ran back through the mud in a panic, one hand on the damp wall to guide her. Heart racing. Breath shallow and strained. Terrified of what she might meet in the darkness.

After a few minutes, her pulse slowed, and she realized with mounting horror that she hadn't been counting her return steps. She was truly lost now. She stopped and tried in vain to make out something, anything. When she saw a faint glow in the distance, she wasn't sure if it was real or only her imagination. But her eyes locked onto it, and she moved forward.

The light grew brighter quickly, and in moments Aiya was nearly blinded as Yulda came around a bend, holding a lamp high.

"Aiya, is that you?" she called. "Are you alright?"

"*Shenasti*, Yulda!" Aiya said, relieved. "Where have you been? I've been looking for you, and now I'm so turned around that I'll never find Dan again."

"I know where he is, don't worry," Yulda said, her eyes glittering in the light. "In fact, I think I know a lot more than that. Come with me."

As they tromped through the mud, Yulda explained, "Once, when I was down here before, I heard voices. I thought it was Domar, so I hid, but no one ever appeared. Just now, I heard something again. Not voices but something else, like a bird caught in the rafters. So I decided to explore and...well, let me show you."

Aiya had no choice but to follow. Yulda's excitement

began to chase away Aiya's earlier dread. They followed a dizzying maze of corridors until Aiya was certain they were hopelessly lost. But Yulda seemed confident that she was going somewhere specific. At last, she paused and said, "There. You see?"

She held the lamp up high and Aiya strained to see past its glow into the darkness. "What am I looking for?"

"There's a grate in the ceiling. I couldn't see it before because I only had a candle, but this lamp is brighter. I think that's where the voices were coming from," Yulda said excitedly.

"Any idea where it leads?"

"If I could sketch it out I might guess, but I have nothing to sketch with. We're very far from Lord Bolen's, though, I'm sure of it. We might even be outside of the city."

Aiya sized up the young woman. "If Dan were here, he might be able to lift you up to reach it, but I'm too short."

"Let's go get Dan, then." Yulda immediately headed back the way they had come.

"Wait!" Aiya cried in a loud whisper. "We should mark this tunnel so that we can find it again."

"Why? I know where it is."

"How can you possibly know?" Aiya protested, but Yulda was already on her way, and she had to hurry to catch up.

"Don't tell me you know where we're going."

"Of course I do. Do you not?"

Aiya wasn't sure whether Yulda was mad or incredibly gifted. But when she saw a familiar glow ahead, she looked at the young woman beside her with awe. "How did you do this?"

Yulda shrugged but looked pleased.

It didn't take much to convince Dan to join them. The prospect of a way out was too enticing. In the end, Aiya had the best balance, so she climbed on Yulda's back and then onto Dan's shoulders. Moving to a standing position on a swaying foundation with nothing to hold onto was more difficult, but at last she stretched to her full height and reached the grate.

Grasping the iron bars that crossed the frame, she lifted the grate just enough to raise her head and peek into the dark room above. There were windows, and the darkness was that of night instead of the suffocating blackness of underground. Aiya breathed the fresh air with relief.

"It's some kind of a cellar," she called down to Dan in a loud whisper. "It's quite large, I think. There's no one here. I will take a look."

She carefully pushed the grate higher and moved it to the side. The hole it covered wasn't very large, but she had no problem pulling herself up through it. For most of the soldiers, however, it would be impossible. Wherever they were, this couldn't be their escape route.

Aiya sat on the edge of the stone floor, her feet dangling in the hole. The cellar hadn't been swept clean recently, but her boots were caked with mud and bound to leave a trail that even a casual observer would find suspicious.

"What is it?" Dan called up from below.

"Shh, watch out." She unlaced her boots and let

them drop below. Wiping the dirt from her hands onto her trousers, she stood and surveyed the room.

Stacks of crates and an assortment of barrels obscured the view of the stairs. Shelves lined the walls, and above the nearest one a small window was outlined in gray—a sign that night was coming to an end. The other walls were lost in shadow. This was an unusually large cellar, and Aiya knew at once that they were still in Endvar. No small kitchen or public house on the outskirts of the city would need a cellar this size.

A twittering sound drew her attention up to the rafters. It was too dark to spot the bird Yulda had heard, but Aiya blessed it anyway for drawing the girl's attention.

She tested the nearby barrels until she found one light enough to move. It was slow work, but she managed to scoot it under the window with minimal noise. Climbing onto the barrel gave her just enough height to peer through the window.

Outside was a large courtyard ringed with buildings standing gray and quiet in the darkness. The rain puddled at eye level on the stones. All was quiet and empty, but that's not what made Aiya draw in a quick breath.

She scrambled down and hurried over to the hole in the floor. Kneeling, she called down to Dan.

"We are under the guard complex."

"You're certain?"

"Completely."

"If we're at the guard complex, that means we're

close to the eastern gate," Yulda said with anguish. East brought them closer to Ardania, but no nearer safety.

"There is food here," Aiya said. "Give me a few moments to send some down for the soldiers."

She tried to take things that wouldn't be easily missed. She found an old flour sack in a corner and filled it with apples, dried venison, and a sticky paste that had a nutty flavor. It might be easier for the weaker soldiers to eat than something that required more chewing.

Water was another matter. As near as she could tell, the barrels were all full of ale. In their dehydrated state, Aiya couldn't guess what the ale might do to the soldiers.

Returning to the hole, she called, "There's no water here. I need to go upstairs."

"Wait! Is there a rope or something you can lower down? Let me help you."

"I don't think you will fit through the hole," Aiya said. "Yulda yes, but not you. It's too small."

The sound of murmuring voices came from below, and then Aiya could just make out that Yulda was trying to climb onto Dan's shoulders. The poor girl was awkward and shaky, and at one point she kneed Dan in the head as she tried to bring her leg up to his shoulders.

Aiya snickered in spite of herself. "Let me help." She lay on her stomach and lowered her arms. She was just able to reach Yulda's arms and help stabilize her as she tried to stand, but it required much more hauling and laughter to get her through the hole and into the cellar. Yulda's laugh was high and staccato, and the sound of it made Aiya laugh even harder. She buried her face in her sleeve to stifle the sound.

Yulda started to pull her legs through, but Aiya stopped her.

"Take your boots off first. We don't want to leave a muddy trail."

Yulda obeyed, but Dan called back in annoyance when one of her boots struck him, leading to another peal of giggles from the young woman.

"Fool woman," Dan growled. "Just—be careful, you two."

Feeling lighter of heart, Aiya and Yulda padded across the stone floor in their stockinged feet until they reached the stairs. These were made of wood, and Aiya prayed that there was no one sleeping in the kitchen above to hear the creaking as they ascended.

The kitchen was cold and lifeless. Clearly, it hadn't been used in days. A mouse skittered across the tabletop where lay the remnants of a meal that had been abandoned halfway through its preparations: brown potatoes and strips of discolored mutton piled in pie tins.

Yulda stiffened, and Aiya recalled the horrors she had witnessed in Bolen's kitchen. But there was no one else in the kitchen, nor even a sign that there had been any fighting.

Aiya moved to the outside door in search of a pump. It was unnerving to slip outside, even in the dimness of early morning. She felt as if all the empty windows of the barracks were dark eyes watching her, and it was difficult to resist the urge to frequently check over her shoulder. But there, a short distance away, stood a pump.

Dashing back inside, Aiya called for Yulda to look for a bucket or pitcher. Soon they were filling pitchers and basins with water, cringing as the water splashed against the stones in the stillness.

"If only the hole were larger, we could just fill a barrel and be done with it," Yulda grumbled on their fourth trip to the cellar.

"How would you and I move a heavy barrel full of water?" Aiya asked with amusement.

Yulda looked at her with a gleam in her eye. "But if the hole were larger, it wouldn't be only the two of us. Dan would make short work of one of those barrels, don't you think? That would be better than pacing down there like a caged animal."

Aiya smiled. Dan was growing increasingly agitated below. The more he groused at them to hurry, the more Yulda found occasions to stop and stretch dramatically after depositing a load near the cellar drain. But only within view of Dan. She worked quickly and efficiently elsewhere. Aiya knew she should have chided the young woman for teasing him so, but instead she found herself chuckling. It was a welcome feeling after so many days of fear.

After they had lowered the water carefully through the hole, Aiya did one last search of the kitchen and added to their stores as many candles as she dared. Then she and Yulda dropped back down into the tunnel and surveyed their stores.

"When they get stronger," Dan said, "we'll need to

move them. There's no sense letting them rot in that muck when they can be on dry ground with easier access to food and water."

Aiya looked at him sharply. She had hoped that finding these stores meant Dan could assuage his conscience about leaving the soldiers. Instead, he spoke as though he planned to be there to nurse them back to health. But she said nothing. She shouldered a large jug of water while Yulda picked up the sack of food. She would have to find the right moment to remind Dan that the best chance for these men to survive wasn't finding food and water...it was finding a way out.

Six

General Grammel was expecting him. The armed soldiers standing guard outside his office looked knowingly at each other as Merek approached. They let him pass but watched him with hands resting on their hilts.

Good, Merek thought. *He should be worried.*

Merek had no intention of doing anything more than talking to the general, however. He had stewed over this meeting much of the night and then again in the early morning when he'd given up on sleep and cleared his head on the practice field. As much as he wanted to challenge Grammel, there was more at stake than his wounded pride.

His boots thumped firmly on the scuffed wooden floor as he stepped inside Grammel's office. Captain Firl was speaking, looking more gray in the early morning light than Merek remembered from the last time they'd met. He trailed off as soon as Merek entered the room.

Captains and clerks filled the room, and they too grew still as their eyes turned to Merek. There was a moment of heavy silence before General Grammel spoke.

"We'll adjourn for now," he said, nodding curtly to his captains. It took only a moment for them to gather their clerks and file out of the room. Firl nodded to Merek as he passed, and Captain Orri managed a smile in greeting. But Merek only had eyes for Grammel.

When they were alone, Grammel looked Merek over for a moment before speaking. "So, Captain Strong, I hear you've been playing the hero again."

"If I'm the hero, what does that make you?"

Grammel grunted and leaned back in his chair.

"What I don't understand," Merek continued, "is why you would punish the princess. I never thought you were a cruel man, but convincing the king to ignore his daughter when she needed him most was despicable."

"Is that what he told you?" The corners of Grammel's mouth twitched, almost like a smile. "I see. You still think the king can be trusted. If you weren't so wrapped up in your little theatrics, you might have realized that the king is not the man he once was."

"No, Grammel. *You* are not the man you once were. I remember you as a man of honor who loved his king. Now I see a jealous fool who fills his head with lies, even poisoning him against his own daughter so that he doesn't concern himself for her welfare—"

"Rubbish!" Grammel's face reddened. "I wanted the king to go to her, even though I knew it would play into your drama. It made me sick thinking what a glorious moment it would be for the legendary Captain Strong.

But even knowing that, I hoped he would go. I begged him to go. Any price would be worth it if it meant he left that accursed tower."

Merek paused. This wasn't the scene that he'd imagined after his conversation with Sindal. "You *wanted* him to go?"

"Oh yes! I visit him almost daily with some new excuse to drive him out of that tower. But he refuses to leave."

"He said that you convinced him to stay so as to slight me."

"That's no surprise. He blames others for his behavior when it suits him." Grammel rubbed his forehead. He seemed genuinely frustrated.

Merek faltered. The king had seemed so lucid the previous night that he hadn't even questioned if he were trustworthy. Now he wondered how much of what Sindal said could be believed. "And what of the tales that I planned the ambush against the princess? Did those not come from you?"

Grammel's eyes hardened. "The king and I have had many discussions about your motives and whether or not you are as incorruptible as you seem. You must admit, Strong, that the likelihood of one man rescuing the princess alone when a dozen soldiers failed to keep her safe is highly preposterous. Especially when you consider that you were two days away with presumably no prior knowledge of the attack. The rescue makes for a good story, and I'm sure the people will be speaking of it for weeks. But it's a farce to those who see your aspirations for what they really are."

Merek clenched his jaw to keep from saying what he was thinking. Any explanation of how he rescued Ria would just sound like a weak excuse. And he didn't owe this man an explanation.

"So you planted false notions about me in the mind of a man which you say is failing."

"False?" Grammel smiled shrewdly. "We'll let the king be the judge of that. It must be trying for you that not all of us are taken in by your lies."

With great effort, Merek pushed away his anger. This wasn't supposed to deteriorate into personal attacks. It was time to redirect the conversation. "If you would agree to leave the tale-spinning alone for a time, I have more pressing matters to discuss."

"Oh? I can't imagine what you might have to say that would interest me. But, as you are here…" He gestured to Merek to sit.

Merek sat on the edge of a hard, wooden chair, incapable of relaxing in Grammel's presence.

He's not the enemy, he reminded himself. *You need his help.* He took a deep breath.

"For some months my men have been tracking questionable activities in Endvar, uncertain whether they posed a threat to the citizens at large or just a few private individuals. The closer we get to uncovering their purposes, the more we drive them to act."

"Is that right? Do go on," Grammel said, unmoved.

"By now, Captain Wott will have spoken with Captain Alrek about mobilizing the garrison at Endvar in anticipation of a possible attack. We've found where the enemy is hiding, and if all went well in my absence, they may have already flushed them out. But I suspect this isn't the end of the matter. I want to bring a larger company of soldiers with me when I return. With your permission, of course."

"I see." General Grammel leaned back in his chair, pressing his fingertips together and frowning. "So if I understand you correctly, you've only recently learned of this plot?"

"We identified the major players over the summer, but only recently did I learn that they plan to move against the city," Merek affirmed. "However, at the same moment I also learned of the impending attack on the princess and thought that it deserved my immediate attention."

"How very convenient."

"Convenient?"

"I suppose that if I asked if you are aware that Endvar has been attacked, you would claim ignorance. After all, you were far from the city, away on a rescue mission. *Very* convenient."

Merek stood in alarm, knocking his chair to the floor. "Endvar has been attacked?"

"Not just attacked," Grammel growled, his voice rising. "Endvar has fallen. I received word this morning, and I find it questionable at best that the man charged with defending it was far away playing hero on an errand that smells of deceit."

"What news of the city? The people? My soldiers?"

"The enemy took the gates and sealed the city before my garrison could get there. But you probably already know that."

Merek glared at the general. He was in great danger of hating this man. "Don't waste my time with meaningless accusations. If you truly believed I had any part in this, you would have had me arrested."

Grammel reddened. "If it were up to me, you would already be in chains. But it seems that only the king can authorize your arrest, and as I said before, he doesn't always discern between truth and lies. But I know more than you think I do, Strong, and if I get one whiff—"

Merek didn't wait for Grammel to finish his sentence before he strode to the door and flung it open. "How soon can I expect you in Endvar?" he said over his shoulder.

"How soon—?" Grammel sputtered, standing. "You are not my commanding officer, Strong!"

"Are you coming or not?" Merek demanded from the doorway.

Grammel's eyes narrowed so that they nearly disappeared under his heavy eyebrows. "We leave tomorrow. Pray the city isn't a pile of ashes by the time we get there."

Seven

Ria squinted at the scaffolding high overhead where men moved blocks of stone into place. She could just make out in silhouette the squealing pulleys that they used to lift the heavy stone.

"How far up are they going to go?" she wondered aloud.

Neither of the young men answered her. Not that she really expected them to. They were guards. Their job was to stand in front of a door, not answer questions from a precocious princess who didn't have the good sense to ignore them.

"Until they run out of stone, do you think? Or perhaps until they all drop from exhaustion?" she mused. "Surely they can't be following a plan. Only a madman would dream up a tower that destroyed his favorite garden and then lock himself away in it."

The guards shifted uncomfortably.

"Ah, so you *can* hear me." She smiled. "I wasn't sure.

I promise I won't tell the king what you said about him being mad. It will be our secret."

Ria was rewarded with a look of panic on the soldiers' faces before the door opened and Martin stepped out.

"I'm sorry to keep you waiting," he wheezed, sounding weaker than when Ria had last seen him. "Your father had a difficult night and I wanted to be sure he was in good spirits before you saw him."

"He's my father, Martin. I shouldn't be kept from him in good spirits or bad."

"Perhaps." Martin ushered her into the tower. "But I must act with prudence, for both of your sakes."

Ria didn't argue further, for the sight before her took her breath away. Her father's beloved garden—the place of so many happy memories—stood before her in shadowed ruin.

"Oh Martin!" she said mournfully. "Could you not have stopped him? What was he thinking?"

Martin shook his white head, stooping slightly as he mounted the stairs that ran along the curving wall. "It seemed a harmless distraction at the time. I thought he would abandon it long before now. But he is determined."

As they passed through to the next level—a sparsely furnished room that Ria surmised served as Martin's living quarters—voices drifted down from higher above on a third level.

"General Grammel is with the king now," Martin explained. "But your father wanted you brought to him at once."

"How very devoted of him," Ria said sourly. She hadn't forgiven her father for ignoring her the previous evening. But she hadn't yet decided whether or not to punish him for it. Walking through the dying garden below had sobered her considerably.

"Thank you, sire," Grammel's voice became clearer as they mounted the final steps to the upper floor. "I will send word as soon as I arrive. And as to the other matter...?"

The king's answering sigh was heavy. "I wish I knew what was best. When you speak, it seems clear that you are right. But then—" He cut off as Martin and Ria entered the room.

Sindal was dressed in an amber dressing gown, reclining on a cushioned couch that had once belonged in his sitting room. He jumped to his feet when he saw Ria, his face erupting in a wide grin. "Oh my darling! You're home!"

Ria rushed to him, all bitterness banished in the warmth of her father's embrace. Ignoring the pain in her shoulder as he gripped her, she buried her face against him and breathed in his familiar scent. Now she was truly home.

"Oh Far, I missed you so!"

"I've missed you too, Ria! It's been too long!" He cupped her face with his hands and kissed her forehead. "That Artem is committed to stealing you away, I'm certain of it."

Ria felt a chill as if she'd been doused in cold water. "Far, I was touring Danvir's Wall, remember? I came home from my foreign tour months ago."

The king's face darkened briefly, then he smiled again. "Of course. That's what I meant. You must sit here now and tell me all about it."

With a quick bow, General Grammel and Martin left them alone, but not before Martin whispered to Ria, "I'll be close if you need me. If he appears agitated, best to leave quickly."

With those words filling her with foreboding, Ria sat on the couch near her father.

"So tell me, what do you think?" he asked, gesturing with wide arms to encompass the tower room. Furnishings from his bedchamber had been brought to fill the room, but they looked out of place as though they didn't feel comfortable with the arrangement. His desk sat too close to the window and the couch, and both were crowded out by the large bed which so dominated the space that there was scarcely room left against the wall for his standing mirror and dressing screen. Despite the cavernous ceiling overhead, Ria felt stifled and cramped. Thinking of Lotta's words, she reached for Sindal's hand.

"You mentioned a surprise in your letters, but I didn't expect something quite like this. Wherever did you get the idea?"

"From you, actually." Her father's blue eyes danced with delight. "In one of your letters you spoke of standing atop Danvir's Wall and the breathtaking awe you felt as you surveyed the countryside. I was so moved by your description that I decided to build a tower so that on the day we celebrate my twentieth year of reign, I might look out over all of Albon and see my people. It will be a monument to my rule which will be remembered for generations, signifying the end of Danvir's days of war and the advent of Sindal's days of peace."

Ria stroked his hand, tracing his veins and coarse blond hairs. "I've seen such towers on the castles in Branvik and Ardania. They are very impressive. But why would you build a tower over your mother's garden? It's been a love of yours as long as I can remember. It broke my heart to see it dying just now."

Sindal's hand clenched into a fist. "You sound like the rest of them...Galinn and the others. It's mine to do what I wish. Of what use is a garden to me?"

"What use? It's a place of life and beauty. You taught me that without beauty we are nearer to death than life. Surely, you don't want to see it destroyed: to see it fall to ruin?"

"Bah!" her father said, pulling his hand away and rubbing it through hair that needed trimming. "Death is everywhere, even in the garden. Death makes life possible. I'm not afraid of death."

Sensing the need to change the subject, Ria affected a cheery smile. "Well, no matter. Let's not argue. What's done is done, and you seem very comfortable here."

She felt dishonest saying these words when what she wanted to do was chide him for being a fool and demand that he return with her to the Hall. It wasn't like her to hide her true feelings from her father, but his manner stopped her. Made her speak delicately.

She hated it.

At the topic of his comfort, however, Sindal relaxed and reached for her hand again. "I *am* very comfortable," he agreed. "All that I need is brought to me by Martin, and I have the most extraordinary view. Come and see!"

He stood and pulled her to the nearest window. Ria didn't want to enjoy it, but when she looked out, her eyes widened with pleasure. The view truly was magnificent. Ria had never seen Albon from this height and was amazed at the changed perspective. The people were miniature, and the buildings looked flat.

"I can see all the way to the city gates!" she said with a laugh. She looked for landmarks and familiar shops. "Look! There's that hideous fountain I fell into as a little girl. And I think I see Pedr's bakery." She grinned with childlike wonder. "I should spend hours here if I were young again."

"It's not too late," her father said, placing a hand on her shoulder. "I had hoped you might join me here. When it's finished there will be another chamber like this one above us. You might sit at your window all day and play your harp all you like."

Ria recoiled at the thought. "Oh Far, I could never lock myself away in a place like this. I should die of boredom with only myself for company, and would likely drive you—" she caught herself before saying *mad,* "—to tears with my incessant chatter."

"I would enjoy your chatter. It gets lonely here at times. Please Ria, I've missed you so." The creases around his eyes looked pronounced with sorrow, and Ria noticed more gray around his temples than she remembered.

But Ria wasn't even tempted. "I'm sorry, Far. I cannot live the life of a hermit. And you shouldn't either.

Come back with me to the Hall and resume your place. I miss you too and have so much I need to tell you!"

A shadow passed over her father's face. "Of course, you're still young. You have much to see and do before the world loses its charm for you. You may visit me here as often as you like. Bring your harp and play for me. Tell me of the silly things that occupy your time."

Ria blinked, astounded. Did her father think she was a little child? "They're not silly things, Far. They are essential to my safety. My escort was attacked on our return from Endvar—"

"Yes, yes, I know all about that," Sindal said dismissively. "How fortunate that Captain Strong was there to rescue you."

"Yes, it was fortunate," Ria said, irritation rising. "That's something else I want to talk to you about. I've considered my marriage prospects and made my choice. I've decided that I'm going to wed Captain Strong."

She had expected dismay. She had hoped for pleasure. She hadn't planned for rage.

"What's this?" Sindal demanded, his eyes hardening as he stepped closer. "If this is a jest, it's a tasteless one, Ria."

"I do not jest." Ria stood up straighter in defiance. "I've made my choice and ask for your approval. I should think you would be happy I didn't choose one of the brainless oafs who've been parading through Albon hoping to catch a throne."

"Better one of them than a conniving traitor," he spat.

"A traitor? Don't be ridiculous. Merek is a good man

and a true friend to you. He'll be as noble a king as you are someday."

It was the wrong thing to say. The king purpled with rage, eyes bulging. His heavy hand struck her across the face so fast that she didn't have time to flinch. Ria staggered backward from the blow, her shoulder flaring with pain as she tensed to catch herself against the window ledge.

"He will never..." Sindal said, panting with the intensity of his anger, "sit upon my throne!"

Ria ducked to avoid his fist, but he grabbed her hair and yanked her head back. She yelped with pain, fear rising at the ferocious look in Sindal's eyes. This was not her father. This was a stranger—an animal—and he terrified her.

"What did he do to you?" he demanded. "What lies did he tell to convince you to wed him?"

Ria couldn't speak, the strain on her neck making it difficult to breathe. With her good hand, she groped on the desk next to her and grasped her father's heavy seal. It was a poor excuse for a weapon, but it was all she had to defend herself.

"Foolish girl! How could you disrespect me this way? You spoiled, careless child! You disgust me!"

Ria gasped for breath, gripping the seal while she tried to find the courage to strike her own father. She closed her eyes against the spittle flying from his mouth, but she couldn't block out his angry words.

"That man will never take you into his bed, do you understand? Or is that what this is about? Have you already spread your legs for him? Are you carrying his filthy child? If you think that I will allow a common bastard to be my heir—"

And then, blessedly, hands were pulling them apart. Soldiers came between them, and Ria opened her eyes to see General Grammel grappling with her father.

"Get out!" Grammel yelled as she stumbled to gain her feet. She vaguely recognized the two soldiers she had teased rushing to her side to steady her. As they went down the stairs, they passed old Martin heading toward the king's chamber. His face was pale and his expression grim. He didn't spare a glance for Ria.

Sindal's bellows followed her all the way to the outer door of the tower.

"Leave me; I'm well enough," she said weakly to the soldiers once they'd escorted her out. They hurried back inside, and Ria slumped against the wall. She breathed in huge gulps of air, trembling despite the warm sunlight on her face. Only then did she notice that she was still clutching her father's heavy seal with the Thorodan crest.

A wave of nausea passed over her. She couldn't bear the thought of returning inside the tower, so she slipped the seal into a deep pocket and shakily started for her rooms. She hugged herself as she walked, her father's hurtful words ringing in her ears and her eyes burning with unshed tears.

Biren met her at the door to her room.

"Oh, my lady!" She took Ria by the arm and helped her sit. "What happened?"

Ria just shook her head, not trusting herself to

speak. She collapsed into a chair and curled her legs up beneath her.

"I'm so sorry, my lady," Biren said, draping a warm throw around Ria's shoulders and pressing a cup into her hand. "I never suspected there might be danger, or I would have requested an escort."

Ria sipped the wine and winced. Gingerly, she probed at her lip. It was tender and tasted of blood.

"Here." Biren gave her a cool wet cloth, and Ria pressed it against her swollen mouth, wondering how bad it looked. She didn't have the strength to stand and seek a looking glass.

"Shall I tend to your hair?" Biren offered cautiously. But Ria's scalp ached where her father had tugged, and she shook her head.

Long minutes passed—hours even?—but Ria couldn't stir herself. She thought Biren might have spoken to her, but she couldn't think of what she'd said. She could only hear her father's accusations and see the murderous rage in his eyes as he loomed over her. She sipped at the wine, waiting for it to ease the jittery feeling in her limbs. She'd felt this before, after confronting the thief in the inn at Cillith. She never expected her own father might make her feel the same.

Thinking of those events in Cillith pulled her mind at last away from thoughts of Sindal. As if a detached part of herself had returned, she became conscious again of her surroundings and stirred, looking for Biren. Her maid was folding linens but dropped them as soon as Ria moved.

"How may I help you, my lady?" she asked uncertainly, coming to her side.

"I must speak with Captain Strong. Will you please send word for him?" The king's opposition made it even more vital that she explain herself to Merek. She hadn't realized Sindal's feelings of jealous suspicion had grown so strong.

A flush appeared in Biren's cheeks. "I'm sorry, my lady. I forgot to tell you that the captain left this morning before you were awake. He sent this note." She retrieved an envelope from a side table.

"What?" Ria said in frustration. "I told him to see me before he left. Can the man not do one thing I ask?"

"You did sleep very late," Biren said apologetically.

It was true. Ria had slept long and hard, making up for weeks of difficult travel. The physician had approved when he saw her upon waking, saying that the rest was good for her. But she'd missed her chance to speak to Merek before he left, and no amount of sleep was worth that.

Ria took the note and moved to the window seat where the light was best, settling against a damask cushion. How long had she been sitting in a stupor? The sunlight of before was lost behind a growing bank of clouds, making it as dim as dusk. Merek's note was short, only a few lines, and addressed her with her formal title. Ria sniffed a little at that.

Princess,

 I regret that I can't keep our appointment, but I'm sure

you'll forgive me under the circumstances. I trust that you will handle the challenges ahead with customary grace and sound judgment. You've proven yourself more than capable and have earned the devotion of this faithful servant.

Until we meet again,

Captain Strong

"What is this? Challenges ahead? What is this cryptic message?" Ria thrust it back at her maid.

Biren shook her head as she reviewed the lines, equally bewildered.

At that moment, the door burst open and Lotta erupted into the room like a seismic event. "I will kill him! I swear I will kill that man with my own two hands!"

Ria was startled. She had never seen Lotta enraged, not like this. It took her a moment to realize who she was talking about.

"You can't talk about killing the king, Lotta," she said. "That's treason, you know."

Lotta stood above Ria and lifted her chin to inspect her face. Her eyes blazed with fury. "Who does he think he is, hurting my girl? I don't care what his excuse is. If he thinks he has demons now, just wait until I've finished with him."

Ria suppressed a smile and winced at the soreness in her lip. A part of her was amused at the thought of Lotta charging her way into the king's lair and unleashing her wrath on him, but she shook her head. "No, Lotta. You really mustn't talk this way. He wasn't himself. Now that I know what he's capable of, I'll be more careful." Her voice was strong, but inwardly, she shuddered to think of going to that tower again.

Ria gave Captain Strong's note to Lotta. "Tell me, what do you make of this?"

As Lotta scanned the lines, her demeanor changed. The anger dimmed, and she grew very serious. "This is what I meant to speak to you about before I heard—" She paused, lines around her mouth forming as she pursed her lips. "There is grim news from the east. Endvar has fallen."

"What?" Ria stood in alarm, suddenly towering over the plump woman. "What do you mean by 'fallen'?"

"I don't know much, but it seems there was some kind of attack. General Grammel is preparing the army as we speak." Lotta's voice was tinged with fear.

Ria had no room for fear. All she felt was extreme annoyance. "And no one thought to tell me? Strong? Grammel? My father? No one! Am I the last in this house to know?"

This was not acceptable.

Ria brushed past Lotta and Biren, indifferent to whether or not they followed. She made her way through the Hall and out into the courtyard, ignoring the servants who looked askance at her swollen face. The breeze tossed her hair, loosened by her father's grip so that it drifted down to her shoulders.

Walking down the hill to the barracks gave her time to plan her words for General Grammel. With her father indisposed, it was vital that she establish her authority with Grammel. The fields around the barracks were alive with activity. Soldiers and horses were outfitted in full battle gear, and wagons were being loaded to capacity with provisions. There was an expectant tension in the air. It had been many years since Rahm had gone to war.

Ria searched among the many uniforms for General Grammel and found him in a thick crowd of high ranking officers. They parted to make way for her.

"Your Highness." Grammel greeted her with a small bow. He was an impressive sight in his shining armor and heavy mail. Suddenly, Ria felt foolish demanding to be included in his plans. What did she know of war? Even her father's impaired wits couldn't be much worse than her inexperience.

She raised her chin and tried to speak with authority. She was easily his height, but he must have been twice her size all the same. And far more commanding.

"General, I would like a word."

"As you can see, I'm very busy, Your Highness."

"Then I'll keep this brief. I don't want to delay your departure any more than you do, but I *will* speak with you now."

A look of irritation flashed across his face, but Grammel dismissed his captains and turned to give her his full attention.

"Forgive me for not intervening sooner," he said, glancing at her mouth. "I've asked Martin to have a guard in the room whenever you visit your father in the future."

"That's not your decision. If a guard is present, it will be because I wish it. But that's not what I'm here to speak to you about. You know that my father isn't a well man. I want you to send your troop reports to me. I'll keep him apprised of the situation in Endvar as his health allows."

Grammel's eyes glinted with humor. "Last time I checked, the king was my commander. Until that changes, I'll report to him and him alone. I would suggest you seek your amusement elsewhere."

Ria flushed hot with the insult. "Watch yourself, General. Captain Strong treated me with respect on our wall tour and educated me in the areas where my experience was lacking. I see no reason why you shouldn't do the same." She thought it best not to mention the arm-twisting she'd had to do to get Strong to agree.

"Well," General Grammel said with a patronizing air. "This is nothing like a wall tour, and I think you'll find that I am nothing like Captain Strong."

"Oh I already knew that," Ria said acidly. "But I wonder if you know that it's an indictment of your character and not a compliment."

Grammel's face darkened briefly, and he looked as if he were considering carefully his next words. "Your Highness, I would suggest that you don't ally yourself too closely with that man. He's not the friend to your house that he once was."

Ria stiffened. "Thank you for your time, General. Your perspective is always so illuminating." She dismissed him with a curt nod, though in hindsight she couldn't be sure that he hadn't already dismissed her by turning away and hailing a passing messenger boy.

Ria sighed as she walked away from the unpleasant general. It would be extremely challenging to convince him to look to her as a leader; she really had no idea where to begin.

As she ascended the hill to return home, she heard a man call for her.

"Your Highness!"

Captain Talen jogged toward her from the direction of the barracks.

Ria smiled weakly. She liked the genial, curly-haired man. He was her father's First Captain over the Peacekeepers, and although he was a trifle dull, he possessed a sincerity that she respected. It helped that he laughed at her jests.

"Yes, Captain?"

"I don't mean to disturb you," Talen said, breathing heavily from his jog, "but I've been trying to seek an audience with the king for some days now, to no avail. I was hoping you might entreat him on my behalf." He glanced at her lip covertly.

Ria sighed inwardly. Perhaps she should have stayed in her room until the swelling went down.

"Of course. What's the matter?"

"It concerns some criminal activity taking place in Cillith. He's aware of the situation, but there've been some recent developments I need to share with him."

Ria knew well that crime was increasing in Cillith, remembering the intruder she'd discovered in her rooms when they'd stayed there during the wall tour. "Captain, I can't guarantee that the king will see you. But if you will inform me of the situation, I may be able to do something."

Talen shifted uncomfortably, hesitating to say what

he was thinking although Ria could see it plainly on his face. He didn't trust her abilities any more than Grammel did.

"I'm no fool, Talen," she said firmly, "but if it would make you feel better, write it all out in detail. That way nothing will be missed." That would also give her a better chance of discussing the situation with her father's advisors. She wouldn't tell Talen, but she had no intention of returning to the tower unless it was absolutely necessary.

Talen considered this and nodded. "I'll have my clerk compile the information, though it may take some time." He looked up at the gray sky and grimaced. "I have another task to tend to first, and it will not be pleasant."

"Such is our lot, though, eh Captain?" Ria said with a half smile that felt more like a grimace. "I find that the more unpleasant the task, the sooner it should be finished so as to limit its damage."

"Of course, you're right," Talen said, smiling in return, but it was clear that he was troubled.

As he jogged away, Ria turned back to the Hall. With her own advice ringing in her ears, and the weight of her father's seal in her pocket, it was time to find Galinn.

Eight

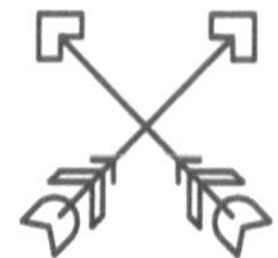

Merek led his soldiers northeast at a quickening pace, trying to cover as much ground as possible before the darkening clouds opened. He and Rorden had met Captain Eldar and his company in the late afternoon. They were still making their way toward Albon with the wounded Captain Drenall and his men who had survived the ambush, but when Eldar and Drenall heard Merek's news about Endvar, they decided that Drenall and his men should carry on alone so that Merek's soldiers could return with him to Endvar.

They were quiet as they rode, grim thoughts of home and fears of what had happened to the city hanging over them. When the rain began, it quickly accelerated to a downpour, limiting their visibility and making it dangerous to continue further in the premature darkness.

Sheltering under a stand of trees, Merek ordered his

men to make camp, as meager as it was. They had no tents, and he put them to work building fires as much to give them something to do as anything else. Eventually, all the soldiers were huddled around smoking campfires, talking very little and taking whatever comfort they could from the limited warmth.

Merek found Rorden sitting on a log, shaving wood chips idly with his knife. Merek sat beside him and looked at the growing pile of shavings at his feet.

"Are you planning to stuff a mattress with those?" he asked. "You'll wear out your knife first."

Rorden smiled weakly. "It's a nervous habit, sir." He laid the knife in his lap and rubbed his eyes with the heels of his hands. "How did this happen? After all we did to uncover this plot, it didn't make a difference. We failed!"

Merek understood the young man's frustration. He'd spent most of the day reviewing the past few months, wondering how he could have stopped the recent events from unfolding. *We didn't fail*, he wanted to say. *I failed. I failed you, I failed Wott and Dan and Aiya and Imar and Lord Ogmun and the whole cursed city.* But he didn't stop there. He had failed Ria, the king, and every citizen in Rahm who now had war at their doorstep.

That's what he'd told himself for the first few hours of their journey. But what he found himself saying to Rorden now was, "We didn't stop the attack, but we certainly haven't failed. If they've been coordinating this for as long as I suspect they have, we couldn't have stopped them anyway without a larger force. They were ready for us. We've been at peace too long and have neglected our borders. War was bound to come. We just have to do everything we can to end it—quickly, and on our terms."

"Yes, sir," Rorden nodded. He picked up his knife and resumed shaving the stick to a point.

Merek wished he could believe his own words so readily. What he said was true. The many parts and pieces that led them to war now were not his fault alone. But he still had trouble sleeping that night, and it wasn't from the constant rain dripping on him from the thick canopy of trees which had only just begun to shed their leaves.

The rain didn't let up all night, and the morning light was delayed by the storm. Nevertheless, Merek had his men up early preparing to ride by the dim light. As they packed up and tended to their horses, a call sounded out in the camp.

"Riders approaching!"

Merek jogged to the edge of the glen with Rorden close at his heels.

A few miles away, soldiers approached around a bend in the road that curved behind a small hill. Merek squinted against the rain. "Can you see who it is?" he asked.

After a pause, Rorden answered confidently. "That's Captain Talen's banner, sir. It looks like he has about a dozen men. What do you think they could want?"

When the prison cart rolled into view, Merek's heart clenched with dread. "No, surely not," he murmured.

"What is it, sir?"

Realization washed over Merek as a wave of nausea,

followed by an urge to fight. "If I'm not mistaken, Sergeant," he said through clenched teeth. "They're here for me."

"For you?" Rorden frowned. Then he took in the prison cart, and his eyes widened in disbelief. "You don't mean—"

"Grammel said the only thing stopping him from having me arrested was needing to convince the king. It appears he finally got his wish. Curse this rain!" Merek said vehemently. "If it hadn't slowed us down, they might not have caught us."

"What do we do, sir?" Rorden asked, a hint of panic creeping into his voice.

Merek turned his back on his approaching doom. "Let's ride out to meet them."

"Sir," Rorden said, grabbing at his arm. The young man looked angry. And afraid. "This isn't right," he said in a harsh whisper. "Flee before they get here. We can fight them off if we must. We have the advantage."

"No, it's too dangerous. Even if you survived, you would be enemies to the crown. The only thing that matters now is saving Endvar."

"But if you go with them, you'll be hanged. Surely you know that!"

Merek *did* know it, and it took everything he had not to draw his sword and fight for his freedom. "Maybe not," he said, managing a faint smile that felt more like a grimace.

Captain Eldar was approaching, so Merek instructed him to have the men mount up. Then he pulled Eldar aside and said quietly, "Whatever happens, don't let Rorden do anything rash."

Eldar raised a questioning eyebrow, but when Merek didn't elaborate, he just nodded.

They rode toward the approaching party in two columns, with Merek and Eldar at the head. With each passing second, as they drew closer to Talen and his men, Merek's indignation grew. What had he done to deserve this? He'd given his very blood to defend his country, had seen countless friends die, and had worn out his life in the service of the king. Even now, he was on his way to defend Rahm against her darkest threat in many years, and one man's petty grudge would lead to this? Dishonor, imprisonment, and likely death.

His anger against Sindal grew with a fierceness that blurred the edges of his vision. Sindal could have stopped this at any time. He could have kept Grammel in his place. He could have listened to Merek and been a king instead of cowering in a tower listening to fools.

Merek was angry with Talen too. How could the man have accepted an assignment like this? Apparently this was a day to be betrayed by old friends. Merek had never realized that Talen was a man with no integrity.

No, that wasn't fair. He knew Talen, and he knew this would be giving him no pleasure. But it felt good to be angry. Anger gave him the strength to face what was coming.

When they were close enough to speak, both companies halted. Merek said nothing. He wouldn't make this easy for his friend.

Former friend.

Talen didn't speak either. Instead, one of his lower captains, dressed in the brown uniform of a peacekeeper, produced a document and began reading in a loud voice.

"Captain Merek Strong, by order of the king you are under arrest for high treason," he called out.

The reaction from Merek's men was immediate: audible gasps, and a few muttered curses from the ordinarily disciplined group. Even Eldar shifted uncomfortably in his saddle. No one had expected this. Merek didn't spare a glance for the man reading the writ. He only looked at Talen, who held his gaze with an inscrutable expression.

The officer continued. "From this moment forth, you are hereby stripped of your rank and office and are ordered to surrender all weapons and personal property. You will submit yourself to the custody of Captain Talen, First Captain of the Peacekeepers, to be transported to the king's prison where you will await trial."

The shame of the words burned in Merek's ears, but he fought the urge to look away. When he spoke, it was to Talen.

"When did you become Grammel's errand boy?" he called. "I know this is his work. Why isn't he the one getting his hands dirty?"

The other men grew silent, waiting for Talen's answer.

Talen raised his head, curly hair clinging to his forehead in the rain. "I serve my king," he said simply, but there was a look of determination in his eye.

"Sindal never would have approved the writ if

Grammel hadn't pushed him to it. You know this, just as you know that if I return with you now, it will mean my certain death."

"It was out of my hands as soon as the king signed the writ. Don't be a fool. No good can come from resisting."

The unmistakable sound of a sword being drawn drew Merek's attention. Surprisingly, it wasn't the youthful Rorden, but the mature Eldar who brandished his weapon.

"These are unjust charges, and I will not stand by while you take this innocent man!" Eldar bellowed.

Merek was stunned. Even more so when Eldar's challenge was answered by the echoes of dozens of his men drawing their swords in kind.

Talen's men immediately drew their own swords, glancing uneasily at their commander.

Merek didn't want his men to fight—soldiers killing each other was always a waste, especially when their country was at war—but he didn't tell Eldar to stand down. Not yet.

"You're outnumbered four to one," Merek continued. He and Talen were the only two who hadn't yet drawn weapons. To draw his sword would be to cross a line from which he and his men could never return. "I don't want to see blood spilled here any more than you do. Turn back now, and not one soldier need fall. Allow us to go to Endvar and save the city."

Talen kept his eye fixed on Merek, but he raised his voice so all could hear. "Any man who inhibits Captain

Strong's arrest will be considered a conspirator and charged with sedition!"

Merek's men stood firm. He felt a rush of pride for their courage.

"Your words don't scare them, Talen," he said. "These aren't unseasoned soldiers who have never grappled with true fear. These are my best men, the ones I've chosen to serve with me on the wall. I see the uncertainty in your men's eyes. They know this isn't a fight they can win."

He moved his horse forward. After a pause, Talen responded in kind. They met in the center of the road between the two forces.

"Why did you bring such a small force?" Merek asked, speaking low so that only Talen could hear. "You know me. Did you think I would surrender willingly? It's almost as though your heart wasn't in it. Turn back. Return to Albon and say you couldn't catch us in time."

"I didn't need a larger force," Talen said wearily, "because I knew you would come peaceably. At this moment, your men are free to continue on without you. But if you resist, not only will they be charged with treason, but also every man who serves under your command will be suspected of being tainted by your seditionist activities and will be treated accordingly."

"Every man?" Merek was shocked.

"Every single one," Talen affirmed grimly. "In every city from here to the farthest reaches of the northern forest."

Thoughts flashed through Merek's mind of Dan, Stefan, and every other soldier who served under him all over the country. At best, they would be forced to denounce him, give up their commissions, and leave the army under a cloud of suspicion and dishonor. At worst, they would find their fate with him at the end of a rope.

Merek could never do that to them. And Grammel knew this. He cursed under his breath.

"Stand down, Eldar," he called over his shoulder with great effort. "Take your men and continue on your way."

"But sir!" Eldar protested.

"That's an order!" Merek barked. He did not want his men's last memory of him to be watching him get shackled and locked behind bars.

"Yes, sir," Eldar said reluctantly. The soldiers sheathed their swords, and Eldar gave the order to move out.

Merek felt his last hope for survival go with them. It leaked away from him, leaving him tired and suddenly aware of how wet and cold he was.

Talen, looking considerably relieved, motioned to one of his men to bring the prison cart forward. The wheels clattered as it rocked on the uneven ground. Seeing it, Merek had a brief moment of panic, considering how he might fight his way free before they trapped him in that box.

Instead, he dismounted and held out his hands for the iron shackles. They fitted into place roughly, their metal cold against his wet skin.

Now that he had committed to this course, Talen's expression softened. "I know you fear the worst, Strong, but it may not end that way."

Merek scoffed. "You're a fool, Talen. When has anyone ever been cleared after being arrested for treason? And worse, it will be a military trial, so the man who will pronounce judgment will be the same man whose lies put me here in the first place."

Talen just shook his head. A soldier opened the door of the cart. It was open to the air on all sides, but still drier than Merek, soaked through as he was. The soldier seemed hesitant to approach.

"Sir?" He gestured toward the cart.

Merek closed his eyes, summoning the strength to go against his every instinct. Submit, instead of fight. Choose prison over freedom. Death instead of life.

A strong hand grabbed his arm, and he tensed, eyes snapping open.

"Have courage, friend," Talen's voice sounded in his ear. "I don't know what fate holds in store for you, but I do know this. The Merek Strong I know would never give up hope, no matter how small the odds or how dark the night."

Talen stepped away from him as if he'd said too much. Merek watched him go wordlessly, then gritted his teeth and climbed the steps.

NINE

Ria pushed away the bowl of cooked grains that had once been hot and welcoming on this dreary morning when copious rain poured down the windows and necessitated candles being lit indoors. Now the cereal was cold and lumpy, having been only half finished. Ria was too distracted by the documents and ledgers before her to pay much attention to her breakfast.

Galinn saw the motion and gestured to a servant who hurried forward to remove the bowl from the table.

"Would you care for some refreshment, Your Highness?" Galinn asked. "It's long past noon, and I fear you're overtiring yourself."

"Is it that late already?" Ria said distractedly, opening the book of accounts she was looking for.

"I'll dismiss these people if you wish, so that you may rest and eat," he offered.

Ria looked up from the table and blinked to clear her

vision. At the other end of the great hall, the crowd of people was growing. Word had gotten out that there was finally someone to hear the petitions that had gone unanswered by the king for so long.

Galinn had not only accepted her offer of help, but had been grateful for it: relieved that there was finally someone with whom he could share the burden of stewardship in the king's absence. At first, Ria thought that it might take a few hours to see to the most pressing needs. But there was so much she needed to learn, that by nightfall they had barely begun. So, she'd risen early the next morning and joined Galinn and her father's clerks in the great hall, surprised to find that a small crowd had gathered during the night.

As she looked over the group of people, she saw several of them had produced baskets of food. They'd known it would be a long day.

"Bring me a basket with simple food," she said to Galinn. "I won't tarry in feasting while they wait."

The steward nodded, and after a time a servant produced a basket overflowing with three kinds of bread, fruit, cold lamb, and a handful of delicate pastries with flaky crusts. It wasn't exactly the humble fare she'd had in mind, but she didn't complain.

When Ria had considered where to sit to hear her people's petitions, she hadn't given her father's throne even a passing glance. She wasn't the king, and she wouldn't posture herself as a usurper. So she had settled for a practical alternative, asking for the large feasting table to be brought in and inviting her father's clerks, councilors, and treasurer to join her.

Somewhere between a land dispute and needing to chastise a lesser noble who was reported to have been engaged in questionable dealings with a group of Delth miners—Rahm's rulers had a long memory when it came to the violence of the Delth, and any business or trade with them was still illegal—a small disturbance took place at the other end of the hall.

A few minutes later, Galinn murmured to Ria. "Your Highness, it seems there's a young boy demanding to see you. He says you know him, that he traveled with you on your return to Albon."

"Is it the cobbler's son?" Ria perked up. "Yes, I do know him. I can't see him just now, but fetch Biren. She'll know just what to say."

Ria turned her attention back to the man standing before her. "It seems that this isn't the first time that you've been guilty of trading with the Delth," she said in a firm voice. "I'll send two officers to check on you regularly in the future. If they find even a whisper of illegal activity again, you'll be stripped of your title and your lands. Is that understood?"

Ria didn't actually know if it was an appropriate response, but she had little tolerance for nobility who defied the crown to seek their own gain. The balding man nodded and bowed his head respectfully, ears red with shame.

Ria looked up to greet her next subject, but her attention was caught by the sight of Biren hurrying toward her with Finn at her heels.

"I'm sorry to interrupt, my lady," Biren said, breathlessly, "but I thought you'd want to hear this." She nodded to Finn.

"Yes?" Ria asked. "What is it, child?"

Finn spoke in a rush. "I was on my way home and saw my uncle the miller and remembered that my far had to ask him about the new roof he just put on because ours just started leaking horribly during all this rain—"

Ria's eyes drifted to the windows where rain streamed incessantly against the darkening afternoon sky. She should ask Galinn if there were any parts of their roof that needed mending before the heavy rains of autumn started. This storm was just a precursor to what they could expect in the coming months.

Ria heard 'the captain' and her attention snapped back to the boy just as he finished with, "—chained like a prisoner. Why? What has he done?"

"Which captain is that, Finn?

"Captain Strong, of course! After he found you in that barn and brought you home safe, why would you have him arrested?" Finn flushed with agitation.

"I did no such thing, Finn. You must be confused. The captain left Albon four days past. He's well on his way to Endvar now, I'm sure."

Finn shook his head. "It was Captain Strong; I know it. He saw me and waved to me a little, but it was hard because his hands were locked up. And then the other captain with curly hair told me to get away from the cart."

Ria started. Captain Talen had said that he had an onerous task ahead of him when they'd spoken last.

Could what the boy said be true? She turned to Galinn. "Do you know anything of this?"

"Nothing, Your Highness. But I'll look into it."

"Do," Ria ordered. "And quickly."

"Will you help him?" Finn asked, his eyes wide with worry. "He didn't look very happy."

"I'm sure the princess will do all she can," Biren said soothingly. "Now, thank her like a gentleman with a nice fine bow, and I'll see if there's anything I can get you from the kitchens."

Ria watched them go and tried to focus on her next task, but she felt a great unease that wouldn't pass until she heard back from Galinn.

It was an hour before Galinn's man returned, wet from the rain. Ria dismissed the merchant with whom she'd been speaking. Her discomfort grew at the sight of Galinn's expression. The steward had perfected the art of unflappability, but it could be trying at times like these when she was anxious for information.

Bending and speaking in a low tone, Galinn said, "I'm afraid what the boy says is true. It seems that Captain Strong was apprehended early yesterday by order of the king."

Ria felt his words as a shock through her whole body. She stood in alarm.

"Where is he?" she asked urgently.

"He's imprisoned under Captain Talen's charge. Shall I inform Talen that you wish to speak with him?"

"No, but order a carriage. I'll go directly. I'd rather he didn't know I was coming."

Ria eyed the basket of food and grabbed it. She felt a

twinge of guilt as she turned her back on the crowd of citizens, who had all come to their feet as their princess swept out of the room. But Ria knew that whatever their concerns, she could do nothing for them until she had seen Merek for herself.

Ria had never had an occasion to enter the prison before, though she'd seen it from a distance her whole life. It sat on a bluff overlooking the city: a large squat stone building whose pillared facade did nothing to take away from the bleak flatness of the other three walls, broken up only by small slit windows. Ria shuddered to think of Merek trapped in one of those dark cells. Anger surged within her, and for the first time in her life she felt as if she could commit an act of violence, though she couldn't decide whom against.

The sergeant who greeted her at the entrance was speechless at the sight of her and seemed uncertain what to do.

"I'll see Captain Talen immediately," she instructed, and he scurried away to his commander's office.

Ria followed the sergeant, and pushed through the door before he could speak.

"Thank you, Sergeant. You are excused," she said briskly.

Captain Talen sat at the desk, an expression of surprise shifting to one of wariness as the princess entered. He stood and nodded to the sergeant to leave.

Ria had worked over what she would say on the

drive, but in the moment her prepared thoughts flew from her.

"Where is he?" she demanded. "I want to see him, and I swear to you that if I don't like what I see, it will be on your head, Talen."

"Your Highness," he said, moving forward to offer her a chair. "I didn't expect you. Please, sit. I'm afraid I don't get many royal visitors, so I hope you'll forgive the untidiness."

"I'm not here to discuss the state of your office," Ria said derisively, remaining standing. "I'm here to discuss the fate of Captain Strong. Of what crime has he been accused?"

"I assure you," Talen said calmly, "that I have the matter well in hand. I'm sorry you came all this way, but you needn't concern yourself, Your Highness. This is a military matter and one that is being attended to at the highest level."

His calm refusal nearly made her choke with rage.

"How dare you?" Her words tasted like fire in her mouth. "This man has saved my life. The crown owes him a debt of gratitude, and you presume to tell me it's none of my concern why he's chained in here like a criminal?"

Talen regarded her steadily for a moment. "Do you consider yourself a friend to the captain, then?"

"A truer friend than you, presumably."

He blinked. Her words had struck a chord. So he *did* feel a measure of guilt for his behavior.

"My apologies," Talen said, and his demeanor changed. "I hope you can understand my reticence to speak of these things. I'll do my duty to my king, but Strong is still my friend. I don't want him to suffer needlessly."

"Of what crime has he been accused?" Ria repeated, more calmly this time.

"The highest crime," Talen grimaced. "Treason."

"Treason!" Ria felt winded. Treason meant certain death. There was no going back from such a charge. "But, how?" she asked, sinking into the chair Talen had offered.

"It appears that for some time he has been conspiring with a nameless enemy, likely by means of a band of Khouri criminals. Upon searching his quarters, a small fortune was seized, as well as a number of valuable Khouri gemstones."

"That's troubling," Ria admitted. "But is it enough to justify treason?"

"Alone, perhaps not. But that's not all." Talen moved to a locked cabinet and retrieved several sheets of paper that he laid on the desk. "This is perhaps the most damning piece of evidence."

Ria looked over the notes. She recognized some street names in Endvar, but at a glance she couldn't make sense of it all. "I'm no soldier, Talen. What am I looking at?"

"It's a plan to assault the Wall Guard and seize Endvar's eastern gate. Do you recognize the captain's hand?"

Most of the writing was unfamiliar, but there were notes in the margins critiquing the plan in handwriting that she did indeed recognize.

"There must be an explanation for this," she said, trying to push away the dreadful feeling settling over her. "Have you asked him about it?"

Talen shook his head, retrieving the documents and locking them safely away. "That's not my place. General Grammel will see to all that when he returns, but I've learned that Strong was secretly training a remote group of soldiers to climb the wall in order to carry out this attack."

"Yes, I know about the climbers," Ria said. "But it was purely a defensive measure, to identify weaknesses and anticipate future attacks."

Talen looked at her sharply. "How do you know of this?"

"Captain Strong told me of it while we were on our wall tour," Ria said. *Curse him for not telling me everything,* she thought. What was the meaning of this plan to attack Endvar itself?

"Do you know where these troops are located? They are unnamed in these documents, and I would have them questioned."

Ria hesitated. For all that Talen claimed to be Merek's friend and appeared to be sharing openly with her, she still didn't trust him. It was by his hand that Merek was imprisoned, after all.

"I can't say. But Talen, what if this is an unfortunate misunderstanding? What if it is no more than...a training exercise? You know him as well as I. What you describe isn't possible."

"Perhaps," Talen said doubtfully. "But how do you explain the money and the gemstones? I was skeptical myself until I heard that Endvar had fallen. I understand that even the king was unconvinced until then. With this threat, the mounting evidence was too much to ignore."

"Then I will speak to my father," Ria said, standing. "Surely there's something that can be done. But first, I want to see Strong."

TEN

Merek sat on the stone floor of his cell, looking up at the slit window high above him. The meager light coming through waned toward evening. It wouldn't be long before his cell would be completely dark.

The stones used in constructing this building were too perfectly cut and fitted to consider climbing. Even if he tried, the window above was barred and so small only a child could slip through. But the cold air coming from it made it feel three times its size.

Merek wrapped the blanket tighter around his shoulders. It was at least clean, and the soup he'd been given earlier had been warm. But still, he shivered with the cold.

In addition to his weapons, Talen's men had confiscated his boots, his belt, and his uniform coat. He missed the coat the most. He was still wet from his ride in the rain, and could have used the extra layer of warmth.

His feet without their boots were growing numb with cold. The single cot was too short for him to lay on comfortably, so he sat on the cold floor instead, the blanket wrapped around his shoulders, trying to stop from shivering. He would have to ask for another coat—or a second blanket—if he were ever given the opportunity. He hadn't seen Talen since he'd entered the cell. The thick walls and the solid oak door insulated him from the rest of the prison so that he sat in silence hour after hour.

At first his thoughts had been for Endvar and the people he'd left behind. That's what he'd clung to in order to ward off despair as he'd been carted through the city street like a common criminal. Humiliating and degrading as it was, it seemed a small thing when he compared it to the unknown suffering of people he cared for. People he had failed to protect.

But as the heavy door shut with a final boom, and the iron key sounded in the lock, he'd suddenly understood that his own situation was no less desperate. Forced idleness was a new experience for him, and an unwelcome one. The more his body was still, the more his mind raced, parsing out the events of the past days, weeks, and even months that had contributed to his incarceration. It was maddening.

Eventually, the sleepless nights of the past week caught up to him, and his pacing led to sitting in an exhausted stupor against the wall. He must have dozed because he woke to the grating sound of a key in the lock and discovered himself lying in a tight ball on the floor, his face to the wall.

A familiar voice sounded like something out of his dreams.

"Captain Strong, this is twice you have ignored one of my summons. I hope you aren't making it a habit. Oh don't look at me like that, Talen. You may do what you will, he'll always be a captain to me."

Merek turned and scrambled to his stockinged feet, clutching at his blanket with one hand and his trousers with the other.

Ria stood in the open doorway with Captain Talen at her side. For a moment, he was so astounded by the sight of her that he forgot to be ashamed at his own pitiable state. The last time he'd seen her, she'd been battered and weary from days of hiding, injury, and hunger. Now she was well-rested and groomed like the princess she was. Even with her left arm wrapped in a proper sling, she projected an aura of strength in the small room. How had he forgotten how lovely she was? She wore a gown of deep blue, the hood of her ermine cloak thrown back to show the glinting of jewels in her tightly bound hair.

"Ria!" he blurted in shock. "What are you doing here?"

Talen's eyes flickered at Merek's familiar use of her name, and Merek felt momentarily chagrined. Then again, why should he worry about such things now?

"I'll pretend that you had something more welcoming to say," Ria said, looking him over with a critical eye that made him feel very exposed. She turned to Talen. "As melodramatic as this scene is, I would prefer a fire and a chair. Wouldn't you, Captain Strong?"

She fixed her gaze on Talen, daring him to challenge her. For all the lightness in her tone, her eyes smoldered with anger.

"I suppose," Merek answered.

"Good. I'm glad we agree. Your office will do quite nicely, Talen. Come, Captain." She'd called him by his title more times in the last two minutes than she had in the past month. She was doing it intentionally to goad Talen. If Merek hadn't been feeling so wretched, he might have smiled.

Talen signaled to a soldier outside who stepped forward with shackles for Merek's hands and feet.

"Really, Talen, is that necessary?" Ria protested, her warm breath puffing mist in the cold air of the cell.

"I'll concede to your request, Your Highness," Talen replied as the soldier locked the cold iron into place around Merek's ankles and wrists, "but I insist on certain terms."

Ria frowned but didn't object further. Looking Merek over again, she said, "You assured me that he wasn't harmed, and I see that's true, but I'm not sure I would agree that he hasn't been ill-treated. Where are his boots? His coat? He's fairly blue with cold."

"It's standard to remove those items in these instances," Talen explained. "The coat belongs to a military office he no longer holds, and his belt or the laces on his boots could be used to..." he hesitated, "...to do himself harm."

Ria's eyes narrowed, and she spoke deliberately. "Then you will get him a *new* coat and return his boots without the laces in them."

It embarrassed Merek to be spoken about as if he wasn't there, but there was nothing he could say to improve the situation, so he stayed silent. When he was firmly shackled, the soldier took him by the elbow and shuffled him out the door. The corridor outside his room was warmer than his cell had been but also darker as it was only lit by a few sconces. With cells on either side, there were no windows to let natural light into the stone corridor.

With each step up the stairs, the air grew warmer, and Merek thought longingly of Ria's mention of a chair and a fire. Would Talen bend to her will that easily? What had she said to him to allow this visit?

When they entered Talen's office, he blinked a few times from the brightness. A warm fire danced in the fireplace and oil lamps around the room cast a cheery glow. The soldier holding his arm stopped just inside the doorway, waiting as Talen cleared away the contents of his desk and locked them away in a cabinet.

"I'll give you one half hour. If you need anything," he hesitated, glancing back and forth between the two of them, "I'll be right outside the door."

Ria nodded her head toward the door in dismissal, her rigid posture doing nothing to mask her barely contained fury. As soon as the door closed, she rounded on him.

"After all we've been through together, how could you not have trusted me, Merek? What else have you kept from me?" she accused.

Merek was stunned. "You're angry with *me?*"

"Of course I'm angry with you! Why didn't you tell me of your plans? Your pride is so insufferable!"

"Well, the next time I'm arrested and thrown in prison, I'll be sure and inform you first," he said, feeling defensive.

"That's not what I mean," she snapped. "The hidden money, the plans to attack Endvar, the jewels—"

"Jewels? What jewels?"

"Gemstones they found hidden in your house. Something that proves you have ties to Khourin."

"Of course I have ties to Khourin!" Merek said, exasperated. "I've rented a room from two Khouris for years! If they found Khouri jewels, they must be Aiya's or Imar's. Does no one think these things through before they rush to condemn a man to his death?" He moved to run his hand through his hair but was brought up short by the chain that attached his shackled wrists to his ankles.

Some of the anger in Ria's eyes dimmed at the sight of the chains. "Then you must tell Talen. Tell him everything. Explain that it's all been a misunderstanding."

Merek shook his head. "This is less about proving anything to a reasonable man like Talen and more about General Grammel eliminating a threat. His opinion is all that matters, and he's convinced that I am conspiring for the throne."

Ria exhaled loudly in frustration and walked to the window, looking out at the blustering rain. "You should have said something to me sooner. Perhaps I could have done something to prevent this. But now..." She tapped a fingernail against the glass. Softly, she moaned, "Now everything is ruined."

Merek moved closer to the fire, basking in the first real warmth he'd felt in days. His hands and feet were so cold that the heat bathed them in sharp pain, but he stood as close as he dared, hoping that at least his clothing might dry. "I don't know about 'everything'. From where I stand, my future is rather bleak. But I don't see how that would concern you."

Her reaction was fierce and unexpected. She whirled around, and the fire in her eyes raged. "You are such a fool, Merek Strong! How does it concern me? There's no way I can marry you now, even if by some miracle you were to escape the gallows. Even if my father is lenient and stays your execution, you will still be tainted by the accusation. How could a man like that ever become king?"

Merek felt as if the breath had been knocked from his lungs. "What are you saying? You want to *marry* me?"

"Well I can't now, obviously!" Ria said, throwing up her hands and stalking back to the window.

Words were slow to pierce Merek's shock. "And you're angry with *me* for keeping secrets? When were you going to tell me?"

"That's why I wanted to see you before you left Albon. But instead of coming as I asked, you ignored my summons and—" She shook her head in frustration, then leaned her forehead despondently against the glass. When she spoke again, her tone had lost some of its bite. "I would have said something sooner, but I wanted to talk it over with my father first. I almost said something about it that night on the wall in Haldin. Do you remember? The moon was so beautiful it very nearly loosened my tongue."

He was grateful her back was turned, and she couldn't see his face. Of course he remembered. He held the memory of that night close to his heart, with so many others of their time together, never daring to give them his full attention.

"Yes, I remember that night."

She glanced over her shoulder at him, and a playful sparkle glinted in her smile. "That's why I insisted we go to Haldin, you know. So that I could see you in your home. There's something that comes from knowing a man's people that really solidifies his character, don't you think? After all, I'd been going through great lengths to see men like Hegrin in their home territory, it was the least I could do to offer you the same courtesy."

Merek wasn't sure whether to be flattered or offended that he was being compared to Hegrin. "And all that time we were together after your party was ambushed? You never thought to say anything?"

Ria shook her head, the jewels in her hair flashing with the light. "By then I'd made up my mind not to say anything until I'd spoken to my father. It seemed best under the circumstances."

"So you kept news of your plans to yourself until we returned, and then you spoke to your father," Merek said, a connection coming together in his mind.

"It...didn't go well." She shuddered.

Merek sighed. Suddenly, it all made sense. Why Sindal had turned against him at last. Why now, when

Grammel had been pushing him for months. It wasn't the news about Endvar. It was his daughter choosing Merek as a husband. If Grammel wanted to convince Sindal that Merek was conspiring for the throne, Ria had just given him glaring proof. And with that realization, Merek lost the last thread of hope that he would ever be free.

Chuckling at the cruel irony, he pulled a chair over to the fire and collapsed into it, his head hanging heavy in his hands.

"What is it?" Ria asked, stepping forward. "What's wrong?"

Merek closed his eyes. How could he tell her what he suspected? It wasn't her fault that her father's mind had been poisoned against him.

As it turned out, he didn't need to say anything. Ria was too clever not to reach the same conclusion he had.

"No," she whispered, blanching. "No, it can't be. Do you think my father turned against you because I told him I've decided to marry you?"

"I understand that many fathers are protective of their daughters when it comes to marriage."

"I never thought...But...your arrest...that means this is all my fault!" She gasped and rushed to his chair and knelt before him. "And if you are hanged, that means—"

"No! You can't think like that," he said sharply, cutting her off. He looked at her tortured expression and said fervently, "No matter what happens, promise me that you will never think that."

Ria grasped his hand and looked up at him with

shining eyes. "What a blind fool I am! Can you ever forgive me?

The tenderness of her touch left him speechless. Heart swelling, he reached out a manacled hand to gently brush a tear from her cheek.

"Of course I don't blame you. Grammel is persistent. Sindal would have turned against me eventually." Merek's voice was thick with emotion. It was hard to believe that she could feel the same way he did. Yet here she was before him, dark eyes wet with tears, speaking of marriage and a future they may have had together. Could she really have loved him this whole time? He felt such a mix of emotions—surprise, excitement, bitterness, loss, hope—that he couldn't properly feel any of them.

Ria closed her eyes and rested her head on his knees. "Curse my father and his demons. If only...What should we do, Merek?" Her voice sounded very small and afraid.

Gingerly, he rested his hand on her hair. He wished he could just hold this scene forever, sitting with her in this way before the heat of the fire. For a moment, he could almost—not quite, but almost—imagine that they were sitting in front of their own hearth in a scene of domestic contentment in the life that they could never have.

"I suppose it shouldn't make a difference now," he said, "but knowing that you care for me, that if things had turned out differently between us we might have had a future together—"

At his words, Ria stiffened and pulled away. "I didn't mean..." She blushed furiously and moved quickly to stand. "I should have said—Oh dear, I've been a blundering...How can I explain?"

The ugly truth of what she was about to say hit him with such force that he felt sick with it. Merek's fleeting dream of happiness withered in a heartbeat.

"My requirements for marriage..." she began, and her formal tone was more hurtful even than the words he knew were coming.

"Stop," he said. "You don't need to explain. I'm sorry...I misunderstood." His throat suddenly felt very dry.

Ria blushed again and backed away, clinging to the wall behind her as if she wanted to flee. "I do think very highly of you, you must understand. You are my friend and—"

"Please, you needn't explain," Merek repeated hoarsely. "I didn't mean to suggest...Forget I said anything." He couldn't bear to hear any more, feeling a new chill inside that the fire couldn't warm. Why did it hurt him so? Moments before he had assumed she didn't care for him. Why should it be so painful to have it confirmed?

The silence between them was heavy and uncomfortable. There was nothing more to say, so Merek stood.

"Thank you for your kindness. I'm quite warm and dry now." It wasn't completely true, and Merek was loath to return to his dark cell, but even that would be preferable to enduring this new tension between them.

Ria looked pained, but their time was drawing to a close. Whatever more she might have said, there was no time for it. Instead, she picked up a basket from the floor near Talen's desk.

"I brought something for you," she said. "Talen disapproved, but I'm not inclined to do things to please him these days. Perhaps I'll bring you another one tomorrow just to spite him." She smiled playfully and then looked away, her cheeks reddening.

Merek cursed himself for his rash words. He could face the gallows easier than he could face her changed attitude. But the damage was done. In a moment of recklessness he had ruined everything, and it sickened him.

When Talen entered the room, he had Merek's boots —laceless now—and a heavy coat that was even warmer than his uniform coat had been. He frowned when he saw the basket in Merek's hands but didn't object.

Ria busied herself at Talen's desk as the exchange took place, then called out as the guard started to take Merek away.

"Wait!" With a flourish, she finished scribbling something down, folded up the paper awkwardly with her one good hand, and hurried over to where Merek stood in front of the fire.

With others present, her posture was controlled and commanding again. She slipped the note into his manacled hand and he noticed a dark spot on her upper lip. A bruise? How had that happened?

"I'm not finished with you," she said firmly. She paused, as if considering saying more, then frowned and left the room.

As soon as the door closed behind her, Talen stepped forward, holding out his hand. "The note, please. I did tell her that everything had to go through me first."

Merek's fingers tightened around the paper. Talen could have taken the note for himself, and Merek appreciated this small courtesy. Instead of handing it to Talen, he tossed it into the fire. Whatever she'd written had been meant for his eyes alone. He wouldn't risk further humiliation by sharing it with another.

Talen frowned as if measuring this act of defiance. As the flames caressed the edges of the paper, they curled into blackness and soon were engulfed. Satisfied, Merek turned his back on the fire and shuffled out of the room.

Ria leaned against the soft interior wall of the rocking carriage, watching the gloomy prison recede against a backdrop of rain and mist. She blinked back tears of frustration. She'd made a fine mess of things. What an utter fool she'd been. Lotta had tried to warn her, but she hadn't listened. Ria had known that Merek might not initially agree to the marriage, so she'd been prepared to be persuasive. But she had anticipated reasoning it out with him in a calm, comfortable setting. With refreshments. Not blurting it out angrily while he sat in chains in prison.

And then, after all that, he'd misunderstood her intent. His tender words had been so unexpected that she'd responded without thinking. And with all the delicacy of a cudgel.

Perhaps he'd only spoken out of desperation, but the pain in his eyes as she'd fled from him had been real. Whatever hope she'd offered had left him more wounded when she cruelly retracted it than he'd been when she first saw him in that dreadful cell. She'd gone to get answers to her questions and reassure him that he wasn't alone, that someone was fighting for him. Instead, she broke him worse than Talen and Grammel had.

The thought made her eyes swim again, and she angrily swiped at them with her sleeve. Not for the first time, she was relieved that she had insisted on making the trip to the prison alone. She needed a moment to compose herself before returning to the Hall, for when she got there, there was business to be done. And—her stomach stirred unpleasantly at the thought—it would include a visit to her father.

ELEVEN

Aiya felt a gentle nudge against her shoulder bringing her out of a restless sleep.

"It's time," Dan murmured, then stepped over her to wake the sleeping Yulda.

At last. Aiya sat up at once, reaching for the knapsack she'd been using as a pillow. She and Yulda had been waiting for what seemed like days—it was hard to know for sure in these underground tunnels—waiting for Dan to decide that the other soldiers were healthy enough to be left. With any luck, the three of them would find their way to safety, then Dan would return with help for his friends. But it might be days before his return, and he wanted to be certain that some of the men were strong enough to tend to the others in their absence.

Aiya pulled on her boots and stuffed the makeshift blanket—half of an abandoned one they'd found while searching the tunnels—into her pack. Over the past few days, they'd discovered more signs that these tunnels had been recently inhabited. Aiya was grateful for every scrap of blanket or clothing they found as the temperature never rose above a steady chill. But the cache of abandoned weapons—with cracked blades or broken shafts—had most captured Dan's interest.

"You're ready, then?" Aiya asked, tying her knapsack shut.

Dan rubbed the back of his neck and glanced at the men huddled in groups in the dark cavern. "I won't be going with you, Aiya. I'm staying here."

Aiya stood to face him, a feeling of dread squeezing her stomach. "Explain, please."

"Jax and I—" Dan began, pausing as Yulda joined them. "We've spoken to some of the men, and they agree that we should stay and try to seize the southern gate."

"Oh, not this again!" Yulda scoffed in a harsh whisper. "I thought you'd put that idea to rest. Tell him what a foolish plan this is, Aiya!"

Aiya just looked at Dan, wide-eyed with disbelief. They'd spoken of this before, but he had agreed that getting these men to safety was more important than trying to fight the invading forces. After all these days they had waited, now he was changing his mind? Aiya felt a sense of panic at the thought of leaving him behind.

"You two go," Dan insisted. "Try and find a safe route out of these tunnels and back to Rahm. Tell the garrison that we'll attack the southern gate in five days' time."

"Attack how? With sticks and stones?"

"We have weapons..."

Yulda snorted.

"...of a sort. Jax and I have picked over them. There are plenty sound enough to overpower a handful of soldiers. If we don't act now before the larger army gets here, we may never have a chance to reclaim the city."

"For the love of St. Judith's eleventh toe, Dan," Yulda exclaimed. "What was the point of nursing these men back to health just to send them to their deaths? You don't even have proper weapons!"

Dan frowned at the girl. "These men are soldiers. They each know their own life is better spent by taking back the city. They're not afraid to die if it means saving Endvar."

Yulda threw up her hands in disgust. "Stop trying to be a hero, Dan. You're just going to get yourself killed!"

Aiya watched her stalk away, for once glad the young woman had spoken her mind.

"Will you talk to her? Try to explain?" Dan asked Aiya.

"Explain what? How can I explain to her that after begging her to join us at great personal risk, you're now abandoning us both?"

"What? I'm not abandoning—"

"She trusted you. We both trusted you," Aiya said hotly, anger rising unchecked by days spent in this dank hole. Any respect she'd felt for Dan was evaporating under the heat of it. "Where I come from, someone who sends two women unprotected into enemy land would be ashamed to call himself a man."

Dan's eyes narrowed. "You think I want this?" he hissed. "I've tried to find another way, but there just isn't. You and Yulda must go and warn the garrison. Our attack will fail if the garrison isn't there to secure the gate as soon as we seize it."

"Then forget the gate and come with us," Aiya begged. "What you suggest is too dangerous. Too many things may go wrong and you'll all be killed. Let us save these men now, then return with a larger force to do this plan."

"It could be too late then," Dan said, shaking his head. "Can't you see? This is our last chance to stop a war." The expression in his eyes was unyielding.

Aiya pressed her lips into a thin line. "Very well, then. This is goodbye." She lifted her knapsack onto her shoulder and scanned the darkness for Yulda. The former kitchen maid was skulking at the far end of the cavern with a makeshift pack of her own, made of an old shirt, and a lamp in one hand. The darkness behind her marked the tunnel where they would begin their search for an exit.

"Aiya," Dan stopped her with a hand on her arm. She paused but felt such hostility toward him that she couldn't meet his eyes. "I'm not trying to be a hero."

"Good," she said flatly, looking straight ahead. "Because when you die in five days' time, there will be no songs or poems written to honor your sacrifice. You and your men will be forgotten, and the only thing Yulda and I will remember is your folly. The man who could have saved all these soldiers but instead sent them to their deaths on a fool's errand. Until even that, too, is forgotten."

Aiya shrugged off his hand and walked away. A part of her felt sick for saying the hateful words, and she didn't look back at Dan so that she didn't have to see the hurt in his eyes. Her anger gave her the strength she needed to join Yulda and stride boldly into the yawning darkness.

Morning brought meager light into Ria's bedchamber. The rain had continued all night, and heavy clouds clung to the city and chased away proper dawn. As the memory of her visit to the prison the previous evening washed over Ria, so did a feeling of dread. *It seems to be a common companion these days,* she thought grimly, throwing back the warm bedclothes.

Biren was quick to attend her, insisting that she take time for the movements the physician had given her to regain motion in her shoulder. They were painful, and left her panting with effort, but Ria obeyed. Not being able to use both arms freely was a considerable nuisance.

Rather than returning to the great hall, Ria grabbed her lap harp—covering it to protect it from the rain—and moved resolutely in the direction of the garden. Although Merek wouldn't be tried as long as General Grammel was away from the city, she couldn't bear the thought of leaving him to languish in prison. Nothing else would be accomplished that morning until she had petitioned her father for his release.

The guards let her in this time without any objection. When Ria entered the tower, she paused again at the sight of the dying garden. It seemed even more cruel now, with the sound of rain beating upon the stone. All this lovely garden needed to live was so close, yet impossibly out of reach.

Ria found Martin in the second floor chamber, dozing on a small couch before a dim fireplace. Had the king had a difficult night that kept the old man awake? Or was Martin simply growing too old for the rigors of service? Ria thought about slipping past him to the upper room, but as she passed, he stirred and woke.

"Your Highness," he greeted in his dry, raspy voice. "I didn't expect you this morning." He gathered himself to stand, his movements excruciatingly slow.

"I just need to see my father briefly, Martin," Ria said. "No need to trouble you."

"Of course," Martin said, patting about his person. Either taking stock or searching for something, Ria wasn't sure. "And, where are your guards?"

"Guards?"

"I can't allow you in that room without some protection. Not after the king's behavior. Your safety is paramount, Your Highness. The soldiers downstairs can escort you if you'll wait for me to summon them."

"Don't trouble yourself." Ria gestured to the lap harp. "I only wish to play for my father. I'll call for help if he becomes excited." Before Martin could object, she walked briskly past him to the stairs.

Sindal sat in his shirtsleeves in front of a glowing fire, a cup in one hand and a quill in the other. On a table at his elbow rested an open notebook, and Ria waited for him to finish writing before she spoke from the doorway. Into her mind flashed an image of his enraged face the last time she'd seen him and the horrid words he'd shouted. Her mouth and scalp had healed, but her heart was still bruised. She felt a surge of anger and the harp felt slippery in her hand. She breathed deeply to calm herself. She couldn't afford to provoke him this time. There was too much at stake.

"Good morning, Far," she greeted, stepping around an overturned chair and a pile of books to come closer to the circle of firelight. If she'd thought the great hall was dismal in the persistent rain, it was nothing compared to the empty gloom of the stone tower. Low hanging clouds obscured the windows, and most of the heat from the fire was lost in the dark recesses of the cavernous ceiling.

Her father didn't look pleased to see her. "You again? What trickery do you have for me today?"

She regarded him a moment before responding, trying to decide if she should be subtle or blunt. "No tricks today, Far. I thought I would play for you. Though I'm afraid it won't be to your usual standards with my arm injured as it is."

Ask me about my injury, she thought. That would open the door to telling him about the ambush and rescue, and perhaps soften his heart toward the man who had saved her life. But Sindal just grunted and leaned over to scratch something down in his book.

Ria picked up the overturned chair and brought it closer to the fire. She sat and placed her small lap harp on a stool before her. Gently slipping her left arm out of its sling, she tried a few warm-up scales. Oh, how her shoulder ached! It wasn't quite as taxing as the physician's exercises, but she wouldn't be able to keep it up for long.

As she played, she tried to engage her father in conversation, but he wouldn't respond to her naturally. Instead, he grunted or ignored her entirely to scribble in his book. Was it a diary? She would have to remember to ask Martin about it.

As her shoulder tired and Sindal continued to stonewall her efforts at conversation, Ria became impatient to address her true purpose.

"I went to the prison yesterday and saw an old friend there," she began.

Her father shot her a dark look but said nothing.

"It's wrong, you know. Locking him away like that. He's been nothing but loyal to you, and I owe him my life. We should be honoring him before the people, not charging him with unspeakable crimes."

Her father's grip around his cup tightened. He didn't look at her when he spoke, merely gazed into the fire. "His heart is black. So black to have turned you against me. My own daughter."

Ria took a deep breath and let it out slowly. "I'm not against you, Far. I'm as faithful as I ever was. But you're confused. You see deceit and treachery where those who love you would show only loyalty and honor. Now an innocent man is doomed to die after doing no wrong other than serving his king."

Sindal didn't answer. Ria finished the melody, letting the music fade into the stillness. When he still didn't speak, she placed her harp gently on the floor, and stepped over the stool, coming to her knees before her father's chair.

"Far, I'm begging you. Release Captain Strong from prison. Restore him to his position, and clear his name."

"Why should I do that?"

"Because he's your friend and mine. Because he has served you well for many years. And if that weren't enough, because he saved my life!"

Sindal's blue eyes were full of suspicion. "And earned your favor in the process. Marriage is a fine reward for saving your life."

"If you have questions about his conduct, let's you and I work them out together. But release him now. Don't make him spend another day in that place."

One hand reached out to trace her jawline. "How does he have such hold over you? I see clearly how his eyes have long been on the throne, but I never imagined he would turn you into his whore to make it happen."

Ria blinked at the insult, her face growing hot. "Oh Far, you're a bigger fool than I thought." She rose to her feet, repulsed suddenly by the man before her. "You can't see the truth when it's plain before your face. Your petty jealousies will cost a worthy man his life while you sit up here locked away, ignoring your people while your country goes to war. You're an embarrassment to the crown!"

Sindal's face reddened, and his eyes flashed murderously. With a bestial growl, he barreled out of his chair toward Ria, then stopped short, looking warily at the long knife she held defensively before her.

"You will *not* touch me again," Ria breathed, anger and fear making her heart race. "And lest you think I'm still inexperienced at defending myself, know that Captain Drenall took great efforts while I was away to teach me how to best a skilled opponent." It wasn't strictly true. After the incident in Cillith, he'd tried to show her a few things, but she was still recovering from her injury and hadn't taken much time to practice. She held her father's eyes unflinchingly, however, hoping that he wouldn't suspect her bluff.

"This man sent you here to threaten me, and still you think he's innocent?" Sindal shrank away from her, glowering.

"I came here of my own accord, to beg for his life. The knife was just to make sure you behaved. I don't want to hurt you, but I will *not* allow you to hurt me again," Ria said fiercely, her voice shaking from the fire coursing through her veins.

The passion of rage died a little in Sindal's eyes, and Ria thought she saw a flicker of shame. He turned away from her. "Leave me. I see now that it's not your fault. He's deceived you, and you can't see the truth. But he will pay for turning my own daughter against me."

Ria lowered her knife, feeling suddenly weak. Somehow, her effort to plead for Merek's life had only cemented his death. She heard it in her father's resolve. Feeling shaken, she turned and stooped to pick up her fallen harp. As she did so, the king's heavy seal pressed against her leg beneath the folds of her dress. Now would be the time to return it to her father, but she left it resting in her pocket. Hoping her father couldn't see the shadow of deception in her eye, Ria left the chamber with her shoulders straight, fighting the urge to run.

TWELVE

The mud beneath Aiya's boots was soft and deep. She'd spent so much time watching her feet that she neglected to notice when Yulda stopped in front of her. Aiya bumped into her with a stifled grunt.

"What is it?" she asked.

"Look up there," Yulda said, her voice tight from lack of use.

Aiya followed her gaze to an unexpected pattern of shapes high on the tunnel wall. They were at an intersection of sorts, and the yellow markings almost reminded her of—

"It's writing! Some kind of message," she said with interest, sidling past Yulda. "You won't be able to read it, so give me the lamp and I will try."

"Why would you say that?" Yulda demanded.

"Say what?" Aiya asked, surprised at the girl's sudden anger.

"That I can't read it."

"Do you read Ardanian?" Aiya asked, confused. "I didn't mean to offend. You may read it if you like." She handed the lamp back to the girl.

Yulda's expression softened. "No, I don't read Ardanian. I thought you meant—" She cleared her throat, abashed. "Forget it."

Aiya's gaze lingered on the young woman, but Yulda turned away and said nothing more. Aiya turned back to the writing, raising the lamp high above her head, and peered at the letters.

After a moment of silence, Yulda asked, "Can you read it?"

"Reading and writing is much harder than speaking. But I might—" Aiya looked at the first group of characters and tried to parse out the root word. "I think it's something to do with direction. Down, perhaps?"

Yulda drew closer and looked at the yellow marks. Part of them had been smeared by moisture on the earthen walls, making them less legible. But even with some of the letters difficult to read, the next word was more familiar.

"This part is talking of water," Aiya said. "Is it a direction to find water? There must be some close with all the mud."

Yulda cocked her head, considering. "Might it be falling, not down?"

"I suppose it might. Why?"

"Falling water," Yulda mused. "Or, a waterfall?"

Aiya turned to the young woman, impressed. "You may be right. Now the question is, did they want to warn away from the waterfall? Or direct someone toward it?"

"There's only one way to find out." Yulda moved down the tunnel with more purpose.

It didn't take long before Aiya questioned their decision. The mud grew increasingly deep, making a sucking sound with each step as they fought its grip. The walls of the tunnel were not simply damp, but had tendrils of water running in rivulets down to the floor.

"Be careful!" Aiya warned. "I've heard tales of underground rivers that will sweep you away before you know they're there."

"I don't think so," came the breathless reply as Yulda fought through the mud at a quickening pace. "This tunnel has been used. Quite a bit, I'd say. One pair of footprints or two might be a coincidence. But so many boots have crossed this way recently that it's surely a safe passage. We may have even found our way out!"

But we don't know what's waiting for us when we get there, Aiya thought, wishing Yulda would move with more caution.

After a few moments, Aiya asked, "Why did you get upset when we found the writing on the wall? I was under the impression that only Rahmish nobility studied foreign tongues. Most commoners do not learn them, do they?"

Yulda didn't answer for a moment. When she did, it was with a tone of resignation. "Not foreign tongues, no. But they can at least recognize the difference between Rahmish and Ardanian, can't they?"

"You cannot read Rahmish?" Aiya guessed.

"It's as foreign to me as your own language."

"But that's not so shameful. In my country, many people do not read and write."

"But your country isn't Rahm. Here we have schools for all children, no matter their lack of wealth or status. Unless you are too feeble-minded to learn, then there's no place for you and your family is anxious to find you whatever occupation will not require any sort of wit," Yulda said bitterly.

"You are not feeble-minded," Aiya said firmly.

Yulda stopped and turned to her. "Then why do the letters dance around and make no sense? The only other child I know who couldn't learn them was the tanner's son, but he still drools and soils himself like an infant."

Aiya shook her head. "I don't know, but I do know that you're not feeble-minded. Perhaps it's a problem with your eyes."

"No," Yulda said, continuing to walk. "My vision is fine. Better than most, in fact. I can see something once and remember it in perfect detail. It's just letters and numbers that make no sense."

Aiya paused. "You can remember things in perfect detail? What sort of things?"

"People, places. Without even trying, I see the details around me, and can remember it all. I can't read street signs, but if I've been somewhere once, I can find my way back even through an unfamiliar city."

"That's how you've always known where we are in the tunnels," Aiya realized with awe.

Yulda didn't answer.

"Yulda? Might I teach you some Ardanian? Not the letters, but some phrases? It might be helpful if we are discovered."

Yulda shrugged, but she cooperated as Aiya taught her some common phrases that she thought might be useful like, 'Please help.' 'Hungry.' 'I am lost.'

This occupied both of their minds as they trudged through the muck. The way became even more difficult, and Aiya sensed that they were moving gradually uphill.

Then Yulda stopped and gasped. "Look! Is that light ahead?"

It was difficult to tell. The light from the oil lamp made them blind to subtleties in the darkness. However, when Aiya simply glanced ahead rather than looking directly, it did seem that part of the darkness wasn't as black as the rest.

"Careful," she advised, but she too had a hard time keeping herself from breaking into a run. Together, she and Yulda hurried toward the gray shadow. It was further away than it had first seemed, and they panted trying to hurry through the mud.

As they drew closer, Aiya became aware of a deep rumble building in the earth around them. At last, the tunnel opened into a large cavern, and the rumble became a roar. The faintest hint of light illuminated remnants of an ancient rockfall. Some of the rocks had been cleared away, but the largest boulders remained, and the opening could only be reached by climbing up the monoliths.

Dousing the oil lamp, they left it sitting between two

rocks against the cavern wall. If they ever came back this way, they would need it. Fresh cool air blew through the gap, bringing a faint trace of mist as they climbed. It was easy for Aiya to scale the rock in her trousers, but Yulda struggled with the awkwardness of her dress. Eventually, Aiya had to climb back down to help her up.

The opening was wide enough for several men to pass through and almost as tall as the height of a tree. They stood together at the top, awed by the sight before them.

They'd indeed found the waterfall, emerging from a small grotto behind it. Large boulders lay scattered about the floor of the grotto like broken teeth from a rock giant out of the old stories from Aiya's childhood. The waterfall itself wasn't very wide, but it thundered from a great height above them onto a bed of jagged rocks far below. It was dizzying to be so close, feeling the rock around them reverberate with the force of it, the spray wetting their clothes and hair. They clutched each other's arms to steady themselves.

"I've never seen anything like it," Yulda said with wonder.

"Nor I," Aiya breathed. "It's no wonder they had to smuggle supplies into the city. It would be impossible to get a wagon through here, even if one could manage that narrow track." She pointed to a small trail carved into the side of a cliff that moved away from the grotto and disappeared around a bend.

"Is that our route then?" Yulda said warily, eyeing the steep drop to the turbulent creek below.

"I see no other way to get down," Aiya replied. "But

we won't follow it for long. It's bound to take us to people, and people are what we want to avoid. I just hope our way isn't too rough. We have only three days now to find the garrison."

"Hmph. It would serve Dan right to leave him and his men to be butchered," Yulda grumbled.

"Yulda!" Aiya snapped. "Don't say such things!"

"Why not? You were angry with him too," she insisted defiantly.

"Yes, but I don't wish him harm...or the others. I disagree with his choice, but I'll do all that I can to help him." With that, Aiya began picking her way down the large rock where they stood.

After a pause, Yulda followed. Aiya regretted her harsh words to the girl, but she regretted her words to Dan even more. He *was* a fool, but he had been a worthy companion, and he didn't deserve to be treated that way. She dearly hoped those would not be the last words she ever spoke to him.

As they emerged from the grotto and onto the small track, they discovered that a gentle rain was falling—something they hadn't noticed when they were surrounded by falling water. Wishing for a cloak and hood, or even a heavier jacket, Aiya glanced up at the steel gray sky, barely illuminated with the onset of dawn.

"I do hope we can get a glimpse of the sun to know where we're going," she said.

"That's easy," Yulda said, her tone still a little sulky. "This is the Vifar River. If we follow it, it will lead us directly to Rahm."

"How can you be so sure?" Aiya asked doubtfully.

"I told you, I can remember things I've seen. What is a map but a kind of picture?"

Aiya still had doubts, but she decided to trust the girl. She had led their way through the tunnels and found a way out. This wouldn't be nearly as difficult, would it? Trekking through unknown wilderness in a country with whom they were now at war. Trying to sneak back into Rahm with only three days to find a force to rescue Dan and his soldiers. No, not difficult at all.

Merek dug the sharp end of a small rock between the stones, scratching at the mortar until it began to flake away. It was laborious work, and he seemed to scrape more skin from his fingertips than mortar as he wore away at the rough stone.

He perched more than four feet up the cell wall, and counted it a small victory that he'd been able to make it that far. He'd already fallen several times, so at moments like this he had to be very careful that the force he applied to the mortar didn't knock him off balance. Slow. Tedious. But he appreciated the distraction, and he had nothing better to do. So he scraped at the wall with a rock he'd found embedded in the sole of his boot, carving out a new handhold for his upward progress.

The small window was still high above him when he heard his food slot open. *Finally.* He heard the familiar clatter of a bowl against stone as his evening meal was thrust into the cell.

He held still on the wall, waiting for the sound of the slot closing. It didn't come. Instead, he heard an oath from the soldier outside his door and footsteps as he ran back the way he had come.

Merek considered moving down to a safer height. But the soldiers were quicker than he expected, and before he had negotiated his descent, the door squealed open.

"I demand to see the king," Merek said, turning his head to ensure the soldiers could hear him. His voice was raspy, and it hurt to speak. For two days he'd been yelling this phrase repeatedly, trying to provoke a response.

They were responding now. A heavy weight struck Merek's ankle, knocking his foot free from its precarious hold. He slipped and fell, hitting the ground hard and feeling a great tearing sensation in his ankle as it buckled under him. He lay on the stone floor for just a moment, gritting his teeth against the pain. Then the soldiers fell upon him. Something hard connected with his face, knocking his head back against the stones. Head swimming, he rolled onto his side, knees tucked to protect himself from their thick boots.

After several excruciating minutes, with Merek using every ounce of self control to resist the urge to fight back, he heard a familiar voice.

"Stop! What is this? Step away from that man!" Talen cried.

"He was climbing the wall to escape, sir," one of the

soldiers protested. Merek opened one eye, but his vision was blurry. Three hazy forms stood over him, with a dark shape on the floor near his head that looked vaguely like a club. That must have been what knocked him from the wall. At least they hadn't used it to beat him.

"And just how was he going to escape?" Taken shouted, his voice ringing with scorn. "Through the window? Or through the door that you left wide open? You two, help him to his feet. You, bring some water to clean up this blood."

Rough hands grabbed Merek under his arms, but he waved them away, slowly coming up onto his knees on the hard stone floor. He paused there, spitting out blood and waiting for the world to right itself. Feeling his teeth with his tongue, he was relieved to find he hadn't lost any. His lower lip was torn, his ankle ached fiercely, and his hips, back, and ribs felt bruised when he moved. But he didn't think the soldiers' hearts had been in it, so all in all it wasn't too bad for a beating.

Talen dismissed his men with a growl and crouched before Merek, holding out a moist rag.

"What is the meaning of this?" Talen demanded.

Merek took the rag and sat back against the stone wall. He cleared his throat in an effort to speak. "It's not easy for a man to get your attention. I've been shouting myself hoarse for two days. Thought I'd try a different approach."

Talen shook his head. "You are an idiot. I haven't been here for the past two days. And the guards— they're trained not to respond to the prisoners.

Except," he noted, looking Merek over, "in certain instances."

"So I gathered," Merek said, wiping the blood from his face. It had stained the front of his clothing, and his mouth was tender, making it difficult to speak.

"So, Strong, what was so important that you had to risk your life to get my attention?" Talen grumbled.

"First, help me to the cot," Merek said. "This floor is as cold as death itself."

Talen braced him up with one shoulder and helped him limp over to the cot. His right ankle wouldn't take any weight, but he could still move it. Just a sprain then. A painful annoyance.

"I need to see the king," Merek repeated. "If you have any compassion for an old friend, you'll arrange it."

Talen shook his head. "That won't be possible. The king sees no one. Not me, and certainly not you. Where do you think I've been these past two days?"

"You petitioned the king?" Merek looked at him in surprise. "For me?"

Talen scowled, but when he sat next to Merek on the cot, Merek realized the scowl wasn't for him. "I know it's unorthodox, but I can't in good conscience send a friend to his death without knowing for certain that he is not simply on the wrong end of a personal grudge. The princess seems convinced of your innocence, and I thought that if the king would see me, he would hear two voices dissenting from Grammel's."

It didn't change anything, but knowing that Talen believed him innocent made a difference to Merek. Suddenly, he didn't feel so alone.

"I have to try to make my case. It's the only hope I have now."

"I'm telling you, it won't happen. The king refuses to see anyone. I've heard that even the princess has been banned from the tower."

This was grim news indeed. If Sindal wouldn't even see his own daughter, Merek had no hope of gaining an audience with him. Though, to be honest, even if he gained an audience he had little hope that anything he said would change the king's mind. But he had to try.

He rubbed his face and sighed.

Talen glanced at him with a curious expression. "You know, Strong, the princess seems to care a great deal about you. She'll have me flogged if she sees you in this state."

Merek didn't answer right away. Should he respond to the unasked question? Or should he point out that the princess was unlikely to see him since she hadn't returned to the prison since her first visit. This suited him well enough, since he couldn't think of their last meeting without feeling ill with shame.

"What's your point, Talen?"

"It just makes me wonder, that's all. Why should she care so much? And why does her father seem so intent on having you behind bars? It's a very intriguing puzzle."

"You spin such sordid tales, you should have been a minstrel," Merek said drily.

Talen snorted. But in a serious tone, he added, "Be careful, my friend. I don't know what you've done to attract the wrath of such powerful men, but I'm afraid your allies aren't strong enough to fight them both."

"So it would seem." Merek's words died off into heavy silence.

After a moment, Talen stood and clapped him on the shoulder. "Let's get that ankle wrapped before it swells. I'm in no mood for a flogging."

Thirteen

Ria sat on the floor of her father's study surrounded by books, folios of loose sheets of paper, and half a dozen scrolls of ancient parchment that were so brittle the outer edges flaked off when she touched them. Sindal's desk, chairs, and tables had been removed to the tower, but Ria was grateful to find that all the cabinets and bookcases remained with their contents untouched.

She knew her search would be more efficient if she just told her father's clerks what she was looking for. They could find what she needed in the archives—or even here in this room—faster than she could hope to, but she didn't dare ask for help. Not for what she was considering. If she were going to succeed—and she had to, or more than one life would be at stake—then absolute secrecy was a must.

Footsteps sounded from down the hall, and Ria casually turned over a few papers she'd been collecting and slid them beneath her. Then she turned her attention back to an open book. It was one of several biographies of her grandfather, King Danvir. She'd only meant to skim, but she kept finding herself drawn into his story and losing her purpose.

At a knock at the door, he glanced up to see Captain Talen standing in the doorway. Whatever question he'd been about to ask died at the sight of her sitting on the floor in the middle of what appeared to be a ransacked room.

"Yes?" Ria asked distractedly. She was still irritated with the captain, and seeing him made her feel a twinge of guilt. How many days had it been since she'd visited Merek? She'd intended to return, but Galinn had started receiving the first reports from General Grammel—and fortunately had the good sense to give them to her rather than taking them to the tower—and she'd found herself woefully unprepared to respond. Any spare moment she'd had since then, which were already too few, had been spent trying to fill the very large gaps in her knowledge.

To be honest, Ria welcomed the distraction because she was ashamed to return to the prison. What would she say to Merek? How could she possibly bring him any comfort when it was her fault he was in chains? Then there was the matter of her botched marriage proposal. She'd tried to explain herself in the note she'd written before she left the prison, but now she worried that it had been too rushed and insensitive. And how should she interpret his unexpected response? Did he have feelings for her? He didn't actually *say* he cared for her. Perhaps that wasn't his intent any more than it was hers. The unanswered questions arising from that awkward conversation, and the inevitability of having it again, kept her from returning to the prison. She'd never realized she could be such a coward.

And here was a reminder of her cowardice standing before her, clearing his throat. She shot him a glare.

"I'm sorry to disturb you, Your Highness," Talen began apologetically. "Galinn said I would find you here. I was wondering if I might have a word with you, about a certain friend of ours."

Ria arched one eyebrow. "You call him 'friend' now? That's a strange word for someone you have shackled and locked away in a cell." She knew that she was being unfair blaming Talen for carrying out orders, but she couldn't understand how he'd had the stomach to do it.

Talen didn't flinch at her sarcasm. Ria sighed and closed her book.

"Come in. I can offer you a bit of rug if you care to sit. I'm afraid this room's more comfortable furnishings have recently found a new home elsewhere."

Captain Talen stepped into the room, looked skeptically at the piles of academic refuse around her, and remained standing. Ria was possessed with a sudden urge to join him and stretch her legs and back, but the pile of papers under her backside kept her firmly on the floor. Talen was the last person she could afford to let into her confidence.

"How is Captain Strong?" Ria asked, craning her neck to look up at the curly-haired man.

"He is…" Talen cleared his throat. "Incarceration does not agree with a man like Strong."

"I've never met a man with whom incarceration did agree, Talen."

"Quite so, but I was wondering if you've had any luck with your father. Strong seems to think a king's pardon is his only hope. Grammel has made up his mind, and he's not often inclined to change it."

Ria considered her answer carefully. "I've met with my father. He requires further convincing, but I know him. He's not a cruel man. I think in the end he will decide to be lenient."

Talen's eyes flickered with hope. "You think so? That would be very fortunate, my lady."

"Don't speak a word of this to Strong, mind you. I would hate to raise his hopes if it doesn't work out."

"Of course." Talen made as if to leave, his countenance considerably lighter than it had been when he entered.

"Captain," Ria stopped him. "There is a matter that you may be able to help me with. Please, sit." She moved aside a stack of books and maps to make room for him on the rug.

While he sat and awkwardly crossed his legs in the small space, she retrieved a small packet of letters from her sling. It had proven to be a convenient carrier, and one she never had to worry about setting down and forgetting.

"These are Grammel's reports from Endvar. With my father unwell, it's my duty to represent him and advise the general. I've discussed it with my father's advisors, of course. But if you have time to review the reports, your perspective as a trusted officer would be appreciated as well."

Talen's eyes gleamed. "I'm honored that you seek my counsel, Your Highness, but I expect that General Grammel won't care much for it. A general must have a certain autonomy over his forces and feel free to make decisions as he sees fit."

"Of course," Ria conceded. "But did you know that King Danvir never had a general? He and his father before him commanded the armies directly."

Talen nodded. "I expect there were some advantages that way, but it certainly made the royal line more vulnerable, don't you think? Your father's decision to appoint a general has proven to be a wise choice in protecting the crown."

"So says the military man," Ria said drily, handing him the envelope.

Talen took the packet from her and scanned its contents.

Ria didn't wait for him to finish before summarizing the important points. "The general hasn't yet been able to confirm who holds the city. Some reports indicate Ardanian, but they don't wear uniforms from the royal army, and there are witnesses who described an unusually large number of Khouris present when the city fell. It may mean that our enemy doesn't represent any kingdom or acknowledge any border." She thought of Domar and suppressed a shudder. She wanted to believe that his employer wasn't Artem, but after her father's behavior, she couldn't be certain of anything. "Whoever it is, they have repelled Grammel's attacks and have responded by retaliating against its citizens. Namely, the noble class."

Talen must have seen that part of the report, for he just nodded. Ria had been sickened to learn of the gruesome beheadings of poor Lord and Lady Ogmun, as well as some minor nobles whose names she didn't recognize.

"Has General Grammel sought to communicate with them?" Talen asked. "Tried to learn their purpose and intent?"

"All emissaries have been rebuffed. Whoever it is these men are serving, they're not interested in having a conversation with the general."

"Can't Grammel just storm the gates and win the city back? Surely he can overwhelm whatever force holds it."

Ria squinted at Talen. "When was the last time you visited Endvar, Captain? It's a considerable stronghold, and even with their small numbers the enemy has the advantage in every way. In the end, it may come down to a large-scale assault, but I would like to have a city standing when they're through."

"I see. In short, this puts General Grammel in a situation where to attack brings death to Endvar's citizens, but to do nothing means giving the enemy a chance to amass a larger force."

"Precisely. Either way, I fear that we're playing right into the enemy's hands. It would be preferable to meet them on open terrain where Grammel's numbers have the advantage. The longer he waits for them to come out and meet him, the more time they have to entrench themselves in the city."

"But if he attacks the city now, the cost to the citizens of Endvar would be catastrophic," Talen said grimly. "We would have to be prepared to accept enormous losses."

"You see why every viewpoint is helpful. I would be interested to hear your recommendations, Captain."

Talen paused thoughtfully. "Might I take this with me?" he asked, holding up Grammel's report. "I'd like to examine the details more fully before committing myself."

Ria looked at him appraisingly. He seemed so genuine and sincere. "I suppose you may. I know its contents well. But don't keep it too long. I'm anxious to make a decision and send a response."

Talen agreed and tucked the packet away into his coat. Ria rose to bid him farewell, coming up to stand directly on the loose papers she'd tucked under her, trusting that her full skirts would obscure them adequately. As she watched Talen leave, she was struck by what a singularly selective thing trust could be.

Rorden watched the glowing sky grimly. Endvar wasn't directly visible, obscured as it was by the terrain, but the fires burning within her walls illuminated the night sky behind the hills.

If only the garrison had received Wott's command before the gates had been sealed. If only they'd found the tunnels sooner. If only the princess hadn't insisted on touring the wall and pulling Captain Strong away for all those weeks. It seemed that no matter what they did, the enemy had stayed one step ahead.

"You see that there?" the soldier next to him asked.

Rorden blinked away the light from his eyes and looked where the man was pointing. There was movement against the blackness of the trees. A man with a cart was driving up the road toward their camp. That was odd. Since General Grammel's army had arrived, a whole host of tradesmen, merchants, and craftsmen flocked to the city of tents almost daily. But not usually in the early hours of the morning with dawn still a long time away.

The guard beside him straightened and moved toward the perimeter of the camp to intercept the cart.

"I'll come with you," Rorden said, his curiosity piqued. Anything to take his mind off the brooding thoughts that had occupied him lately.

The driver looked up as they approached, torchlight dancing across his fleshy features. He peered uncertainly at the two soldiers silhouetted before him, then at the camp beyond.

"State your business, sir," the guard called in a neutral voice.

The driver of the cart pulled his mule to a halt, grumbling when it didn't respond right away. "I have something to say to the man in charge," he said, raising a hand up to shade his eyes against the torchlight.

"I'll hear your business first, sir," the guard replied in

that same neutral voice. Not a challenge, but not particularly friendly either.

The driver glanced behind him. "Can we at least get to a fire to warm up? I'm afraid one o' them might not make it if she sits in the cold much longer."

The soldier's sigh was almost imperceptible. Dutifully, he walked toward the bed of the cart. "What have you got, then? A couple of sows? Some chickens? The campmaster won't be up for a few more hours. You can bring your—"

The guard cursed and jumped back from the cart, looking up at the driver.

"What's the meaning of this?" he demanded in a harsh whisper. "Have you no shame, man?"

"No, it ain't like that!" the man pleaded. "They ain't mine; I never seen 'em before tonight! I'm just a farmer what lives down in the Vifar valley. Then they come knocking at my door all wet from taking a dip in the river, they says."

The rest of the farmer's words were lost to Rorden because at that moment he rounded the cart and saw what had so startled the guard. Two women lay huddled under a quilt. The younger of the two presented a ghastly image in the torchlight with hair that looked as though it had been cropped by a butcher's knife, the woman's scalp narrowly avoiding the blade. He recoiled at the sight of the wretched creature, but then moved closer and recognized her companion hidden in shadow.

"No. It can't be!" Bounding up the side of the cart— the driver hollered at him as he rocked it with his weight —Rorden gently turned her face toward the light.

"I know this woman," he said excitedly. "Tell me, where did you find her?"

"Oh, well, if that isn't a piece of luck," the farmer exclaimed, sounding relieved. "I told you, I didn't find 'em. They found me. Knocked on my door last night. Wet and cold as drowned rats, they were. Me wife, she brought 'em inside and gave 'em dry clothes, but they wouldn't stay to warm up proper. Said they had to get to the garrison before daybreak. Asked for directions and would o' tried walking if I hadn't hitched up Insel here." He nodded to the mule.

"You say you know this woman?" the guard asked, coming closer to inspect the two figures.

"Yes, she's...a friend," Rorden answered, stopping short of telling her connection with Captain Strong. There was no use plaguing Aiya with the same cloud of suspicion that hung over him in camp. All of Captain Strong's men were regarded with wariness by Grammel's soldiers, but none as much as Rorden. As much as people loved a hero, it seemed they loved seeing him fall from grace even more.

Rorden looked at the young woman next to Aiya. "I don't know who this girl is, though," he said, taking in her pale skin, and the ravaged remnants of her hair. Then she shifted and opened her eyes, and sudden familiarity ignited his memory.

"What—? How—?" He staggered in disbelief.

The young woman's eyes widened as she focused on him. She pushed herself up on one elbow with great effort, and when she spoke, her speech was sluggish. "Well, how do you like that? We tell him to take us to the garrison and he finds us the most useless soldier in the whole army. Aiya," she said, nudging the sleeping woman. "You won't believe who we've found."

Aiya stirred and opened her eyes, but they were glassy and unfocused. Rorden leaned forward, ignoring Yulda's gibe. "Aiya, are you well? It's me, Rorden." He brushed her cheek gently, and her skin was cold and waxy beneath his touch. "We must get you warm. When was the last time you ate?"

Aiya's eyes fluttered closed again, and her face slackened. Yulda sniffed. "Happy to see you too, kind sir. When do I get my royal welcome?"

Rorden looked at the girl, a sharp retort on his tongue, but she looked so pitiful with her tufts of hair illuminated like a patchy halo that compassion overcame him. "Let's get you both to a warm fire with something hot to drink, and then you can tell me everything."

Yulda must have seen the pity in his gaze because her expression changed from haughtiness to great self-consciousness, and she ducked her head as the farmer started to move the cart forward. They had barely moved a few feet, however, when she stopped him.

"Wait! I almost forgot! You must send troops to the southern gate at first light. Dan and the other soldiers are planning to attack, but there must be troops ready to enter the city once they seize the gate."

Rorden glanced at the other soldier, but he'd made no more sense of her words than he had.

"Are you daft? Did I not speak loudly enough? Dan is alive. In Endvar."

"Sergeant Dan!"

"No, your uncle Dan," Yulda replied snidely. "Of course I mean Sergeant Dan! We found some other soldiers who survived, and they decided to attack the southern gate. But they'll need reinforcements to hold it." She suddenly yawned and closed her eyes. "We must send troops or they'll all be butchered—don't tell Aiya I said that." She slumped back onto the bed of the cart as it began moving again. "Please, Rorden, send the troops. Dan is a fool, but he's a good fool."

Fourteen

"Your Highness, Captain Talen is here to see you."

Ria glanced up at the servant and was surprised to realize that dusk had fallen. Where had the hours gone? The windows of the great hall now served as black mirrors reflecting the princess and her entourage seated around the table in lively discussion about the economic effect of war they could expect to see throughout the kingdom.

Talen waited at a respectful distance, and Ria left to speak with him directly. She steered him away from the murmur of conversation at the table, looking for a bit of privacy in the busy hall.

"You asked me for my recommendations," Talen began when she was satisfied that they were far enough from listening ears. He handed over a sheaf of notes. "We need to draw them out. If we can convince them to leave the stronghold, then we can use Strong's wall climbers to take back the gates."

"But how do we draw them out? They refuse to respond to requests to parley. They have no incentive to leave the city until they've amassed a force large enough to contend with ours."

"The size of the force isn't the issue. It's getting them away from the city so we can take back the gates and seal off their support. Grammel needs to call in additional units, but keep them hidden so the enemy doesn't know the size of our army. When they attack, they'll be prepared for a force half the size of the one we'll have, and then we'll go behind them with the climbers and take back the city. They'll be trapped."

Ria considered this. It was risky. Its success hinged on a small group of soldiers who had trained for a covert assault but had no practical experience. But Grammel's plan of attacking Endvar with brute force and no consideration for civilian casualties was no better.

Ria looked over Talen's notes more closely, noting where Grammel's extra troops would need to be hidden, how long it might take for them to arrive, and how big of a force the wall climbers could feasibly overcome.

Here, she glanced sharply at Talen.

"You show an astute mind, Captain."

"Thank you, my lady."

"I'll have my clerks draw up this plan and send it to General Grammel immediately. Thank you for your contribution."

He nodded respectfully.

"Captain, before you go," Ria said, producing a sealed envelope bearing red wax imprinted with her father's seal. "I believe you'll wish to act on this order immediately."

Talen took it from her, eyes widening. "Did he..?"

Ria smiled. "Enclosed you'll find a king's pardon for one Merek Strong, as well as orders reinstating his rank and releasing all seized goods back into his hands. And various and sundry items, I didn't read it fully."

Talen grinned. "Thank you, Your Highness. I'll act on it at once. And," he added, lowering his voice, "should I suggest that he put some miles between him and the king just in case His Majesty should change his mind?"

Ria grimaced. "It may be advisable. But Captain, I wish to see our friend before he leaves, if you would be so good as to instruct him accordingly. And mention that if he fails to answer this summons, I will cheerfully send you to arrest him again."

Talen laughed, openly relieved. Ria smiled in return but couldn't feel completely at ease. Yet. As he walked away, considerably lighter of step, she resisted the urge to wipe her sweaty palms on her skirt.

Sleep didn't come easily to her that night. She sat for a long time in front of the fire, until it died out and the cold drove her to bed. But even then, she slept fitfully, dreaming of dark threats and desperate escapes. When she woke in the deep hours of the night, she gave up on sleep altogether. Wrapping herself in a heavy blanket, she moved to the alcove near the window and curled up on the padded bench.

Outside, the grounds were lit in pockets by braziers tended by the night guards. Ria rested her head against the cool glass, thinking to herself that it hadn't been that long since she'd found her father in a similar posture in the middle of the night. Was this going to be the way of things for her? The thought made her grimace.

She refused to believe that she was doomed to her father's same fate. There had been no mention of madness or even unusual sleep habits in the biography about Danvir.

But perhaps Danvir wasn't burdened by a guilty conscience.

No. She would not feel guilty about what she'd done. It was the right thing, she was sure of it. If her methods had been questionable, well, it was an exigent circumstance.

Her insides twisted. That was a dangerous line of thinking. A slippery slope that she couldn't afford to flirt with if she were going to be the queen she hoped to be someday. It threw into sharp relief the fact that she couldn't do this alone. She needed a companion to account to: a partner to provide clarity. Someone she trusted who would be her compass when she was so wrapped up in a problem that she couldn't see which way was up. And even more importantly, someone who knew her so well that he could see when she was lost in the first place.

Aiya slowly became conscious of the sound of rain dribbling down the side of her house.

No, not her house.

Her house was destroyed, burned to the ground. Her eyes snapped open as the memories of recent days flooded her mind.

She was in a small tent, laying on the ground in someone else's bedroll. Two other bedrolls lay next to her, but these were both empty. Rain pattered gently against the canvas and dripped steadily from the ceiling. Where was she?

The events of the previous night were hazy. She remembered following the river to Danvir's Wall late in the afternoon and discovering that the grate covering the culvert was half rusted away. Half swimming and half being swept away by the Vifar River, she and Yulda managed to pass through the grate, but then struggled to escape the current and make it to shore. She shuddered as she recalled the moment of panic when she lost her bearings and couldn't right herself. But Yulda was a strong swimmer and had dragged her to shallow water.

Yulda. Where was the girl now?

Aiya sat up, looking at the coarse woolen dress she wore and vaguely remembering a farmer and his wife with strong hands and a pronounced lisp. As she reached for her boots—still wet from her swim—she wondered what the farmer's wife had done with their clothes.

Aiya tried to move quickly, but her fingers were swollen, and she struggled with her laces. Finally she got her boots tied and hurried out of the tent. She wasn't surprised to find herself in the midst of an army camp— that was the only explanation for the tent—but she was surprised at the silence. Where were all the soldiers? Where was the bustling activity?

The tents appeared to have been staked in a corn field. The trampled stalks of corn hadn't yet been swallowed by the mud, for which she was grateful as it kept her boots from sinking with every step. She followed an alley of sorts between the tents until it led to a larger lane. The smoke from cookfires was visible not far away, and she started to head that direction when the sound of voices stopped her.

Aiya turned and recognized Rorden and Yulda—now with a brown scarf wrapped around her head to hide the ruin of her hair—talking together in earnest. They glanced up and saw her, and both of their faces relaxed into smiles.

"Aiya!" Rorden called out, engulfing her spontaneously in a hug. She stiffened momentarily before reminding herself of his affectionate ways. "I'm glad to see you back on your feet again. Yulda told me all about your escape."

"And Dan? Has someone gone to help him?"

Yulda and Rorden exchanged a worried look. "Captain Eldar led a company of men—all that's left of Endvar's Wall Guard—to the gate this morning, but there's been no sign of activity."

"None?" Aiya felt weak.

Rorden's lips tightened. His dimples made it difficult for him to ever look truly serious, but this was the most grim Aiya had ever seen him.

"They'll stay until it's dark, but they don't dare do

anything more without orders from General Grammel. He didn't exactly authorize their movements today."

"This General Grammel, is Captain Strong with him?"

A look of pain flashed briefly across Rorden's face. "Aiya," he said softly. "There have been strange happenings of late. It would be wise to keep your connection to Captain Strong quiet."

"Why?" Aiya asked sharply. "What has happened?"

Rorden glanced around to ensure they were alone. "Captain Strong has been arrested."

Aiya recoiled. "What?"

"He's being held in Albon on charges of treason."

"This can't be possible," Aiya said in disbelief. "What you're saying can't be true."

"I don't believe the charges are just," Rorden muttered, glancing back toward the main avenue. "None of us do. For that our whole company are just short of being seen as traitors ourselves."

"But...why? I don't understand." Captain Strong's conduct had always been above reproach.

Rorden jerked his head in the direction of the main part of camp. "If you ask me, I think General Grammel is behind it. He hasn't openly condemned the rest of us, but the other soldiers keep their distance. We're given no tasks of any meaning. Until you two got here with word of Dan needing support, that is, but even that was more a matter of volunteering, you might say."

Yulda added, "I'm not even a soldier, but just being with Rorden has marked me as surely as if I had the plague."

"Well, it doesn't help that you look the part," Rorden said, smiling a crooked smile. He nudged her shoulder playfully, but Yulda just glowered at him, her cheeks reddening.

"Do not tease the girl," Aiya said firmly, looking around for a place to sit. She was beginning to feel light-headed. A ring of large stones sat around a campfire, now cold and untended. She moved toward them but stumbled over a piece of errant firewood that had drifted from its stack. A hand grabbed her elbow and steadied her. She looked up in surprise. The older soldier seemed familiar to Aiya, but she didn't know his name.

Rorden saluted the man sharply. "Captain Eldar, sir. Do you have word of Dan and the others?"

The captain looked at Aiya. "Is there any chance the attack was not to take place today?"

"We discussed no contingencies," Aiya said, but in her mind she cursed Dan for not having done so. *What am I supposed to do now?*

"Then I'm afraid they are lost to us," Eldar said darkly. "Forgive me, miss, but if you're feeling well enough, General Grammel would like to speak with you both."

A wave of sickness passed over Aiya. What would she say to the man responsible for this unspeakable offense against Captain Strong? But if he could help Dan and his men...

"Of course."

Rorden squeezed her shoulder. "Just remember what I said. General Grammel is no friend to Captain Strong."

"You aren't coming?" Aiya asked.

"It's best if Sergeant Rorden doesn't come," Eldar explained. "And miss, I've told the general very little of you. I'll leave it up to you to decide how much he needs to know."

The warning was clear. Aiya nodded her understanding and fell into step beside Yulda, following the officer to the heart of the army camp.

GENERAL GRAMMEL WAS A THICK-SET MAN WITH A RUDDY complexion whose brow was so heavy it seemed knit together in a permanent frown. As the two women entered his tent, however, he smiled at them.

"Ladies, I'm glad to see you so well. I trust that you're being well tended?" He invited them to sit around the large table. An aide rushed forward to clear two chairs of stacked papers and rolled up maps.

Aiya sat obediently next to Yulda, feeling dwarfed by the large chairs and the powerfully built man who sat across from them. He nodded to another aide scratching on a tablet.

"Now, which of you works for Lord Bolen?" he asked, looking back and forth between them.

"I do, sir. I mean, I did," Yulda corrected herself, her voice small.

Aiya glanced at her. The girl seemed to be visibly shrinking in her chair.

"And you are...?" He turned to Aiya.

"I have a shop in the city, sir. Or rather, I did. It burned during the attack."

He looked at her with interest. "You speak our language well. Have you lived here long?"

"Ten years, sir. Thank you." She adopted the same meek tone as Yulda. The general seemed to be trying hard to be pleasant, as if he expected them to be intimidated. It was usually best to give people what they expected when you planned to lie to them.

"Tell me, how did you manage to escape the city?" General Grammel asked, turning back to Yulda.

She answered by telling of the attack on Lord Bolen's house and how she managed to survive. When she got to the part where she escaped, she looked uncertainly at Aiya.

General Grammel turned his attention to Aiya. "You and this sergeant were together?"

"I was in the market when the soldiers attacked," Aiya explained quickly. "A soldier —Sergeant Dan, he called himself—protected me. We hid in a brassworker's shop, until Yulda discovered us."

The general seemed to accept her brief account and spent the rest of the time questioning Yulda. As her tale took them into the tunnels, he slowed its telling with frequent interruptions. Aiya's presence was only required to recount the conversation between Behni and Master Domar. Otherwise, she sat quietly and waited as the time drew long, feeling increasingly weak and wondering how long it would be before she could get a proper meal.

When the general finally stood, he took each of their hands gratefully, his beefy hands swallowing theirs. "Sergeant Dan and his men acted bravely. Choosing to sacrifice themselves in the hope that they could save the city was noble and all that I expect from my soldiers."

"So you mean not to go after them?" Aiya asked.

"I'm sorry. But don't despair that they are lost. Their sacrifice will be remembered, you can be sure of that."

Aiya managed a weak smile, but inside she felt as if there were cracks threatening to tear her apart. Wrapping her arms around her middle, she escaped out into the fresh air with Yulda quick on her heels.

Fifteen

Merek stood in front of the looking glass and inspected his appearance. He'd chosen to keep the beard that had grown during a week of imprisonment, but it was now trimmed close and tidy, his hair shorn respectably short. Bathed and dressed in a clean uniform, one wouldn't guess that he'd so recently been a condemned man sleeping on a prison floor and beaten by guards.

He'd been shocked when Talen had come to him the previous night with word of his pardon and release. It had seemed such an impossibility that he'd scarcely dared believe it. The rest of the night passed as a blur: receiving the property that had been taken from him—it was immensely satisfying to lay hold on his weapons again—returning to his room above the barracks, and sitting for some time alone perfectly still, trying to believe that soldiers weren't going to burst into his room and carry him back to prison. Eventually, he decided that if that was going to happen, at least he could enjoy some sleep before it did. So he laid down on the bed—a real mattress!—and slept the hardest, longest sleep of his life.

The next morning, he'd half expected to wake and discover it had all been a dream. But when he found himself still in his own bed, in his familiar rooms in Albon, the stupor of the previous night fled, and he jumped into action.

Sending instructions to have a horse prepared for him, Merek set about cleaning away the signs of his recent humiliation. His body still ached from the beating, and he struggled to walk without a limp, but he was glad to see there were no visible marks that his clothing and beard didn't cover.

He told himself that was why he kept the beard. That, and he was leaving Albon as soon as possible; etiquette wouldn't demand it of him once he left the city walls. But there was a part of him that whispered it was something more. An angry part, still seething from betrayal. It was dangerous, he knew, so he buried it and straightened his coat, turning his back on his reflection.

Talen had been very direct about the princess wanting to meet with him. Had there even been mention of a threat? He wouldn't be surprised. But this was a meeting he would keep in any event, even though he anticipated it with a mixture of eagerness and foreboding. He was ashamed when he thought of his careless words the last time they'd met, and he knew that, awkward though it may be, his mind wouldn't rest until he'd cleared the air between them.

"Your Highness, Captain Strong is here to see you. Shall I send him in?"

Ria looked up from the notes she'd been jotting down and blinked to clear her vision. Her restless night hadn't precluded an early start, and she was already feeling the effects of a lack of sleep.

"Captain Strong? Here?" she asked sharply. She'd intended to visit him discreetly, not have him come up to the Hall. She glanced across the room where Galinn conferred with members of the household staff. The great hall was quieter this morning as she'd finally worked her way through the line of waiting citizens and could meet with petitioners at her leisure, if such a thing existed anymore. But this was still too public a space for such a private meeting.

"I'll see him in the library," she said to the servant.

"My apologies, Your Highness, but Count Orlin is waiting for you in the library."

"Ah, yes, of course. That won't do." Ria had forgotten about the Ardanian ambassador. "Take Captain Strong to my sitting room. And," she added as her stomach gurgled noisily, "bring some breakfast."

Ria's pace quickened as she approached her sitting room. The sun had finally emerged after the long storm, and the sitting room was warm and lit with a watery light.

Merek stood at the window, his back to her, posture erect, basking in the sunlight.

Ria paused in the doorway, feeling a release of some

of the tension she'd been carrying. "If I had known it would take an arrest for you to respond to my summons, I would have thrown you in prison weeks ago."

He turned as she spoke, and his lips twitched briefly in a smile. His dark blue uniform and neatly trimmed appearance gave him such a commanding air that it defied any memory she had of the wretched man in prison.

He greeted her with a stiff bow. "Good morning, Your Highness."

Ria ignored his formality, rushing to him with a wide, beaming smile and grasping his hands affectionately. "Dear Merek, let me take a look at you. Are you well? Did they treat you abominably?"

Merek's expression softened.

"I'm quite well, my lady. Thank you. Talen didn't say as much, but I suspect I owe you my life for interceding with the king."

"If you do, then I merely consider my own debt to you repaid. Please." She gestured toward the two chairs sitting on either side of a small table.

"You aren't wearing your sling," he observed as he sat.

"Yes. My shoulder isn't fully healed, but I no longer need to immobilize it. What a mercy! But I'm more concerned about you. You move the way I did after my fall, as though you are so battered you're barely holding yourself together."

"It's nothing. I'm not as young as I once was, but it'll soon pass."

Ria gritted her teeth. "Curse that man. I told him that you were not to come to harm!"

"It wasn't Talen's fault," Merek said quickly. "If anything, it was my own. But that's not a topic I care to discuss today," he said, raising a finger as she opened her mouth to interrupt. "If you merely wish to satisfy yourself that I'm well, then you've seen all you need to see, and I'll excuse myself. I'm anxious to return to Endvar as soon as possible."

A pair of servants entered the room bearing trays.

"Will you join me for breakfast, Strong?" Ria invited, as the servants laid out a basket of warm biscuits, pastries, fluffy eggs, and fresh cream.

Merek barely glanced at the food, his right knee bouncing slightly in agitation. "I really don't have the time, Your Highness."

"Very well then." Ria waited until the servants left, closing the door behind them. The silence between her and Merek felt too quiet, as if the very room waited for her secrets. Her hand strayed to a tendril of hair behind her ear, twining the strand around her fingers as she began. "The last time we met, in Talen's office, I'm afraid that I—"

"Please don't think anything of it," he interrupted crisply. "We were both under great stress and said things we didn't mean."

"Oh." Ria paused. "Of course. But...what did you think of my note?"

Something flickered in his eyes. "I didn't read it."

"Why not?"

"Talen wanted to read it so I destroyed it in the fire. I didn't want to embarrass us both."

Discomfort tempered Ria's irritation. This was going to be harder than she thought.

"Well, to be blunt, Merek, I *do* wish us to wed. I know that there are a few impediments to this, namely my father's opposition, but I'm increasingly convinced that this arrangement is best for the future of Rahm. Wedding a man of your character and life experience will be of great benefit to me as I prepare to rule as queen and will reassure the people that the throne is secure and the Thorodan line will continue. I assume you've had sound reasons for avoiding marriage in the past, so I ask that you consider your duty and reconcile your opposition for the good of our kingdom."

She had prepared that little speech during the night, and was pleased that she remembered it now. The room grew still.

Merek watched her steadily, his expression inscrutable.

"No," he said simply.

"I beg your pardon?"

"No, I cannot marry you."

"Cannot? Or will not?"

"Does it matter?"

"Yes, it matters! You can't simply refuse me without giving an explanation."

"This is not the time to..." Merek glanced at the door as if he wanted to leave. "Aside from your father's objection—which is more than a mere 'impediment'—I cannot marry you because it would be the worst kind of lie."

Ria's insides twisted. "I don't understand."

With another impatient glance at the exit, Merek leaned forward, resting his forearms on the table. "To you, marriage is contracts and agreements and political maneuvering. To me, marriage is..." he paused, searching for the right words. "...a woman who gives up wealth and comfort for a humble life in the forest to be with the man she loves. Bearing his children and nursing him for years when tragedy robs him of sense and he doesn't even know her anymore."

The retort Ria wanted to give died in her throat at his sincerity. She thought of Merek's mother and looked down at her hands, feeling a flush rise in her cheeks.

"What you describe may be good enough for you," Merek continued gently, "but it's not what I want. And someday you may not want it either. You're young, with much of life ahead of you. Someday you'll regret binding yourself to a man so much older than yourself."

Ria's head snapped up. "You doubt my constancy? You think I'll be unfaithful?"

"I merely doubt your experience. You're in the prime of your youth, with so much of life ahead of you. I fear that a union between us would only be tolerable at best."

"I don't care about your age!" Ria moved aside the basket of cooling biscuits and reached for his hand. It was a bold gesture, and he stiffened at her touch but didn't pull his hand away. His hand was large and tanned, with callused fingers and strong knuckles. Her own looked small and slender by comparison.

She looked into his eyes and willed him to listen. "You're the only person I respect well enough to offer my hand in marriage. You're the only one I trust to rule with me. With our country at war and my father's health ailing, I want some certainty in my life. You could give it to me. Just say 'yes,' and let's be done with this!"

Merek patted her hand as he pulled his own away, and she felt a surge of irritation at the patronizing gesture. "Ria, you've done me a great honor. I don't deserve your good favor, and I don't share your same confidence that I'm fit to rule. But I wish you the best and know that someday you'll find a man who captures not only your favor but also your heart. And then you'll be grateful that I didn't let you make this mistake."

"Mistake?" Ria scoffed. "I'm not some flighty milk-maid. I have neither the temperament nor the convenience of letting my heart dictate my future. I'm a princess and someday will be queen. There's no room in those titles for the simple affections of a commoner."

Something flickered briefly in his eyes, and then it was gone. His expression hardened into resolve. "You may not always feel that way. I could never accept being responsible for your misery. I've seen what joy marriage can bring and would feel hollow trying to live anything else."

"This is foolishness," Ria said dismissively. "Stop thinking of marriage as strictly a matter of the heart. Many marriages succeed with less respect than you and I share. I'm confident that we could be happy and do much good for our people. Consider your duty. Rahm needs you. *I* need you to lead her at my side."

Merek shook his head and stood. He moved to the window and looked out across the rolling green pastures, wet from the recent rain. He didn't speak. He didn't have to. She'd seen that look of determination before. He would not be moved. She thought again about his words in Talen's office. Looking at him now, with his proud profile and controlled presence, there was no hint of the tenderness he had shown there.

"You are not convinced."

"No. Someday, you'll thank me for it."

Ria sighed. Perhaps she should feel embarrassed at being refused, but all she felt was acute annoyance.

"The food is getting cold," she said flatly.

Merek blinked and turned toward her as if shaking off a heavy thought. "Forgive me for keeping you from your breakfast. If that's all you require, I'm anxious to see your father before I depart. So if I may beg your leave—"

"My father?" Ria's heart skipped a beat.

"Yes. I don't know when I'll return to Albon again, and I owe him my thanks."

"No! You mustn't see my father," she said, standing in a panic. "Indeed, you shouldn't even be here in this house. You really should leave the city as soon as possible."

He looked at her sharply. "Why? What's wrong?"

Ria's stomach churned unpleasantly. She hadn't planned on having this conversation, but she realized now that she should have been prepared for it. She should have guessed that he would want to see the man who had pardoned him. The man whom he still thought of as a friend.

"It isn't real," Ria said quietly, glancing at the door. She could almost taste the bitter treachery of the words. "The pardon is a forgery. I found some copies of old pardons—really old ones, it's not a thing that's often done—and copied the language, then used my father's seal. I can fake his hand well enough. Well enough for Talen anyway, and since he wanted you released almost as much as I, I took the chance."

As she spoke, Merek's countenance darkened. "Ria, what have you done?"

"I know it was wrong. But it was also wrong to have you arrested in the first place! I couldn't just let you die! And my father wouldn't listen to reason. What else could I do?"

"But this—to forge a pardon in the king's name—this is treason! If anyone finds out, there will be no mercy. For either one of us! And possibly Talen as well!"

Ria cringed at the storm in his eyes. "That can't be helped. I had no other choice. But no one will find out. You and I are the only ones who know."

"What about Grammel? What will happen when he returns and sees the pardon for himself? Or when your father learns I've been freed?" Merek stepped forward until he was towering over her. She resisted the urge to step back, instead straightening to her full height.

"All Grammel will hear is that you've been pardoned. When he returns, he'll be full of glory from winning a war, and will be able to afford to be generous. Unless he returns in defeat, in which case we'll all have far more serious things to worry about. As for my father, he's more reclusive than ever, and there may be a chance he won't hear the news." This was overstating things. Although he was reclusive, it was unlikely that Sindal wouldn't hear of Merek's release eventually. She wasn't sure how she would handle that future day, but that was her problem to solve. "Just to be safe, however, I would suggest that you stay away from Albon until I've had a chance to smooth things over with him."

Merek glared at her. "So I'm to be exiled."

"Well, I guess you could call it that. But just for a time, and only unofficially." It really had seemed a fine plan in her mind. Certainly better than watching him die a traitor's death.

Merek ran his hands through his hair in frustration.

Ria thought she could read his thoughts. King? Or outlaw? Her actions may have just solidified his future as one or the other. But which one? Neither was a future of his own choosing.

"I had no choice," she insisted. "My father was so angry; he wouldn't listen. I tried, but he's not himself. What else could I do? Just watch you die? Watch you be executed as a sacrifice to my father's madness?"

Unexpectedly, Merek gripped her shoulders, and she gasped a little as his gray eyes bored into hers. "Ria, you have to understand. If I'm exiled and you are discovered, there's nothing I can do to help. Justice will be swift. I will likely not even learn about your trial until it is over. There will be no last minute pardon. No friend to come to your rescue."

Ria blinked, trying to break the intensity of his gaze. She felt unexpectedly short of breath, and when she swallowed, her mouth was painfully dry. "Thank you for pointing out the obvious," she said acidly. "I know the risks, Captain."

Merek released her and looked out the window at the sun rising higher in the sky. "I must go. I just wish there was something I could do to ensure your safety. To leave you here with no protection..."

The concern in his voice made her ashamed of her flippant words. "Then you aren't angry with me?" she asked.

"Oh, I'm angry. Angry enough to curse at you if you were one of my men. Of all the foolish, meddlesome, arrogant things to do. Risking your own life just to save mine?"

Ria smiled in spite of herself. It almost sounded noble when he said it like that. She reached out a hand in farewell. "I shall not regret it. Never. We belong together, Merek. In life or death, don't you see?"

"Given the option, I would prefer life," he growled.

"Does that mean you'll marry me?"

He gave a short bark of a laugh. "No. It just means that the next time you have any grand schemes to save my life, talk it over with me first."

When Merek was almost at the door, she remembered something.

"Strong?"

"Yes?" He paused in the doorway.

"I asked Captain Talen to offer some perspectives on the situation in Endvar," she said, watching him closely.

"Yes?"

"Talen told me a few days ago that he didn't know where your squad of wall climbers was located. Yet in his proposal, he mentioned several of them by name."

Merek glanced at her, but said nothing.

"You came up with the plan, didn't you?" she asked. "It was Talen's handwriting, but your design."

A smile tugged at his lips and smoothed the frown on his brow. "Under the circumstances, it didn't seem wise to make it known that Talen was seeking the assistance of a man accused of treason."

Ria laughed. "How wonderfully ironic! I hope Grammel uses it just because it was yours."

Merek grinned, and the room brightened at the sight.

"Oh!" Ria said, before she could stop herself. "There's my Captain Strong! Now I know you really did make it out of that prison."

He grunted and departed with a low bow. But as he turned away, the gleam in his eye told her he was pleased.

Sixteen

The army camp was a festive gathering from a distance, its colored tents and banners reminiscent of a celebration. Merek caught his first sight of the camp stretching out on a wide plain before him as he crested a small rise. The city of Endvar sat quietly in the far distance, a gray shadow against the horizon. It disappeared from view as he descended toward the valley, lost behind the hills.

As Merek drew closer to the camp, even the atmosphere was one of gaiety. Soldiers greeted each other with cheerful enthusiasm. Cooks and their maids laughed with the men as they dished their portions onto tin plates.

This isn't a group that's seen serious battle, Merek realized. Nor did they know what dreariness awaited them when winter set in. He didn't begrudge them their ignorance. It wouldn't last.

Merek attracted stares as he rode through the camp.

He stayed mounted to keep himself above the crowd. Let them see him ride with dignity, rather than slipping in undetected as he would have preferred. He wanted to put to rest any rumors about his imprisonment. Not just for his sake, but for Ria's. The more that people accepted his pardon and reinstatement, the fewer questions would be asked as to how it came about.

General Grammel's tent towered above the camp in bands of burgundy and silver, outlined proudly against a thick forest. It was once Sindal's tent, back when the king had commanded his armies directly. But few in this camp would remember those days.

As Merek led his horse up the wide avenue that led to the command tent, he recognized more of the officers. Several of the men nodded to him in respect. Others refused to meet his eye. *So quick to turn on one of your own,* he thought with a tightness in his belly. But they weren't his concern. The person he needed to win over was going to be far more resistant. It was vital that he gain Grammel's trust, or Ria would never be safe.

Committed to his course of action, Merek nevertheless felt a strong sense of disgust as he caught sight of Grammel's banner—its image that of a boar's head with mouth wide in a fearsome bellow. The two sentries at the tent door looked sideways at him but didn't stop him from entering. They wouldn't stand in the way of a captain of his rank unless expressly instructed. And why would Grammel have issued such instruction when he believed Merek to be locked away in Albon?

When Merek entered the tent, all eyes turned toward the door. Grammel stood abruptly, knocking over a tumbler in his haste and cursing as its dark contents spilled over the table and into his lap. The other officers in the room gaped.

"Strong!" Grammel sputtered. "How did you—? Argh!" he growled, snatching a map off the table and shaking off the liquid.

"Excuse me for taking you by surprise, General," Merek said calmly, enjoying the sight of the flustered Grammel. "It seemed prudent to report here first before going to find my men."

"*Your* men?" Grammel took in his uniform, and his eyes narrowed. "Only a king's pardon could have freed you from that prison, and I would have received word."

"In my haste, I may have passed your rider. I'm sure you'll forgive my eagerness."

Grammel glanced around at the other officers. "Dismissed," he barked, and took advantage of the distraction of his captains shuffling out the tent to straighten his appearance and wipe at the stain on his trousers.

When they were alone, Grammel looked Merek up and down for a long moment.

"Old friendships run deeper than I thought."

"So it would seem." Deception didn't come easily to him. Better to say little and let Grammel fill in the gaps himself.

"Why? If you were freed, why come here? To seek your vengeance?"

Merek snorted. "Every time you open your mouth, you reveal the smallness of your own mind. I came because my city has been attacked and I aim to do everything to take her back."

"*Your* city? You've proven to be a poor steward indeed, else she wouldn't have fallen in the first place."

With great effort, Merek pushed away an impulse to strike the man hard in the jaw. "Shame me all you wish, Grammel. I'm here to stay."

Grammel smirked. "I don't know how you managed to convince the king, but I'm not so easily played. You're not needed or wanted here. *I* will free this city. You won't be playing the hero this time, Strong."

"Don't be a fool, Grammel. I have a company of men that I've trained myself who know Endvar better than any other soldier in your army. You would throw away that advantage out of spite?"

Grammel was quiet for a moment, considering Merek's words.

"You'll be under my command," he finally said. "No acting outside of my orders."

"Agreed. In return, my men have full access to your armory. Much of their gear and weaponry were left behind in Endvar."

Grammel gave a brief nod. "And you won't be joining my captain's meetings."

"What? Why not?"

"Pardon or no pardon, I don't trust you. I won't risk you working with our enemies to undermine our strategies."

"So you would send me and my men into battle blind? I'm a First Captain!"

Grammel smiled thinly. "You may have the title, but it's nothing to me. You have no more place at this table than the boy who cleans my boots."

Merek flexed his hand at his side. He wanted to argue, but he had to find a way to eliminate this friction between them. For the sake of Endvar, but also for the sake of an impulsive princess who had betrayed the king out of the kindness of her heart. Thinking of Ria calmed him, and he was able to speak without malice.

"I'll consent to that condition. For now. But I hope that you'll reconsider it in the future." *If my men and I can live that long.*

"Aiya! Come quickly!"

Aiya looked up from the pair of black stockings she was darning. Yulda hurried to her from between the columns of hanging uniforms and bed linens. The two of them had been assigned duties in the laundry: tedious work that kept Aiya from dwelling on Dan.

"You'll never guess who just arrived in camp," Yulda said, taking Aiya's darning and placing it in the basket next to her. She grabbed her hands and pulled her to her feet.

For a brief moment, hope kindled in Aiya's chest. Perhaps Dan had survived. Perhaps he'd decided not to attack after all and had moved his men to safety through the tunnels. But even as she thought this, she knew it couldn't be true.

Aiya allowed herself to be pulled along by the younger woman. They weaved through the lines of laundry toward the section of camp where the remnants of Endvar's Wall Guard were assigned.

Captain Eldar had allowed the two women to keep a tent there and take their meals with the soldiers. It was an unusual arrangement, and the other laundresses gossiped openly about it. But aside from Yulda, Rorden was Aiya's only friend. She was grateful to have somewhere in this noisy, dirty camp to remind her of home.

"All the camp is talking about it," Yulda said as they neared Eldar's camp. "I wanted to be the first to tell you because Rorden said he's a particular friend of yours."

Yulda moved to the side as they entered the campfire ring in the midst of the Wall Guard's tents. A familiar figure stood surrounded by a group of soldiers, the men chatting and laughing in a more lighthearted manner than Aiya had seen yet.

"Captain Strong!" she breathed, disbelieving. The sight of him was so unexpected—and so welcome—that relief shook her composure like the last tremor shaking a dam near collapse. She blinked back tears, trying to hold them at bay. Through the haze of tears she saw him notice her. He grinned and bounded over to her, gripping her in an exuberant hug.

"Aiya! I couldn't believe it when Rorden told me that you'd escaped. What a miracle!"

Aiya was so startled that she had to remind her arms how to move to return the embrace. The shock of it stopped her tears, at least, and she hastily wiped them away as he released her.

"I could say the same for you, my captain," Aiya said with a little laugh. "We have all been so worried about you. Returning to us now must be a good omen."

Yulda sidled up to Aiya, clearly expecting an introduction.

"And you must be the young maid to whom we owe so much," Captain Strong said, taking the girl's hand as elegantly as if she were of noble birth.

Yulda colored slightly. "Thank you, sir."

"Come, you must tell me of all your adventures," Captain Strong said, steering the two women to the campfire. He made them sit as though they were guests of honor, and then he himself served them the humble stew that was the evening meal.

It was as joyous a meal as any celebration Aiya had ever attended. The air of gloom that had pervaded the soldiers was gone, replaced instead with a heady relief. As they ate, Captain Strong questioned her about the days following the attack: how many soldiers she'd seen, what was the condition of the city, and how they'd found their way through the tunnels to safety. But his curiosity evaporated when someone grimly brought up the ill fates of the soldiers who had stayed behind.

"There will be plenty of time for that tomorrow," he said. "Tonight is a time for celebrating. Old friends have returned safe." He tipped his cup to Aiya.

Aiya felt a warmth at his words; a soft glow deep in her chest. But a part of her felt detached somehow, incapable of fully appreciating his attention. She couldn't forget the way he'd looked at the Rahmish princess. His heart was won, but not by Aiya.

That thought was accompanied with a kind of dull sadness, like an old grief that one grows accustomed to bearing. But this was a weight she didn't have to bear tonight, she decided. She would relax and enjoy the evening. She would be the captain's friend and count herself fortunate for that honor. Of all the things she'd lost, she didn't want to lose another moment wishing for what could not be.

Hours passed and a cold, brisk breeze cleared the night sky, revealing glittering stars. Many of the soldiers retired with the chill, and Aiya found herself growing drowsy before the fire, but couldn't muster the energy to stand and leave this scene of contentment.

"Rorden tells me that you and the girl have taken up work here in the camp," Captain Strong said, bringing Aiya back to alertness. She realized they were alone before the fire, and the captain had taken Yulda's empty place beside her.

"Yes," she replied. "It helps to stay busy."

Captain Strong nodded thoughtfully. "You musn't blame yourself, Aiya. Dan's choices were his own. You couldn't have saved him if you'd stayed."

Aiya glanced at him, feeling vulnerable that he had guessed her thoughts. His proud profile was silhouetted against the firelight. The look in his eye told her these were not idle words. He spoke from experience.

"Perhaps not," she replied softly, "but if I had stayed, I might have convinced him to give up his plan and come with us. Or convinced enough of the other soldiers to change his mind."

The captain shook his head. "Dan is very determined. Stubborn. He wouldn't have listened, and instead you and the girl would have lost your chance for escape."

Aiya could not speak of the guilt she felt when she remembered her final words to Dan.

"I just wish I knew what happened," she said quietly. "Were they defeated at the gate? Or were they discovered in the tunnels? Did the end come swiftly or did he suffer?"

"Don't think on these things. These questions will torment you if you let them...and to no useful end."

"But what if—?" Aiya began, turning to face him in her earnestness. "What if some of them lived? Or escaped? Dan could be alive, hiding in the city, needing help while we sit here doing nothing."

The thought pained her even as it gave her a glimmer of hope. To think of him a captive, or injured and helpless, was almost worse than believing him dead because it meant that not only had she failed him, but every day that he suffered only added to that failure.

"Do you really think that's possible? That he might still be alive?"

"I do." Aiya answered more fervently than she felt, willing it to be true. "He's clever and a capable fighter. More than capable," she added, remembering his skill against Hala. "He nearly bested Behni's Menari warrior."

"Did he?" Captain Strong sounded impressed. "Well, that's something. If he did manage to survive, then we must pray he can keep alive long enough for us to take back the city."

"And how long will that take? I have no experience with armies, but it doesn't seem that this one is doing much of anything."

Captain Strong kicked at a smoldering log with his

boot, shifting it closer to the glowing embers until flames licked its edges. "Grammel is being cautious. To attack Endvar directly will take more than just a large army if we want anything left standing."

He fell silent for a moment, and Aiya became aware of the deepening cold. The dying fire could no longer keep it at bay. Just as she was beginning to think longingly of bed, Captain Strong spoke again.

"You needn't continue to work in the laundry if you wish. You're welcome to stay here with my company. No one will question your place."

"I...Thank you. But I don't mind the work. Besides," she said, smiling wryly, "with my home reduced to rubble and my income with it, it wouldn't hurt to earn a few coins."

"Rubble?" Captain Strong looked at her sharply.

With horror, Aiya realized that she hadn't told the captain about the fire. "Oh! I forgot! You don't know!" She stifled the choking urge to laugh.

"What is it? What do I not know?"

"My home. The shop. It's all destroyed. Behni burned it to the ground. The entire building. I'm quite homeless and penniless now, and I'm afraid you are too."

Captain Strong's expression was unreadable. Surprise, yes, but also a trace of something else. "Homeless, you say?"

"Yes."

"And penniless?"

"I'm so sorry. Imar doesn't know yet either, because

I haven't been able to get word to him in Branvik. I'm afraid there's nothing left."

Captain Strong shook his head in disbelief. To Aiya's surprise, he laughed. "Not nothing. When General Grammel had my rooms searched for proof of dissension, he claimed as evidence a chest of coins my mother gave to my keeping. In trying to seek my ruin, he unwittingly preserved it. I suppose I should thank him."

Aiya listened with relieved amusement. "How fortunate for you! I'm very glad to hear it."

"But it's not just that. You're not penniless either." His eyes shone with excitement in the firelight, and he stood so to better search his coat pockets. "He found something else that—ah!"

Captain Strong withdrew a small lump from his pocket. "I'm not sure how these came to be in my room, but they must belong to you or Imar."

Aiya reached for it, bewildered. When her fingers brushed the soft velvet bag, she recoiled in recognition.

"Those cursed stones!" she hissed. "They will haunt me to my grave! Shall I never escape them?" She shrank back, wrapping the quilt tighter around her.

Captain Strong stiffened at her reaction, and Aiya realized that her words had been in Khouri. He looked abashed. "Forgive me. I didn't mean to offend. Had I known about the jewels—"

"No, do not apologize to me," she said, chagrined at her outburst. "I was surprised, that's all. But please, put them away. I cannot bear to look upon them."

His hand closed around the bag obediently. "Why do you hate them so?" he asked, returning to sit by her side.

Aiya breathed deeply, resisting the urge to jump away and flee now that she knew what he carried. "They bring nothing but death and destruction. First my husband and daughter in Khourin. Now Imar's shop is destroyed and an army has invaded Endvar. Each time I believe I'm free of them, they find me and bring fresh devastation with them."

"You can't believe these jewels are really cursed."

She scowled at the hint of humor in his voice.

"Very well, then," he said, trying to hide his smile. "What would you have me do with them?"

"Keep them if you wish. I don't care. As long as I never lay eyes on them again."

"Aiya, I can't simply keep a fortune of jewels that don't belong to me," he said incredulously.

"Then give them away. Or sell them. Then you can finally buy yourself a proper house instead of living like a common tradesman in a rented room above a shop."

Captain Strong chuckled, tucking the jewels away. "I'm not claiming them for myself, but I'll keep them safe until you say otherwise. As a stewardship, if you will."

Aiya sniffed. There would never be a time when she would want those jewels. Now that she knew Captain Strong had them, she felt a distinct urge to leave his presence. The warmth of camaraderie was gone. In its place, Aiya found her mind wandering to Dan.

As Ria entered the library, the draft from the door caused the flames behind the grate to dance. Of course Count Orlin had asked for a fire to be lit. He was constantly complaining about the climate here in Albon, which Ria thought was unfair considering that the Ardanian capitol city of Rellana spent most of the winter under snow. Perhaps it was the damp that made Count Orlin so miserable. Rellana did have those marvelous southern breezes that blew in from Khourin, which made the wintry air dry, if still bitterly cold.

She wasn't surprised, then, to find Count Orlin huddled near the fire in her father's favorite armchair. He glanced up as she entered and hurried to stand and give her a deep bow.

"You seem comfortable," Ria observed.

"Your Highness. I trust your father is well and you haven't been detained caring for him," Count Orlin said, his accent clipping his words short.

"I haven't seen my father this morning," she replied evenly. She wouldn't apologize for making him wait. She had started the day cross, and her mood wasn't improving. Today was supposed to be the twentieth anniversary of her father's coronation, but instead of spending it in celebration, she was interviewing Count Orlin. With the king withdrawn to his tower, she had to do what she could in his absence. Today that meant getting Count Orlin to reveal all he knew about the conflict in Endvar without sharing too much herself.

Count Orlin moved another chair close to the fire for Ria. He could have asked his aide to do it, or even one of the royal guards who stood in the room, but it was a sign of deference coming from the Ardanian. A clear statement that they were allies, not enemies.

"So," Ria began, settling herself on the edge of the cushion. "What tale do you have for me today?"

The Ardanian man shook his head and looked sincerely troubled. "I'm afraid I cannot confirm the claims you brought to me. The word I have received from King Idan is that he's a friend to Rahm as his father before him."

Ria waited. When he offered no more, she sighed. "I see that you haven't taken me seriously."

Orlin glanced conspicuously at the two guards who stood near the door. "Believe me, Your Highness, that is not the case. It grieves me that my country has lost your trust. King Idan speaks highly of your wisdom and hopes that you will not give credence to these rumors."

"Rumors? These are not mere rumors. Ardanian soldiers have seized Endvar. I have received accounts from two witnesses who managed to escape the city. Their reports are very credible." *Keep to the facts. Don't reveal your suspicions.*

Count Orlin held his hands out, palms up in a pleading gesture. "I beg you not to lay this at my king's feet. Perhaps these are mercenaries hired by a shared enemy trying to drive us to war. Please, for the sake of both our countries, do not rush to judgement."

Ria watched him steadily. In her own heart she wished to agree. She'd spent these past weeks trying to convince herself that what he suggested was true, that Ardania—that Artem—had nothing to do with these acts of aggression. And Orlin seemed genuinely in earnest.

But he was a politician. He knew how to seem whatever suited him at the moment.

"If things are as you say, King Idan must be equally concerned with finding whoever is responsible."

"I am certain he is, Your Highness," Count Orlin nodded, withdrawing a pipe in the serpentine style of the Ardanians.

"Then perhaps it would be helpful to give him the name of Domar." Ria said the name calmly, though her own heart tripped in fear to speak it.

Count Orlin wiped his pipe thoughtfully on the corner of his sleeve, but not before Ria saw the small tremor in his hand.

"Does that name mean anything to you?" she pressed.

"I'm afraid not, but I have some other contacts who are not connected with the king who may know something. Outside of the knowledge of the crown, you understand. I shall make inquiries and inform you the moment I hear anything useful."

"I would expect nothing less." Ria stood. She'd learned enough. "These guards will escort you back to your rooms."

The count eyed the guards and coughed a little. "Is this escort very necessary, Your Highness? I am no threat to you. Surely my many years of loyal service to your father is worth something."

"My people are dying, Orlin," she snapped. "Trust is a luxury that I can no longer afford."

Ria watched the man bow and leave the room. Once she was alone, she sank back into her chair, all veneer of resolve gone. Ironically, Ria did believe the count. She didn't think this was a plot by King Idan to move against Rahm. Idan was a just and even-tempered man, not one to turn on an ally without provocation. But when she'd mentioned Domar's name, Orlin's fleeting expression—of what, surprise? Dread?—meant something. She'd disarmed him, perhaps more than even he realized.

I shall inform you the moment I hear anything useful, he'd said. Not *if* I hear anything useful. Whatever was going on, the ambassador knew—or suspected—more than he was divulging, and Ria was determined to learn what it was. No matter how painful it was to hear. Because if Domar's employer was indeed an Ardanian prince, there was only one man it could be.

Seventeen

"Forty-seven."

"What's that, Captain?"

"There are forty-seven skilled bowmen down there." Captain Eldar nodded at the shadowy figures moving below them in the mist.

Heavy fog had rolled in during the night, bringing with it a chill dampness. The air was clearer on the small hill where Merek and Eldar sat astride their mounts, but below them it was difficult to discern individual shapes.

"Bows would be useless in this fog."

"At least they could die with sword in hand."

Merek didn't respond. He watched the last remnants of Endvar's Wall Guard struggle to coordinate their movements in order to hoist a behemoth tree onto their shoulders. The tree was nearly the height of a man in thickness and had been felled the previous day and stripped of its branches. It would make an impressive battering ram, but the sight sickened Merek. It was never easy to send men to their deaths. But these were *his* men, hand-picked by him to serve on the wall for their skill, valor, and loyalty. They deserved a more noble death than marching hopelessly to slaughter like common foot soldiers.

Across the way was another small hill where General Grammel waited with his entourage: an island in a sea of heavy clouds dotted with dark shapes. The surrounding mist muted color, and Grammel's uniform looked dark gray rather than the deep crimson it truly was.

A mounted officer near Grammel raised a flag on the end of a pole and signaled with three wide, sweeping arcs.

"It's time, sir," Eldar murmured.

Without a word, Merek led his horse down into the foggy soup toward his men. Soon the view of Grammel was lost as the clouds engulfed them, and the shadowy shapes of his men emerged on the road. Each of their expressions was grim and determined as they shouldered the heavy tree. He nodded briefly at Rorden as he passed, feeling a new flare of anger toward Grammel as he thought of the young man's fate. Such intelligence and talent thrown away because of one man's jealousy.

"Steady," he said as some of the men shifted their weight and it sent a ripple effect through the ranks. "We're not far from Endvar, though you can't see any sign of the city in this fog. Pray it holds because it may save your life today. Three divisions will be following to flood the city once we break through the gates. At that point, it will be our charge to hold the gates against a possible retreat."

The men glanced at each other. Breaking through the gates would be exhausting. Even if the fog prevented archers on the city wall from finding their mark, they would be in poor shape to fight fresh soldiers. Either way, Grammel had ensured that Merek and his men would not survive the day.

"Many of you have families in the city and have been anxious for their welfare. Let thoughts of them drive you onward. You've served your king well, and if you should die today liberating the city, take comfort in knowing your families will be free."

And if I should die today, he thought as he urged his horse onward, *at least that will guarantee Ria's safety.* Merek's loyalty to the crown would be unquestionable. There would be no reason to investigate the truth behind his pardon. It was a small consolation, but at least it meant that his death wouldn't be a complete waste. He wondered if Ria would mourn him, but there was no answer to that question that didn't cause him pain, so he quickly pushed it aside. This was no time for sentimentality.

Shapes loomed out of the fog and resolved into buildings: huts and cottages that marked the outskirts of the city. Empty now, as the residents had fled to safety when Endvar fell, they were dark and ominous sentinels lining the highway to the gates.

Merek resisted the urge to glance over his shoulder at the dark windows. It was unnerving the way they yawned lifelessly in the gloom, and the skin on the back of his neck crawled with the uncomfortable sensation of being watched. But he kept his eyes fixed straight ahead as the road inclined in a long ascent toward the gate.

His men behind him struggled with their burden, and he slowed his horse to ease their pace. By the time the gates came into view, each of the soldiers' backs were damp with sweat and their faces were flushed.

The city wall drew closer, a shadowy apparition in the mist. A shout sounded from somewhere at the top of the wall, sending a chill through Merek as he spotted archers running into position, their bows drawn. He raised his shield. At some point, he would have to step aside and let his men face the brunt of those arrows alone. But he would wait as long as possible.

He snapped down his helm. The archers on the wall shifted excitedly as he approached, but none of them fired.

What are they waiting for? He'd hoped to draw some of their fire to give his men a chance for their first approach, but they didn't seem interested in wasting arrows on him.

The buildings on either side were larger here, and he felt their mass hemming him in...funneling him to the waiting enemy.

At last he could go no further without dangerously shortening their approach.

Eldar called out from far back in the fog, the signal that the troops were in position behind them. All was ready.

Trying to shake the feeling of dread in his stomach, Merek moved his horse off the road, closer to an abandoned tavern whose sign creaked as it swayed in the fog.

He drew his sword and was about to issue the order for his men to advance, when he stopped.

Just ahead, the massive gate was opening. Merek cursed inwardly. It would be horribly ironic if the enemy troops decided to come out and face them now after all the times Grammel had tried to draw them out. Now, when his men were weighed down by a massive burden with no weapons in hand.

But no, this was no army. Men, perhaps ten of them. They were followed by two soldiers with their swords drawn, prodding them through the gate. Merek strained to see through his helm's eye slit and the thick fog.

They were a ragged bunch, stumbling and shuffling along in bare feet. Many of them were shirtless, their hands bound and their exposed skin flushed pink in the cold. Uncertain, Merek watched and waited. It wasn't until one of them emerged, powerfully built yet shorter than all the rest, that a dark suspicion took root in his mind.

These were *his* men. Dan and the others. The soldiers who had hoped to mount a brave attack to take back the city. And they were being paraded in front of him like livestock before the butcher.

The Ardanian soldiers ordered the captives forward into a ragged line. A smattering of murmurs beside him told Merek that his men had recognized them too. What was the enemy's purpose? Did they hope to bargain using the Rahmish prisoners?

Merek's mind raced, trying to find a way to save his men without abandoning their mission.

"Be prepared to run," he spoke in a low voice to the

soldiers beside him. "I'll engage the enemy and give our men a chance to escape, but you must follow quickly with the battering ram to distract the archers."

A murmuring chorus of quiet assent came in reply. An expectant tension grew as neither Ardanians nor Rahmish moved. Then, responding to a call from atop the wall, the Ardanians raised their swords and began chopping down the bound men before them.

Merek's blood ran hot with their screams, and he spurred his horse forward. Arrows flew from above, some directed at him but most aimed at the defenseless men. In the precious seconds it took Merek to reach them, four of them fell.

He slammed his horse into the first Ardanian, stopping his sword from falling again. The man fell to the ground, but his companion was quicker on his feet and pushed one of the Rahmish soldiers in front of the horse. Merek cringed as the man fell with a scream beneath the beast's hooves.

He swung his sword at the Ardanian, who stumbled and fell to the ground, his sword skittering away from him across the stones.

"Clear the road. Now!" Merek yelled to the surviving Rahmish prisoners. Those who could move huddled behind his horse for protection while arrows rained down from above, glancing off his armor and his stallion's chest plate. He backed his horse awkwardly away from the gate, careful not to tread on the surviving soldiers. With a chilling cry of pain, his stallion took three arrows in the neck, and Merek clung to his mane in order to avoid being thrown, his sword falling to the road below.

The yells of his men told him the battering ram was approaching. Unarmed, Merek tried to turn his horse out of their path, but the animal fought him, jerking the opposite way. Hastily, Merek slipped out of the saddle and landed clumsily on his feet. The stallion collapsed in a heap, his blood pooling on the stones.

"You'll be needing this, sir," a familiar voice greeted Merek. He turned to see Dan holding his sword.

"Good to see you alive, Dan."

"Thank you, sir."

The volley of arrows lessened as the archers above focused on the men with the battering ram. They had almost reached the gates.

Three other men besides Dan sheltered next to Merek's fallen horse. They looked pitiful in their soiled rags, but there was a fire in their eyes that showed that they were ready to fight. Merek handed Dan a knife to cut their bonds.

"You need to get off the road. Grammel's army is just behind us. Make for the outer villages. I'll search for any wounded and follow."

"Sir, they're here," Dan said urgently.

"What do you mean?"

"They're here, everywhere." He glanced up at the darkened windows of the pub looming over them.

The men with the battering ram ran past with a terrific shout.

"Now! Go!" Merek ordered, and the little group of survivors ran toward the nearest building with Dan in the lead as the soldiers rammed the gate. The resounding boom shook the earth, and many of the men staggered with the force of it, their shouts of courage faltering. But they didn't drop the log.

Merek heard their cries to regroup, but he didn't watch their second approach. Instead, he moved among the wounded, checking for any signs of life. Arrows protruded from some of the bodies, but most had sword wounds deep in their chests or necks.

With another earth-shattering boom, his men rammed the gate again. Arrows continued to rain down on them from above, but the fog provided some protection and only a few found their mark. Another approach, and this time the loud crack of splintering wood split the air.

Merek's men shouted in triumph. The gates held, but wouldn't for much longer. Merek ran in a crouch to his horse, watching for any sign of Grammel's men. At this rate, they might be through the gates in only one or two passes. Where was Grammel?

Merek's crossbow had been crushed beneath his horse when he fell, but his bow was still intact. He cut the lashings and slung his bow and quiver over his left shoulder.

Suddenly, a horn sounded in the fog. Merek turned, disoriented.

It came from behind, but it was not a Rahmish horn.

The rainfall of arrows immediately ceased. Merek's men halted, looking around in confusion. Was it a trick of the sound echoing in empty city streets? Merek stepped further into the fog, away from the gate.

A dull roar grew around him, then burst into chaos as Ardanian soldiers poured out of the abandoned buildings: rivers of armed shadows obscured by fog. There were hundreds. And he and his men were trapped between them and the city wall.

Curse you, Grammel, and then he could spare no other thought for the fool. Two soldiers were upon him, while the others ran past and attacked his confused men from behind.

"Leave it! Arms to the rear!" Merek called, hoping some of his men would hear. He disarmed one soldier and thrust his sword into the other one's side. The first soldier returned with a long knife, trying to catch Merek while he yanked his sword free, but with a swift kick against the man's knee, Merek sent him to the ground. Another soldier emerged from the fog, and Merek parried his blow with such force that the Ardanian stumbled backward and fell over his dead comrade. Before Merek had finished with him, another soldier was upon him. And another.

Breathing heavily, he drove his bloodied sword again and again into the enemy, looking for places of weakness between the dark gray plates of the Ardanian armor. The underarm, back of the neck, or even behind the knee if he was desperate.

As he fought, Merek tried to get a glimpse of how his men were faring, but the fog impeded his vision. By the sounds around him, he knew it was a bitter fight.

But the fog also prevented the Ardanians from coordinating their efforts, diminishing their advantage. Instead of a slaughter, it was turning into a melee with individual pockets of fighting while the rest of the host blundered around uselessly trying to find the action.

All at once the fog brightened, making Merek squint as he faced down three Ardanians. The sun appeared overhead as a gray ball through the mist, turning the fog blindingly white. His enemy paused, blinking. Merek attacked, driving them back against the wall of a nearby hut. One of the Ardanians fell under his sword, while another swung at Merek with a spiked club. Merek raised his shield arm and staggered back from the force of the blow. While he recovered his footing, the other soldier grabbed a pitchfork leaning against the hut and thrust it toward Merek. Merek leaped back a breath too late, and two of the tines pierced his leg.

He yelled with the white hot pain and wrested the pitchfork away from the man, driving it into the chest of the soldier who had raised his club again. The third man faltered, seeming stunned to realize his comrades were dead and he was unarmed. He tried to skirt around the building away from Merek, but Merek's dagger found him first.

Merek paused to look at his leg. It was bleeding, but not so copiously that it was an immediate threat. He tore a strip of fabric from the uniform of one of the dead Ardanians to staunch the blood. As he tied off the makeshift bandage, the scrape of a boot against stone sounded nearby. He looked up, but it was too late. He barely registered the spiked club before it crashed down on his head.

His helmet rang, and Merek fell forward onto his knees, head erupting with sickening pain. His vision swam, and he had a vague impression that the enemy was raising his club again. A voice in his mind shouted at him to act, but his body couldn't respond.

Then a shape rammed into the enemy soldier from behind, tackling him to the ground. Merek blinked, trying to clear his vision. The new shape was flesh-colored: a shirtless man without a uniform.

With great effort, Merek removed his dented helmet and breathed in the damp misty air to clear his head. One eye was clouded with blood, but the other could just make out Sergeant Dan delivering a death blow with the Ardanian soldier's own club.

Merek wiped the blood from his eye. Dan had returned. Without weapons, armor, or even boots, he had joined the fight and saved Merek's life.

"Thank you, Dan," Merek groaned as Dan helped him to his feet. He closed his eyes as the world tilted beneath him, willing it to be still.

"My pleasure, sir."

When Merek felt steady again, he opened his eyes.

Dan frowned at him in concern, his breath puffing white in the cold air. His face and shoulders glistened with sweat and blood. This was not the first enemy he had killed today.

"Are you all right, sir? That's an ugly cut on your head."

"Help me wrap it, I can barely see."

Merek's head flared anew with pain when Dan touched it, but he worked quickly, and soon Merek could rub the blood away from his eye and keep it clear.

"Where are the others?" Merek asked. "Did they make it to safety or ignore orders as you did?"

Dan grinned. "We're members of the King's Wall Guard, sir. We'll not back down from a fight, especially when our own are outnumbered."

Merek shook his head and smiled grimly. "I understand that's what got you into this mess to begin with."

Dan just grunted. They moved cautiously around the hut in the direction of the main road. The battle was moving further into the outskirts now, and Merek worried about his men getting isolated if they didn't stay together.

Just as they engaged a large enemy soldier who stood nearly as tall as Merek, another horn sounded. This one Merek recognized.

"It's about time, Grammel," he grumbled through gritted teeth as he slammed his fist into the enemy's face and pushed him toward Dan who now carried a sword and shield. His head still rang, and his movements were slow, but there would be no rest until Grammel's men secured the area.

The sun blazed high in the sky now, clearing the mist, but the air was still cold and frost clung to the shadows. Merek and Dan jogged out onto the main road just in time to come to the aid of Rorden and two other soldiers who were being swarmed by enemy soldiers.

Rorden took a second glance when he saw Dan: ragged and barefoot, yet wielding an Ardanian sword and shield with as much ferocity as though he were fully armored.

"Remind me to tell you how ridiculous you look

when this is all over, Dan," Rorden called as he threw an enemy soldier to the ground and planted a spear in his chest.

Dan just growled, locking blades with an Ardanian and driving the man back against a building, shattering the glass of a storefront window.

With the clearing of the fog, Merek got a better sense of the flow of battle. Fighting amongst huts and cottages was profoundly different than on open terrain. It was clear, however, that the Ardanians were pulling away to contend with General Grammel's larger force, much to the relief of Merek's beleaguered company.

The street quieted as the last of the active fighting died away. The large battering ram lay discarded where his men had dropped it. Bodies littered the road, many of them clustered around the abandoned log where Merek's men had been attacked unawares.

"Rorden, Dan," he called.

The two men were ducking into doorways to ensure that no more Ardanians hid in the shadows. They turned and jogged to him, looking weary but determined.

"Organize the men to get the wounded off the road. Move them to the leeward side of that log in case the Ardanians return. Then search for whatever wagon or cart or two-wheeled barrow you can find that might help us get these men back to camp."

"Yes, sir." They saluted in unison.

"Oh, and Dan," he said, looking down at the sergeant's feet which were scraped and purple with cold. "Find yourself some boots."

Dan nodded sheepishly, then jogged away.

Merek went with Rorden to search the nearest of the fallen Rahmish soldiers, but as soon as he bent over the first one, a wave of nausea surged over him, and he vomited onto the street.

"Whoa!" Rorden jumped back. "Perhaps you should rest, sir."

Merek straightened, wiping his mouth with a sleeve. His planned retort didn't come because it was all he could do to stay upright. His head felt like it had been cleaved open, and his vision wavered.

"I'm no physician," Rorden continued, peering at him more closely, "but that head wound is as bad as any I've seen."

Merek just grunted. Of what use was a commander who couldn't command?

He busied himself instead, counting the number of men who had not only survived the battle, but were well enough to walk. Fourteen. Fourteen men remained in fighting shape from his original company, and one of those was Dan, who shouldn't have even been there.

"Aiya will be pleased to see you, Dan," he said.

Dan glanced up at him from where he was removing an Ardanian soldier's boots. "Did she make it then? She and Yulda? Are they safe?"

"You'll have to hear the whole story from her," Merek said. "She hasn't been herself for worrying about you."

Pink spots appeared in Dan's cheeks. "She wasn't happy with me when she left. She called me a fool and accused me of trying to be a hero."

"Of course you were trying to be a hero," Rorden said

cheerfully. "No sense in trying to survive when you can die in glory, right?"

"Well, she was right about one thing. We were no match for the Ardanian army. They poured into the city and filled the guard complex shortly after she left. We were trapped. Had no hope of escaping with only a handful of broken weapons."

"So you chose the smart route, I see," Rorden replied.

Dan just glowered at him and turned back to his search.

Hooves clattering on stone drew Merek's attention as General Grammel and two of his captains rode into view.

"Captain Strong! You survived, I see."

Disappointed? Merek thought. But he just answered with what he hoped was a sharp salute. As sluggish as his movements felt, it was difficult to tell.

"Permission to move my wounded men to safety, sir."

"We're rounding up the last of the enemy now. What a weak attempt at an ambush," Grammel scoffed. "Prepare your men to resume their assault on the gates."

"My men," Merek protested, "haven't the strength of numbers to lift the log, let alone move it with any force. If that gate is going to fall today, you'll have to supply your own men to do it. Sir," he added belatedly.

Grammel's heavy brows knit together beneath his shining helmet. He made an impressive sight in his polished armor and flowing crimson cape with a matching plume atop his helmet that fluttered in the breeze. He surveyed the road with its dead and wounded and appeared to take in for the first time the small number of men from Merek's company who were still in fighting shape.

"I expected better from a company under the command of the legendary Captain Strong."

"Expected better?" Merek said hotly. "You sent us into a trap and then were slow to come to our aid. We were outnumbered as much as six to one, and yet my men still managed to inflict that many times more casualties on the enemy. These men deserve commendation from you, General, yet you act as if I'm asking to take them for a pint of ale at The Seven Moons."

Grammel's complexion darkened to its familiar purple hue. But whatever angry words he was prepared to say, they died on his lips. Another horn sounded, this one from inside the city. Grammel's eyes widened as he looked to the wall.

Merek turned to see the gates opening and row upon row of Ardanian soldiers marching out to meet them. He spared a glance for his men and was relieved to see that they were all safely off the road. If they stayed there, they might not be cut down like children before the enemy army. The army which was far, far more numerous than they'd been prepared for.

His head pounded with the rhythm of their marching. They would be upon them in moments. One of Grammel's captains blew three long notes into a brass horn, followed by two short ones, alerting the rest of their troops. Even if Grammel's troops could get there quickly, they were hopelessly outnumbered. Merek stood in the midst of the three horsemen, feeling distinctly disadvantaged on foot as he faced down the oncoming host. Planting his feet, he drew his sword.

"Go save your men, Strong," Grammel growled.

"Excuse me, sir?" Merek glanced up at him in surprise.

"You've bled enough for one day." He spoke with grim resolve, his voice lacking its characteristic edge. "Get your men to safety. That's an order."

Merek didn't move. "With all due respect sir, this fight was mine before it was ever yours."

General Grammel grunted. "So be it."

Eighteen

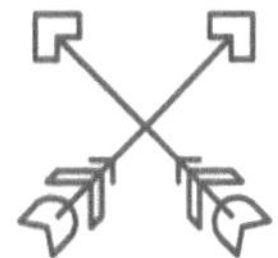

The smell of freshly baked sweet rolls filled the carriage. When Ria closed her eyes, she could almost imagine she was back in Pedr's bakery with the large brick oven radiating warmth instead of jostling along in a drafty carriage, huddled in a heavy cloak.

"Are you tired, my lady?" Biren asked.

Ria opened her eyes. "I was trying to dry out my toes by picturing myself sitting next to Pedr's oven. It almost worked."

"Their bakery is probably the only dry place in the city," Biren observed, looking out at the sheet of rain running down the window.

Ria had enjoyed her visit to Lotta, though she felt a little guilty for spending so much time away from the Hall. It would probably have been better to invite Lotta to visit her instead, but she enjoyed the break from her duties as much as the company. Besides, it was the only way to enjoy Pedr's rolls fresh from the oven.

The carriage bounced through a pothole and gave a terrific lurch. Ria and Biren yelled in surprise as they fell against each other, sliding into the wall. The carriage skidded along the street until it ground to a halt tilted at an absurd angle. Outside, men's voices shouted to each other over the rain.

Ria groaned, moving to untangle herself from her maid.

"Are you quite alright, my lady?" Biren asked.

Ria pushed against the wall to sit up. "Just a little jostled. You?"

The door to the carriage opened above them and a sergeant dressed in the green of the Royal Guard poked his head in.

"Your Highness, are you well?"

"Quite well, Brandel, considering how we've been tossed about."

"My apologies, Your Highness. The rear axle is damaged. There's a tavern nearby if you'd like to wait while the driver brings another carriage."

"How far are we from the Hall?" Ria asked.

"Not more than half a mile."

"Very well, we shall walk. Biren, I hope you don't mind getting a little wet," she said, drawing the hood of her cloak lower over her brow.

It was more awkward to exit the carriage than she'd expected, requiring an undignified climb out the door above them. It was only with both the guard and the driver's assistance that they managed it. At least the rain meant the street was empty of witnesses.

Sergeant Brandel insisted on accompanying them to the Hall, despite Ria's insistence that they were close enough to manage on their own. Rain slashed at her long skirts as she walked and seeped through her cloak. Despite her generous hood, Ria blinked against the water pouring into her eyes, struggling to see more than a few feet in front of her. She walked as quickly as she could, trying to avoid the puddles that stretched the entire width of the street. Long before they reached her family's estate, she regretted her decision.

As they passed through the gate, a rider overtook them at such speed that Sergeant Brandel pushed the women aside protectively. The rider pulled his horse to a sudden stop and looked back at them, as if he'd just realized they were there.

"Hold there, man!" Brandel shouted angrily. "Watch where you're going!"

"My apologies," the rider called. "I have an urgent message for the king."

"It's the king's daughter you nearly ran down, you fool."

Ria lifted her hood from her brow. "I will hear your message, soldier." She wiped her face with a wet sleeve in a fruitless effort to stem the tide of water running down it.

The young man looked her over and nodded decisively. He dismounted and bowed briskly.

"Your Highness, I bring news from Endvar." His countenance was grim.

Bad news, then?

Ria frowned. "Very well, soldier. Let's go inside and get out of this cursed rain. I'm sure whatever you have to say will be better heard in front of a warm fire."

She began walking across the courtyard, but the messenger didn't follow.

"General Grammel is dead," he said. "The enemy has routed our troops and many of the officers were slain."

Ria stopped in her tracks. "I understood that this enemy was too small to contend with our forces, that they refused to fight because they could barely hold the city."

The soldier shook his head. "They've received reinforcements and now number in the thousands."

"Reinforcements from where?"

"Ardania, Your Highness." He withdrew from an inside pocket of his coat a torn piece of violet fabric. Embroidered on it was a crest that Ria recognized well. She fingered it, tracing the familiar symbol of the royal house, anger welling inside her.

Here was the proof she was looking for.

"There's no room for doubt, Your Highness. It's an Ardanian force, and there is no hope of regaining the city without additional reinforcements."

It made no sense. Why would Artem attack Endvar? Trade with Rahm was vital to Ardania's prosperity, and taking the city would cause a costly conflict that risked far more than Endvar was worth. Ria considered the Hall and the dry clothes waiting for her. She turned instead to the lodge where visitors to court were housed.

"I wish to hear everything, soldier. But first, there is

someone I must see. Go on to the Hall. I'll hear more from you when you have dry clothes and food in your belly." She turned back to her companions. "Biren, tell Galinn to tend to our guest's needs. Sergeant, come with me."

She started toward the lodge, then stopped and turned back.

"Soldier?" she called over the rain to the young man reaching for his horse's bridle.

"Yes, Your Highness?"

"Any word of Captain Strong?"

The young man shook his head. "I can't say, Your Highness. He wasn't among the survivors, but hasn't yet been found among the dead."

"Yet?" she asked sharply.

"The speed with which our troops withdrew necessitated leaving many of our fallen behind."

Ria shivered. The thought of Merek being abandoned on the battlefield was too horrible to consider, but if he hadn't been accounted for with the survivors...

"There's something else you aren't telling me. What is it?" She knew this wasn't the place for such a conversation, but she couldn't bear to wait if the news was foul.

Something flickered in the young man's eyes. He looked down at his boots. "I shouldn't speak beyond my official task, Your Highness. I don't know all the facts."

"But you know something. What is it?"

"Only that Captain Strong led the assault on the city. The rumor is that he and General Grammel were surrounded, cut off from our troops when the General fell. Only the General's death has been confirmed, but it's presumed that the captain did not survive."

Ria's insides twisted. *It can't be true. Not Merek. He wouldn't do something so mundane as get himself killed.* She knew these thoughts were childish, but in this moment she drew strength from them. And for now, she needed strength. She wouldn't believe the worst until she knew for certain.

With a heavy weight settling around her heart, she hurried across the courtyard to the guest lodge.

She didn't normally visit the lodge, and the servants at the door jumped when they recognized her, ushering her quickly out of the rain. A fire blazed in the entrance hall, warming the dark paneled room. A handful of visiting nobility gathered in pockets of lazy conversation, but these all stopped as the doors shut loudly behind her.

Ria threw back her hood, sending a shower of rain cascading to the polished wooden floor. The men and women in the room stood in surprise, forgetting to bow at the sight of the drenched princess.

Arin, the lower steward who administered to the needs of court visitors, appeared at her side. "Your Highness, what a lovely surprise. May I take your cloak? Please, warm yourself by our fire, and I'll bring you some mulled wine."

Ria ignored his invitation. "Clear the room," she said, as one of Arin's men slipped her dripping cloak from her shoulders. "We are not to be disturbed."

The occupants of the room—lords and ladies as well as one or two wealthy merchants—were so taken off guard that they didn't even protest. Gathering their servants and children, they exited the room, throwing curious glances at the princess as they departed.

Ria spoke quietly to Sergeant Brandel as the guests filed out. "Bring me Count Orlin, and tell the guards they needn't be too gentle with him."

The sergeant performed his task quickly, and it wasn't long before Ria heard a loud scuffle down the hall. She stood in front of the fire, her wet clothing dripping on the stone hearth.

Two guards entered the room, holding Count Orlin between them. The man looked disheveled and alarmed, and his aide followed behind speaking in a high voice to the sergeant.

"You may not handle the count this way!" he cried in his heavy accent. "As a diplomatic officer, Count Orlin is under the protection of your king."

"Any violence against me," Orlin said, struggling to keep his voice calm, "will be seen as an act of war against my kingdom, according to the terms of the treaty signed by King Sindal himself."

"Your kingdom," Ria said, pitching her voice so that it carried to the end of the room, "has already violated the treaty through acts of aggression against Endvar. Any protection you may have once been afforded is now forfeit."

"Your Highness!" The thin man straightened at the sound of her voice as he was bodily marched down the hall. The guards deposited him before her, releasing their hold. Count Orlin smoothed his rumpled clothing, glowering at the guards who stayed within arm's length.

"Your Highness, I am certain your father would not approve of this treatment. I recognize that you are young and inexperienced, but you must be careful not to succumb to such gross disregard for the alliance between our two kingdoms!"

Ria's anger flared at his oily insults. "You have trespassed on our hospitality for too long, Count Orlin. Do you dare try and tell me that you don't recognize this crest?"

She produced the fabric torn from the enemy soldier. The count regarded it impassively. "Either you are aware of these hostilities and have been lying to me," Ria said, switching to Ardanian, "or you no longer hold the ties with your king that you once did. In either case, you are of no more use to me."

As she spoke, Orlin's eyes narrowed.

"I assure you, Your Highness, that King Idan isn't complicit in any threat against your good country. If I might be permitted more time, I may be able to uncover whoever is responsible for this intrigue."

"I don't have the luxury of time. And neither do you. These are acts of war against the most important city on our borders. As such, I hereby declare all Ardanian citizens within our borders enemies to Rahm. Any citizens will be arrested, and their property will be claimed by the crown as spoils of war."

Count Orlin blanched. "Your Highness, I must urge you to not overreact. I feel for the people of Endvar, I do, but to declare war against an ally is—"

"Do you know just how many Ardanian merchant ships are currently docked in Rahmish ports? Or how many of your caravans are making their way across this kingdom as we speak? That is a loss of great riches indeed. I will answer aggression with aggression, and Ardania will suffer greatly for it."

For the first time, the count looked truly troubled. He blinked rapidly and cleared his throat. "I assure you, Your Highness, that won't be necessary."

"I'm not interested in assurances. What I want is answers. I want to know why Ardanian soldiers have attacked Endvar." She waved the Ardanian royal crest emphatically.

Orlin glanced at the guards uncomfortably. Continuing in Ardanian, he said, "I may have learned something that would explain these reports, but you have to understand that this is all conjecture. I have nothing substantial to support it. The information I do have comes from sources not connected with the king. That is to say, what I'm about to tell you is not even known by him."

"I understand. King Idan is not culpable. Go on."

The ambassador rubbed his smooth chin thoughtfully. "As you may someday learn, succession is not always a painless affair. Particularly when one has an ambitious sibling."

Finally, he was getting to it.

"You speak of Prince Artem." Ria felt a coldness in her middle but kept her voice firm.

Orlin nodded briefly. "As a way of...diverting the prince's talents, King Idan assigned him command of the armies shortly after his coronation. It was more an honorary role than anything else, but the prince relished it. Some of my sources suggest that he may have been training some soldiers secretly for a special purpose. Something that he wanted to keep from the king."

"And it includes Endvar?"

"I've recently learned that there may have been covert activities taking place inside the city for some time now."

"You expect me to believe that Artem sent an army against Endvar without Idan's knowledge?"

Count Orlin shrugged smoothly, straightening his coat. "The king has many soldiers stationed in the far reaches of the land. It wouldn't be difficult to siphon some away without drawing attention until one has amassed a force large enough to take a city."

Ria thought of how little she knew about Rahmish troop movements. She vaguely knew there were multiple garrisons in various parts of the land, but she had no idea how many soldiers that included and certainly wouldn't know if some of them were moved. It was possible that Idan was as overwhelmed as she learning how to assume control after his father's death. A cunning man like Artem would easily be able to take advantage of the situation for his own gain.

"So you're telling me that Artem has led an attack on Endvar without the sanction of King Idan?"

"As I said, this is only conjecture. But it would explain the item you are holding."

Ria shook her head. "It makes no sense. Starting a war with a stronger neighbor? A powerful ally? What is his purpose? To prove himself to Idan by increasing Ardania's lands? Or to create such an indomitable reputation that he challenges his own brother for the crown? What does he hope to gain by going to war?"

Count Orlin glanced uncomfortably at her. "I can't say for certain, Your Highness."

"Try."

Orlin sighed and seemed to shrink a little. "I suspect he has long had dreams of seeing himself on the Rahmish throne. One way or another. When he failed to secure a marriage alliance with you, this may have seemed the most promising alternative."

"Impossible." Ria suppressed a shudder. It was an audacious move, and if it were anyone else, she would call it foolish and doomed to failure. But Artem wouldn't engage in such an enterprise if he didn't think he could succeed.

Ria turned away from the ambassador so that he couldn't see her expression and moved to the tall window. The current of rain running down the panes turned the outside world into a warped wonderland of shifting grays. Idan was a fool to have given Artem such power, but one thing about the ambassador's words rang true. Idan would never risk outright war with Rahm. But would Artem? He'd always been more cunning than Idan, and the violence against the nobles did have a certain air of dramatic cruelty. And what about the ambush? Could he have really intended Ria harm?

I suspect he has long had dreams of seeing himself on the Rahmish throne, Orlin had said. Could their whole relationship have been a farce? Was she no more than a means to satisfy Artem's greed from the beginning? Heat crept up Ria's neck and cheeks, and her anger flared so hot she felt she could spit sparks.

But she wasn't the same young woman who'd been taken in by his lies over two years earlier. Calmly, she turned back to the ambassador. "Write to your king and explain everything you have told me," she said. "Order your sources to testify before him of their involvement and everything they know of this plot. With your emissary I will send my demands that Artem withdraw his troops or risk the imprisonment and seizure of all Ardanian citizenry and assets in Rahm."

Count Orlin clasped his hands together submissively. "I understand. Our king should know these things. The witnesses, however, may be hard to procure. You mentioned a man before by the name of Domar. A man like that with the connections he has...One does not simply expose him and his workings without dire consequences."

Ria was unmoved. "That's not my concern. You will produce the witnesses and inform your king. Whatever follows is the natural consequence of doing business with a man like that. I have a city to save."

"I agree, Your Highness. You're right, of course. But one must tread delicately in these matters lest the innocent suffer as well."

"And what of Endvar's innocents?" Ria rounded on him. "What of the children who were cruelly beheaded after watching their parents tortured? I'm tired of listening to your half truths. If you want to prevent all out war between our nations, you will do as I demand."

Ria couldn't bear to hear one more word from the

man. She turned to the guards and ordered in Rahmish, "Take him to the prison. When he's willing to cooperate, I'll consider him a guest again. Until then, he is under arrest."

The count stiffened. "Your Highness, I am trying to cooperate, but you must listen—"

"Go. Get him out of my sight."

Orlin's face flushed pink with anger as the guards grabbed him.

Ria almost smiled when she thought of Captain Talen's confusion when the guards arrived with the foreign ambassador. "Take heart, Count. Better men than you have spent time in that prison and emerged in one piece." But at the thought of Merek, her humor died. *Merek missing. Lost in battle.* It was too much to contemplate.

As the guards hauled Count Orlin from the room, Ria spoke to Sergeant Brandel. "How badly damaged was the carriage, Sergeant? Will it take long to repair?"

"I can't say, Your Highness. Many of the blacksmiths and wheelwrights have gone with the army camp."

Ria thought she detected subtle envy in his tone.

"Do you wish you were there? With the army?"

"I'm happy to serve where I'm needed, Your Highness."

"Which is no real answer at all," Ria chided. "You sound like Count Orlin."

The sergeant's lips twitched briefly. "It's an honor to serve you, my lady, but it's been many years since we've faced a serious enemy. I'm as anxious as the next soldier to be a part of things."

Ria nodded. "If you can be that honest every time I ask you a question, you may see the battlefront sooner than you think."

Brandel looked at her in surprise. "Your Highness?"

"I need a carriage, Sergeant. And soon. Because you and I are going to Endvar."

Despite the rain outside, Ria's room was warm and stuffy. She opened the window, letting the cold night air pour in. The ringing sound of metal across the courtyard announced that a blacksmith was working late to repair her carriage.

So much of the courier's report simply didn't make sense. Why didn't the Ardanians push further into the country while they had the advantage? By all accounts, they'd stopped their march just past the Hoggen bridge, despite having a clear path to the village beyond. What was Artem's game?

The last time they'd met, Artem had been cool and distant. The only emotion he'd shown was a glint of humor when he'd introduced his new bride: a lovely young thing who'd watched Ria with suspicion, she'd said very little and excused herself quickly. Ria had felt the weight of Artem's gaze through the evening, but whenever she met his eyes, his expression was impassive. Was he plotting against her even then?

As much as his betrayal hurt, it was a relief to know the truth. Now that her dark suspicions were confirmed, she could view him squarely as an adversary. But that didn't make it any easier to guess his strategy, and the revelation had added little to the conversations with her father's advisors. She still had no idea what to do.

Beside the window seat stood her harp, regal in the light glowing from the fireplace. Ria reached out a hand and gently ran her finger along the strings. They produced such an elegant sound that she sighed involuntarily. Gone were the days when she spent hour upon hour playing uninterrupted. There was once a time when it was as much a part of her daily routine as eating or sleeping. But those days of indulgence seemed a lifetime away.

She brushed the strings again, and again, and soon her fingers idly picked out a melody.

If this was what it meant to rule a country, she could almost understand her father's desire to lock himself away. No time to herself, only endless demands piling on top of each other until the days ran together as one. Of course, supporting an army at war didn't help with that. Now it was time to go visit the warfront and appoint a new general, with the man she would have chosen missing.

Not dead. Surely not that.

Her fingers stopped their idle motion, and the music died out in the stillness of the room. A floorboard creaked behind her, and Ria turned, expecting to see Biren.

A man stood on the opposite side of her chamber, half hidden in the shadow near her wardrobe. She tensed, her heart fluttering with panic. His countenance was so haggard in the dim light that it took her a moment to recognize him.

"Far!" she exclaimed with relief. "You startled me! How long have you been standing there?"

"Don't!" The king's voice was husky. "Don't stop playing, please. I miss it so." He moved haltingly out of the shadows, as if he was burdened with pain or exhaustion.

Ria cringed at the sight of him. He'd lost weight in the weeks since she'd seen him last, and his skin sagged in dark patches under his eyes. His hair and beard were unkempt and filthy, his lips caked with dried spittle. His fingernails were brown with grime as he reached forward a hand to stroke her cheek.

But his eyes were bright and intelligent, and Ria tried not to flinch at his touch.

"Far?" she whispered.

"You look so like your mother. Tell me, why do you look at me with such fear?"

"Nonsense," Ria said, her jaw tense under his touch as she fought the urge to step back.

"Yes, I see it. Fear. Even disgust. Is my company so awful? Can you not bear my presence?"

Ria swallowed. "I'm only tired, Far. Why did you come?"

Sindal sighed, and Ria turned her head away from his putrid breath. He lowered his hand from her face and turned to stroke the strings of her harp.

"I am not well, Ria. I can see it in the faces of those around me. I see it in your eyes."

"Nonsense. We're worried for you, that's all, but you're as healthy as you ever were."

"In body, perhaps, but not in mind. What sort of man spends his days in a stone tower instead of with the daughter he loves?" He coughed a short laugh.

Ria took courage at his words. This was the father she knew, not the wild man she'd met in the tower.

"Then come back to me," she said. "Leave that accursed tower and come home. It can't be healthy to spend your days locked up alone. Your mind needs activity. You need to feel the love of your people and immerse yourself in their needs."

"No. No, I cannot," he said with a heavy sigh. "It is for the best. There are gaps in my days, things I cannot remember. And they are increasing. When my mind returns, I sometimes find that I have done...unspeakable things."

The darkness of his tone made Ria shudder. He turned away and stood before the fireplace. The fire was warm enough, but Ria was growing chilled before the open window. She closed and latched it, then reached for her shawl for warmth.

"I'm sorry if I hurt you," her father said, his back still to her. "I don't remember, but sometimes I write things down when I am...not myself. I was so very angry, but I don't even remember why."

This admission, and the pain in his voice, filled Ria with compassion. Her throat constricted with emotion, and she hurried to him, wrapping her arms around him from behind and resting her chin on his shoulder.

"Tell me how I can help you. You needn't suffer this alone. Let me help."

"No. There's nothing you can do, except continue to fill my place here. I spoke with Galinn before I came to see you. I'm proud of you," Sindal said, lifting one of her hands to his lips. "You will be a better monarch than I ever was."

Ria let this sink in. He knew. He knew what she'd been doing to fill his place. And he was proud of her.

"What about Captain Strong?" she asked hopefully.

"Don't concern yourself about him. Grammel will see to his execution. It's a messy business, and you needn't be involved."

Ria recoiled at his words. So he didn't know everything. She withdrew her arms and stepped away. Suddenly she felt anxious for him to leave. The sickening realization that it would be best if her father never left the tower again filled her with self-loathing.

Sindal turned, and she struggled to meet his eyes, hoping he wouldn't read the guilt in them. "Ria, I came here to ask that you don't visit me again."

"What? Why?"

"It's not safe for you. I don't want you to risk it. I cannot promise that I will not—just swear to me that you will stay away."

"But you're my father!" Ria protested. "I'm your daughter! You're all the family I have!"

"Exactly! Don't you see?" He gripped her shoulders and she flinched, but his touch was firm, not violent. "You are all the throne has now. Rahm has already lost her king—"

"No, Far, you're not—"

"—and at a time like this she needs a leader. If something were to happen to you, with no heir to take your place, it would be devastating. We would be plunged into a civil war, and our enemies would be upon us in a moment, taking advantage of our weakness."

Ria thought about how she had bungled through these past weeks and wondered if the kingdom would be that much worse off without her.

"If this is my last act as king, and as your father, then let it be this," Sindal said firmly. "Give me your oath that you will stay away from the tower."

"This is so hard," she pleaded. "I can't do it alone. If I could have your guidance at times, or—"

"I know. I know that it's a high cost. But there are many good people who will help you. You must promise me never to set foot in that tower again."

Ria looked into her father's eyes. There she saw the man she knew and loved. It made her want to weep. "I will. I will respect your wishes, though it breaks my heart to do so."

Sindal nodded sadly and kissed her tenderly on the forehead before turning to leave.

"Far?"

He paused at the door.

"I'm not giving up on you. Don't get too comfortable in that tower."

He smiled and bowed his head respectfully. It was a gesture of honor, and Ria's eyes were pricked with tears as she raised her fingers to her lips in parting.

Nineteen

"Watch your step, Your Highness."

Ria grimaced as she sank ankle deep into thick mud. The rain had finally stopped during the night, but the series of storms had left the camp sitting in a thick soup.

This was Ria's first time in an army camp, and she raised her hood to get a better look as Sergeant Brandel assisted Biren from the carriage. It was a hive of activity with soldiers, tradesmen, and civilians sharing far too little space for such a large population. Some of them glanced her way, but most ignored her, too intent on their purposes to be distracted by curiosity. None of the faces were familiar, but the sight of a blue uniform marking a member of Endvar's Wall Guard filled her with a sudden melancholy. There had been no word of Merek, and it was assumed that his body had been claimed by the enemy.

The thought nauseated Ria and robbed her of breath.

He didn't deserve such an end. She quickly focused on her surroundings to divert her attention from thinking about him. There would be time to mourn later, but now she had work to do.

Overwhelmingly, her impression of the camp was one of filthiness. Mud clung to clothing, climbed up tent walls, and was flung by the wheels of passing carts. She grimaced as she stepped through the deep wheel ruts.

"The general's tent isn't far from here," Brandel said.

"Yes, I saw it as we approached. Take Lady Biren to find the campmaster and see to our tent while it's still light." The command tent rose proudly in the distance, its bands of crimson and silver rippling in the cool breeze. But it was missing something. The pole out front was bereft without Grammel's banner. They would have removed it for his burial. Now it was up to her to determine whose banner would fill it.

No sooner had she finished speaking than an officer stepped forward and saluted. "Welcome, Your Highness. I trust that your journey was comfortable."

Ria looked over the man, taking in his stiff posture and generous gray mustache. "Thank you, Captain..."

"Firl, Your Highness."

She eyed the insignias on his uniform. "You're one of Grammel's first captains?"

"Yes, Your Highness. There are but two of us remaining."

He said it as calmly as if he were discussing his breakfast, but there was an edge of alertness that betrayed him, as if he expected to replace Grammel as general. Well, if he were going to put himself forth for consideration, she would give him a chance to show his abilities.

"After I get settled, I would like to meet with all the first captains and lower captains. Can you arrange that?"

"Of course, Your Highness."

A passing soldier took a second glance at Ria and stopped.

"Your Highness!" He stepped toward her eagerly. "Have you received word of Captain Strong? I remember you were particularly interested to hear of him."

Ria recognized him as the same courier who had brought news of Grammel's death the week before. The anxious knot in her stomach tightened. "I've had no word as yet."

The soldier grinned. "Then you'll be happy to hear that he's alive. Returned to camp this very morning."

"Alive! Are you sure?" The knot loosened hopefully.

"I saw him myself not an hour ago in the surgeon's tent."

Ria turned to the mustached captain for corroboration. He nodded. "It's true. Captain Strong and another soldier returned just today, surprising us all. It's an omen of luck after such a desperate loss." Firl's words were cheery enough, but his eyes looked cautious.

"I wish to see him. Immediately," Ria ordered as relief coursed through her, leaving her limbs tingling.

"Of course. Let me escort you."

Ria lifted the hem of her skirt and half-trotted in the direction of the surgeon's tent. The courier's words raced through her head. Alive! It was more than she could have hoped for, and yet she had hoped all the same. The surgeon's tent was quite a distance away, and the mud sucked at her boots with each step. Her heart thumped with excitement as she hurried along.

Captain Firl tried to reclaim her attention, but Ria cared nothing for his attempts at conversation. She interrupted his wishes for her father's good health to ask, "What is the captain's condition? Captain Strong. How does he fare?"

Captain Firl's mustache twitched in a frown. "I believe he's well, but the soldier with him isn't as fortunate. You can judge that for yourself, however." He nodded to a long rectangular tent as they approached. The canvas appeared to have once been white but was now varying shades of brown, the lower edge nearly black where the heavy fabric rested against the earth.

Ria's footsteps slowed. For a moment she feared what she would find. Just the thought of entering the tent with its horrors made her feel weak.

The nearest flap opened and her breath caught as a familiar figure stepped out. It was *him*. Alive and well, not injured or on the brink of death as she'd feared. At his side was Rorden and the Khouri woman, and the three of them were engaged in a serious conversation. Ria paused, not wanting to interrupt, but fairly bounced with glee while she waited.

Merek gripped the small woman's shoulder, and she looked up at him with...gratitude or grief? Ria couldn't tell, but she was getting tired of waiting.

"Thank you, Captain Firl," she said to her escort. "I believe your services are no longer required."

As she approached the tent entrance, the Khouri

woman noticed her, then ducked back inside the tent. Rorden saw her next. The expression on his face brightened as he murmured to Merek, then followed the Khouri woman into the tent.

Strong turned, blinking with surprise. Ria gasped a little at the ugly wound on his crown. It was scabbed and oozing angrily. Despite that, he seemed well and whole without significant injury, though his breastplate was filthy and stained. Ria looked him over and sighed with satisfaction.

"Captain Strong."

"Princess," he returned, his gray eyes soft with weariness. "I didn't know you were in camp."

"Only just." She wanted to weep and laugh at the same time but was suddenly conscious of having an audience. It wouldn't do to appear too playful, particularly if the mustached captain was watching, so with great effort she swallowed her exuberance.

"So," she said, taking in the bruises, dirt, and dried blood that marred Merek's face. "Are you trying to make me a widow before you've made me a bride?"

He looked at her sharply. "I wasn't aware that it was my place to do either."

"Oh dear. I do hope that knock on the head hasn't affected your memory."

"Believe me, that I would remember." He smiled, and it was all she could do not to throw her arms around his neck. Instead, she laughed and grasped his hands warmly.

He immediately winced and she dropped them.

"Forgive me."

"No matter. Only a sprain."

"It's just that you gave me such a scare. For days I feared that you'd fallen. I can't tell you how wonderful it is to see you alive and well."

"It's good to see you too, Ria. Truly. But why are you here?"

"General Grammel is dead."

"I know. I was there when he fell."

"Of course," she said, suddenly self-conscious. "I'm here in my father's place to name his successor."

"I see." Merek stepped off the path to make room for a passing soldier. "Forgive me, I'm not used to seeing you act in this particular arena."

"You're not the only one. I'm afraid it will take some convincing to get these soldiers to follow me. Will you help?"

"I'm at your service, of course. Only, please, no more talk of brides and widows. They don't know you as I do and have no appetite for your jests."

"Who said I was jesting?" Ria said with a wink and was rewarded with a reluctant laugh.

As they walked together through the camp, Merek outlined briefly why it had taken so long to return. When the full strength of the enemy force came upon them, he and Grammel were separated from the rest of the troops. Some of his men tried to get their wounded companions to safety, but others joined in the fray despite the horrible odds against them.

"Dan saved my life more than once that day. He could have moved to safety with the others, but he wouldn't leave me despite having no armor and only scavenged weapons. I lost track of him shortly after Grammel was killed. When I found him again, he'd lost his shield fending off an Ardanian with a wicked cudgel." He limped a little as he walked, and Ria wondered what other injuries she couldn't see. She wanted to press him for more, but feared her intrusion would be unwelcome.

Instead, she jumped forward in the story. "And after our forces retreated? What did you do then?"

"We hid by day, trying to work our way past the enemy undiscovered at night. We made good progress at first, but after the second night Dan's fever set in and I could scarcely move him. If Rorden hadn't found us yesterday, I'm not sure we would have made it."

"Will he live, do you think?"

"His only hope now is in losing his arm," Merek said grimly. "Even if he survives, I'm not sure he'll agree it's worth the price."

It sounded rather melodramatic to Ria. To live was worth any price, wasn't it? Certainly the price of a limb. But the dark look in Merek's eye made her keep her thoughts to herself.

As they walked, they gravitated toward the quieter paths on the fringes of camp near the woods. When the command tent came into view, Ria paused for a moment to take advantage of the semi-privacy.

"This evening I'll be meeting with all of the captains to appoint the new general. I hope that you'll be there too."

"Of course."

A loose strand of hair brushed against her neck, and

Ria deftly looped it back into place. "Merek, what I mean to say is that I would like *you* to be the new general. Before you say no," she said hastily as his expression clouded over, "let me finish. I know you care nothing for honor and titles, but this is—"

"I accept."

"—not the time...wait, what did you say?"

"I'll do it."

"Oh. You will? Thank you." Ria meant it, but felt deflated that her argument was cut short. "But...why? You denied my father. I expected you would deny me as well."

Merek rubbed his eyes. "When your father asked me, we were at peace. It didn't feel right to leave my post where I might do some good to sit in an office in Albon getting fat and full of myself."

Ria smiled at the unlikely image. "But now?"

"Now we're at war," he said simply. "I accept your appointment, Your Highness." He bowed his head gravely, then stifled a yawn. "If you'll excuse me, I have some matters to attend to before this meeting of yours."

"Of course." Ria was so delighted that she raised up on her toes and swiftly kissed him on the cheek. He caught her before she could pull away, and held her for a moment against him, her cheek resting against his warm neck. He smelled of earth and sweat and blood, but Ria closed her eyes and breathed it all in, relishing in the reality that he was alive.

"I was so afraid for you," she confessed quietly. "I didn't want to believe that you were lost, but when there was no word of your return...." She pulled back to give him a teasing smile. "I should have known that it would take more than an army to kill my Captain Strong."

"Hmm." He frowned as he released her, but his gray eyes were bright. "You hold me in such high esteem that I'm doomed to disappoint."

"You shall never disappoint me. Though you might want to find a clean uniform before greeting your captains tonight. *General* Strong." The look that crossed his face made her laugh. "Get used to it, Merek. Everything is about to change."

"May I get you anything, my lady?" the young woman asked uncertainly.

Aiya gave her a little smile. Captain Strong's directive that she be allowed to remain with Dan and whatever she wished should be granted had clearly confused the surgeon's staff. A foreign woman dressed in humble working clothes but being granted all the consideration of nobility? Clearly this young assistant had decided to err on the side of caution.

"A stool would be nice," Aiya answered. She considered telling the girl that she was no noble lady but decided it might be simpler this way. Servants didn't ask nobility impertinent questions.

Dan lay on a stained cot, his fever keeping him unconscious, but restlessly so. His eyes tracked ceaselessly beneath his lids. Occasionally he opened them, looking about with a glassy, delirious stare. He wore only a pair of filthy, tattered trousers. The rest of his clothing had been lost in imprisonment, according to Captain Strong's brief account.

Aiya still didn't know the details of how Dan and his men had been found in the tunnels. Eyeing the many bruises and abrasions on his body, she wasn't sure she wanted to know. She tried not to look at the putrid limb. It had been crushed, the captain said. Crushed by a beastly man wielding a studded club. The bones of the forearm and elbow were shattered. But what was worse was the mottled color of the swollen flesh. The arm had died, and if the surgeon didn't take it soon, it would kill him.

"What is that you're giving him?"

The young woman had returned with a wooden tumbler. "It's a sleeping draught. To help when they..." she trailed off, glancing across the tent to the large surgeon's table.

Aiya took the tumbler from the girl and dipped a finger in the liquid to taste it. Alarmed, she muttered a curse.

"You cannot give this to him."

"But the surgeon said he will need—"

"Not this. His heart is too weak battling infection. If you give him this, he will not survive the surgery."

Aiya dumped the contents of the tumbler onto the dirt floor of the tent, adding it to the bodily fluids and waste collecting near the wounded and dying. She went to the large cabinet where the girl had prepared her concoction. Without asking for permission, she opened tins and jars, sniffing and tasting the contents in an effort to find something useful. She didn't recognize the

Rahmish names for many of the items, but she knew them well enough by smell or taste to identify their Khouri counterpart.

She found an unused mortar and pestle and began grinding some jeshi root, vaguely aware that the young woman was talking in earnest to the surgeon and gesturing accusingly toward Aiya. Aiya worked in a panic, worried that at any moment she would be thrown out of the tent. As the surgeon approached, she added a few drops of cinet oil to the paste. She glanced up at the surgeon. He was a beefy man who wore a bloodstained apron over his generous belly and looked as if he would be equally comfortable slaughtering animals.

Instead of demanding that she stop, the surgeon watched Aiya for a moment. Then he turned to the young woman at his side.

"Do as she says," he said, then returned to his work.

Aiya was as surprised as the young assistant. Bolstered by his words, she asked the girl for items, and the assistant got them much quicker than Aiya had. When she was finished, Aiya spooned out a small amount of the orange paste.

"We'll place this under his tongue. It will help with the pain, but it will not slow his heart so much."

No sooner had they finished than the surgeon appeared at Dan's cot with two soldiers. They lifted his cot and carried him to the table—a large wooden slab stained and scarred from heavy use.

Aiya shuddered as they lifted Dan onto the slab, reminded again of a carcass before the butcher. Leather straps bound Dan's legs, chest, and left arm to the table, but it wasn't enough. When the surgeon pierced the flesh of the dying arm, Dan's eyes flew open and he strained against the straps.

His bellow was so primal—full of fear and pain—that Aiya nearly fled from the tent. Instead, she swallowed her own horror and stepped close to his head, shushing him as she would a child. She stroked his brow, and his panicked eyes locked onto hers, pleading with wild desperation.

Aiya felt as though her insides were being squeezed out of her, and she tried to ignore the sounds and smells of the surgeon's work. It was best not to look, so she stayed at Dan's head and tried to calm him with her touch and her voice. She spoke in her native tongue because that was what flowed naturally from her lips. After a time, his eyes closed again, and she sang songs from her childhood while gently stroking his hair clotted with sweat and blood.

Sooner than she expected, the surgeon called for the cauterizing iron, kept hot and waiting in the brazier nearby. Aiya bent close to Dan's ear, trying desperately to reassure whatever part of him might be listening. He tensed but didn't wake when the hot iron seared his flesh. Aiya gagged against the smell, burying her face against her sleeve. But then it was finished, and the surgeon pronounced it a job well done.

Aiya tried not to look at his arm as they moved Dan back to his cot, but the very absence of it made it hard to look at anything else. The young assistant returned with a blanket, and together they covered him properly. Aiya didn't feel well, but she couldn't leave his side. What did a soldier do when he can no longer fight? Could Dan redefine himself again, as he had when he'd left his brothers' theater troupe and joined the army? These questions plagued her as evening descended and brought with it a new grief. The grief that Dan would awaken to a crushing disappointment that life would never be the same. And the worry that although he had survived, he may wish that he hadn't after all.

TWENTY

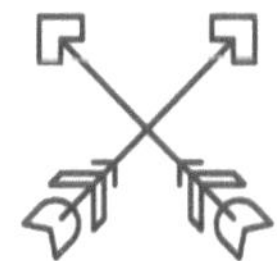

Merek woke to darkness and a distinct feeling of confusion. He was lying on his back, but not sleeping on the ground. Where was Dan? Slowly, the memories of the day trickled through to his consciousness. Dan was safe. Merek was in his tent in the army camp. And Ria. Had he just dreamed that she'd been there?

No. It wasn't a dream, and he was supposed to join her captains' meeting.

He sat up quickly, wondering how he came to be sleeping on his cot. He vaguely remembered Rorden helping him with his armor and coming to the tent with the intent of changing into a clean uniform. But by the look of things, he must have only managed to remove his boots before collapsing in exhaustion. Feeling ashamed for having slept, he pushed the fog out of his mind and moved into action.

Dressing was challenging with his sprained wrist,

but this was no time to coddle injuries. As he pulled on his coat, he felt a wave of nostalgia. No longer would he be wearing the blue and gray of the Wall Guard. As general, he would adopt the red and gray of the army, with more decoration and pomp than he was used to. He wondered how the other captains would take the news. There were only one or two who could have seriously considered themselves poised to take Grammel's place. But then again, it was a rare man who achieved high rank without also having an overdeveloped ego. Since the other captains were of noble blood, their sense of entitlement was likely to be even stronger.

He sighed as he tried for the third time to tie his cravat with his wrist injured as it was. It would be a challenge to get some of these men to follow him, but he and Firl had fought together at Durr's End, and young Orri had always treated him with respect. With their support, the others would come around.

However, there was no way his cravat would cooperate without another hand. Stepping out of his tent, he was relieved to see Rorden sitting at a nearby cookfire.

"Good evening, sir," Rorden greeted, getting to his feet. "Do you have an appointment?"

"Yes, and so do you. But first, help me tie this wretched thing so I don't look like a foot soldier fresh out of training."

As Rorden helped him tidy his appearance, Merek regretted not having a private moment with the young man to warn him of what was about to unfold. He cursed himself for falling asleep. What would Ria say when he arrived late? Something humiliating, most likely. And marvelous.

"You seemed pleased this evening, sir," Rorden said, as he straightened the shoulder seams of Merek's clean coat. "Feeling refreshed after your rest?"

Merek just grunted. He must stop thinking of Ria that way. He scooped up handfuls of water from a nearby barrel to splash his face. Again and again. It was bracingly cold, but effective in rinsing away the blood and dirt of battle...and ridding him of any idle thoughts of the princess. No matter how affectionate her flirtations, he knew her true feelings. There could be no future with her that didn't leave him feeling sick with artifice.

Feeling more composed and presentable, he set off for the command tent with Rorden at his side. They passed dozens of cookfires with soldiers huddled around them for warmth and companionship. The camp was settling in for a long, cold night.

Staked torches lit the pathway and braziers flanked each side of the command tent, bathing the area with light. Guards stood on each side of the door, their presence encouraging curious passersby to hurry on their way.

And there was much to be curious about. As they approached, Merek heard voices raised in anger from inside the tent.

"Even if you overlook the fact that he hasn't served with the army in many years, there's still the question of his recent arrest and imprisonment."

Merek froze. He knew that voice. Firl was one of

those he'd assumed would be with him from the start. This wasn't a good beginning if *he* was questioning Merek's leadership.

Ria's voice came in response, and though she wasn't as loud as Firl, she was clearly angry. Whatever had been said before Merek's arrival, it had pushed her dangerously far.

"I would have expected a man of your 'untainted character', as you call it, to hold yourself above gossip. You speak of things you know nothing about. Strong is as loyal to the crown as anyone in this room."

"No one in this room doubts his loyalty," a calmer voice interjected, "but we aren't the only ones who will spread gossip, are we? Think of the thousands of soldiers who need to have utmost faith in the integrity of their commander. Isn't it better to appoint a general who is above such tales?"

"Don't presume to patronize me, Orri," Ria snapped. She *was* angry. "I may not have bloodied my sword in battle, but do not make the mistake of thinking I don't know a man's character or ability to lead."

Captain Firl scoffed audibly. "With all due respect, Your Highness, my groom has more experience than you."

Merek cringed. Firl didn't understand the character of the woman he was goading. If he wasn't careful, Firl would be decommissioned before the night was over.

"There was nothing respectful about that statement, Captain." Ria's voice dripped with disdain. "May I remind you that every single one of you serves in his post at the pleasure of the crown, and in this moment, that means me."

Merek hurried through the tent door to stop Ria from saying something she would later regret.

Inside, Ria stood at the head of the large table. She leaned forward with her hands pressed against the wood, her posture defiant, and her eyes flashing furiously.

"And furthermore," she said, her voice rising, "it will someday mean Captain Strong himself. After we are wed, *he* will be your next king. If that is not reason enough for you and all the soldiers under your command to follow him without hesitation, then I invite you to use the door at once."

She raised her arm to the door where Merek had just entered. He froze, stunned into immobility at her words. All eyes turned to him. The shock that went through the room was palpable. The captains at the table grew silent, their aides standing behind them shifting in excitement.

Merek walked stiffly toward the table, trying to keep his face impassive. He hoped they couldn't see the anger that threatened to erupt just under his skin.

"I understand that it's uncommon to have a female member of the royal family presiding in this tent," he said quietly through clenched teeth. "But I don't recall that it gives anyone license to sit when she is standing, do you, Captain Firl?"

As one, the captains stood, many of them begging Ria's pardon for the insult.

Ria met Merek's look and gave a small nod. There

was a hardness in her eyes, but no apology. No shame or acknowledgement that she had just performed an act of deceit, even betrayal. Only infuriating confidence.

Well, he had expected humiliation. But this was so much worse.

In the silence, Orri cleared his throat. "Sir, we didn't mean to offend. The princess invited us to speak openly. But if we had known of your...personal connection, we would have been more delicate."

"I value honesty, but I will not tolerate disrespect," Merek said sharply, directing his anger at Ria toward the table of captains. Taking a deep breath, he tried to make his tone more measured. "It's never easy to bury a leader and accept new command in the middle of a campaign. I won't hold the words you've spoken tonight against you. But tomorrow is a new day, and I expect to see the same respect that you would offer King Sindal himself if he were here."

Ria nodded. "Very well, General. I see that you have everything in hand, and I believe I am in your chair. So this is goodnight. Please let me know if I may be of further assistance."

The men bowed as Ria breezed out of the room, barely sparing a glance for Merek. Had this been her plan from the beginning? Were her tender words earlier in the day just to manipulate him into this position? As Merek watched her leave, his anger gave way to suspicion, and that brought a much blacker feeling to his heart.

The cold night air felt soothing against Ria's burning cheeks. She shouldn't have allowed herself to be so provoked. But the fire burning inside her was difficult to extinguish and her mind raced with all the things she wished she'd said to those arrogant men.

Ria followed Sergeant Brandel to where her tent had been erected. It wasn't as large as the general's tent, but there was plenty of room for Ria's trunk and two proper cots. No sleeping on the ground this time as she had during the wall tour.

When she entered the tent, Biren was stoking the brazier that had been lit for warmth and light. Ria assumed this was a luxury few in the camp enjoyed, but she was grateful for it. The chill weather had a taste of winter to it, and the warmth would be welcome.

"I asked for pallets to keep your belongings out of the mud," Biren said as Ria entered. "But I don't know if they'll find any to spare."

"I suspect we'll just have to get used to living with mud for a while," Ria said, warming her hands at the fire.

"How did the captains accept your announcement?"

"Not as well as I'd hoped." Ria grimaced, removing a glove and inspecting her fingernails. "I'm afraid I did a very foolish thing."

She recounted how the captains' initial amazement had soon turned to resentment, much of it subtly directed at her.

"The more they slandered Strong's character, the more angry I became. There was nothing I could say that would put their objections to rest...until I told them that he was to be their future king."

Biren gasped as she opened Ria's trunk. "Did he agree, then? Do you have an understanding?"

Ria felt sick. "No. Nothing has changed between us. That's why it was an extraordinarily foolish thing to say. And what's worse, it was at that exact moment that Strong entered the room."

"Oh dear."

"Indeed."

"How did he react?"

Ria cringed inwardly as she remembered. "Like he was made of stone. He was either so stunned that he couldn't be upset, or he was angrier than I've ever seen him."

Biren lay Ria's dressing gown on her cot next to her nightdress. "I'm sure you'll make amends. He'll understand you only meant well."

"Yes, of course. Tell Rorden I'll need to speak with him in the morning. For now, I think I'll find some dinner."

"Wouldn't you rather I bring you something?"

"No, not tonight." Ria exited her tent, and Brandel fell into step behind her. "Sergeant, go. Get yourself some food. I will not wander far."

At the nearest campfire, Ria found a group of three older soldiers sitting together in quiet conversation. She sat near them on an overturned barrel, and they fell silent.

"Good evening. Would one of you gentlemen know where I might get some dinner?"

The men glanced at each other and shrugged. One of them stood and left without a word.

Ria tried to engage the other two in conversation, asking of home and their families, but they were unwilling to say much. The third man returned with a plate of tough, stringy meat, half a potato, and a slice of crusty bread. Ria accepted it graciously, and made an inner commitment to allow Biren to find her something more suitable in the future.

After a few more minutes of awkward attempts at conversation, the man who'd brought her meal spoke up. "Is it true that Captain Strong is our new general?"

The other men perked up with interest.

"He is," Ria answered. "He assumes duties immediately, though the official appointment ceremony is yet to be determined."

"That's a fine choice," said a man with white hair growing in a ring on the top of his head.

His companions agreed. "Couldn't ask for a finer man."

Hearing that they were ready to accept Merek without misgiving loosened the knot in Ria's stomach.

"Is it true that he will be our next king?" one of the men asked. "They say the princess announced it herself."

Ria started. *They think I'm a maid, not the princess.* But of course, why would the princess join them unaccompanied at their campfire?

She considered her words carefully. "Yes, that's what the princess said."

One of the men snorted. "Can you imagine? I used to

serve with him before he was First Captain. I never thought of him as a king."

"I don't like it," another said, shaking his head and picking at his teeth with a fingernail.

"You just said he was a fine choice!" one of his companions ribbed him.

"As general, aye. But king? He's no more noble than you or me. As common as they come. A king should be something special. It should be in his blood."

Ria pressed her lips together tightly. Saying what she thought had already gotten herself into too much trouble for one night. But she didn't have much appetite for her humble meal and soon excused herself from their company.

TWENTY-ONE

All was dark in her tent when Ria woke to the sound of voices outside. There were still embers glowing in the brazier, so she must not have slept long. But the air held the biting chill of deep night.

Biren was asleep, and Ria didn't want to wake her, so she reached for her thick dressing gown and boots before going to the tent door.

"Sergeant?" she called softly through the flap.

The voices stopped. Brandel spoke. "I apologize for the disturbance, Your Highness. You have a visitor. I asked him to return in the morning, but he refused."

"Who is it?" Ria asked, although there was only one person in this camp who would be brazen enough to wake her in the middle of the night.

"It's Captain Strong, Your Highness. Er, that is, General Strong."

Ria untied the laces of the tent flap and drew it aside. She raised an eyebrow at the newly appointed general.

"What is it?"

"Forgive me for waking you. I wanted a word in private." Merek glared at Brandel.

"And it couldn't wait until morning?"

"I'm afraid not."

"Very well," Ria sighed and wrapped her dressing gown more tightly around her. "Come in. It's freezing out there. Try not to wake Biren."

She drew back to let him enter the tent, letting the flap fall but leaving the laces undone. She folded her arms against the cold and looked him over. He was still dressed in the uniform he'd worn previously that evening, but the cravat was gone and his shirt was loosened at the top. His stone exterior was gone too, replaced by a simmering anger that seemed intensified in the harsh shadows from the glowing embers.

She searched for a jest to relax them both. "I'm surprised at you, Strong. I would have expected more decorum than to come to a lady's tent in the middle of the night."

"It can't damage my reputation any more than you did tonight."

"Don't be ridiculous—"

"Please," he said wearily, lifting a hand to silence her. "I'll keep this brief. I don't wish to be here any more than you want me here, but this needs to be said while it still can."

His words filled Ria with dread. But whatever criticism of her character—impulsive, immature, inexperienced—she knew he had a right to say it after her behavior.

Merek ran a hand through his short black hair. When he looked at her, his gaze was so piercing that she found it hard to meet his eyes and fidgeted with the lace around her cuff instead.

"I've been trying to understand," he began, "why you would compel me into this impossible situation. Why you would make such an outlandish claim when you and I both know that there is no betrothal between us. Then I remembered a conversation from some months back, and it finally made sense. I think I understand you now, and can even understand the reason for the deceit, but I cannot condone it. So I came here privately to tell you that I refuse to be your pig farmer. You'll have to find someone else because I won't do it."

Ria looked at him in surprise. "I'm sorry, my what?" Of all the things she'd expected to hear, it wasn't that.

"Your pig farmer. A warm body taking up space in a chair so that you can be free to do whatever you wish as queen."

Something about his words did sound familiar. And then Ria remembered the private laughs she and her father had shared about her marriage prospects. Had she ever mentioned those conversations to Merek? Perhaps there had been one dinner party...but this was ludicrous. How could he even think she'd been serious?

"Is *that* what you think this is about? You think I want a brainless oaf as a husband so that I can indiscriminately exercise all the power of the throne?" She would have laughed if his expression hadn't been so fierce.

"I watched you in that tent pushing those men into doing what you wanted just as surely as you've coerced me," Merek growled. "And it worked. I'm trapped. Forced into playing your little game, pretending to be betrothed because to tell the truth would undermine any credibility you have in this camp. So I will play along. But I must make it clear to you right now that I will not marry you. When all this is over, the lie ends." Some of the fire died in his eyes when he was finished, as though the words were a relief to speak aloud.

Ria blinked with astonishment. How had he misunderstood her so completely? "You can be such a fool, Merek Strong. Do you even know me at all? I don't want a pig farmer. I want an equal who will speak to me as you are now. I want your wisdom and experience; your honesty and courage. I need your frankness, your perspective, your confounding ability to be infuriatingly...*right*. You provide balance for me in a way no one else does. I want you by my side to lead, not standing forgotten in the shadows."

"Is that what you tell yourself? Pretend that you'll listen to me in the future when you don't listen to me now?"

"Shh." Biren's breathing changed rhythm, and Ria eyed her sleeping form. "Of course I listen to you," she whispered.

"Do you? I've been clear on the subject of marriage, and yet you ignore my wishes and announce to the camp that we're betrothed, turning me into a complete fool in front of those I'm supposed to lead."

"I'm sorry for that," Ria conceded. "I didn't intend to say it, I swear to you. I was just so angry with Captain Firl and wanted to put him in his place. He and Orri were resisting your leadership, and I wanted to unite them once and for all."

"There are better ways. You can't inspire loyalty with gossip. Now it looks as though I've seduced you into promoting me instead of earning the position through my own merit."

"That's laughable. No one will believe it."

"Just wait. In a camp this size, you'll be amazed at the stories that come to life after tonight."

"Well it certainly doesn't help that you sought me out in the middle of the night," she said with half a smile, tossing her hair behind her shoulder.

Merek glowered back. "There was no other way to talk to you without being overheard. We can't speak of this again. I'll go along with your scheme for now, but as soon as I say it ends, you will retract the lie. Blame me if you must. Claim that I was unfaithful to you. Whatever it takes to preserve the honor of the crown."

The prospect of shaming him further made Ria feel wretched. She couldn't do that to him. "I have an even better idea. Make it be true. Agree to marry me, and stop this charade. Am I really that repulsive that you can't even consider it?"

He snorted softly. "You know it isn't that."

"Then why are you so adamant against it? I apologize that I imposed on you, and I won't hold you to an agreement you didn't make. But the best solution may be simply to put your prejudices aside and agree to be my husband."

Merek closed his eyes. "How to make you understand..." When he opened them again, his expression was so frankly intimate that Ria forgot for a moment that they weren't alone in the tent.

In a low voice taut with restraint he said, "Have you never loved another so deeply that your very lifeblood seems tied to them? That you can recognize their footstep apart from any other outside your door, and your heart leaps at the sound. You can be in a crowded room and without seeing them, know instinctively where they are from moment to moment as they move through the group." He searched her eyes expectantly, but whatever he was looking for he didn't find because his face fell. "If you had felt this as I have, you wouldn't have to ask."

His intensity gave Ria pause. Clearly he spoke from experience. And she felt ashamed because she did not. For as much as she thought she had once loved Artem, she realized now that it paled in comparison to the love Merek described. She and Artem had shared only a shallow passion rooted in false impressions. What Merek spoke of was something else entirely, and Ria knew at once that she had misjudged him. Into her mind flashed an image of the lovely Khouri woman and the need in her eyes as they'd stood together outside the surgeon's tent. Was she the desire of Merek's heart? The thought that they might share a bond so intimate pricked her with envy.

But she wouldn't yield without a fight. "It's true that

I haven't felt what you describe," Ria answered honestly. "If your heart belongs to another in that way, then it's unfair of me to ask this of you. But perhaps if you—"

"Not another, Ria! My heart belongs to you!" Merek hissed in exasperation. "Every waking moment I think of you. When I'm away from you, every thought is how I might share this moment with you. What you would say if you were there. I hear your laughter in my mind, and it's the most beautiful sound, but it tears me apart because it's only a memory. And then when we're together, my whole being is alive with your presence. But it only pains me further because it isn't the same for you." He raked a hand through his hair and shook his head. "Do you really not see how you torture me with your talk of marriage?"

Ria's words dissolved on her tongue, awed by his passion. She'd never seen him so vulnerable. So unguarded. It was unsettling.

But also an opportunity.

Taking a deep breath, she stepped closer to him. Close enough to touch. She looked into his eyes, and with all the tenderness she could muster, whispered, "Then don't fight it. Marry me. Make me your wife. It's what we both want!"

He regarded her for a moment with eyes darkened by the night, but his jaw was set, and she knew his answer before he spoke. "No. It's not...the same. What you wish of me I cannot give. I can't be an indifferent partner, united in purpose but not affection. And what I wish, you cannot give either."

"I'll give myself to you freely and honor you as a

wife. I swear to you!" She tried not to blush under his gaze, but she felt the heat rising in her face, and it was only with great effort that she didn't turn away. "Please, Merek. I may not be able to give you my heart as you wish now, but I will try. With time, I'm sure that it will come. I can learn to love you as you love me; I'm sure I can!"

She reached for his hand, but Merek shook off her touch, stepping away from her and moving toward the tent door.

"Don't!" Ria called out. She cringed, glancing at the corner where Biren slept and whispered, "Please don't go."

He hesitated, his face half turned toward her, his profile outlined in the fading firelight.

She racked her mind for the right words to keep him there. Somehow she knew that this conversation would not happen again. If she ruined it now, she wouldn't be given another chance.

"I learned some time ago not to let my heart speak for itself," she began, "and as a result, I'm afraid its tongue is rather foreign to me. I don't know what I feel. But I do know that although I have chosen you to be my husband because of your strength of honor, your wisdom, and your character, I'm not indifferent to your virtues as...a man."

His shoulders were tense, and a part of her longed to reach out and touch them, smooth the tension away with her fingers. But was this the touch of a lover? Or the touch of a friend? She couldn't be sure. She didn't dare act on her impulse for fear of deceiving him. To pretend affection that she didn't feel would be the worst betrayal of all. So instead, she settled on truth.

"I offer you all that I have and all that I am, with a promise to become what you want me to be."

Merek turned at last, but she could see that he wasn't moved. "You don't understand. I'm not asking you to become anything other than what you are. You owe me nothing. But I can't marry you when you don't love me. Even if you did grow to love me, I would always wonder if your affection was genuine or merely a force of will. I can't live with that doubt. It would be a black corruption of what I feel for you and would destroy us both."

"Is there nothing I can say to make you change your mind?"

"Is there nothing I can say to make you understand my heart?"

In a moment of decision, he stepped toward her.

Ria realized what he was going to do only a breath of a moment before it happened. One hand reached toward her tentatively. She'd seen such strength from those hands, yet he touched her with such gentleness: brushing a strand of hair behind her ear and moving his fingers to the nape of her neck. He cradled the back of her head as he turned her face toward his.

She froze, her breath stilled. Gently, tenderly, his lips brushed hers. She closed her eyes. His lips were warm, with the faintest scrape of whisker, and the salty smell of his skin bringing an image of powerful labor under a cold sun. Her heart pounded in her ears, yet still she didn't dare breathe. She felt the nearness of his body as a tenseness in the distance between them. Then his lips left hers and his voice sounded low and soft near her ear, sending a tingle down her spine as his breath brushed her neck.

"This isn't the life for you. You would regret it, and I would never forgive myself for your misery."

And then it was over. A cool breeze blew between them as he released her and stepped away. Ria opened her eyes to see his retreating back as he walked out of the tent and disappeared into the night.

TWENTY-TWO

Darkness brought a sharp chill to the Dimm Forest. The rain had stopped at last, but the clearing of the skies made the temperatures plummet. The glowing windows of Stefan's home and scent of cooking food enticed him with their promise of warmth. He climbed the steps and scraped the mud from his boots before pushing open the back door.

"Far!"

"Far's home!"

A chorus of squeals greeted Stefan as he stepped into the small kitchen. Three beaming faces rushed him, the unruly brown heads of his youngest children burrowing into his side as they commanded his attention.

"Evening, Far." Adisa smiled at him from the cookstove. His oldest daughter already had half the village talking about what a beauty she would be in a few years.

Stefan untangled himself from the web of arms and legs and stepped over the youngest who'd fallen to the floor. "I missed you too, Myrun. Watch your brother there, Roki." He bent to give his wife a swift kiss on the cheek, earning him a smile.

"Right on time," Veln said. "You always know right when the food is ready to be served. Not a minute too soon, nor a moment too late."

Stefan grinned. "That's because I can smell your lovely cooking all the way down at the guardhouse, and it calls me home as surely as dusk brings the cows."

Veln laughed and retied the loosening apron around her middle, shooing away the little one pulling at the strings. "Did you see the boys out in the yard? I expected them half an hour ago. No doubt they're swinging from the hayloft."

"Should I go round them up?" he offered.

"Never mind. As soon as we sit down, they'll come charging through the door wondering why no one called for them."

She proved to be prophetic. As the last of the venison dumplings were served into the chipped stoneware bowls, the door burst open and two energetic boys pushed their way into the room, followed by the slower shuffling step of their oldest brother.

Veln shot her husband a satisfied look, then barked orders at the boys to hang their wraps and hats before sitting down to eat. The noise level of the room—which had already been significant with five children settling in for the evening meal—more than doubled with the addition of Stefan's three older sons. With an effortless ability honed by years of experience, he ignored the cacophony and listened to Veln as she discussed the day.

"Runa came by asking if I'd seen their best milking goat. Disappeared in the night with no sign of it anywhere."

Stefan grunted and bit into a thick crust of warm bread. Such tales had been increasing of late. The whole village was feeling skittish, looking for signs that bandits had been visiting in the night. Stefan couldn't say for certain if their claims were unfounded.

"I saw Lars walking to the river with Svana today."

Stefan looked up. Karn's eyes shone with excitement as she gloated over this piece of news. Lars kicked her under the table, an act that earned him a sharp rap on the head from his mother.

"What's this?" Stefan asked.

Lars glowered at his sister. "She wanted to see the river, Far. That's all."

"I told you to stay away from the river while it's running so high," Stefan warned.

"We didn't get close. Besides, the rain has stopped."

"It doesn't matter. It's still rising with the runoff, and it'll be days before it drops. Was that cobbler boy such a bad influence on you that you don't remember how to listen to your far?"

"No," Lars grumbled, eyes lowered to his bowl.

"If Svana is worth impressing," Veln added, "she won't ask you to do something so reckless. Any girl without sense isn't worth the attention of a Falbrook."

Stefan watched Lars pick at his dinner. He was the same age as Stefan was when he and Merek had left the village to join the army. Stefan couldn't imagine sending his boy away, but at the time he'd thought of himself as practically a man. He wondered how long it would be before Lars was courting one of the village girls seriously. Or worse, when one of the village boys came around asking for Adisa. *That* was a frightful thought.

All at once, a thundering roar sounded in the distance, growing quickly as if it would swallow the house. The floor and table shook, the bowls and cups rattling. The children looked to Stefan and Veln, faces drained with fear. Myrun burst into tears and threw himself into his mother's arms, his cries drowned out by the fearsome sound. It couldn't have been more than a minute or two, but it felt like an eternity before the sound died out and the shaking stopped.

"Well then. All in one piece?" Stefan asked brightly, hoping his children couldn't hear the fear in his voice.

"What was that?" Adisa asked, her eyes wide.

Stefan stuffed the last of his bread in his mouth and stood. "I don't know, but I'll find out. You all stay here and lock the doors. Finish your supper and mind your mor."

Veln looked at him sharply over Myrun's head. "You're leaving now?" She glanced pointedly at the frightened faces around the table.

"May I go too, Far?" Lars asked.

Stefan looked down at his hopeful expression. "I'll take Lars," he said, and stroked Myrun's head gently as he moved to the door.

Lars jumped out of his seat with excitement, pulling his cap down over his ears and wrapping a muffler around his neck for extra warmth. Stefan reached for a lantern that held a thick, new candle.

He looked back at Veln. Her face was grim, and he knew by the look in her eyes that she wasn't pleased that he was leaving. She was proud of his position as captain, but only when it didn't cause her much trouble. But she said no more, turning instead to tend to Myrun with a calm voice and gentle smile.

The night air nipped at Stefan's ears and nose as he stepped outside. Through the trees he saw a bobbing light coming from the direction of their nearest neighbor.

"Did you hear that?" Odun asked when he joined them, his breath forming a cloud that glowed as he raised his lantern to get a good view of Stefan and Lars. "It sounded like it was barreling right through my house."

"You and Nella all right?"

"Fine. You think it might be an earthquake? I've never felt one, but Nella said that's how her uncle described it."

"Can't say. I've never felt one either." But it felt wrong to Stefan. Too...substantial.

There was no moon, and the light of their lanterns didn't illuminate much. Soon they were joined by others: men from the village wanting to know what had caused the noise and the shaking. They spoke in whispers to each other, sharing what they'd heard and guessing at its source.

They were following the trail in the direction of the river, skirting around a small hill, when a voice cried out ahead. Stefan hurried past the other men to the front of the group. Three men stood in the middle of the track, mouths agape.

Ahead of them was a solid wall of mud, taller than the height of a man. It blocked their path and extended into the darkness in both directions. Stefan raised his lantern, but couldn't make out the full size. It looked like the whole hillside had collapsed, bringing a torrent of mud, trees, boulders, and debris with it.

Stefan moved off the path, leaving his excited neighbors behind. He pushed his way through the forest, following the path of the mudslide. The ground was relatively level here, but the volume of debris and the force it must have had as it moved...

Stefan's heart sank when he reached the wall. The mudslide had pushed right through it, swallowing it up as though it were nothing.

A curse sounded beside him. Lars looked at him with wide eyes, as if equally surprised to hear what he'd said, but this was not the time to worry about his son's language.

Stefan handed Lars his lantern. "Go to the guardhouse and call as many soldiers as you can. Quickly!"

As the boy hurried off into the night, Stefan turned back to the yawning blackness that had appeared where the wall used to be. Beyond that blackness lay bandits who had already been getting restless. Without a wall to keep them at bay, how could he protect his people?

Twenty-Three

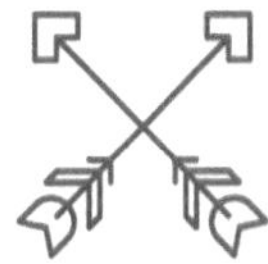

"It almost seems a shame to go through such effort, doesn't it?" Ria asked as Biren tightened the laces of her dress and arranged the tucks and folds in her skirts. "I'll only be covering it all up with a heavy cloak anyway."

"Careful, my lady. Next you'll be asking for a pair of trousers."

"Hmm, might I add a pair under my petticoats for warmth?" Ria teased.

"It has gotten miserably cold, hasn't it?" Biren left the skirts and began brushing out Ria's hair. After a moment of silence, she asked, "Did you sleep all right, my lady?"

"Not as well as I would have in my own bed, that's for certain. Why do you ask?" Ria hoped her breezy tone hid her discomfort at the question. Not only had she been awakened in the night by Strong's unexpected visit, but she'd lain awake for a long time after he left, her thoughts spiraling into frustration. She hoped Biren had slept through it all. This was one secret she had no intention of sharing with anyone.

"You just look tired, and your spirits seem a little troubled this morning. No doubt a good meal will fix that."

"No doubt," Ria answered, though she very much disagreed. She squinted into the small looking glass perched on the top of her trunk. It wasn't as large as she was accustomed to, but served the purpose well enough to show that she had dark shadows under her eyes.

Curse you, Merek.

When Biren finished her hair, Ria exited her tent with a determination to be lively and energetic. She made an effort to greet the soldiers and staff she saw, and even stopped to join a game of sticks and bobbers. The children didn't seem to notice her cheerfulness was forced and brightened like daisies in summer when she joined them.

But her heart simply wasn't in it. She couldn't get Merek—and how very much she dreaded seeing him—out of her head.

Unfortunately, there was no way of avoiding him.

"Did you still wish to speak with the general this morning?" Biren asked as Ria wandered through the camp market, feigning interest in a variety of ointments to protect her skin against the chill wind.

No, she did not wish to speak with the general. Not until she had more time to sort things out. A part of her was indignant that he'd taken the liberty of kissing her. But at the same time, she was so struck by his tenderness that she couldn't truly feel put upon. More than anything, she felt confused. The kiss had been so fleeting that she couldn't even say whether or not she'd enjoyed it. And if she had, what did that mean? Was it a sign of her true feelings? Or just a sign that she hadn't enjoyed a man's touch in a very long time? A part of her was horrified that it had happened. But another part of her, she admitted, wanted it to happen again, curious to see how a second kiss would feel.

There was no way she could face Merek with these thoughts battling in her mind.

"Yes, thank you, Biren. Time has quite slipped away from me. Let's not delay any longer, shall we?"

Whatever her personal feelings, she would behave as a princess.

As they approached the large tent striped with crimson and silver, a small crowd clogged the pathway. Couriers, clerks, and even tailors and cobblers vied for the privilege of outfitting the new general, all waiting for a chance to be heard. As Brandel firmly encouraged them to move aside for the princess, they straightened and bowed respectfully. Ria nodded and smiled as she passed, noting that she had seen many similar scenes as people waited upon her father. Perhaps being a general wasn't all that different from being a king.

The inside of the tent was even more crowded. Soldiers and aides hurried back and forth on errands for the uniformed men gathered in the center of the tent. There, standing around the large table, Merek bent over a map with his captains. Their conversation seemed intense, but they spoke in low tones to each other, the sound of their voices not carrying over the activity around them. Again, Ria was reminded of the swarm of activity that surrounded her father in the days when he had cared about being king.

Her thoughts snapped back to the present as Rorden approached.

"Good morning, Your Highness. I trust you slept well."

Stifling a sigh, she smiled.

"Thank you, Rorden. Will you please inform the general that I need to speak with him?"

"Of course." Rorden bowed and returned to the table to speak quietly into Merek's ear. Ria held her breath, waiting for him to look at her. That first eye contact would communicate much of where things stood between them. She tried not to think about the previous night, knowing that she wouldn't be able to hide the flush in her cheeks if she suspected even for a moment that he was thinking of it too.

Merek didn't even look up. He spoke to Rorden, and then turned back to the table. Ria was disappointed. And annoyed.

So that's the way it's going to be, is it? Well, if there was one thing she would not put up with, it was being ignored. Nonetheless, she dutifully waited until Rorden returned. The apology was written on his face before he even spoke.

"Forgive me, Your Highness. Captain Strong—that is, *General* Strong—regrets that he can't receive personal visitors at the moment. Scouts reported enemy troop movements early this morning, and the general is in the midst of coordinating a response. I'm sure you under-stand that his attention can't be diverted no matter how desirable the diversion."

Very good, Rorden, Ria thought. *How well you sweeten your commander's message.* She was certain Merek's words had not been so complimentary.

"This is not a personal visit," Ria said. "I have infor-mation concerning the enemy that may be of use."

As she watched Rorden return to deliver her reply, she was reminded of learning to read and write Ardanian as a child. Speaking had come more easily for her, so her tutor had forced her to practice her writing skills by forbidding her from speech for an entire week. She was only allowed to communicate by writing in Ardanian, and Lotta and Sindal would respond by writing in reply. Although effective, it was also laborious and frustrating. Rorden was no better than her little writing pad, passing messages back and forth in far more time than it would take to speak freely.

This time, after Rorden delivered her message, Merek paused, considering. He looked up at Ria at last. His face was so impassive, she could read nothing in his eyes. She tried to smile a little, but it faltered before his stoic gaze. Feeling distinctly unwelcome, she approached the table anyway. It appeared that her fears of being reminded of his passionate words the previous night were unfounded. Indeed, he seemed to have buried them so deep that only marginal tolerance remained.

"Forgive me for keeping you waiting, Your Highness."

Ria was so taken aback by his coolness that she felt unsure how to proceed. It was an unfamiliar feeling for her, and she desperately tried to find her footing.

"I don't mean to intrude, but I have information that may be of use to you."

"We're most honored by your presence, of course, and are eager to hear anything you might share."

Ria's lips tightened at his clipped formality. *I will go along with your scheme,* he'd said. But this was not the attitude of a man to his future bride. It was the attitude of a man trying to dismiss a woman whose company he could not endure.

A serving maid appeared at the table's edge bearing a platter of food. As she set it down, Merek smiled kindly. Watching the girl curtsy in return, Ria fumed. *A small gesture of gratitude for a servant girl but no warmth for a princess? Well then.*

Finding strength in her indignation, she began. "The Ardanian ambassador has shared some information with me that I found illuminating. It seems likely that the enemy forces are led by Prince Artem, the younger brother to King Idan."

"Is he a young man with golden hair and hands that look as though they've never seen a day's hard labor?"

Ria was surprised at this astute description. "You know of him?"

"I've seen him," Merek said. "He emerged from the gates after Grammel fell, just long enough to sneer at the carnage before returning to the city. He hasn't been seen outside the walls since."

Merek's tone betrayed a clear distaste for the man

and the first sign of emotion he'd shown since Ria entered the tent. Oh yes, he would not like Artem.

"I'm not surprised that he would shun the battle-field. I expect the idea of combat is too coarse for him. He prefers a more…intimate stage." It gave Ria no pleasure to think of Artem, let alone to speak of him. But she was rewarded with a flicker of something in Merek's eyes.

"You know him personally?"

"Oh yes," she said airily. "Did you not know? We were nearly betrothed not two years past."

Merek looked at her sharply, a small crack appearing in his stone exterior. "He was your suitor! Why haven't you mentioned this before?"

"Why? Are you jealous?"

"No, of course not!"

"Oh, that's a pity." Ria arched one eyebrow. "I should like to see you jealous."

The other men chuckled appreciatively, and Merek smiled at the ribbing, but the smile didn't reach his eyes. Ria, however, couldn't have been more pleased with the change of mood at the table. Feeling far more comfortable, she continued with her tale.

"I was surprised to learn that Artem leads this campaign. This isn't really his style. He's more the spider who spins webs and ensnares his prey when they least expect it rather than using direct force to get what he wants. Subtlety, cunning, those are his weapons. But if you've seen him yourself, then Count Orlin must be right."

"What else does Count Orlin say?"

Ria moved around the table and claimed the chair at the head for herself. It was clearly the general's chair, and Merek's own coat was draped across the back. As if he had invited her to sit, Merek removed his coat and placed it on the arm of the chair to the left. With a nod at his first captains, he and the rest of the officers sat, their attention turned to Ria.

"By all appearances," she began, "King Idan knows nothing of this aggression. Artem has been given command of the armies and has been moving troops outside the notice of the king. And because Artem is Artem, there's good reason to believe that he is not simply interested in Endvar, but rather has designs to take all of Rahm."

Judging by the looks on the captains' faces, this wasn't a surprise.

"You already know this?" she guessed.

"We've suspected as much," Merek replied, his tone finally beginning to lose some of its stiffness. "Grammel assumed that the enemy hadn't already spread beyond Endvar because it didn't intend to do so. Either Endvar alone was the prize, or they didn't have adequate support. But it was always possible that there was more to it than that. The amount of activity we've seen lately suggests that they're coordinating quite a large force on the Ardanian side of the border. There would only be one reason for such a force."

"He must not be very skilled in war," said one of the captains—a man who looked as though his face had been smashed by a brick. Alrek, Ria thought his name was. "Their attempts to extend past Endvar have been inconsistent and uncoordinated, as if there's no clear leader and the captains can't make up their minds."

"Yet, the taking of the city was expertly planned and executed. It makes no sense that penetrating further into Rahm wouldn't have also merited the same foresight. What is his game?" This from the mustached Firl who had so provoked her the night before. Merek had apparently forgiven him of his mutinous talk the previous evening.

Ria settled back in the chair as the discussion turned toward battles already fought and how they might deflect the Ardanian prince's purposes. While the officers argued, she took the opportunity to study the men in the room. In addition to Firl, Orri had also been allowed to stay. They had either overcome their misgivings or hidden them carefully because they now treated Merek with respect. There was another man there whom Ria remembered vaguely from Endvar, an older man with three fingers on his left hand that were no more than stubs. But his eyes were keen and thoughtful. It seemed that all the men at the general's table were intelligent and experienced. Ria just hoped they were loyal too.

Surreptitiously, she watched Merek. Though his attitude was one of control and strength, she saw traces of the weight he carried. The sleeplessness of worry. Suddenly, she felt ashamed that she'd added to his stress; increased his troubles with her behavior the day before.

His right hand rested on the arm of the wooden chair, mere inches from her left. Unbidden, her mind traveled back to the previous night and the moment when his fingers brushed her neck ever so gently, followed by his lips on hers. She watched him speaking to his captains, and the thought of sharing such an intimate moment with him excited her. Knowing him in such a way was an honor higher than many she'd enjoyed in a life of privilege.

Merek turned to her and met her eyes. She instantly blushed at the direction her thoughts had gone. Clearing her throat, she frantically tried to think of what had been said. The rest of the table was silent, waiting for her response.

"Forgive me, gentlemen. I'm afraid I lost track of the conversation for a moment. It's difficult to focus with an empty stomach, isn't it?" Her cheeks burned, and she longed for some fresh air.

"Captain Alrek wondered if we can consider King Idan an ally," Merek said.

"The ambassador and I have both attempted to contact Idan for assistance," Ria answered. "There's a strong likelihood that Artem will intercept our messengers, but if by some miracle they don't go astray, I expect he'll come to our assistance."

"With what army? If his brother has stolen his own army out from under his nose, of what use is the Ardanian king?" Firl said dismissively.

"Not his entire army," Ria said. "You can rest assured that King Idan has adequate force to bring his brother in line." She spoke confidently, but her memory of Idan and Artem's relationship gave her unease. Idan had a soft spot for his brother that might not serve him well as king.

"Eldar," Merek said, addressing the man with the missing fingers. "See if there's a man among your ranks who would be able to sneak past the enemy and make his way to King Idan as an emissary. He would need to be well-acquainted with Ardania to stay off the main roads but still find the king quickly."

Eldar nodded and murmured instructions to his aide behind him. As the conversation moved to details about scouting parties and anticipating the enemy's next move, Ria grew restless. She needed to stretch her legs, but there was one more thing that needed to be said before she left.

Ria stood, and the men at the table quieted and stood in respect. "I'll leave you now, but General, I'd like a private word before I go."

Merek nodded reluctantly, and followed her to the far corner of the tent. Here lay a cot with bedding carefully folded at its foot, clearly unused. The previous general's belongings had been removed, but the new general hadn't yet settled in. She was glad of that. She felt less intrusive that way.

"Your Highness, this isn't the time—"

"Relax, Merek. I don't wish to discuss last night's events any more than you do. That is not my chief concern."

A look of relief mingled with sheepishness flashed across his face. Ria almost wanted to laugh but felt too keenly the gravity of what she was about to say. She turned her back to the crowd in the tent so that her words couldn't be overheard or observed by anyone but him.

"Have you given much thought to spies?" she asked, speaking barely above a whisper. "I mean, here in the camp."

"Should I?"

"With Artem leading the enemy's forces, you absolutely must. I may not know much of warfare, but I do know him. He will have infiltrated this camp before you even left Albon."

"You tell me this apart from my captains," he observed.

"No one should be above suspicion. How well do you know them?"

Merek looked over her head at the men gathered at the table behind her. "I trust them completely. Several of them are from my own guard in Endvar."

"Which means they were in a position to be influenced even before this conflict started."

He frowned. "What you suggest...I cannot suspect my own captains of treachery. Especially not after what Grammel did to me. I refuse to think that of them."

"You're an honorable man, Merek. That's one of your greatest virtues. But your enemy is not honorable. If you cannot think the way Artem does, then he'll always be two steps ahead of you. Please—" she hastened to add when he shook his head. "Just promise me that you'll be very careful whom you trust."

Merek sighed. "I'm not completely new to this, Ria. I should think you would know by now that I know how to be discreet when the occasion calls for it."

Ria colored at his words. "Of course," she said stiffly. "I didn't mean to suggest otherwise. If you'll excuse me—"

"Wait." Merek rubbed his eyes and stifled a yawn. "Ria, I owe you an apology. My actions last night were not those of a gentleman."

Now? Ria thought crossly. *You want to do this* now? "I said I didn't want to discuss last night."

"Yes, of course." He cleared his throat uncomfortably. "But…if you can find it in your heart to overlook my poor behavior, I would be indebted to you."

He glanced up and, seeing the eager attendants who were restlessly waiting for their conversation to end, bowed to Ria and left her.

Ria was speechless. From passion to coldness to awkward apology—she felt as though she were a spinning top, never sure where she would land and which side would be facing up. She watched him walk away from her, proud and erect. No sign of the momentary weariness of a moment before.

Did you mean it? she wanted to ask. She resisted a sudden urge to rush after him and demand, *Did you mean what you said last night?* Somehow that question had taken on vital importance, because his words had moved her in a way she hadn't realized until that moment when he was trying to pretend they hadn't happened.

TWENTY-FOUR

Aiya found the apothecary's stall to be a wonder of both possibility and gross negligence. Some of the tonics and powders he sold the soldiers who came to him to treat the various fungi and rashes cropping up in camp would have been humorous if they hadn't been so appalling. But every so often, Aiya found a gem. A lump of hettin root or shavings of dried bear intestine, carelessly mixed in with the useless and forgettable. She never let the apothecary know how pleased she was with these finds. If he had known their true worth, he would have charged her double.

Aiya stowed her purchases away in her satchel and started back to the surgeon's tent. The surgeon had been so impressed with the poultices she made for Dan, and how quickly his wounds were healing, that he'd almost begged Aiya to leave the laundry and work for him. She'd agreed, but only on condition that Yulda come too.

The poor girl hadn't made any friends with the other laundresses, preferring to observe their idle chatter with a mixture of fascination and disgust. Yulda carried such a hardness about her. She seemed incapable of relating with the other girls whose heads were full of soldiers and gossip about the princess.

The princess and the captain. No, not captain. General. Aiya hadn't seen Strong since she'd heard the news. That suited her just fine. The less she thought of him, the better. Her days were full of tending to Dan and teaching Yulda the recipes to various tonics, ointments, and poultices.

"It's just like working in a kitchen," Yulda had said, and after less than a week she was not only learning quickly but even improved some of Aiya's methods with her own techniques.

As the makeshift marketplace fell further behind her, the ground underfoot hardened into less traveled paths. Aiya had made this trip many times in recent days, and each time she tested herself by picking a different route back to see if she could find her way in the labyrinth of tents, supply wagons, and horse corrals that made up army life. She walked swiftly, knowing that she would be missed in the surgeon's tent. There were battles almost daily now, skirmishes for townships as the Ardanian force pushed out from Endvar. By the steady stream of wounded keeping them busy, Aiya gathered that the Rahmish resistance wasn't going well. Or perhaps that was what victory looked like? The wounded in victory would be just as bloody as in defeat, wouldn't they? She heard little about the battle as a whole, but the dispirited attitudes of the soldiers she tended gave her a grim picture of the drama playing out on the field.

Aiya skirted around the edge of a clearing—one of dozens in the camp—where individual divisions gathered for meals, weapons practice, or to mourn their dead. This particular yard was the last before she reached the surgeon's tent. As she passed, Aiya glanced at the two soldiers sparring with each other and then stopped in her tracks.

One of the fighting soldiers was Dan. He wielded a sword with his left hand, and his movements were slow and deliberate. His right sleeve dangled uselessly from the place just above his elbow where the surgeon had removed it. His face was thin and strained with exertion, a mere shadow of the man he had been weeks before when they'd hidden together in the city.

Aiya felt a surge of awe mingled with irritation. How did he find such drive, pushing himself far beyond what a reasonable man would do? He continually surprised her, and that was a pleasant sensation. But it was also foolish considering that he had recently battled a deadly infection.

Aiya turned to the soldiers watching the contest. A dozen men gathered at the edge of the circle, giving Dan and his opponent room to move about freely. One of them she recognized from the surgeon's tent, where he had often visited his brother. He noticed her and smiled.

"May I?" Aiya asked, gesturing to the soldier's sword.

Startled, he handed it to her. It was heavier than

she'd expected, and she had to grip it with both hands to hold it out before her. Feeling dwarfed by the thing, she approached Dan from behind.

His opponent noticed her first, and with a pointed nod of his head gestured to Dan to look behind him. When Dan turned, his determined expression turned to one of bemusement.

"I have often been told that I speak your Rahmish language very well," Aiya said, "but somehow you still don't understand me. So I will try to speak a language you do understand." She pointed the sword in the general direction of his chest. "Now, when I say the words 'rest' and 'avoid exertion' do they sound clearer to your ears?"

Dan smiled and coughed a small laugh. "I hear your meaning clear enough, Nurse Aiya. But I've been discharged from the surgeon's tent, so I thought a little warm-up exercise would do me good."

"Discharged?" Aiya dropped the tip of the heavy sword onto the hard ground. "But you still need daily poultices and clean bandages! I will speak with the surgeon. You're not ready to return to duty."

"This is a war camp. They need the beds for the truly wounded. I can walk. I can even handle a sword. That's as good as being fit for battle." Dan moved to the edge of the yard and hung his practice sword on the rack where other soldiers selected weapons of their own.

"Not to me it isn't," Aiya insisted, following after him. "I will bring you your daily poultice, then. You have much more healing to do, and if you make your body work too hard to do it, it will just take longer."

"Personal visits from the nurse, eh, Dan?" A nearby soldier looked up and leered at Aiya. "When you're finished with her, send her to my tent. I'm sure I can show her a thing or two about the strength of a real man."

Aiya gave him a withering look, her cheeks warming with indignation, but the man just laughed and stepped closer.

"What? You think this one-handed cripple can give you anything I can't?"

The man's laugh was cut short in a heavy grunt as Dan plowed into him. Aiya jumped back in surprise. The two men sprawled in the dirt, Dan pinning the larger one to the ground with the stump of his right arm pressed against the man's neck.

Dan's pale complexion flushed red, blotchy and angry in the cold. "A *real* man doesn't talk to a lady that way. And if I ever hear you talking about her like that again, you'll find out how it feels to have your throat cut by a one-handed cripple." He pushed against the man's throat for emphasis and the other soldier sputtered and coughed, gasping for breath.

Aiya was too horrified to speak. Dan was going to get himself hurt. Just the sight of his wounded arm stump pushing against the other man made her weak. How much pain it must be causing him!

But she stood rooted to the spot, unable to intervene. Her life had been full of men like the lecherous soldier, but she had never once been so forcefully defended. Imar would have steered her away and forbidden her from returning to this part of camp. Tupin would have responded with subtle threats given with a smile, not this show of force. An unfamiliar feeling of gratitude washed over her. And pride that Dan was her friend.

When the man offered a ragged nod, Dan relented. He scrambled off the soldier and stood. "Thank you for letting me practice with you today," he said to the man's gaping companion. "I think I'll find another yard tomorrow."

Dan slumped a little as he walked away, and the bright color drained out of his face, leaving him deathly pale. Aiya rushed to his side, holding his good arm to help him stay upright.

"You shouldn't have done that."

"Maybe not." He winced.

"Let me see your arm."

"Not here. They might still be watching."

Aiya snorted gently at his pride, but obeyed. She led Dan into the surgeon's tent, then made him sit on a stool in the corner.

She frowned when she lifted his sleeve and found his dressing stained with blood.

"I wish you hadn't done that. Certainly not for me."

"It needed to be done. Men like that...well, it's best that you don't know what they're capable of."

Aiya laughed. "Oh, Dan. If only you knew me from another life, you wouldn't think you needed to protect me so."

Dan grunted. "I don't know about that. A fair lily that grows in a field of weeds is still a lily, isn't it?" He met her eyes, then turned away, blushing. "Someday I'd like to hear more of your story."

"Perhaps you shall," Aiya smiled. "But not yet. Because then I'll no longer be that fair lily you imagine me to be." She turned her attention back to unwinding the soiled dressing but worked with her mind full of lilies and a smile on her lips.

Merek would be hard pressed to admit it, but he actually enjoyed having Ria present for his captains' meetings. He thought at first that he'd ruined their friendship after that disastrous night where he'd confessed his heart to her. Kissing her had been the most heartbreaking thing he'd ever done. She'd been so stiff and cold—her lack of affection for him shockingly clear—that the kiss extinguished any lingering hope he'd had that she might care for him. At the same time, his resolve against marrying her had been strengthened. The thought of a lifetime of such unreturned affection made him ill.

The next few days had been painfully awkward as they were both unsure of how to treat each other. He'd hoped that she would decide to leave the camp and return to Albon, but now he was glad she hadn't. She'd become a welcome fixture in the command tent. She liked to tease and make light of things—him, specifically —but she never detracted from important conversations and always knew when it was time to listen and observe. When she shared her observations, they steered the discussion in productive ways. Merek found her presence a comfort in a way and missed her when she didn't attend.

At least, that's how he ordinarily felt. But this night she'd begun the evening cross, and her mood was not improving.

"Remind me again how half a dozen men are going to overwhelm the thousands who are occupying the city?" Ria asked in a critical tone, picking idly at the tines of a jeweled hair comb in her hand.

Merek and Rorden looked up from the map of Endvar before them. They'd been discussing the merits of an attack on each gate, trying to determine if seizing the eastern gate and cutting off the Ardanian support was most critical first, or if it would be wiser to seize control of the southern gate so that the Rahmish armies could flood the city. Ria had detached herself from the conversation, moving her chair to warm herself near the flaming brazier.

"There won't be thousands still in the city when our climbers attack," Merek said patiently, though she already knew this.

"Oh, that's right. Because you're going to sacrifice hundreds of your troops in a faux retreat, hoping that the Ardanians won't be able to resist coming out of the stronghold in full force in order to gain ground against us. It's really a shame that there isn't some other way to accomplish the same purpose without risking all those lives and potentially devastating my countrymen."

Merek could feel Rorden's questioning look. The bitterness in Ria's tone communicated more than her words did. They were the only three people in the tent.

He'd chosen the late hour intentionally so that they wouldn't be disturbed, but he was beginning to think it had been a mistake. Perhaps the princess would be more civil in the morning after a good night's rest.

"It's a calculated risk with acceptable losses."

"It's not acceptable to me, and it shouldn't be acceptable to you, either. You're not—" She glanced at Rorden and cut off.

Rorden coughed, a dry hacking sound that had worsened in recent days. The sound spoke of dreadful things to Merek; men being laid waste by long exposure to the cold of winter, their numbers dwindling from illness before they even reached the battlefield.

Ria turned her back on the men and moved nearer to the flame. As Rorden's coughing fit died down, Merek joined her. The firelight glinted off the jewels of the comb she held. Its twin was still embedded in her hair.

She followed his eyes and explained, "It was giving me a headache. This smoke doesn't help either."

The weather had turned cold enough that the braziers were almost always lit, providing much needed warmth but creating an almost permanent haze of smoke in the tent. The vents in the ceiling didn't work well when the tent flaps were laced up tight as they were now to guard against unwanted visitors.

Warming his cold hands at the fire, Merek said quietly. "We need to be able to trust each other, Ria, and that means speaking freely. Say what's troubling you."

"You're not thinking clearly, Merek. You know I'm right, and if I were one of your captains, you wouldn't hesitate. Sentimentality is clouding your judgement."

"Sentimentality?" Merek smiled. "I'm not sure anyone has ever accused me of that before. Well, Your Highness, *you* are the one who appointed me general. If you don't like the way I lead, you're welcome to appoint another instead."

"Maybe I will," Ria said, raising her chin to look at him with eyes brightened by the fire.

"Be my guest."

"In fact, you may pick him yourself."

"How generous of you."

"On our wedding day."

Merek froze.

A smile appeared on Ria's lips. "After all, as a new husband I'm sure you'll have more important things to engage your time."

How could she switch from irritation to saucy seduction so quickly? He couldn't respond to her challenge in front of Rorden, and she knew it.

Ria turned away from the fire. "Rorden, you're a clever man. If I told you that there was a way we could entice Prince Artem and his troops out of the city without putting our own soldiers at risk, what would you say?"

Rorden glanced between the two of them. His voice was rough from laborious coughing. "If it's as you say, I expect I would recommend such a course of action."

Ria shot a triumphant look at Merek.

"What the princess has failed to mention," Merek interjected, "is that she wants to use *herself* as bait to draw the enemy out of the city. But putting her safety at risk makes it an unacceptable option."

"Putting my safety at risk is exactly why it would work," Ria insisted. "Artem wouldn't be able to resist the opportunity, and he would bring troops with him to further strengthen his display of power."

They'd discussed this multiple times, and it always came down to the same thing. The very aspects of the plan which made Ria push it were the same aspects that caused Merek to reject it.

"The next queen of Rahm shouldn't be placing herself at risk. I will not yield on this."

Ria growled in frustration. "What good am I to my people if I don't do what I can to protect them? Don't think I don't see the hypocrisy. You risk yourself without hesitation, going out to battle with a head wound that hasn't ceased weeping and a shield arm that cannot bear a shield."

Merek opened his mouth to argue that he was experienced with taking risks in battle and improvising when things went awry, but Rorden spoke first.

"It's getting late. Maybe we should leave this matter and decide instead how to get a message to the north."

Welcoming the diversion, Merek returned to the table. Rather than just sending a courier to notify Stefan's men that they were needed, Merek wanted to choose someone he could trust to deliver memorized instructions with utmost secrecy. If Ria was correct in assuming that there were spies in the camp, he couldn't risk even a slight chance of the enemy finding out about the climbers. If they lost the element of surprise, it would be a quick slaughter.

You see, Ria, I do listen to you, he wanted to point out.

But she was acting churlish, and he didn't want to respond in kind. He did respect her courage in suggesting that she be the diversion they needed. It was misguided, but honorable all the same.

Ria joined the two men at the table, but her mood was sullen, and she contributed little to the discussion. Merek hadn't realized she'd fallen asleep in her chair—well, *his* chair—until she began snoring softly, her knees drawn up to her chest.

"Let's adjourn for the night." He stood, stifling a yawn, and Rorden rubbed his bloodshot eyes.

"Will I be joining you tomorrow, sir?"

"No. Continue our work from tonight. I don't want these documents to leave your person, do you understand? And," he added as an afterthought. "See the apothecary about that cough, will you?"

"Yes, sir."

After Rorden left, Merek turned back to the sleeping princess. She carried such a heavy burden for someone so young. Though, he realized, when he was her age he was already a sergeant and well on his way to becoming captain. Perhaps he was unfairly punishing her for her youth and inexperience.

But no, it was right that he wanted to protect her. What kind of man would intentionally send the woman he loved into harm's way? They would have to find another way.

Merek tidied the papers on the table, selecting the more sensitive ones to burn in the brazier. As the paper caught fire, brightening the room with flashes of light, Ria stirred in her sleep.

She gasped, a panicked look in her eyes. "Oh!" she said, blinking rapidly as if unsure of where she was.

Merek fought a smile. "Rough sleep?"

Ria settled back into her chair. "I had a most disturbing dream. More a memory, actually." She shuddered and fell silent, but her expression was still troubled.

"Would you like to talk about it?"

"It was nothing. Just a girl I saw on the streets of Rellana." She paused for a long moment before continuing. "She had no nose. I think she might have been beautiful once, but her nose...it was just gone. It was a ghastly sight. I was with Tollana, the younger princess, and she was so appalled at the sight of this young woman that she ordered the guards to remove her from our view. Toll was usually so tender-hearted that I was stunned by such cruelty. I told her so when next we were alone. That's when I learned that it was shame that caused her to react in such a way. Not shame for herself, but for her older brother, Artem."

Ria yawned and stretched, then hugged her knees again, tucked up under her long skirts. Her gaze was distant. "Artem was possessive of the women that he...kept. When he grew tired of them, he disfigured them in some way so that no other man would want them. The more fond he was of one, the more hideous he would leave her."

Merek felt a wave of disgust for the blond prince with his strong jaw. He watched the last of the papers curl and blacken, listening to Ria's story.

"Those who survived were marked forever as once

belonging to him. Ironically, this gave them a kind of infamy. Disfigured as they were, they nonetheless commanded the highest prices in their trade. Other girls began to mar themselves to pretend that they too had been wanted by the prince. Eventually the king learned of it and confronted his son, putting an end to the practice, at least as far as Toll knew. It was then," Ria said drily, "that I began to doubt Artem's suitability as a husband...handsome face and clever words notwithstanding."

In the silence that followed, Merek asked, "And this is the man whom you trust to honor a flag of truce and guarantee your safety?"

Ria sat up straighter in her chair. "I don't trust him. I will never trust him. But I trust *you*, and if you're with me I know that he won't harm me."

Her words pleased him even as they frightened him.

"I wouldn't be with you. With so few climbers, it's best if I join them."

Ria narrowed her eyes. "I see," she said flatly. "Of course, I should have guessed. You'll rush into danger at the first opportunity. The more risky, the better because who is going to tell you 'no?'"

Merek sighed. "It's late, Ria. We both need rest. Let's discuss this another time." He reached for her cloak and pulled out her chair so that she could stand.

"Are you throwing me out of your tent, Captain Strong?" Her eyes glittered.

"As delicately as possible, Princess. And it's General Strong now."

"Hmm, I don't see a general's uniform." She eyed his

captain's coat critically, then turned her back to him and held out her arms for her cloak. "Besides, you'll always be Captain Strong to me. The hero who saved a princess hiding for her life."

Merek draped the cloak around her shoulders, brushing away a strand of hair that had come free before it could be trapped by the heavy fur trim.

She turned around to face him, her eyes pleading. "I want to do this. Let me draw Artem out of the city, making it safer for you and the climbers. We can end this together and go home before it's time to light the New Year lanterns."

It was hard to face her fury, but this begging was even worse. Merek closed his eyes and ran his hand through his unkempt hair.

"Perhaps I *am* being sentimental. Tactically, there's much about your suggestion that makes sense. But when I think about giving you into the hands of that... that man...I think I could give up anything else if it means keeping you away from him."

"Even letting Rahm fall?"

"I wouldn't let that happen."

"You can't do it all, Merek," Ria said firmly. "You can't save the world and protect everyone you love all by yourself, and I refuse to watch you destroy yourself trying. You may be my general, but I'm still your queen. Or, almost," she added with a half smile.

She left him there alone with the dying embers. As the cold of the night closed in around him, he reflected on her words and wondered if she meant them as a promise, or a threat.

TWENTY-FIVE

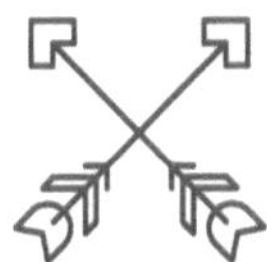

Count Orlin, Ardanian Ambassador to Rahm, was not suited to life in prison. In the month since he'd been arrested, his complexion had paled to an ashy hue, and he'd lost enough weight to accentuate his already pronounced features. His nose now looked hawkish on his gaunt face as he entered Talen's office, and his sharp eyes darting around the room only strengthened Talen's impression of a dangerous bird of prey.

"Good day to you, my lord," Talen said with a brief nod. "Please, come sit by the fire and warm yourself. You're alone today?"

A sigh of pleasure escaped Orlin's lips as he settled himself into the proffered chair. "It is amazing how one appreciates the small comforts after being denied them so long."

"With all due respect, sir, you have been denied very

little. If Vinter brings one more rug or cushion, we'll have to move you to a larger cell."

"Do you have any larger cells?" Orlin perked up at this.

"No," Talen scoffed. "Where is Vinter today?" Talen didn't care for Orlin's aide and the conniving way he'd backed Talen into a corner, insisting that because Count Orlin hadn't been stripped of his diplomatic status by the king, he was still entitled to the hospitality afforded the office of ambassador. Once Talen had conceded to a change of clothes and a fur rug, Vinter had expanded that to include a mattress, padded stools, an upholstered chair, a writing desk, and various improvements to the ambassador's diet.

Yet, still Orlin dwindled. As his flesh seemed to fade, however, his mind was sharper than ever.

"Vinter is on an errand for me. It will just be the two of us today."

"You don't wish our conversation to be transcribed? How will you add it to your grievances with which to petition the king?" Talen lightened his tone with humor, but in truth, Orlin's growing documentation of his treatment in the prison did concern him. The princess had ordered Orlin's imprisonment and then promptly left the city. Talen feared that if Orlin ever secured the attention of the king, he might have a hard time justifying the lengthy imprisonment without the princess there to offer her support.

Orlin rubbed his hands before the fire. "You and I both know that the king will not hear my petition. My sources tell me that he has refused food and drink and turns away all visitors, even you."

"Something tells me that you aren't simply giving up your appeal."

"No. No, I'm not. But I am coming to realize that I need to address my grievances to someone who has the power to do something about it."

"Not the king?"

"Nor you either, I'm afraid." Orlin said. "No, I see now you are only a puppet whose master has cut the strings. I am making my appeal to the highest authority—excuse me, the highest *functioning* authority—in this land."

A knock sounded on Talen's door, and he glanced up in surprise. His aides knew better than to disturb him when he was questioning the ambassador. Orlin, however, smiled as if this interruption were expected.

"Come!" Talen commanded. When the door opened, it revealed Vinter's face, but only for a moment. Satisfied that his master waited inside, Vinter ducked aside and held the door open as Lord Hegrin swept into the room.

"My lord!" Talen blurted, coming to his feet. "What brings you here?"

Lord Hegrin filled the room as much with his haughty air as the voluminous layers of fine fabrics that hung from his shoulders. He didn't seem surprised to see Count Orlin.

"Captain Talen, it has come to my attention that a political ally is being held here against his will. As a concerned member of the king's court, I've made it my aim to investigate."

"Count Orlin's imprisonment was ordered by the princess herself."

"Indeed. Where is the arrest warrant that I may examine its veracity?"

Talen bristled. "With all due respect, I'm under no obligation to share it with you, my lord."

Lord Hegrin's thin lips tightened. "You needn't be so testy, Captain. I merely wish to be of service. In the princess's absence, and with the king indisposed, it's important that diplomatic relations be tended with care. Don't you agree?"

"Diplomacy is not my concern, my lord."

"Precisely my point."

"If I might be of help," Orlin said, rising to his feet with a steadying hand resting on the back of his chair. "Lord Hegrin only wishes to provide some much needed oversight to my detention. If he were in possession of all the facts—"

"I'm the one who provides oversight here," Talen said firmly. "Lord Hegrin's presence is not required. Until I'm informed otherwise by her Royal Highness, it would be grossly inappropriate to discuss these matters with him present."

Hegrin's eyes narrowed, but Talen held his gaze steadily. He feared he was walking a thin line by disrespecting the nobleman, but he also knew that Hegrin held no authority over him. Unfortunately, during the princess's absence, he wasn't sure it mattered.

"I'm disappointed, Captain. Perhaps you don't fully understand my position. Would you care to discuss it over dinner this evening?"

"I'm afraid not."

"Very well. Another time then, perhaps." Hegrin turned to Orlin and offered a small nod. "If there's anything I might do to assist in your comfort, please do not hesitate to send word."

Orlin thanked him and turned back to Talen with a look of triumph in his eyes as Lord Hegrin stalked out of the room. Talen felt that something important had just taken place, but he wasn't sure just what it meant. It was an unpleasant sensation, so he settled back in his chair and tried to look more confident than he felt.

"It's not wise for you to make enemies with someone as powerful as Lord Hegrin," the ambassador chided.

"It's not wise to let him wipe his dirty boots on me either, as he seemed to expect."

"He is uniquely poised to make your life very difficult if he so desires."

"How do you figure that?"

Count Orlin stroked his long nose. "Have you not considered how important Lord Hegrin would become if something were to happen to the princess?"

Talen looked at him sharply. Did he mean it as a threat? "Lord Hegrin's son could make a claim to the throne, but so could half a dozen other nobles who trace their lineage back to Albon the Great through other lines."

"But none of those nobles are as ambitious or powerful as Lord Hegrin. It may be his son who claims royal blood, but you can believe that the father would be very well served to see his son take the throne."

"It's highly unlikely. The princess is in good health,

and as soon as she marries, Hegrin's claim will be insubstantial."

"Is that right?" Orlin's eyes glinted. "Unless, of course, there are those who would oppose the princess's choice. If she were to choose, for example, a commoner who was recently condemned a traitor, there may be those who would rather see the likes of Lord Hegrin come to power."

Talen's spine stiffened. "What's this?"

Orlin shrugged. "Perhaps it's nothing, but I've heard rumors that the very man the princess has named to replace General Grammel has also gained her hand in marriage. An old friend of yours, I believe? Captain Strong has certainly risen far from his humble beginnings."

Talen held very still to avoid betraying his surprise. It irked him that Count Orlin was still obviously well connected despite being in prison. "If that's the case, then I'm sure all of Rahm will rejoice at the news. He's a good man and a loyal servant of the crown."

"Perhaps. But a word of caution, if I may," Orlin said, rising to his feet. "These are uncertain times for your people, with your king withdrawn to his tower and the threat of war in the land. They'll be looking for a strong leader who can assume the throne unencumbered by scandal or the taint of madness. Under the circumstances, it would be wise to not make enemies of important people."

"I can understand why you didn't wish to have this conversation recorded by your clerk," Talen said in disgust. "If you were not already under arrest, what you've said here would be enough to hold you on suspicions of conspiring against the throne."

Again, Count Orlin shrugged. "And yet I *am* already under arrest, so there is nothing for me to lose by speaking the truth."

But what are you trying to gain? Talen wondered to himself as he summoned a guard to escort the ambassador back to his cell. Why align himself with Lord Hegrin? Did he truly think the people would reject the princess if she chose to marry Captain Strong? And could the rumor be true, or was it merely the ambassador's creation?

Alone, Talen permitted himself a small smile. When Strong had been imprisoned, Talen had suspected there might be more to his relationship with the princess than he'd admitted. It appeared Talen was right after all. He would have no trouble recognizing Strong as the future king, and with a king's pardon, surely the scandal Count Orlin referred to would not materialize. Would it?

Of one thing Talen was certain. He needed to find out what was really going on, preferably from a source more reliable than a disgruntled ambassador with suspicious intent.

Twenty-Six

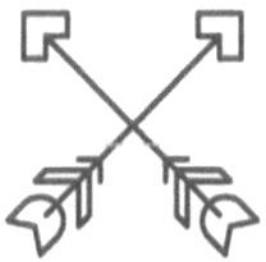

"Rider approaching!"

Rorden squinted into the distance. The forest was a shapeless mass on the other side of the valley. Clouds hung low against the treetops, and a few white flakes fell from the leaden sky. It had turned unseasonably cold, and the air bit his lungs with each breath.

There was motion against the trees, a rider bearing Alrek's mark. Rorden followed General Strong to meet him, with two of the newly appointed first captains on their heels.

The rider reined to a stop when he recognized the general. His horse was panting from the hard ride, steam rising from its glistening neck.

"Captain Alrek has gained the bridge, sir, but he's struggling to hold it. His men are faltering, and if he doesn't receive reinforcements soon, it will be lost."

"What of Captain Salvin?"

"No sign of him, sir."

"He may have been caught in the ravine," Captain Audon said at Rorden's left.

Strong grunted. "Send a company to find out what happened to Salvin. If the ravine is impassible, have them circle around on the other side of the village. They'll have lost the element of surprise, but it's too late for that now."

"Yes, sir," Audon replied crisply. His eyes were bright with the anticipation of joining the fight. He returned to where his lower captains were waiting, men who had once been officers in the Wall Guard. The sound of his deep voice rang out over the valley as he barked orders to his men.

Strong turned back to the rider. "Do you know whether Orri's men have reached the promontory?"

"Yes, sir. They're clearing it without significant resistance."

"Good. Thank you, soldier."

This news cheered Rorden. It was the first time in days that they'd gained ground against the enemy. Now if they could just hold it long enough to wait for the additional troops the general had summoned from around the kingdom.

The sharp sound of a horn rolled across the hills. At the same time a flag appeared on the nearest rise. Rorden swore softly, glancing at his commander. He'd hoped it wouldn't come to this.

Rorden watched the signals, parsing out the message from a distance. "Additional enemy troops are on the move, sir," he said. "At least two thousand have left Endvar."

General Strong slammed his helm down over his face. "Eldar!" he growled, turning his horse.

"Here, sir!"

"Are your men in position?"

"Yes, sir."

"I know you were hoping they would get a respite today, but we need them now."

"Yes, sir." The captain gave the order and another horn sounded, this time from close at hand. Far in the trees, out of sight where they stood, a signal would be passed on to Eldar's men to come out of hiding and engage the new enemy troops.

But they wouldn't go alone. Riding back to where the rest of the army waited, Strong shouted, "Captain Firl! Come. We ride to Alrek's aid."

The men shouted their approval as the call went through the ranks. The order was given, and as one the foot soldiers set off at a steady pace, the mounted cavalry behind them waiting restlessly to begin their march.

Rorden watched the host until they'd skirted around the trees and disappeared from view. He felt a keen mixture of envy and relief. There was a part of him that wanted to be in the midst of battle, fighting alongside his fellow soldiers. But there was an increasingly larger part of him that preferred discussing strategy and tactics with General Strong over engaging in the actual conflict. He was a respectable soldier, he knew, but seeing a battle as pieces of a whole, that was a gift. And what's more, General Strong trusted him.

Trusted him with things he didn't trust anyone else with. That was worth more than all the renown in the world.

The last of the units had gone out with Strong, so Rorden joined the other stragglers and support staff in heading back to camp. His first stop was the tailor who had fitted the new general for his uniform. Although General Strong hadn't complained—Rorden suspected he felt sentimental about the Wall Guard blue and wasn't in a hurry to give it up—Rorden had thought the delay unconscionable and told the tailor so.

Next, he visited the draper. Aiya had helped him choose fabrics for the general's banner, and Rorden was delighted to see it almost finished. Strong had been surprisingly disinterested in Rorden's designs. Perhaps he hadn't yet considered that when he became king, his crest could very well supplant the Thorodan crest that had flown over Albon for generations. Not at first, of course. But someday, perhaps.

That thought excited Rorden more than any other. Living in Albon among luxury, serving the future king, and possibly being able to properly court Biren. They would see a lot more of each other if he accompanied the general to the capital. If not, Albon was full of promising young women who would be eager for his attentions.

The future king.

Rorden smiled to himself. He'd been shocked to hear the words come out of the princess's mouth. And he wasn't the only one. Whatever agreement existed between the two of them, judging by General Strong's reaction, the princess had spoken out of turn. She was going to keep the general's life interesting, that was certain.

Rorden hadn't decided what to make of their relationship. There didn't seem to be an increase in tenderness or affection between the two of them. If anything, there was a—perhaps not *coldness*, but at least a stiffness between them in recent days. Rorden shook his head. He couldn't begin to understand the motivations in a relationship like that. But it wasn't his place to judge, was it? As long as he got to be a part of the general's new royal life, he wouldn't complain.

It was with these thoughts on his mind that he entered the command tent, but it wasn't empty as he'd expected. Princess Honoria stood alone at the table, a sheet of paper in her hand.

"Your Highness!" Rorden blurted in surprise. "I didn't expect you."

She smiled when she looked up, but her eyes narrowed briefly as she looked past him. "You're alone, then?"

"Yes, my lady. The general won't return for some time."

The princess sighed, and her expression darkened. "Was it too much to hope that he would wait to go to battle until he'd properly healed?"

"You needn't worry, my lady. His injuries aren't serious."

Her lips twitched. "Ah, that's the crux of it, isn't it? As long as a man can walk and drag a sword, he's fit for duty. I suppose that it's a common enough sentiment for you soldiers, but I'm still getting accustomed to it."

Rorden wasn't sure what to say. Did she seek his reassurance? She didn't seem fretful, though. More...pensive.

"Is there something I can help you with?"

She fixed her dark eyes on him in an appraising look. "In fact, there is. I've been waiting for an opportunity to speak to you alone."

Rorden wiped his nose, trying desperately not to fidget under her gaze.

"Tell me about this," she said, waving the sheet of paper she held.

Rorden recognized it immediately. His mouth went dry. He'd been so proud of his design, but under the critical eye of the princess it seemed rustic and unpolished.

"The general needs a crest now, Your Highness. Serving with the Wall Guard, none was ever required."

"I don't recognize this style."

"It's patterned after the weaving styles of the north. I spent time there over the summer and thought it was fitting."

"It doesn't look much like the other noble crests."

"With all due respect, my lady, that's the point. General Strong isn't from a noble family. To design a crest that mimics nobility seemed inappropriate."

Her eyes flashed. "Inappropriate? To design a noble crest for the man who will be king someday? You disappoint me, Sergeant. I thought you had more respect for General Strong."

"It's not a matter of respect, my lady," Rorden insisted. "Or rather, it is, but not in the way you think. Please, if I may speak freely?"

"I'm listening."

"In my youth, my father entertained many noble families when they traveled to our coastal city. Forgive me, but I usually found them selfish, proud, and incapable of understanding life outside their own privileged experience. When word spreads that our future king comes from the most humble background, there will be many—particularly in the noble class—who will see it as a personal offense that you've chosen a commoner. They'll see it as a betrayal of the loyalty they've shown the crown for so many generations. It may be very difficult for some of the people to accept him."

"So you wish to highlight his common beginnings? Flaunt his shortcomings? How will that help?"

Rorden coughed, the pain of it deep in his chest. "Patterning General Strong's crest after the accepted pattern for noble families would look like we're trying to hide his common status. Instead, I think we should emphasize that he's not one of them. Make it clear that you prefer him over all the nobles in the kingdom, and you're not ashamed of who he is."

The princess tapped her lower lip thoughtfully. "The gossip would be as fast and fierce as a wildfire."

"But it would burn away quickly because there would be nothing more to fuel it. Much would depend on you, my lady. If you can embrace who he is, instead of trying to make him be something he's not, the people will follow your lead."

She looked at him closely. Perhaps he'd been too bold. But he'd given this much thought, and she'd given him permission to speak freely.

"I think I'm beginning to see why General Strong values you, Sergeant," the princess said, her face relaxing.

Rorden smiled, feeling a surge of pride and relief. "Thank you, Your Highness."

"Now I need you to do something for me. You heard the general's words last night. He's making decisions based on concern for me rather than strategic advantage. He admitted as much himself."

Rorden's smile faded. This was a conflict he didn't want to be caught in. "If he won't listen to you, Your Highness, I don't expect I'll be able to change his mind."

"I don't want you to change his mind. I want you to help me contact Prince Artem. It must seem official, as if the general and I are united. Once the invitation is accepted, Merek can't stop it from happening."

Rorden recoiled from the thought. "I can't be party to such behavior, Your Highness."

"Why? You agree that the diversion would be far more effective in drawing Artem out of the city. I can see it in your eyes. Help me make it happen."

"You're asking me to betray General Strong's trust."

"I'm asking you to do what he would do himself if he were thinking with his head instead of his heart. Taking back the city is vital to cutting off Artem's reinforcements. Think of the lives that will be saved!"

Rorden turned away for another coughing fit. Princess Honoria frowned. "Winter has come early. How much success can we hope to have if our numbers dwindle due to illness? The sooner we take back Endvar, the sooner we can end this conflict!"

"Not like this." Rorden shook his head. "Not through deceit or forcing the general's hand."

Her lips turned down in disapproval. "You refuse to help me, then? I'm disappointed in you."

"No, I don't think you are," Rorden said, taking a chance in a last attempt to avoid alienating her. "With all due respect, Your Highness, I think you wouldn't want it any other way. You wouldn't want a man in my position being so easily influenced to betray the general."

It was a gamble, but something flickered in her eyes and a smile tugged at the corners of her mouth.

"Perhaps. Rest assured that I'll remember this conversation, Sergeant."

Rorden felt an easing of the tension. He knew that he was right to refuse, but how did one refuse a princess? He shuddered to think of how much harder it would be when she was queen. Getting caught in domestic squabbles between two such powerful people would not be pleasant.

One of the guards posted at the entrance ducked into the tent. "Forgive the interruption," he said, addressing the princess. "There's a woman here to see the general. When I told her he wasn't here, she asked to speak with Sergeant Rorden."

The princess looked cross for only a moment, then nodded. "I'm sure whatever business she has can be completed quickly. Please send her in."

Aiya entered the tent, but hesitated when she saw the princess. Rorden greeted her with a smile and tried to ease her discomfort.

"How have you been, Aiya? The general will be sorry he wasn't here to see you. It seems we don't get to see you much anymore."

Aiya smiled in return, her lovely brown skin flawless even after weeks in a rough army camp.

"You're far too important now, Rorden," she teased. "I apologize for interrupting. I wanted to see the general, but perhaps it's better this way. You can tell me if I have cause to be concerned, or if I'm just being a fool."

With a nervous glance at the princess, she continued. "Dan is healing well, but he still has great lengths to go. I fear that he hasn't considered his future. He sees the troops going out each day and waits for his turn. I don't want to be the one to tell him that there's no place in the army for a one-armed man. But someone must, don't you think?"

Princess Honoria listened with interest as Aiya spoke. "You speak of Sergeant Dan? The officer who saved Merek—Captain Strong's life when Grammel fell?"

"Yes, my lady," Aiya replied.

"From what I've heard of this man, he's as loyal and courageous as you could ever hope to find. Isn't that right, Rorden?"

"Yes, I suppose."

Rorden was puzzled to see her eyes alight with excitement.

"He seems to think that he's the same soldier he was before," Aiya continued. "I fear that someday when the truth comes crashing down on him, it will crush him.

But the longer we let him pretend, the heavier that truth will be."

"If his fight to be battle-ready is keeping him going, I'm not going to take that from him," Rorden said. "Better to face bitter disappointment when he's stronger, don't you think?"

"But he needs to finish healing. He's pushing himself to learn to fight with his left hand, with no shield, when what he should be doing is resting."

"I don't know this Dan," the princess interjected, "but I'd like to make his acquaintance. It must be very frustrating to feel like you're the only one who has nothing to contribute." She looked pointedly at Rorden, but he felt that he was missing an important cue. Was she speaking of herself? "A man with that much determination is surely one who could be trusted to do anything asked of him with complete discretion, don't you think, Rorden?"

Something clicked in Rorden's mind, and he finally understood the princess's meaning.

"Yes, indeed, Your Highness. Aiya, we may have an assignment for Dan that would allow him to continue healing while still giving him something worthwhile to do. Not only worthwhile, but of extreme importance. Do you think he's well enough to travel?"

SHADOWS GATHERED AROUND CAMP AS DUSK FELL, MUTING colors and bringing with it the feeling of homesickness that Ria frequently felt when she contemplated another cold night with little more than thin canvas keeping her from the elements. But she returned to her tent with an inner smile, pleased about the direction things had gone with Aiya and Sergeant Dan. Not only was Dan proud to have purpose again, but Ria recognized a tenderness in Aiya's manner toward him that gave her an unexpected feeling of satisfaction.

At last she had done something useful.

And it wouldn't be the last time. Rorden had refused to help her send word to the Ardanians, which complicated things. It would have been simpler with his assistance, but she could manage without him. She was the future queen, after all. She didn't answer to Rorden or Merek or anyone else. If she wanted to arrange a meeting with Artem, that was her right.

She'd have to act quickly, before Merek returned. She didn't trust Rorden to keep their conversation confidential, and once Merek learned of it, he would try to stop her. But Merek wasn't in camp and likely wouldn't return for a day or two. By then, it would be too late.

Ria found Biren visiting with Sergeant Brandel outside her tent, a basket on one hip showing that she was returning from the laundry. They didn't see her at first, and Brandel's smile was unguarded and relaxed. *If you look past the balding hair, he's actually quite handsome,* Ria realized with amusement. *If Rorden isn't careful, he may have competition.* Unsurprising. The other women in camp were artisans, tradeswomen, and members of the peasant class. None of them approached Biren's level of refinement.

But refinement didn't lend itself well to danger.

Biren paled when Ria told her about her plan. "My lady, I don't feel comfortable with you putting yourself in harm's way."

The three of them stood inside Ria's tent as daylight faded outside, a solitary lamp casting dramatic shadows against the canvas walls.

"The danger is minimal," Ria said more confidently than she felt. "It's a small risk if it means we can take back Endvar."

"I have to agree with Lady Biren," Brandel said, his brows drawn together with concern. "Your Highness, if you insist on approaching the Ardanian camp, let me muster up a larger escort to ensure your safety."

Ria shook her head. "It won't do. A larger escort would only alarm them. One squad only."

"Then allow us to deliver the message for you," Brandel suggested. "You can stay here rather than putting yourself at risk."

"Without my presence, they won't take the message seriously. It must get to Artem directly, not be discarded by some lower captain who thinks it's a ruse. Besides, I speak their language fluently whereas I assume you don't?"

"But my lady," Biren interjected. "Don't you think you should wait and consult with General Strong? He's far more experienced than you in matters of war and surely would have a safer approach."

Ria suppressed a grimace. From Biren it would never be intended as an insult, but she was tired of being told that Merek knew better than she did. "In this matter,

Strong is wrong, and I can't wait for him to listen to reason. We must act tonight. Can I count on you both?"

Brandel looked at her and nodded reluctantly. "I'll do whatever I can to protect you, Your Highness, but I still don't agree with your methods."

"Noted. Biren?"

Biren bit her lower lip. "I merely fear for your safety, but I'll do as you ask."

"Thank you. We'll simply approach a lowly sentry on the far outskirts of the camp, allow him to be assured of my identity, and deliver my request for a meeting. By the time he recovers from his surprise and thinks to notify his superior, we'll have disappeared into the darkness again. If all goes well, we'll return long before daybreak. If not, Biren, you will notify Rorden to mount a rescue."

"As you wish, my lady," Biren said miserably.

Ria looked away from her maid's worried expression, suppressing her own uncertainties. She felt a thrill to be doing something meaningful at last. She would not let Biren's caution prick her with doubts now.

TWENTY-SEVEN

It took longer to find a suitable mount than Ria expected. By the time Sergeant Brandel returned with a horse, Ria was fidgeting with anxiety. Biren had found a pair of trousers which Ria wore under her gown. She opted to keep her gown in order to appear as regal as possible, but there were no side saddles in camp and the trousers would be necessary so that she could sit astride comfortably with her skirts bunched around her.

Deep night had descended when she and Brandel rode quietly into the trees behind her tent with half a dozen soldiers surrounding them in a guard formation. The soldiers were unknown to her, but Brandel had assured her that they were trustworthy. They circled the army camp, not to avoid the sentries posted at the perimeter—the guards let them pass without comment —but rather to avoid the attention they would have attracted moving through the main part of camp. Biren would sound the alarm if they didn't return by daylight, but Ria didn't want to alert anyone prematurely. If all went well, they would return in a few hours none the worse for wear with events set in motion that would bring about the end of the war.

Riding around the camp took much longer than if they had passed straight through, but with every jingle of bridle or snort of the horses, Ria was glad they'd taken this longer route. They moved through the trees, staying close to the edge of the forest to be less visible as they skirted the open fields.

While waiting for Rorden the day before, Ria had had plenty of time to examine the maps with which Merek had planned their most recent assault. She knew regaining the Hoggen bridge would give them a strategic advantage, but it was a little less clear how an indirect approach through the neighboring ravine was better than the more obvious route through the wider valley. However, she didn't need to know the strategy behind his tactics. She only needed to know where the current fighting was taking place so that she could avoid running into Merek.

At this thought, a wave of trepidation passed through her. Was she doing the right thing, going behind his back like this and forcing his hand? Immediately she was filled with indignation. She wouldn't need to force his hand if he would listen to her. When she had turned the tide of the war, he would—begrudgingly, she was sure—admit that it was worth the risk.

The little entourage left the valley and ascended a small grassy hill, making Ria glad to be riding astride as she gripped with her knees to hold steady in the saddle.

She didn't trust her horse. The young stallion shifted uneasily beneath her, as if sensing her discomfort. She wished there had been time to find a nice docile gelding in the camp.

As they began their descent, Ria looked up at the sky where clouds had parted to reveal a mosaic of stars. The light was welcome, but the extra chill was not. The night air bit at her nose, and she was grateful for the warm muffler wrapped around her neck and ears. Even with the extra layers and her heaviest ermine cloak, she struggled to keep her teeth from chattering.

As if reading her mind, Brandel asked, "Are you all right, Your Highness? If you wish to turn back, it's not too late."

"Not at all, Sergeant. It's merely the cold. How much further until we reach the river?" The thought of wading through the icy water made her cringe, but Brandel had assured her that he could manage both horses and she needn't dismount for the crossing.

"Not far now," Brandel answered. "On the other side of that ridge to the left is the Hoggen bridge. We'll stay to the right and skirt around that far hill where the Vifar widens out."

Ria nodded, thinking of the map she had examined yesterday. She wondered if Merek was on the other side of the hill with his troops right at that moment. Had he succeeded in pushing the Ardanians back and securing the bridge? It would be a significant victory for the Rahmish.

But not as significant as they would have if her plan worked. If Artem agreed to meet with her and they sent climbers into the city while his back was turned, they would only need to seize one gate to have a good chance of taking back all of Endvar without a long and costly siege.

It's the right thing to do, she repeated to herself, trying to ignore the niggling doubt which suggested otherwise. There was a small part of her that protested that a future queen shouldn't be sneaking behind her general's back. This sort of a decision should be made together, not in secret with a small cohort of conspirators.

As they skirted around the last hill, the bulky outline of Endvar came into view, silhouetted against the night sky. Braziers burned at sentry posts along the wall, but other than that the city lay dark. In the foreground, the sight of tents rising in clusters around glowing fires made Ria's heart beat faster.

The Ardanian camp.

Her throat went dry, and Ria suddenly balked at the sight of her enemy. But her horse moved relentlessly forward, following Brandel's lead. Ria resisted the urge to pull on the reins and flee back the way they had come. This was her plan. She would see it through even though her heart pounded in her ears and she felt sick with it.

It was understandable she was nervous. It didn't mean she was making a mistake.

Her horse sidled in agitation beneath her.

The Vifar river spread out below them as a dark gash in the land, the last barrier between her and the enemy army. Brandel reined his horse in, and the other soldiers gathered closer for instruction.

"There's a sandbar about a quarter mile that way,"

Brandel said quietly. "We'll cross there and approach the camp through those trees. They'll keep us hidden until the last moment."

Ria peered into the dark but couldn't distinguish many details. She was grateful for Brandel's calm when she felt jittery in her skin. They moved quietly toward the river bottom with Brandel and two other soldiers in the lead, four more bringing up the rear. Thick trees lined the banks and leaned out over the water. Soon the ground sloped gently to a wide sandbar that sat like a pale streak in the starlight.

The sound of moving water grew louder as they moved out from the cover of trees. Brandel stopped at the edge of the sandbar and dismounted.

"Here we go," Brandel whispered. "Give me your reins, and I'll lead the horses across."

Ria obediently handed over her reins, hoping her horse would be steady. She grabbed the pommel, jolting from side to side with each step of her horse.

If the cold water shocked Brandel, he gave no sign of it. He simply murmured soothingly to the horses as they moved through the water. When water splashed into her boot and ran down her ankle, Ria stifled a yelp and lifted her feet. She tucked them against the body of the horse, feeling distinctly foolish.

What was she doing, sneaking through a black river in the middle of the night with only a handful of guards and the enemy a stone's throw away? She was no spy. She couldn't even manage the discomfort of a little cold water. She glanced up at the sentry fires of the Ardanian camp. It wasn't too late to turn back. The only harm would be to her pride. Brandel and Biren would be discreet. Merek would never have to know what she'd attempted.

They reached the other shore, and Ria grasped for her horse's mane as he scrambled up the bank. *I'm having misgivings*, she would say to Brandel. *Perhaps we should reconsider.*

But just as they emerged onto the beach, a shape rose out of the darkness and darted toward them.

"Brandel!" Ria cried as her horse tossed his head against the threat.

Another shape ran toward the soldier on her right and Ria's horse shied away. She gripped the pommel tighter, trying to stay upright.

There was a grating sound of sliding steel as a man shouted in Ardanian, "Grab the woman! I'll get the horses."

Brandel was caught between the horses with no free hand to draw his weapon.

In a moment of quick decision, he tossed Ria's reins back at her and ordered, "Flee! As fast as you can, and don't look back!" Then he yanked her mount hard on the bridle and slapped him on the shoulder.

The moment cost him.

One of the shadowy figures was on Brandel in a moment, knocking him to the ground. Ria's guard closed in tighter, and she couldn't see Brandel or his attackers. Her eyes strained against the darkness.

"This way!" a soldier directed from behind.

Her hands fumbled, searching for the reins, her heart pounding in her throat. Another shadow loomed out of the night, and her horse reared. Ria shrieked, grabbing his mane and clinging with all her might.

A man beside her—Rahmish or Ardanian?—cried out in pain.

A space opened nearby, and Ria's skittish horse bolted down the beach, away from the fighting.

"After her!" a man shouted in Ardanian.

More shapes with glinting blades lunged for her out of the trees, faceless under hoods. Cold water splashed against her legs as the stallion stepped into the shallow water, rearing again. She could hear nothing over the desperate sound of his whinnies...could think of nothing more than trying to keep her seat.

One man grabbed her leg, and she kicked out, trying to shake it free. Hands reached for Ria on the other side —two, four maybe, they moved too fast—seizing her and trying to pull her from the saddle. She fought against them, but they were too strong.

She grabbed for her knife, but her fingers were stiff with cold, and it slipped out of her grip. She kicked as someone hauled her to the ground, but her foot only hit water, spraying it ineffectually. Ria writhed against the man who held her, and he tightened his grip painfully, pulling her toward the beach.

Just as they stepped out of the water something hit against her hard, knocking her to the ground and pushing the air from her lungs. Cold sand pressed against her face and hands as she pushed herself up. Steel scraped against steel and thudded against flesh.

Someone was fighting with her attackers.

Someone had come to her rescue.

She scrambled out of the way. Faintly, she could just make out Brandel's balding head. She thought she recognized others of her escort but couldn't be sure.

Her attackers had forgotten her for the moment, distracted by Brandel and the others. Ria hurried to her feet and lunged blindly for her horse, but he tossed his head and jerked away. Blessedly, the reins brushed against her fingers and she seized them, pulling against his thrashing head with a strength she didn't know she possessed.

"Go, my lady!" Brandel called. "Run—" This last word was punctuated with a hard grunt.

Ria scrambled to find a stirrup, but it was too late. Rough hands grabbed her and pulled her away from her horse.

She screamed involuntarily. This was not supposed to happen. She had a plan. No one was supposed to get hurt.

"I have her," a deep voice said in Ardanian, clamping his hand over her mouth.

"The others?" another voice answered.

"All dead but this one."

All dead? The scuffling behind Ria ended with a thump and a moan. She twisted to see what was going on, but the hands which held her were too strong.

"Bring them both. Captain Mischa will want to see what we found."

"The last of the wagons are loaded, sir."

"Already?"

"Most of the wounded are Ardanians. Our troops fared far better."

"Well then." That was something. Merek looked out over the valley where Endvar lay cold and dark. He'd climbed this ridge while Eldar's men saw to the fallen, taking advantage of the respite from the cries of the dying. In the dark, the task of seeking out the wounded from among the dead could take longer than the actual battle. It was a grim task, and one which Merek was glad to leave to those of lower rank.

"Gather the Ardanian wounded to claim as prisoners. Alrek can escort them back to camp. His men deserve the break after their fight today."

Eldar and Firl's troops had strengthened Alrek's men just in time to hold the bridge, and when night had fallen the Ardanians had pulled back. The reprieve had given Alrek's forces a chance to withdraw, leaving the bridge in the hands of fresh men. It was a victory, but still Merek felt disappointed. He'd hoped that the crucial bridge battle would have drawn Prince Artem out of his stronghold, but neither success nor failure had yet enticed him out.

In the distance, faint pinpricks of light illuminated the enemy's camp. It wasn't a large force on this side of the city, only a few thousand. More were in the city proper, and spies reported that a larger host camped on the Ardanian side of the border.

Merek thought he could make out the turrets that marked Lord Ogmun's estate and felt a twist of grief thinking of the kind man and his wife who had died so brutally. Grief was quickly followed by anger. As long as the enemy had Endvar to protect them, they had no reason to come face the Rahmish army on fair ground.

A siege was out of the question. With unrestricted access to Ardania, the enemy could gather fresh men and supplies, rendering a siege attempt useless. Merek, too, was summoning fresh troops from around the kingdom in anticipation of the Ardanians pushing further into Rahm. But the Ardanians seemed content to only make a token show of force. Likely they hoped the long winter would do their fighting for them, and they could emerge from the city in the spring refreshed and ready for battle when Merek's forces would be depleted and haggard from exposure.

Merek feared that was exactly what would happen if he didn't succeed in drawing the enemy out soon.

Could Ria do it? he wondered. And if she could, should he let her? The thought made his skin crawl, but he had to admit that it was the kind of risk Danvir wouldn't have hesitated to take, and Merek would have admired him for it.

But Danvir was a seasoned soldier. He would have fully understood the risks and would have known how to handle himself if something went wrong. Ria had many fine qualities, but she was no soldier.

Twenty-Eight

Ria climbed awkwardly up the hill to the enemy camp, flanked on either side by Ardanian soldiers. The darkness made the uneven terrain difficult to see. Her hands were bound before her, and a leather strap had been placed in her mouth to make it difficult to speak. It tasted of sweat and horse, and she gagged on her own spit.

With her hands bound, she couldn't hold her skirts up, and they caught on her boots and snagged on surrounding brambles. The fourth time she fell, she hit her knee hard on a rock. Tears sprang to her eyes, and she whimpered in pain. She considered refusing to go on, but the enemy soldiers hauled her up and made her keep going, even as she leaned on one for support until the pain passed.

Brandel had a quieter time of it. She worried that it was because he was so injured from his beating that he couldn't protest. But she was glad he was alive. When she thought of the other soldiers lying dead on the riverbank, her lungs felt constricted.

It was her fault this had happened. Brandel had warned her not to go through with her plan, but she hadn't listened. Why hadn't she listened? Now Brandel and the others had paid the price for her pride.

And her pride wasn't doing her any good now.

Saliva pooled around the corners of her mouth. Her hands were going numb—either from cold or being bound too tightly, she wasn't sure. Now she was an enemy hostage with no one the wiser except poor Biren who wouldn't report her absence until the night was spent. That was hours away.

With longing, Ria thought of Merek. He was so close, just on the other side of the western ridge. If only he knew of her danger, he would race to her aid. But he would never know because she'd insisted on keeping her plans from him. She had insisted that she could do this alone.

Ria, you stubborn fool. When will you stop expecting the world to bend to your will?

She couldn't waste another moment chiding herself, however, for they were approaching a sentry and the light from the torch offered her the first view of her captors. The soldier on her right had a bulbous nose and shaggy hair peeking out from under his dark helmet. The soldier she had leaned on for support wore his hair long in two braids. He said nothing, but his eyes were sharp and alert.

The sentry eyed Ria and frowned at their mounted leader as the prisoners passed. "Found some stragglers, then? I thought all the action was at the bridge tonight?"

Ria didn't hear the Ardanian officer's response. Passing through the border of the camp filled her with such dread that she felt it as a wave of sickness radiating from her middle. If it hadn't been so many hours since her last meal, she probably would have emptied her stomach out of nervousness.

With each step she drew closer to the enemy and further from safety. With each step she regretted wearing a fine gown to announce her status and wished she was instead invisible as a humble servant. Did they know? Had they guessed who she was? Now that she was a captive, her original message seemed pointless. What good would it do to arrange a meeting with Artem when she had already delivered herself into his hands? Instead, she felt instinctively that she needed to protect her identity.

They didn't walk far before the leader of their group dismounted. He continued on foot to a nearby tent in the Ardanian circular style with a peaked roof. Ria was shepherded inside and looked desperately for Brandel.

He was bruised, and his whole left side was stained with blood. But he managed to keep his feet and protectively drew closer to her despite bound hands. Ria focused on the ropes binding her own hands so as to not think about Brandel's blood leaking out of him. For once, her mind was so full of panic that it chased away any hint of fainting, but she angled her body away from the sight just in case.

The Ardanian in charge—she thought he might have

been a sergeant—loosened the leather thong in Ria's mouth. Her jaw ached, and her cheeks felt raw.

"Now," he said in halting Rahmish. "You will speak your name and say why you came to our camp."

Ria glanced at Brandel, hoping he would follow along. "My name is Biren. I'm a maid to Princess Honoria of Rahm. As you can see, I'm no threat and do not deserve these bonds. Your men killed six of my guard without provocation. I demand that you release me at once and return our horses that we may return to our business."

The Ardanian cocked his head at her tone. He had heavily lidded eyes which gave him an air of boredom. "What is your business?"

"It's of a private nature and doesn't concern any member of this camp." Ria held the man's gaze in spite of her fear. She hoped he couldn't read the lie in her eyes.

The Ardanian stepped close enough to Ria that she could smell his stale breath. "Your business doesn't matter. Now you are a prisoner. Sit." He grabbed a low backed chair—practically a stool—and placed it before her.

The command was mild enough, but his eyes held a warning.

"I prefer to stand," Ria replied, her mouth dry.

The Ardanian glanced from her to Brandel. "This is your guard? He does not look well. How much more can he bleed tonight? Mm?"

Ria sat obediently. Brandel—who wasn't offered a chair—followed suit, collapsing on the ground beside her. She hated to capitulate to this man, but Brandel seemed grateful for the rest.

The Ardanian smirked and nudged Brandel with his boot.

"What do you have to say? Will you tell me your purpose?"

Brandel lifted his head with effort. "She is who she says. I can add nothing more, except that mine was simply an assignment of protection. We pose no threat to anyone."

Bless you, Brandel.

"Why would a simple maid be granted such protection? Someone else must have known of your purpose to allow you to bring so many soldiers with you on this 'private business.'"

"My lady wishes to keep me safe," Ria answered.

"By sending you to the enemy camp in the middle of the night?"

"The camp was not our aim. It was merely an unfortunate risk of proximity." In her mind, Ria frantically strung together a story in case the sergeant should press her. A secret meeting with a member of the Ardanian camp. But who? What would resonate with him? A cousin of some sort? A secret lover? Biren had spent a long time in Ardania with Ria. It was not implausible.

Thinking of Biren gave Ria fresh anxiety. How long before she would go to Rorden for help? Could it be as late as midnight yet? There were still so many hours until dawn. Now her instructions seemed foolish and naive. She'd never believed that they would actually need to be rescued.

Curse her reckless pride, but it was all she had now. Could it somehow save her?

"I warn you, sir, that we're expected back in our own camp soon. If we don't return safely, troops are prepared to come to our aid. Release us, and we will return peacefully."

"What is your name again?"

"Biren."

"Lady Biren, shall I just kill you now and return your body to them instead?"

Ria felt the blood drain from her face. She suddenly realized that she was completely in this man's power, and she'd given him no reason to keep her alive.

"Kill me, and you ensure your own death," she said forcefully. "The Rahmish army will come down on your head so fast that there will not be so much as a spearman left alive in this camp. And when they are finished with you, you'll have to answer to your own prince. He would never stand for it."

The Ardanian's eyes narrowed. She wondered if she had spoken too quickly, but he must have understood her meaning because he turned and approached one of the soldiers. He spoke softly in Ardanian, but Ria understood every word.

"Go to Captain Mischa. Tell him we have a prisoner who claims to be a maid to the Rahmish princess and hold the interest of Prince Artem."

"Sir," the soldier replied. "If she is who she says, she would fetch a high ransom. Are you sure you want me to go to the captain?"

The sergeant glanced back at Ria, who quickly looked at the floor as if she hadn't been listening.

"You suggest I don't tell the captain? That we keep her to ourselves?"

"It would be a pretty bounty indeed, with only the three of us to share in it. We kill the soldier—he's half dead anyway—and hide her away so they never know there was another prisoner. There are plenty of places in the city where we could stash her and no one would ever know."

"What of the sentry? He knows we have her. He'll ask questions."

"So we pay him off. Easily done."

The sergeant scratched at his neck and looked up at the ceiling where the spiral pattern in the cloth disappeared into darkness. Considering. Ria strained to hear his answer. She needed to get away from these men, even if it meant she was taken to a higher authority and her true identity was discovered. Better that than being hidden away in some hovel where no one could find her.

"I suppose we don't have to act right away," the sergeant finally murmured in reply. "No need to alert the captain just yet. Let me speak to someone who might be able to help us. If he thinks it's as foolish as I fear, then we'll inform the captain as if nothing else had happened. Agreed?"

The soldier nodded reluctantly.

As the sergeant approached Ria, his eyes were alight with interest. It wasn't comforting.

In Rahmish, he said, "I will send word to the prince, to see if your claim is true. If so, perhaps you will live a little longer." In his lie, he sounded appeasing. Almost kind.

It sickened Ria, and she breathed a little easier after he left.

The two soldiers who remained were silent and soon the minutes stretched long. There was little furniture in the room aside from the chair where she sat. A pallet bed sat near one wall, with a small chest left open at its foot and piled high with cookware and clothing. Weapons in the Ardanian style rested in a corner. A circular shield in pewter gray, a broadsword, and a studded club. If they could reach them somehow, could they fight their way free? With bound hands...no armor...against an experienced foe in full strength...

As if reading her thoughts, Brandel slumped against Ria's leg. She looked at him in alarm. His eyes were closed and his face beneath the dirt and blood was pale. He needed a surgeon soon. He would not survive another fight.

Their best hope was rescue, but that was many hours away. If only she had some way of notifying Merek that she was in danger. He was so close, not more than an hour's ride. But he might as well be back in Albon for all the good it did her. She was on her own.

A footfall nearby made Merek turn from tightening the girth on his horse. The night was dark with no moon, lit only by bonfires tended around the perimeter of the makeshift camp. Shadows moved before the fires, and the ground was littered with the shapeless forms of the dead. On the other side of the bridge, men were digging shallow graves that would be filled at first light.

"No sign of enemy activity," Firl greeted him, his low voice little more than a growl.

"Thank you, Captain. Tell your men to stay alert. They may yet attack when you think the danger has passed."

"You're going back to camp now?" Firl's voice held an unspoken reproof. Grammel's former captains still weren't used to Merek's unconventional ways. He missed the freedom that he'd enjoyed when he'd been First Captain over the Wall Guard. He might be general now, but that didn't mean that he wanted a retinue with him everywhere he went.

"Continue your work here. I'll send reinforcements as soon as I return to camp."

Merek swung up into the saddle, feeling stiff and moving slowly to accommodate his aching head. He couldn't remember the last time he'd slept more than a few hours at a time. It was catching up to him. Gone were the days when he could push himself relentlessly with little effect. He was feeling the first taste of aging, and he didn't like it.

With a yawn, Merek turned his back on Endvar.

Twenty-Nine

Ria gently stroked Brandel's head where it rested on her knee. It was difficult with her hands bound, but she could reach out a few fingers and brush them against his temple. It was a strangely intimate gesture for a man she scarcely knew, but he had defended her with his life and it seemed a small thing in return. His breathing sounded labored, and she had given up speaking to him. What could be said? An apology was inadequate, and she didn't want to tax him. She wasn't even sure if he was awake.

If she thought too much about Brandel's blood leaking onto her skirt, Ria felt ill, so she forced her mind down other paths. As the time stretched long, she thought of hiding in a humble farmer's barn when Merek had last come to her rescue. As panicked as she'd been then, now the memory felt pleasant to her mind. Merek's presence had been so calming. He'd put her shoulder right again, protected her against the enemy, and safely brought her home. His voice calling her name in that darkened barn had been a soothing balm to her frightened soul. What she would give to hear his voice now! To feel his reassuring arms around her!

Those thoughts led to others and soon she remembered that night when he'd confessed his feelings. A new wave of hopelessness washed over her. In a moment of unrestrained vulnerability, he'd offered her his heart. But she had clutched tightly to her own and the moment had passed unclaimed. What if she never had another opportunity? What if she never saw Merek again? What if he never knew how—

"You are not the maid."

Ria's head snapped up. Her thoughts had wandered...had she dozed off? Her head felt groggy and she peered at the soldier with the twin braids crouching before her.

He was so close, she could smell his unwashed scent. She drew back, but his expression didn't seem threatening. He had a leanness about him, his skin stretching tight over his jaw and cheekbones, that gave her an impression of a tanner's hide.

"Who are you really?"

"I've told you who I am."

"I know Lady Biren. You are not her."

Why was he whispering? Ria glanced around the tent.

"Where are the others?"

"They've decided to hold you for ransom and are preparing to smuggle you out of camp before daylight. If you're going to escape, it must be now."

Escape! Ria's heart fluttered at the word. "What do you mean?"

The soldier drew his knife and reached for the rope tied around her wrists. "The others are fools thinking only of their wallets. Once they turn you over to their accomplices they will have lost their prize. How long will it be before they don't even know where you're kept? How you're treated? If you even still live?"

Ria shivered as the rope fell away. Her raw skin screamed in relief, and her fingers tingled as the circulation returned. "Why do you tell me this? To scare me?"

They were speaking in Ardanian. Clearly this man had guessed what the others did not, that she knew their language. There was no sense in continuing the ruse.

The soldier smiled grimly. "I know you're not Lady Biren, but whoever you are, you don't deserve this fate either. Take this, you may need it." He handed her the knife he'd used to cut her bonds.

Ria stared at him. She didn't know whether or not to trust him, but she didn't have much of a choice. "Can you help us escape?"

The soldier looked at Brandel with a mixture of pity and distaste. "There is no 'us.' Your guard is dead."

Ria recoiled, pulling her hands away and standing up with a start. Brandel slumped to the floor awkwardly, his head lolling to the side against the leg of the stool. His skin was ashen, and Ria realized his labored breathing had stopped. She stifled a cry of horror. The soldier was right. Brandel —faithful Brandel—was dead.

"We don't have time to tarry," the soldier said urgently. "They'll return soon. Come with me." He moved quietly to the tent door and parted it slightly. After a moment, he slipped out.

Ria hesitated, looking down at Brandel's body. The bruising he'd suffered looked ghastly in the dim light. He deserved better than this, to be abandoned in an enemy camp instead of honored in a proper burial. One more searing rebuke for her conscience.

Ria followed the soldier out of the tent. The camp had quieted in the hours since she'd first passed through. Few soldiers moved about, and her guide kept to the shadows to avoid them. They skirted around the back of a wagon and a pen that smelled of hogs.

She didn't recognize their route, and it seemed far less direct than the one they'd taken when she arrived. She knew there was a chance that this soldier was not helping her escape, but rather had his own plan and was leading her into a trap. But he was the only hope she had.

At last they stopped beside a small tent that, from the smell, could have only been a privy. Ria wrinkled her nose involuntarily.

The soldier drew close and whispered, "Your horse is staked just beyond that tent. They didn't dare bring it to camp proper until they knew what they wanted to do with you. If you go straight through those trees, you will find the river on the other side. This is where I will leave you."

Ria felt a surge of hope looking out at the empty darkness. "What is your name, soldier?"

"Rezon."

"Why have you helped me, Rezon? I don't even know you."

"But I know you. Or at least, if you are who I think you are, I know that Biren would want me to help you."

"Won't you be in danger for helping me?"

The soldier snorted softly. "These are small-minded men. If they try to hurt me, I will report to Captain Mischa what they attempted to do tonight. They wouldn't dare."

"Unless we kill you outright and steal the lady back."

A shadow loomed out of the night and Ria caught her breath. Instantly, Rezon stiffened and drew his sword.

"So, who is she?" The voice was that of the sergeant from before. "What do you know that we don't?"

Ria didn't wait for the reply. She lifted her skirts and ran.

"Stop her!" the sergeant cried in alarm.

Ria sprinted as fast as her frozen feet would carry her. Heart pounding furiously, she prayed that Rezon had told her the truth and she would find her horse where he said. Before she rounded the privy, she was already winded. Her lungs burned and she gulped for breath. Behind her were muffled sounds of conflict, but she didn't dare look back.

Ahead of her—a faint splash of gray next to a copse of trees—stood her horse. Her excitable, unruly, blessed horse.

She ran toward him and he started, tossing his head and pulling against his tether.

Shh…it's just me, she wanted to say. *I'm taking you home.* She wanted to speak soothingly to him, but all she could do was gasp for air. The sound of her wheezing was loud in her own ears. If there was anyone within a hundred yards of her, she was sure they would find her from her breathing alone.

Ria bent over to cut the rope and nearly blacked out from the blood rushing to her head. Nausea churned in her stomach and she pawed at the rope blindly until it came free.

The horse whinnied and yanked the rope out of her hands, burning her skin. In a panic, Ria grasped for it and pulled hard, ignoring the pain in her hands. She groped for a stirrup, certain every moment that a pair of rough hands would grab her again. The horse danced, and she hopped with him until at last her boot scraped the stirrup and she heaved mightily up into the saddle, her skirts and cloak twisted awkwardly around her.

A shout sounded close by, and her horse bolted into the trees.

Ria chanced a look back over her shoulder and nearly tumbled off the horse's back. She listed to the left, struggling to stay balanced in the saddle with her dress and cloak bunched uncomfortably beneath her. The grove of trees was small here, and soon she broke out into the open with the black river yawning menacingly ahead. Ria ached to know if her pursuers were close, but kept her eyes forward and focused on trying to balance her weight.

The stallion plunged into the river without hesitation. She yelped in fright as cold water splashed her face.

Water churned in a white frenzy, soaking her skirts past her thighs. Her fingers couldn't feel the reins even as she gripped them. Everything was ice and blinding darkness, but somehow she managed to keep her seat.

As she reached the other side of the river, the bank loomed up before her. Ria felt a surge of panic as, with a powerful jump which nearly unseated her, her horse leaped for the embankment, scrambling to gain his footing. Ria slipped in the saddle and gripped with legs and hands, desperate to hang on.

Don't lose me now you devilish creature.

With a jolt, the horse reached the top and gained his footing again, then sprinted through the forest at breakneck speed. Ria clung to him, a new terror washing over her—that of being thrown if her horse stumbled or being knocked off his back by a stray limb.

The sound of hoofbeats and her own breathing drowned out all else. Her hood fell back and her muffler loosened, exposing her face and neck to the sharp sting of branches as they whipped past, cutting her skin. The cold air brought streaming tears to her eyes, and the vapor from her breath froze around her mouth. Still, her horse ran wild.

In the dark around her, Ria imagined movement: shapes lunging for her. Briars tugged at her cloak, and she let out a garbled scream. Were those hoofbeats she heard above the din of her own horse? Or just her imagination?

At last, her mount slowed. Aching, she pushed herself up to a sitting position and flexed her numb fingers. He was spent and didn't fight against the bit when she pulled him to a walk. She tugged at the wadded cloth beneath her, finally untangling herself from her wet skirts and sitting evenly in the saddle. The horse was warm from his hard ride which warmed her thighs and backside in return. But her neck and hands were still bitterly cold—as were her feet which had been thoroughly doused in the river. If it hadn't been for the warmth of the beast beneath her, she was certain she would have been chattering with cold.

For the first time, Ria realized how well she could make out the forest around her. Dawn was approaching, and she was well and truly alone. There was no sign of any pursuers. But poor Biren must have been beside herself. What sort of uproar would Ria face upon her return? With the added daylight, Ria could see that the trees were thinning just ahead, revealing a wide valley.

"You did it. You brought us home," she murmured to the horse, rubbing his neck with gratitude.

As Merek rode, the early morning sky lightened into an icy blue highlighted with streaks of clouds and a few bright, lingering stars. The movement of his ride created a constant breeze that froze his exposed skin and made his eyes water, chasing away sleep. It was rare that he enjoyed true solitude these days, and he felt a momentary flash of gratitude for the simple pleasure of riding alone with no more than the rhythmic sound of his horse's hoofbeats for company.

Suddenly, movement off to the side caught his attention. Merek brought his horse up short. Through the trees came the form of a rider bent over the neck of a gray stallion, bulky under a shapeless cloak and bowed with exhaustion. Who would be returning to camp at this hour? Merek waited as the rider emerged from the trees and he got a better look. Then he swore in disbelief and spurred his horse forward.

Ria looked up when she heard another rider approaching, her pulse racing in alarm. Had they found her after all? Had she made it this close to camp only to be captured again? But when she saw that it was Merek who rode toward her, the anxious knot in her middle dissolved. Now she was truly safe. She wanted to leap from her horse and hug him, but she barely had the strength to sit upright.

"Ria! It *is* you!" he cried. "But how...? What happened?" He quickly took in her appearance, and his frown deepened.

"I'm well enough. Call your men back. I'm safe now."

Merek's eyes flickered to the trees behind her. "My men?"

"The men you sent to search..." Ria trailed off as she understood. Merek didn't know she was missing. He didn't know of what she'd done. She would have to tell him of her folly herself.

"I just returned from the bridge," Merek explained. "What happened here last night?" He led his horse right next to hers, and his gray eyes were sharp like flint. Ria looked away, unable to meet his gaze. When she didn't answer right away, his tone grew wary. "Ria?"

Her breath hitched as she inhaled. "I was only trying to help."

Silence.

The dread in his voice was palpable. "What have you done?"

"A foolish, foolish thing." Summoning her courage, Ria looked him squarely in the eye. "I never meant it to go so wrong. Please believe me. I thought we could approach the camp without being seen, but they discovered us. I don't know how—"

"Approach the camp? Surely you don't mean..." Merek's eyes widened. "Ria, did you go to the *Ardanian* camp?"

She dropped her eyes and nodded. "I intended to send a message to Artem, to arrange a meeting with him." She couldn't bear to see Merek's expression, so she stared at the pommel of her saddle, but his sharp intake of breath was like a dagger in her heart. She kept talking, hoping to forestall his reprimand. "You wouldn't agree, and I was tired of arguing with you about it. I never imagined that they would capture us and—"

"Capture you?" At this, Merek seized her arm. His touch wasn't rough, and there was a part of her that was just grateful to have him near enough to touch, but his eyes...they fairly crackled with rage. "They *captured* you?"

Ria swallowed hard. "Not for long. I escaped with the help of an Ardanian soldier. Biren was to go to

Rorden for help if I hadn't returned by dawn. I thought you knew. I thought you were out looking for me."

"Are you hurt?" His voice was like iron.

Ria shook her head and shivered. Her throat closed on the words that needed to come next. Brandel bruised and gray on the ground. His blood on her skirt.

Merek released her arm with a sigh and ran his hand through his hair. "Oh Ria, what were you thinking?"

"I was only trying to help. I thought I could—"

"You thought you could what? Single-handedly win the war? Alone and completely inexperienced? You thought you could ignore everything I've said and somehow everyone would play into your hands?"

"That's not fair. I tried to reason with you, but you left me little choice. If you had only—"

"So you thought you would contact the Ardanian prince anyway? Do whatever you wanted even if it defied my direct orders?" His mount shifted in agitation with his rising tone.

She lifted her chin, indignation warming her through. "I have every right to communicate with Artem as I wish, and I have every right to arrange a meeting on whatever terms I see fit. You forget your place, Merek Strong. You are not *my* commander."

Merek's glare deepened. "Fine. You may not be one of my men, but this is *my* camp. And if you refuse to comply with my orders, then you're no longer welcome in it."

Ria paused, mouth agape. Her hair was a tangled mess about her shoulders, and her face showed signs of a rough ride, with abrasions on her brow and across the bridge of her nose. Merek's anger pulsed in his throbbing head. He wanted to rage at her for putting herself in danger, but at the same time he felt relieved that she'd escaped without serious harm. He rubbed at his temples to ease the pressure building in his head. He hated himself for what he was about to say, but he knew it was for the best.

"I'll send word to the campmaster to prepare your things to return to Albon. I want you out of this camp today."

A spark kindled in her dark eyes. "You're throwing me out of camp? What makes you think—"

"I can't fight both you *and* the Ardanians. I'm trying to win a war and can't do that with you undermining me at every turn."

Ria winced. "Merek, I need to explain—"

"There's nothing more to explain. Once you're gone, I'll untangle whatever knot you've created and focus on—"

"Confound you, Merek! Will you just listen? This is why I rode out there last night, because it was the only way to get you to pay attention!"

Merek clamped his mouth shut, seething. But he waited for her to speak.

Ria took a shuddering breath and looked at him with eyes shining with pain. "I lost Brandel, Merek."

"What do you mean?"

"He was wounded too seriously and didn't survive. The others, too—"

Merek swore inwardly, feeling a weight like a stone settle in his belly. "How many others?"

"Six in all. I don't...I don't know their names." She looked down at her hands where she held the reins, twisting them as if they were to blame for her foolishness.

Merek took a deep breath to quell his urge to shout. If only his head didn't pound so. He spoke carefully. "Can't you see, Ria? This is an army camp, not your court. People's lives are at risk. When you make foolish mistakes, good men die. That was a selfish thing to do and proves that you have no place making decisions in war."

"You think I don't know that?" She looked up at him, her face pinched in agony. "You think I haven't spent all night berating myself and wishing I hadn't done it? I just wanted to do something! Every time you leave this camp, you go out and fight the enemy. Men die at your hand, and other lives are saved. You make a difference while I sit and wait, fretting to see if you'll return in one piece, wishing that I could do something to help. But this—" she gestured emphatically toward the camp. "This is something *I* can do. And it matters. I could turn the tide of this war! But if I go home, I'm completely useless!" Her voice broke a little with the passion of her desperation.

Merek wanted to comfort her, wanted to reach out across the distance between them and tell her it would all be well. But this was a moment of decision. Steeling himself, he said, "If you really want to help, respect my decisions even when you disagree with them. Support me. Trust me. Stop trying to manipulate me just so that you can get what you want!"

"I don't manipulate you!"

"Oh no?" Merek scoffed. "Then tell me why the entire army thinks we're betrothed!"

Ria blushed. "That was different, I—"

"No, keep your excuses," he snapped. "I'm weary of them, and I'm weary of you. I'm finished letting you toy with me. I can't have you here interfering with so much at stake. I've indulged you too long. Go home where you belong."

"Merek—"

"You said yourself that I should be careful whom I trust. But I trust you least of all."

Ria drew back, her lips parted as if uncertain what to say, her eyes creased with pain. "I only wished to help," she repeated, her voice tight with emotion, "but I understand you clearly enough. I'll leave as soon as I can gather my things. You needn't bother to speak to the campmaster. I believe that is one task I can manage for myself."

She nudged her horse forward, and Merek watched her go.

It was done. He should have been prepared for this from the moment she'd first arrived in camp. He'd been foolish to think that she could stay. This was no simple wall tour where she could play her games with little consequence. She still hadn't learned that in this camp defying him could lead to disaster. It seemed that each time he started to trust her she would do something deceitful and conniving. Sending her away was the right thing to do.

But victory felt sour to him as he watched her ride away into the first rays of golden sunlight cutting through the morning mist. He hadn't wanted to hurt her, and part of him understood that his anger was a reaction to his fear for her safety, but there was nothing to be done about it now. She would be safer in Albon.

He repeated that thought over and over again, but somehow it failed to give him comfort.

Thirty

The cold that gripped Ria's heart had nothing to do with the chill in the air or her wet skirts clinging to her legs. She tried to straighten up as she rode past the sentries, but it was difficult when she felt like any movement might make her unravel completely. Stirrings of wakefulness were beginning to emerge around camp, and she was grateful it was early yet with few people to see her return. By the time she reached her own tent, the sun had just started to rise, bright yet cold.

The tent was unguarded.

Brandel. Ria felt another stab of pain as she stiffly dismounted. Before her feet hit the ground, her tent door opened.

"Oh, my lady!" Biren gasped, her hand to her mouth. "What happened? You look…"

Rorden pushed past her and reached to steady Ria. "Are you hurt, Your Highness?"

Ria shook her head wearily. "I just...need to sit down."

"You're shivering." Rorden wrapped his arm around her, and she leaned into him as he helped her to the tent. The contact was soothing, but still she trembled with cold.

Biren rushed to grab a heavy fur throw and placed it over Ria's shoulders, guiding her to sit on the cot. "Rorden, stoke the fire and put a kettle on the trivet. We need to warm her."

Rorden obeyed as Biren knelt and tugged at the frozen laces on Ria's boots. Once removed, Biren set to work rubbing her legs and feet. Ria couldn't even feel her touch.

"Shall I tell the units to stand down, Your Highness?" Rorden asked. "Did all return safely, then?"

Ria looked up at him and blinked slowly, trying to comprehend his words. "No. I mean, yes. There's no need for a rescue, but I'm the only one who returned."

Biren's hands stilled. She looked up at Ria, and Ria looked away, unable to meet her eyes. She stared instead at her frost-rimmed boots, wanting to get the words out as fast as she could.

"We were attacked crossing the river, before we even reached their camp. Brandel and I were taken, but the others were lost. Brandel was wounded and...there was no one to attend him. He died a few hours later." *His head on my lap. His body leaning against mine.*

She chanced a glance at Biren. Her maid bit her lip with concern, but she didn't rail at her as Merek had.

"I told the Ardanians that I was you," Ria continued.

"It seemed prudent not to tell them who I really was, and yours was the first name that came to mind. In the end, it served me well. One of them said he knew you, a soldier named Rezon. He helped me escape."

Biren straightened. "Rezon helped you?"

"Who is this Rezon?" Rorden asked. "Why would he want to help you?"

"He…" Biren ducked her head. "He's just a friend. We met in Rellana."

Normally, Ria would have tried to tease the tale out of her, but her spirit felt too sick for humor. "Rezon suspected who I truly was," she continued. "The others were considering holding me for ransom rather than reporting the capture to their captain. Rezon didn't want that to happen."

Biren looked away, her expression inscrutable. She began rubbing Ria's feet and legs again, and this time, Ria could feel the warmth of her hands. She was grateful for Biren's ministrations, but at the same time wanted to be left alone. She didn't deserve to be pampered when Brandel was lying cold and abandoned in an enemy camp…when soldiers whose names she didn't know lay forgotten on the riverbank.

"I'm sorry, Biren," she said softly, looking at the top of her maid's auburn head as she bent over her work. "You and Brandel warned me against this plan, but I refused to listen. Can you forgive me?"

Biren didn't look up, but her voice was sad. "There's nothing to forgive, my lady. Brandel served you willingly, and I'm glad he protected you in the end."

In the quiet that followed, Rorden cleared his throat.

"I'll go and dismiss the units, then. I'm glad you're safe, Your Highness."

"We need to get you out of these wet clothes," Biren said as soon as Rorden was gone. She placed Ria's night-dress beside her on the cot. "I assume you'll wish to rest?"

Ria cringed, thinking of Merek's demand to leave. "Dry clothes, yes, but no rest, I'm afraid. Today we return to Albon."

Biren looked at her in surprise, waiting for an explanation. But Ria simply couldn't offer her one. The pain of Merek's rebuke was too raw. Biren accepted her silence and helped her change into a dry gown and thick woolen stockings. Though the clothes were warmer, stripping off her wet ones left Ria exposed. The chill air sank deep into her bones and set her teeth chattering. Biren placed a hot cup of tea in her hands and bade her drink. Her hands trembled uncontrollably until Biren held them in her own, gently helping her press the cup to her lips.

It was a small thing, but her kindness pushed Ria over the edge. Hot tears pricked at her eyes and spilled onto her cheeks. She'd held it together during the terrifying events of the night. She'd kept her feelings at bay when Merek banished her from the camp. She'd remained calm when telling Biren of Brandel's fate. But now, with Biren's soft hands and kind eyes, the last of her restraint dissolved.

Rorden greeted Merek at the command tent looking more pale and haggard than he had the day before. Merek felt annoyed looking at his grim expression. Rorden already knew about Ria, and he would certainly want to talk about her, which was the last thing Merek wanted to do. Merek tossed his reins to the waiting groom and stalked to the tent.

"Is there any word from Salvin or Audon?" he asked by way of greeting.

"Not yet, sir, but I've sent out scouts to see how they fared."

"Firl is waiting for reinforcements to help hold the bridge," Merek said, tugging off his gloves. "Send him a fresh company within the hour."

"Yes, sir."

Rorden helped Merek remove his breastplate and mail, stained with blood and grime from battle. His clothing beneath the armor was stiff with dried sweat, and he felt an instant chill in the cold air. He sank into his chair, closing his eyes for a moment and letting his body relax for the first time in days. But his mind couldn't rest. His argument with Ria spun in his head. He'd done the right thing; he was sure of it. But maybe his timing could have been better. Now that the moment had passed, his angry words sounded cruel in his own ears.

This would change things between them forever.

"Sir?"

Apparently Rorden had waited as long as he could.

"Yes?" Merek pried open his eyes resentfully.

"There's something you should know. Something happened last night and—"

"I already know, Rorden."

"You do?"

"Who else knows of it?"

"Not many, but word will spread, especially with the princess returning in the condition she did."

"Well, it doesn't matter much," Merek said shortly. "She'll be leaving us soon, which is for the best."

"But sir—"

"I don't want to talk about it," Merek warned. "She'll be returning to Albon soon enough." He stood and reached for his old uniform coat.

"The tailor should be bringing your new uniform today," Rorden said. "Would you like to bathe before he comes? I can summon a barber as well."

Merek sighed. He really could have used an hour or two of sleep, but with the camp awakening around him it seemed that rest would have to wait. He reached for a half empty chalice left abandoned on the table and sniffed its contents dubiously. The thin ale would do nothing for his throbbing head.

"I also want to report that we found our messenger," Rorden added. "More than one, actually. Dan and Aiya leave this morning for the north."

"Indeed?" Merek asked, surprised. As Rorden explained how it came about, he nodded. "I should have thought of Dan before. I foolishly thought he might want to rest after all he'd been through."

"He was thrilled to have an assignment, sir. Aiya will keep him out of too much trouble."

"Aiya surprises me. You say she wanted to go?"

"She seemed relieved when the princess suggested it. She's very worried about Dan. I suspect she may be forming an attachment."

Merek snorted. "Don't start. She and Dan have been through a lot together, that's all. Don't imagine more than there is."

"I'm not imagining!" Rorden protested. "The princess told me later she suspected it too. That's why she suggested that Aiya accompany him. They're leaving under the guise of Dan needing time away from camp for his recovery. It's a convenient ruse under the circumstances. For Aiya to join him may inspire gossip, but not the sort that would alert our enemies."

"I must thank them before they leave. Have a bath waiting when I return so I don't soil this new uniform you're so eager to show me."

Merek was glad for an excuse to leave Rorden and his unasked questions. Eldar's company was on the far edge of the army camp where the surrounding hills brought the tents to an abrupt stop. Most of the camp was empty as Eldar's men were still on the battlefield, so he quickly found Dan and Aiya loading saddlebags onto their horses.

Dan was dressed in plain clothes, the right sleeve of his heavy coat tied off where his arm ended. Merek cringed at the sight, imagining how it would feel to lose his arm, but Dan was smiling and talking animatedly. Aiya was dressed similarly in trousers and a coat, her hair tucked under a knit cap.

As Merek approached, Dan's expression lost some of

its levity and he straightened up, saluting with his left arm. Merek returned the salute, then reached his left hand forward to grasp Dan's.

"I wish you well, Sergeant. No one knows more than I the sacrifices you've made for your country. I'm personally indebted to you many times over."

"And I you, sir," Dan replied gratefully. Merek would have to remember to thank Rorden for thinking of a way to give Dan purpose and preserve his dignity.

"Will this be your first time visiting the northern country?" Merek asked.

"I've traveled there once before in my youth, but that was in a very...different capacity." Inexplicably, Aiya snickered at this, as if sharing in a private jest. Dan's cheeks pinked a little, and his eyes shone. It was good to see his humor returning.

"Captain Falbrook is a good man, but he'll be slow to trust a stranger. Especially a stranger with no written orders who wants to take his men."

The humor died in Dan's eyes.

"If he gives you a difficult time, tell him this. Tell him that it snowed the day my father was buried, and Stefan dug the grave because I wasn't there. I expect he'll listen to you then."

Dan nodded, his expression sober.

Aiya stepped forward with a slight curtsy, the graceful movement made humorous in her young man's clothing.

"Dear Aiya," Merek said, squeezing her shoulder affectionately. "If you can manage to bring Dan back in one piece, I may have use for him still."

Aiya smiled. "Dan seems to find trouble as easily as trouble finds him, but I will do my best. And best wishes on your betrothal, my lord —captain—sir," she caught herself and grinned.

Merek's smile felt more like a grimace as he squinted against the bright sunlight, his headache making him long for clouds. Perhaps after Ria left the camp they could finally put the matter of this ridiculous betrothal to rest. So much would be better after she left.

So why did the thought make him feel so wretched?

BIREN PRODUCED A HANDKERCHIEF WITHOUT A WORD AND SAT next to Ria on the cot, one arm wrapped around her shoulders. Ria hugged a fur to her chest for comfort, stifling her sobs in its softness so they wouldn't escape through the canvas walls of her tent. She knew that soon enough she would wash her face and emerge from the tent with a smile she didn't feel. But for now, for this one moment, she surrendered to despair, letting the tears wash away her misery.

All she'd wanted was to be the leader her people needed. Desperately, she'd tried to prove that she was ready to rule. But she had failed. She'd failed Brandel. She'd failed her people. And she'd failed Merek. After all this time, he still saw her as no more than a pampered princess with no real understanding of the world.

Her worst fear was that he was right.

What did she have to offer an army in the midst of a conflict? What experience gave her the right to be heard?

Her paltry efforts had gotten good men killed and put herself in enemy hands.

And what hurt most was the realization that her closest friend—the one person she felt really *knew* her, with whom she could be safe and eliminate any pretenses—had judged her and found her wanting.

Very wanting.

"It might help if you speak of it," Biren suggested gently, her light brown eyes weighted with concern.

Ria groaned and sniffed. "You're so kind, Biren. I don't deserve you. I deserve to be sent home in disgrace, but he didn't even do that. In spite of his anger—in spite of his *right* —he's giving me the chance to preserve my dignity, making it appear to the camp as if I'm leaving on my own terms. I've used him abominably, and still he offers me respect. What sort of man does that?"

Biren didn't answer.

"I've been a fool in more ways than one. I didn't realize until last night when I thought that I might not see Merek again—I've taken him for granted, always assuming he'll be there for me, never worrying about whether or not I've been there for him."

"I'm sure he understands. You're too hard on yourself."

"No, no, no." Ria shook off Biren's touch. It wasn't Biren she wanted comfort from. It wasn't Biren she wanted to say these things to. "I've ruined it; don't you see? I've betrayed him, and he despises me. And how can I fault him? I expect him to trust me, but when have I fully trusted him? He's treated me like an equal, but I've treated him like an instrument to get my way. Or to get *out* of my way. I've manipulated him, and he's borne it until he could bear it no longer."

Biren watched Ria's agitated gestures with bewilderment. "I don't understand."

"I love him, Biren." Ria smiled sadly. "I didn't know until last night. Maybe not even until just this moment. I didn't see it for what it was because it's nothing like I felt for Artem. That was a reckless passion that was easily extinguished and left ash in its wake. But this, this is something different. It's like…a force of nature: the kind that causes rivers to change course and brings mountains to their knees. Irresistible and constant." A warm wash of conviction spread through her as she spoke.

Biren shook her head as if in a stupor. "Are you sure, my lady? You've been through a great ordeal and—"

"I'm more sure of this than I'm sure of you sitting there before me. Somehow, I must tell him before I go. No more posturing. No more intrigue. I'll tell him what's in my heart even if it means facing his rejection. If we're ever going to work together, there can be no more secrets—only honesty, sincerity, and trust. Beginning with me, today."

A smile tugged at Biren's lips. "Well, then. If you intend to have that conversation with him before we go, we'd best do something with your hair."

Thirty-One

Merek's bath ended all too soon. The soaking had restored him and a light breakfast had lessened the pain in his head, but he still felt troubled and could scarcely manage a smile when he saw the tailor beaming at Rorden's side. A uniform in crimson and silver was draped carefully over one arm. His general's uniform.

Merek handled the fabric carefully, tracing the insignias and silver braiding. The tailored coat fit over a new white shirt of higher quality than his old ones. Just wearing the fine fabric made him stand a little straighter as he looked in the tailor's looking glass.

Rorden nodded in approval. "I doubt the king himself has ever looked so noble, sir."

But Merek couldn't enjoy it—not with the weight of his angry words to Ria still clinging to him. Not with the pain in her eyes fresh in his memory.

"If you'll join me outside, sir, I have something else

to show you." Rorden's eyes twinkled in anticipation. Merek knew he meant well, but he wished he could send Rorden away and be miserable in private.

They stepped out into the light.

"Your banner, General."

Two lads unfurled a large roll of shining green fabric revealing a beautiful crest trimmed in brown and gold. It featured three tall fir trees, the center one larger than the rest, with an arrow, a sword, and an ax intersecting in the foreground.

Merek ran his finger along the border. "Why do I know this pattern?"

"It's your mother's mark, altered to suit the border."

Merek was stunned by the beauty of it. He'd expected some flat representation of an animal, a poor replica of a noble's crest. But this. This was a work of art, and every piece of it spoke to him.

"Do you like it, sir?" Rorden asked.

"It's finer than I could have imagined. You've done well, Sergeant. Very well."

Rorden grinned. "Thank you, sir. Princess Honoria suggested the addition of the axe to represent your father."

Merek cringed at the mention of Ria's name. Remembering the intimate moment they had shared when he disclosed his father's story made him feel ashamed of his recent words.

"And this tree that stands out larger than the rest?"

"That represents you, sir. This one represents your father, and this one here is your future son. Or daughter, I suppose. I expect there will be many Strong children filling the rooms at Thorodan Hall." Rorden winked, his dimples deepening. Then he caught Merek's expression, and his smile faltered.

Merek grimaced inwardly. Rorden didn't know that the betrothal was false—that Merek's future didn't include children, let alone royal ones. After what had taken place between him and Ria that morning, he may have just cemented himself as her enemy. The thought made his insides writhe. He still cared for her as much as ever, and as he traced the fine embroidery which cast a subtle sheen in the sunlight, a part of him yearned for the lie, wished that his future was as Rorden described.

Merek dismissed the group to their task of raising the banner and looked to change the subject.

"I saw Dan before he left," he said to Rorden as they returned to the command tent. "His spirits seemed high. You were wise to consider him for this assignment."

"Thank you, sir, but I can't take credit for it. That was also the princess. Her opinions can be very insightful, and I've come to value her perspective."

Merek frowned at the implied censure. The truth was, Rorden was right. Ria had proven time and again her usefulness since coming to the camp, and he'd been impressed with her persistence in filling the gaps in her knowledge. Sure, she was impulsive and arrogant at times, and she never should have acted so rashly the previous night, but didn't he bear some of the blame? How might things have been different if he'd helped her instead of dismissing her?

Guilt twisted painfully in his gut, and he felt a renewed rush of shame over his harsh words.

But how could he take them back now? Had he gone too far to hope to reconcile? Surely she must hate him.

With a sigh, he sank into his chair and rested his head in his hands, trying to sort out the thoughts in his head from the feelings in his heart.

When he looked up, Rorden watched him curiously.

"Do you think we should risk a meeting between the princess and the Ardanian prince?" Merek asked bluntly.

"I think it's worth considering, sir. There are ways that we can limit the danger to the princess."

"Very well. I'm listening."

RIA TUGGED AT THE HANDLE OF HER TRUNK AND GRUNTED WITH effort when it wouldn't move. "How do you move this beast?" she complained.

"I don't," Biren said, stifling a laugh. "This is why we have porters."

"Ah, of course." Ria felt foolish. This was the first time she'd ever packed her own trunk, and she hadn't considered what came next after buckling the straps. Biren had clearly sensed that she needed the occupation, so she hadn't objected to Ria's help. That is, until Ria had tried to help Biren with her own belongings.

"It's not right," Biren had objected, snapping her own lid shut with uncharacteristic defiance. Her cheeks flushed under their light sprinkling of freckles. "Wouldn't you like to fold your blankets instead?"

The shadows against the walls of the tent shifted as morning drifted into afternoon. When Ria had packed all that she could, she paused and surveyed the small tent which had been her home these past months. She would miss it more than she'd supposed. She hated the mud, and she looked forward to sleeping in her own bed surrounded by thick walls that kept out the draft. But still she would miss the camp. An important piece of her life had settled into place here among the mud and frost and smoke. As painful as the growth had been, she was returning home wiser than when she'd come.

"All finished, my lady. Is there anything else you need?"

Ria reached for her cloak. "More courage?" All that remained was to bid Merek goodbye.

Biren's eyes sparkled. "You have more courage than half the soldiers in this camp. He's no match for you."

Ria smiled weakly. "Perhaps once, but now I feel quite undone."

"You might feel better after you've eaten."

"Maybe," she said noncommittally. Her stomach felt unsettled and she couldn't bear the thought of food.

"I'll check with the campmaster about our carriage," Biren offered, "and then see about a meal. You'll need strength for our journey."

When Biren left, Ria looked around the tent and sighed. It was time. She dreaded seeing Merek again so soon. His words still stung. What if he rejected her again? How would she bear it?

She *would* bear it. She would return to Albon willingly. It would be well for both of them to get some distance. But not yet. The thought of leaving with such angry words between them made her feel ill. Maybe she should confer with Rorden and seek his perspective. Then again, it was partly Rorden's fault that Merek was angry at her now. If he had helped her as she'd asked, she wouldn't have felt compelled to—

No, that wasn't fair. Her actions were her own. Rorden had done right to refuse her.

Shame welled up again and with it came a desire to leave immediately—to slink away unnoticed. But she wouldn't take the coward's path. She would face Merek one last time with her head held high.

Ria strode purposefully to the tent door and threw the flap open. At once she stopped, blinking against the bright sunlight. Merek stood there, looking equally surprised to see her burst out of the tent. Ria's heart leaped at the sight of him. She felt as if she were truly seeing him for the first time. He took her breath away, standing there in his new general's uniform, perfectly tailored to his large, muscular shoulders. His black hair and beard were trimmed short and distinguished, and his gray eyes—almost blue in the light—seemed to see right through her. A sense of wonder washed over her, as though she'd just emerged into glittering sunlight after a steady rain. She felt her cheeks warming in spite of herself.

"What are you doing here?" she blurted.

He smiled sheepishly, and she was filled with a sense of longing. She wanted to rush to him, to tell him every-thing she felt. But she kept her feet firmly planted to the earth. There would be time for that. Later. Now, she needed to proceed carefully so that she didn't ruin things. Again.

And why *was* he here, anyway?

Merek cleared his throat. "I don't...I seem to be developing a pattern of misbehaving and then seeking your forgiveness. Much to my chagrin, I find myself in that position again."

Apologizing! For throwing her out of camp? Or breaking her heart in the process?

"Go on." Ria folded her arms and hoped it wasn't obvious that she'd been crying.

"I've had some time to discuss things with Rorden."

Ria frowned. She wasn't feeling particularly favorable toward Rorden at the moment.

"He's helped me see that I may have been unfair in some of my earlier statements today."

On the other hand, Rorden *was* a loyal servant with trustworthy intuition.

Merek glanced at a porter passing by and watching with casual interest. "I came to see if you would reconsider your decision to leave."

"*My* decision to leave?"

"Yes. I find your perspective on the conflict here insightful, and there are some useful tasks to which you are particularly suited."

Ria narrowed her eyes. What exactly was he trying to say? They needed to speak freely.

"Let's discuss this inside, Strong." She stepped back into the tent and waited for him to follow.

The tent walls glowed with the light of the sun, the golden air warmer inside than out.

"Please speak clearly, Merek," Ria said in low tones.

"Your mood is changing as quickly as a spring storm, and I'm dizzy with the effort of keeping up."

He took a deep breath as if searching for the right words. "There's no precedent for this. A general should be able to make decisions without the taint of personal emotion. But with you here, everything is...different. It seemed that much would be easier if you left, but Rorden reminded me that a man in my position shouldn't look for the easy way."

Ria avoided looking at Merek, afraid of what he would see in her eyes if she did. So instead, she looked at the stitching on his uniform coat, following the lines to the decorated embellishments on his chest. The tailor truly had outdone himself. She wondered if she knew him. If she didn't, she would seek an introduction.

"What have you decided, then?" she asked. "Am I to be banished after all? Or am I merely on probation?"

"Forgive me. I was angry that you defied me, but more than anything I was afraid. I couldn't bear the thought of you putting yourself in danger, and said things I didn't have a right to say. In trying to keep you safe, I overstepped my bounds."

"Overstepped? That's putting it mildly." But she felt a spark of hope kindling in her chest.

Merek reddened. "I'm sorry, Ria. The things I said...I understand if you can't forgive me. I'm not like you always knowing the right things to say. And sometimes when I...." He faltered and took a deep breath to start again. "I should have listened to you and considered the merits of your idea with reason instead of sentiment. You were right. I'm not your commander, and it's wrong of me to treat you that way. You're free to leave the camp if you choose, but you're also free to stay if you so desire."

Ria raised her eyes to meet his and held his gaze for a long moment. The anger of before was gone, but she saw clearly the fear. And hope. He wanted her to stay. She was in danger of getting lost in his gray eyes. She needed to think. She needed to take her time—to make sure the moment was right before—

"And what do *you* desire?" she heard herself say. Was it just her imagination, or did his eyes flicker to her lips? Her heart skipped a beat.

"I only wish—" he began, but stopped when she reached out and touched his hand, her fingers brushing his gently.

"What you said about me was true," Ria said, tracing his large knuckles with her fingertips. "I behaved self-ishly and was foolish to think that I could escape the consequences of my actions. I don't fault you for wanting to send me away. Trust is not a thing easily rebuilt, but I'll give you whatever time you need. I owe you that much."

She hooked her fingers into his and reached for his other hand. His stiff posture emanated wariness, but he didn't pull away.

"Don't toy with me, Ria." His voice was edged with warning. "I won't ask you to leave, but please don't...not this..."

"I'm not toying with you; I swear it." She raised her eyes to his and stepped closer, bringing his hands up behind her so that his arms encircled her waist. It was a desperate gamble, but she'd already risked so much—why hold back now? "I need you, Merek. More than I've ever needed another person. I didn't see until last night. My pride wouldn't let me. But once that was stripped away, once I thought I might never see you again, suddenly I understood. It was *you* I wanted at my side. Not because I thought you could save me, but because yours is the face I want to see before I die."

He swallowed, his breath quickening.

Heart pounding, she raised up on her toes, lifting her face so that her lips met his. He stiffened and started to pull away, but she wrapped her arms around his neck and drew him closer, kissing him firmly and insistently. She closed her eyes, trying to communicate the complicated and wonderful feelings she was just discovering for herself.

At last, he relented. He embraced her warmly in return, pulling her close. He kissed her hungrily, moving from her mouth to her jaw, her neck. Desire welled up inside Ria until time seemed to stand still. The sounds and smells of the camp melted away as she reveled in the tenderness of the moment.

"My lady, are you—" Biren stepped into the tent and stopped, gaping at the two of them.

Ria jumped, pulling away in embarrassment. She stifled a laugh at Merek's expression and turned away to regain her composure. Her hands felt cold against the heat of her neck, and she knew she must be blushing furiously.

"Forgive me," Biren stammered, reddening. "I didn't mean to intrude. I thought you might be hungry." She glanced back and forth between the two of them, disapproval and excitement warring in her bright eyes.

Ria bit her lip to avoid laughing. "Thank you, Biren. If you could give me a few minutes to finish my...conversation with the general, I would appreciate it."

"Of course," Biren said, bowing her way out of the tent. "I will return shortly," she added in a veiled warning over her shoulder.

When she was gone, Ria snorted with laughter. "Dear Biren. She's always so concerned about what's right and proper. I'm afraid I've disappointed her again."

Merek leaned in close, speaking softly in her ear. "Then she'll really be shocked to hear what I have planned for you." He kissed her gently on her neck just below her earlobe.

Ria smiled, feeling a tingle where his beard brushed her skin. "And what is that?" She expected him to speak of their future together—of a true and genuine betrothal—and her heart swelled with joy.

So she was surprised when Merek pulled back, looked her in the eye, and said very seriously, "First, we need to prepare you to meet with Prince Artem."

THIRTY-TWO

Captain Talen walked briskly through the royal gardens, a cold rain seeping through the seams of his winter cloak. The gravel path crunched noisily underfoot, and above the steady chorus of rain an old ash tree creaked ominously in the breeze. Ahead of him, the hulking tower crouched like some kind of prehistoric beast watching its prey. In the gray shadows of the waning daylight, the abandoned scaffolding ringing the upper levels of the tower looked vaguely like a dilapidated crown, and Talen couldn't help thinking it mocked the broken king who lived inside.

Captain Drenall met him at the door. The head of the Royal Guard showed no sign of his earlier injuries as he ushered him inside, for which Talen was glad. The ambush on the princess troubled him, especially since the perpetrators hadn't been caught. It galled Talen that the king had not pursued justice for his daughter.

Despite the grim sight of the king's dying garden, Talen was filled with eagerness. These days, very few people were allowed to see the king, so Talen had been eager to come when he'd been summoned earlier that morning.

Drenall stopped beside a graceful dogwood tree whose brown leaves had curled in on themselves. "Captain Talen, before you see the king, I'd like a word."

"Yes?"

"As you know, the king's health is precarious. It would be well for you to avoid exciting him."

"I understand."

"No, Captain. With all due respect, I don't think you do. His Majesty may say things which contradict what you know to be true. You must take great care in determining whether or not correcting him is worth the toll it will place on his fragile state."

Talen paused. "Are you asking me to lie?"

Drenall regarded him coolly. "I'm asking you to use the truth judiciously. For his own sake, you understand."

Talen didn't understand. To him, truth and deception were adversaries. To muddy them together was to deny the very order of law upon which their kingdom was built. Drenall had always seemed a straightforward man himself, but perhaps his close proximity with the court had clouded his perspective.

Talen followed Drenall up one flight of wooden steps then passed through a dim, circular chamber on their way to a second set of stairs. At the top, Drenall paused before opening the heavy wooden door to murmur one final warning. "Remember what I said. Tread carefully."

Talen hadn't laid eyes on the king in months, and at first he didn't recognize the man who hunched over a writing desk near the fire. His hair and beard were long and unkempt, the normally golden tones darkened by filth. His skin hung slackly from his bones, the tell-tale sign of drastic weight loss in a shockingly short time. As he looked up at Talen, he blinked blearily, his eyes couched in dark shadows of exhaustion.

"Captain Talen is here to see you, Your Majesty," Drenall announced, and Talen stepped forward with a crisp bow.

King Sindal did not speak immediately, so Talen offered an introductory, "Thank you for seeing me, Your Majesty. It's a great honor to be permitted—"

"Talen! Of course! I have an important assignment for you." The king gestured toward a plate of soft vegetables and browned turkey leg. "I need you to taste my food."

Clearly the king hadn't lost his sense of humor. Talen chuckled at the jest, waiting for the king's laugh to erupt out of the deep wells of humor that he was so well known for. It didn't come. Talen's face fell as his laugh died away into awkward silence.

"You summoned me to come test your food?"

"Martin says they haven't poisoned it, and Drenall says he wouldn't let them get close enough to try, but how can I know for certain? You'll taste it for me just to make sure."

Talen shot Drenall a look. The older man betrayed no emotion other than a slight flicker of something in his eyes—wariness? irritation?—that passed as quickly as it came.

"Your Majesty, Captain Talen did not come to test your food," Drenall said. "He is First Captain over the Peacekeepers, and he—"

"I know who he is!" the king snapped. "Talen, taste my food, and if it's suitable then I shall believe Drenall here. Otherwise, you will replace him as my personal guard."

Drenall offered a curt nod, indicating that Talen should proceed. Talen didn't know the way of proper testers, and he felt shamefully presumptuous taking the king's food from his own plate. Sindal watched him as he cut a bite from the turkey leg, then sampled the vegetables. The only other sound in the room was the crackling of the fire and Talen was conscious of his own chewing in a way that made him wish for privacy.

Swallowing, he announced, "I taste nothing untoward, my lord." Aside from a generous portion of pepper that made him wish for a swallow of the wine. But whereas the king had not offered it, he said nothing.

Sindal regarded him intently, his forearms resting expectantly on the table. Then he grunted and turned to Drenall. "The poison might act slowly. Watch him. If he makes it through the night, then we'll know the food is safe."

Drenall's tone was even and respectful as he objected. "You haven't eaten in two days, sire. If you carry on like this, you'll have no strength against the winter chill."

The king pushed the plate away from him. "I've

heard that a man can fall to only one bite of simtera powder, with it barely resting on his tongue. I dare not risk it."

"If that were the case, poor Talen would be writhing on the floor as we speak. Yet you see that he's whole and well. A few bites, please, sire."

Clearing his throat, Talen said, "Perhaps we might discuss matters in Cillith while we wait to see if there are any ill effects from the food."

"Cillith?" Sindal barked, turning his suspicious gaze away from Drenall and fixing it on Talen. "Why should I wish to speak of Cillith?"

"Is that not why you summoned me here today?" Talen asked, taken aback. "I've requested an audience with you these many weeks. Thieves are growing more bold and—"

"Cillith doesn't interest me, Captain. I've summoned you today because there's a far greater evil lurking close to home."

Talen straightened. The king's blue eyes were bright and intelligent with no sign of the distracted haze from before.

"You, Captain Talen, have proven to be a true servant of the crown in the past. Can I trust you to perform my will in the face of the darkest threat we've seen in an age?"

"Without question, Your Majesty." A thrill of excited purpose ran down Talen's spine.

"There are enemies among us, right here in Albon, seeking to remove me from the throne. Your prison holds the most dangerous of these, but I'm certain he's not working alone."

Talen nodded, thinking at once of Count Orlin and the uncanny support he had from Lord Hegrin.

"I need you to find out how deep this treachery goes," the king continued. "Until all his co-conspirators are in chains, I shall not rest. Can I count on you, Captain?"

"Of course, sire. I've suspected for some time that he has connections outside the prison seeking his interests. It shouldn't be too difficult to locate them, but I warn you that some of them may be uncomfortably close to the throne."

The king gave a sharp intake of breath. "Just as I suspected. Of whom do you speak? Which of my trusted advisors are guilty of supporting him?" he demanded.

Talen hesitated. "I don't feel comfortable naming my suspicions just yet, sire. Give me time to investigate further. A charge this serious deserves careful consideration before—"

Color rose in Sindal's cheeks. "You speak of the princess, don't you? You speak of my own daughter!"

Talen started. "No, sir, I don't—"

Sindal cursed and threw the plate of food. Talen shied away in surprise, managing to avoid the heavy disc but not the grease that sprayed the front of his uniform. Standing, Sindal pointed a shaking finger at him. "Don't lie to me, man! I know that she's been helping him. Either he's deceived her and she helps him unwittingly, or she has intentionally betrayed me!"

"Not at all, my lord! The princess is not a friend to Count Orlin. Indeed, it is she who ordered his arrest!"

"What was that?" The king peered at him, his blue eyes fierce.

Drenall looked at Talen sharply and stepped between him and the king. "Perhaps Captain Talen should return another time, Your Majesty. You're growing excited, and that's not—"

"What did you say?" Sindal bellowed.

Talen glanced at Drenall, but drew no comfort from the old soldier's expression. Gone was the stoic control, giving way instead to palpable dread. "I said that Princess Honoria is the one who had Count Orlin arrested. She believes he has information about the invasion of Endvar that—"

"Count Orlin! It's not Count Orlin who conspires against me, you fool!"

"Not Orlin? Then who—"

"I speak of Merek Strong, the devious man who once pretended friendship so that he could gain power. This land has never known such treachery as his, seeking to turn my own daughter against me and steal my throne."

Drenall flashed Talen a look of warning, and it occurred to Talen that Drenall had heard these accusations before. What had happened to the reasonable king who pardoned an innocent man? Talen opened his mouth to speak, but Drenall interrupted.

"Of course Captain Talen speaks of Strong too, sire. But as Count Orlin has also been suspected of treachery and the princess herself had him arrested, it's clear that she cannot be involved in Strong's plot. You must not suspect your daughter of any disloyalty."

Talen's eyes widened in disbelief. How could Drenall slander Strong after all he'd done to save the princess? Was this his idea of using truth *judiciously*? Well, Talen wouldn't deceive the king, no matter how upset this made Drenall. "Your Majesty, I have no reason to believe the princess is involved in anything irregular. As near as I can tell, her actions have always been for the good of the crown and the good of the people."

"There, you see?" Drenall said. "Thank you, Captain. Now if you'll—"

"And as for Captain Strong," Talen continued, ignoring Drenall's glare. "I can only guess what rumors you've heard, but I urge you not to listen to them. You pardoned him once because you were satisfied that the charges of treason against him were not credible. I beg of you to trust in that decision."

"That's enough, Talen," Drenall growled. "It's time for you to leave."

"Pardoned him? What's this you say?" A look of horror crossed Sindal's face, his eyes wide with childlike terror.

Talen recoiled. What was going on here? A nagging worry pushed against his mind and drove him forward. "I released Captain Strong two months ago as ordered by you. Do you not remember?"

"I gave no such order." Sindal backed against the wall, knocking over his chair in his haste. The heavy tapestry behind him fluttered as he leaned against it, clutching his hands, the fingernails long and yellowed. "He's free, you say? I am doomed!"

"But I saw your signature, sire." Talen stepped forward in desperation, kicking a pile of discarded books out of the way as he approached the king. "Your seal and your signature in your own hand."

Sindal raised a trembling hand to his face and covered his eyes, letting out a low moan. His knees gave way and he collapsed to the floor, rocking back and forth. "He'll come for me now. He will come. I am doomed."

Talen crouched before him, repulsed by the cowering weakness in his sovereign. "You are not doomed, sire. Captain Strong means you no harm, I'm certain of it. He is a good man who—"

"You too, Talen? You speak for him? Is there no one I can trust?" the king cried. "He has turned all of you against me!"

Hands grabbed Talen's shoulders as Drenall hauled him to his feet. "You've done enough," Drenall muttered in his ear. "Go. And don't return if you know what's best."

Indignant, Talen allowed Drenall to steer him toward the door and out onto the stairs.

"What's going on?" he demanded as soon as the heavy wooden door closed behind them. "You know Strong is no traitor. Why do you vilify him before the king until he's reduced to...that?" He gestured in disgust toward the closed door now muffling the sound of uncontrollable sobs.

Drenall rested a hand against the door as if needing

a moment to gather his own strength. His scarred face was marred by shadow, his voice hard and defensive. "The king sees what he wishes to see, nothing more. If he's intent on making an enemy out of Strong, I can do nothing to stop him. But it seems best not to extend his fears toward the princess as well. As you see, he's hard-pressed to trust anyone. I'll do whatever it takes to keep her innocent in his mind."

"But to feed his fears about Strong—"

"Can do no more harm than his delusions have already done. Trying to help him see reason only drives him further into paranoia. The least I can do is keep the princess untainted by his madness. If he should turn on her as he's turned on Strong..." Drenall shook his head.

"I don't like it," Talen said. "It's as if he never even pardoned Strong! Do you think I should produce the pardon for him to examine? Prove to him that it exists?"

"No," Drenall snapped. "It's too late to help Strong's cause, and if there's any chance it might cast a shadow of doubt on the princess, it's not worth the risk."

"Why would it cast doubt on the princess?" Then Talen remembered the king's trembling hands. The signature on the pardon was strong and confident. "Do you think she forged his signature?"

"I neither know nor care," Drenall whispered fiercely, "but that's what the king will think."

"But that's treason!"

"If she acted outside the law, then I have no doubt it was for good reason. Think about it. You've seen the state of our king. Can you blame her for trying to right the wrong his madness caused?"

Talen's cheeks grew warm with the shame of having been duped. It was a betrayal, plain and simple. A betrayal of the king and a betrayal of Talen's own trust in her. He was a fool for being so easily deceived.

"Talen," Drenall warned as he turned to back to the king's chamber door. "Be careful whom you trust. There are many people in this court who, if they catch even a whiff of your suspicions, would not hesitate to string the princess up for the vultures."

Talen didn't reply, but Drenall's words lingered in his mind as he stalked out of the tower. He liked Princess Honoria. He didn't want her to be guilty of treason. But he had to admit, it wounded his pride to think that she would have taken advantage of his trust. It hadn't even occurred to him to doubt the legitimacy of the pardon, but now, when he thought about her calm smile as she handed it to him, he felt a flush of anger. Had she secretly been laughing at him? Congratulating herself on deceiving him?

An early dusk had fallen with the heavy rain, and Talen raised his hood against the damp. He would find the pardon. He would examine the signature and hope to discern the truth. And then...what? Could he arrest the princess on a suspicion that he couldn't prove? The king would deny the signature was his own, Talen knew. It was as Drenall said. Producing the pardon would only pit the king against his daughter, and Talen couldn't be sure that the king hadn't signed it after all and simply forgotten. His was not exactly a reliable testimony.

No, he couldn't bring it before the king. But he couldn't simply ignore it, either, and Drenall was right that he couldn't trust anyone in the court. Ironically, the only person whom he still felt like he could trust was the princess herself—because he knew that Drenall was right. She may have acted wrong, but she would have meant well. Talen was sure of that. So he would keep the pardon safe from prying eyes until she returned.

Talen's mind was so preoccupied that he didn't consciously notice the two shadowed figures who'd slipped away from the corner of the smokehouse to intercept him until he had already stiffened and placed his hand on his hilt. The first raised a crossbow, but Talen dropped to the stones so quickly that the bolt drove harmlessly into the smokehouse wall with a dull thud. While the stranger cursed and reloaded, his companion rushed Talen. Talen jumped to his feet and drew his sword to meet the other man's blade, the ringing of steel dampened by the thrum of driving rain on the courtyard stones.

The man was a stranger to him, but he fought well, matching Talen blow for blow. Talen drew on his frustration with the king to increase his aggression and soon his opponent faltered. He called out to his companion, but Talen saw the danger and spun out of the way just as the crossbow fired again.

His attacker took advantage of his distraction to reach past Talen's guard with his sword, but the wet cloak slowed his thrust, and in a quick motion Talen dodged. Knocked off balance mid-thrust, the stranger stumbled, and Talen tackled him to the earth. Blade against the stranger's throat, Talen spat, "Who are you? What do you want with me?"

The man glanced in a panic at his companion. Too late, Talen heard the crossbow fire again. But the surge of pain didn't come. Instead, the bolt lodged in his opponent's temple. Talen sprang back, but the man with the crossbow was already running, disappearing into the night.

Cursing, Talen turned back to his attacker, but he was already dead. With a grimace, Talen searched the man's pockets but found nothing useful. Whoever he was, he was smart enough not to carry anything on his person that would incriminate his employer—and Talen knew immediately this was not a simple robbery.

Had these men been hired by Count Orlin? Not overtly, of course, but through one of his connections. Or perhaps Lord Hegrin felt his purposes would be best served by having Talen out of the way. Talen's list of enemies in Albon was growing in number and influence. Even the king could turn against him at any moment. His only remaining allies were far away on the battlefront in Endvar. Perhaps it was time to pay them a visit.

Thank you for Reading!

If you enjoyed *Pain of Betrayal*, please consider leaving a review on Amazon or Goodreads. (Or both for you over-achievers!) Thanks for helping get my work into the hands of other readers like you.

As a special thank you, I'm delighted to share with you a special bonus chapter that didn't make it into the book. After the battle at Endvar, Merek finds himself stuck behind enemy lines trying to get an injured Dan to safety. While these scenes are referenced in the novel, they take place off-screen in order to not interrupt the main story-line. But it marks a change in Merek's willingness to

accept Ria's appointment to general, so I'm excited to share these scenes with you now.

This exclusive bonus chapter is available to download when you sign up for my newsletter at https://caren hahn.com/betrayal. As a special perk, you'll also be the first to know about current projects and new releases.

Here's a short excerpt:

Merek plunged out of the forest and onto the rock, boots slipping on mossy stones. The river was full and running swift, giant boulders channeling it to a narrow chasm that roared violently as it churned between the walls.

Merek leaned in close to Dan.

"We'll have to leap," he said, gesturing to the gap. "I'll go first."

Dan swallowed.

The fog played tricks with perspective, making it hard to see the boulder on the other side. Merek stepped back and took two long strides before jumping, spray from the churning river bathing him as he passed over it. The opposite boulder came up faster than he expected in the dark, making his knees buckle. He fell to the ground with a grunt, pain shooting through his wrist as he caught himself.

Clenching his teeth, he pulled himself up to stand. He'd made it with room to spare. But Dan's legs were much shorter. And he was gravely injured.

Merek stepped back to the edge and realized as he did that he could see all the way to the trees. The fog was clearing, and the moon emerged through the clouds painting everything with a silvery wash like a fine jeweler's handiwork.

A shout sounded from the trees on the other side. They'd been seen.

Want more? Download the full chapter at carenhahn.com/betrayal.

THE HATCHED TRILOGY

Domesticated dragons.
What could go wrong?

"Interesting, funny, dragon drama and I can read it in
public - PERFECT!"

"Super fun, great writing, and nice romantic tension"

"witty banter, sweet romance, and daring intrigue"

"highly recommend"

What do a high-octane mommy blogger, a Wild West romance, and a [possibly] possessed antique doll have in common?

You can find them all in my FREE collection of short stories. Visit carenhahn.com to download your copy!

Acknowledgments

In the late winter of 2020, the global community stumbled under an unprecedented threat with the spread of COVID-19. As individuals and a society, we lost a lot in the ensuing months, and I'm sure the full effects won't be known for years. But there were also some unexpected things that came from it, and this book is one of them. With time and availability a little more fluid than normal, I was seized with the idea to share the Wallkeeper trilogy with the world. It's been quite a journey, and I am so grateful for you readers who've joined me!

Once again, I appreciate the insights and suggestions from early readers. Crystal Brinkerhoff, Rachel Stauffer, Cori Hatch, Carli Schofield, Joan Schofield, Cindy Schofield, Chris Schofield, Jenny Hahn, Sara Epling, Julie Whipple, and Renae Southwick all provided valuable perspectives, and encouraged me each step of the way. Rachel Pickett again helped me tighten the prose with her editing magic, and is endlessly patient when I make the same mistakes over and over again!

Thanks is also due my six children, who not only support my writing, but have patiently endured this intense publishing process when Mom was unavailable and Dad had to pick up the slack. (I should have bought stock in Minecraft.)

Lastly, none of this would have been possible without my husband's support. I mean that figuratively, but also literally because he's taken my words and ideas and transformed them into beautiful covers and interiors. He also created my website, carenhahn.com, and cheerfully solves my random tech problems when I get stuck. Best of all, he believes in me even before I believe in myself.

About the Author

CAREN HAHN is a Fantasy and Mystery author specializing in clean, relationship-driven fiction featuring empathetic characters who are exquisitely flawed. She graduated from Brigham Young University where—between courses on Humanities, English Lit, and  Biblical Hebrew—she squeezed in as many Creative Writing classes as she could. Caren lives in the Pacific Northwest with her husband and six children.

Visit carenhahn.com to learn more about her upcoming projects and download a free collection of short stories.